PRAISE FOR
LEGENDS OF THE
DRAGONREALM

"Richard Knaak's fiction has the magic touch of making obviously
fantastic characters and places come alive, seem real, and matter to
the reader. That's the essential magic of all storytelling, and Richard
does deftly, making his stories always engaging and worth picking up
and reading. And then re-reading.

> —Ed Greenwood, creator of the *Forgotten Realms*®

"Full of energy... Great world building [and] memorable characters...
It's easy to see why Richard has enjoyed so much success!"

> —*New York Times* Bestselling author R.A. Salvatore

"Richard's novels are well-written, adventure-filled, action-packed!"

> —*New York Times* bestselling author Margaret Weis

"Endlessly inventive. Knaak's ideas just keep on coming!"

> —Glen Cook, author of *Chronicles of the Black Company*

Also by Richard A. Knaak

The Dragonrealm

The World of Warcraft

INDIVIDUAL TITLES

The Janus Mask
Frostwing
King of the Grey
Dutchman
Shattered Light: Ruby Flames
Beastmaster: Myth
Black City Saint
Black City Demon

RICHARD A. KNAAK

LEGENDS
+OF THE+
DRAGONREALM
THE GRYPHON MAGE

THE TURNING WAR BOOK TWO

A PERMUTED PRESS BOOK

ISBN: 978-1-68261-380-1
ISBN (eBook): 978-1-68261-381-8

Legends of the Dragonrealm:
The Gryphon Mage
© 2017 by Richard A. Knaak
All Rights Reserved

Interior Design and Composition by Greg Johnson/Textbook Perfect

**PERMUTED
PRESS**

Permuted Press, LLC
permutedpress.com

Published in the United States of America

ACKNOWLEDGEMENTS

I would like to gratefully acknowledge the countless fans of this series for its longevity, with special thanks going to the following supporters:

Adam Harrison, Mary Lewinski, Jon Cazera, Samir Schwayri, and Wade Atkinson for magically adding to the Dragon Masters' ranks.

Matthew Warnstedt, Chris Coughlin, David Zawistowski, Jennifer Alberts, Chad Armstrong, Christopher Oldham, Justin Passmore, William & Brandy Schuster, Kevin Looney, David Moniz, and Jeremy Reynolds for their added contributions to this effort.

William Schuster and Wade Atkinson for additional light editing.

And everyone else who has taken it upon themselves to join in seeing more tales of the Dragonrealm come to life!

–Richard A. Knaak

CONTENTS

CONTENTS

I

SEA OF MEMORIES

The three-masted ship shook as the latest wave crashed against it, but the stormy sea was the least of his problems.

Just ahead of him, one of the beasts landed with a hard thump. His path cut off, he could do nothing to help his remaining companions as the black-clad attackers swarmed around them.

The Gnor, of course, reveled in the fighting despite the odds against him. Circling like the wolves that were their totem, the armored figures pressed the seven-foot-tall creature toward a corner despite his long reach and deadly ax. Two of their number already lay slain, but they did not care. The pack was what mattered, not individual members. The pack would bring the Gnor down, just as they had most of the rest of the crew.

But the Gryphon had no time to worry more about ursine warrior, for the winged beast that had landed in front of the lionbird now closed on him. Worse, it wore a face that might have been a parody of his own if not for the fact that this creature's kind had existed long before its intended victim. The Gryphon might in part look like the beast for whom he had been named, but he lacked its utter ferocity.

"Kill! Kill!" it roared, eagerly lunging a moment later.

The Gryphon dove to the side. The animal's savage claws just missed ripping apart his left leg. He took a swing at the monster as it passed and managed to cut a crimson slash along its flank. Unfortunately, that would hardly be enough to slow it.

A muscular feline warrior suddenly imposed himself between the Gryphon and the winged behemoth. The catman hissed in challenge, drawing the bestial gryphon's attention from his namesake.

"Don't!" the lionbird shouted. "Save yourself—"

The catman paid his warning no mind, leaping forward as the beast did the same. The pair met in a frenzy of claws and teeth, and at first there was no clear domination by either. Although far slighter than his monstrous opponent, the catman moved with such grace, such speed, that he managed to evade not only swipe after swipe by the gryphon, but also the razor-sharp beak.

Near the bow, the Gnor roared a challenge of his own to his foes. Despite his bearlike form, he too had a beak, albeit a shorter, straighter one. When first the Gryphon had met one of the Gnor's kind—Gnor had no individual names but always seemed to know each other—he had wondered how such a being could be. Sometimes, it appeared to the lionbird that some force had long ago blindly experimented with different body parts in a mad attempt to create a superior form of life. Certainly, the Gnor had few rivals when it came to sheer might, but even they had their limitations.

Indeed, even as the Gryphon rose to help his other companion, he saw a pike come under the Gnor's immense arm and pierce the heavy hide. A stream of blood joined the other dark wounds already perforating the giant's body. Yet, the Gnor still managed to bring his ax down and snap the pike in two. With a grunt, he pulled free the head and continued his struggle against his foes.

As that happened, the Gryphon joined the catman against the winged beast. A name suddenly came to the Gryphon's mind. "Aton!

There's one lifeboat left! Get the Gnor and Nadia and go over the side! They want me! They'll leave you! At least on the water, you'll have a chance!"

"Nadia's dead," Aton rumbled. "Nadia's dead..."

The Gryphon clamped his beak shut. Nadia had not only been a member of their group, but also Aton's mate. A sense of horror overtook the lionbird. Aton had no intention of escape.

"You go!" the catman continued. "They fear you! There's something they know that you need to find out! The master guardians—"

A crossbow bolt pierced Aton in the square of the back. The catman stiffened, then, with a sigh, fell toward the slavering beast. The Gryphon tried to grab Aton, but missed.

The fearsome beak seized Aton by the neck. The beast shook the catman's limp body.

With a growl, the Gryphon used the distraction to leap atop the monster. As the winged fury took note of him again, the lionbird dug his own claws deep into the animal's throat.

The Gryphon held on as the creature struggled to free itself of him. The heavy wings flapped, lifting both combatants several feet into the air.

Blood soaked the Gryphon's hands as he tore deeper into the flesh. He felt the animal heave—

A second crossbow bolt struck...only this time its target was the creature beneath the Gryphon.

With a shudder, the winged monstrosity collapsed. The Gryphon barely had time to leap free.

As he landed, the second of the creatures blocked his path to the Gnor. The Gryphon turned to his left and found himself facing three ebony-armored figures. One was the soldier wielding the crossbow. Another was a grim-faced, helmed keeper, one of the sorcerers of the Aramite Empire. In his left hand, he clutched a small, gleaming stone—a Ravager's Tooth—the magical artifact that was also the symbol of the Aramite's horrific, lupine god.

But it was the cloaked and bearded figure in the center who most demanded the Gryphon's attention. The lionbird could not hold back an animalistic growl.

"Shaidarol...Shaidarol..." he muttered.

"D'Shay now..." the bearded figure responded coolly. "not that you will remember that any more than the master guardians remember you. Even for the few short moments you have left. You will forget everything...which, in your case, is probably for the best where your soul is concerned..."

The sounds of the Gnor battling continued behind the Gryphon, but the giant's breathing sounded noticeably ragged. The Gryphon wanted to turn and help, but knew that he could not take his eyes from he who now called himself by an Aramite title...a wolf raider name. "How did you do that...D'Shay? How did you—how—?"

The Gryphon reeled. His thoughts grew cloudy. Yet, a part of his mind still functioned well enough that he knew the cause. He focused one nearly human eye at the keeper and tried through the growing haze to judge the distance to the sorcerer.

"He's very strong," muttered the anxious keeper. "He's still fighting it!"

D'Shay chuckled. "Yes, he was always a stubborn one! He'll die that way now..."

The keeper frowned. "The Pack Leader ordered his capture...he allowed for some damage, but he wants him alive..."

Still wobbling, the Gryphon took a step toward the trio. The crossbowman took aim, but D'Shay pushed the weapon down.

"Too simple, too clean," the aristocratic wolf raider murmured. "His death must be brutal..."

"Again, I must remind you," the sorcerer began...only to gape down at his chest. There, a gleaming blade had easily pierced his breastplate exactly where the heart could be found.

D'Shay removed the magical dagger. The keeper's blood left not a single mark on the blade.

As the sorcerer collapsed, D'Shay casually sheathed the dagger. Even through his foggy thoughts, the lionbird noted that the crossbowman did not appear at all surprised by the murder.

"You will not be brought back to the Pack Leader. You will die here, die painfully, and die aware that the Dream Lands will soon follow…" D'Shay gestured.

The second beast moved closer to the Gryphon, who also noticed at that moment that the sound of battle had utterly died down. The Gnor had to be dead, he knew; the behemoth would have never surrendered.

"You should have never believed in me, Gryphon…never…"

The lionbird could barely think, barely see. Yet, he knew that he had to reach his former comrade, if only to rip out D'Shay's throat before the beast tore out the Gryphon's.

He tried to throw himself at the bearded wolf raider—

The ship lurched sharply. Enemy and ally alike were tossed to the deck. A harsh groan cut through the roar of the storm as the hull of the wolf raiders' hunter ship, lashed alongside the Gryphon's, scraped against the other one.

Trying to take advantage of the chaos, the lionbird again attempted to reach D'Shay. Unfortunately, his legs buckled under him and he nearly collided face first with the deck.

Teeth bared, D'Shay also fought to rise. He grabbed the rail, but could not pull himself up due to the keeper's corpse, which slid into him at the same time.

The Gryphon managed to stand. He bared his claws—then ducked as the second beast tried to fall upon him. The winged monster immediately whirled about in order to attempt a second attack, but by then, the Gryphon had already leaped.

Wrapping his arms around the creature's thick neck, the Gryphon tried to do with the second beast as he had the first. However, his claws only caught feathers and fur as the monster abruptly took to the air. The creature and its desperate namesake rose among the billowing sails.

The Gryphon had a brief and terrible glimpse of the carnage covering the deck of his ship. The bodies of his comrades lay strewn everywhere, including the Gnor, whose bulky corpse hung draped over the rail.

Clutching tightly, the lionbird finally managed to dig one set of claws deep into the gryphon's muscular throat. Still, it was not enough to slay the beast, which began to dive and dart about in an attempt to shake its undesired burden.

A powerful gust threw the pair beyond the two bound ships. The gryphon tried to return to its master, but the gale proved too strong. The two combatants were pushed farther and farther away.

The winged fury fought to keep airborne. Atop the beast, the Gryphon watched as the two ships quickly dwindled into the distance. His head continued to pound and his memories grew more and more hazy. Whatever spell the keeper had started continued to spread through the Gryphon's mind unchecked. What the reason for that was as lost to the hapless rebel as his friends and the ships.

His treacherous mount continued to fly as the storm forced it. Each glimpse below only offered the Gryphon more of the same. Huge waves raced across the open sea. There was no sign of land…

At some point, he blacked out. What finally stirred the Gryphon to waking was the haggard breathing of the creature. The Gryphon felt moistness on his hands and discovered that at some point he had managed to dig both sets of claws into the neck. It had kept him from falling off, but it had also meant that the winged monster that was the only thing keeping him from drowning was dying.

In desperation, the Gryphon glanced back—at where he hoped to find something. He could no longer recall how he had gotten into this situation. His entire past consisted of his name—such as it was—and his current sorry circumstances. He knew that he had forgotten something terrible, but try as he might, he could not resurrect any of those memories.

The beast shivered. For a moment, it ceased flying. The two dropped like stones, their collision with the water prevented only by a desperate *effort from the monster. Even still, the Gryphon knew that it was only a matter of minutes. He searched every direction, only to see more water. Granted, a mist now obscured much of the east, but the Gryphon could hear nothing that hinted of anything but more sea. How he wished that he could have helped save—who?*

Water suddenly washed over him. The Gryphon jolted. He had fallen unconscious again. Worse, though, his unwilling mount had finally given in to its exhaustion and bleeding. Before the Gryphon could pull free, he and the beast collided with the raging sea.

Striking the water was akin to striking stone. Fortunately for the Gryphon, the dying animal took the brunt of the collision. Still, the animal's twisting threw him to the side. He landed in the stormy sea just as another wave washed over both of them.

The wave separated the pair. The winged fury struggled in vain to keep afloat. Even as the Gryphon fought to keep his head above the surface, he saw the creature slip under. The wings thrashed wildly for several seconds, but stilled even as they, too, sank into the depths.

Another wave threw the Gryphon beyond his drowned mount. As it did, he caught a brief glimpse of something on the horizon. It looked almost like land, but he was too groggy to be certain. His head pounded. Every memory had faded away. All that remained to him was his name, which he repeated over and over in his thoughts as he struggled to keep alive.

I am the Gryphon. I am the Gryphon. I am the—

"GRYPHON! SNAP OUT of it!"

The Gryphon knew that male voice, knew it better than the fleeting memories now fading into the recesses of his mind. He had been dreaming of something, but what it was, he could not say. The chaotic noises filling his ears did not help his concentration any more than the insistent voice did.

"You two! Take him with you! Yalak has the way open! I'll deal with this catastrophe and join you immediately after!"

"But, Father!" another male—a younger one—protested. "I won't leave you again!"

"Do it! Find your brother! He can't continue this lone wolf attitude! We live or die fighting side-by-side!"

A feminine voice cut in. "Nathan! Think of yourself—"

"I won't argue with either of you, Gwendolyn! Take him and go!"

Hands gripped the Gryphon by the upper arms. He must have said something, because the initial voice—*Nathan?*—responded, "We'll save them, don't worry, Gryphon! We did it before and we'll do it again…"

"The Gnor, too…" the lionbird managed to respond, one of his buried memories briefly stirring again.

"What's a Gnor?" the second male voice asked.

"Just get him to safety! You saw what happened! There's more to him than we knew, and we'll need to see if we can help him draw that out again! It may be our best hope…"

A sharp pain coursed through the Gryphon. He let out a cry, then slumped as his consciousness escaped him again.

But in his last moment of waking, another voice echoed in his head, the voice of the bearded figure who had evidently betrayed him.

You will forget everything…which, in your case, is probably for the best where your soul is concerned…

2

THE GRYPHON
AND THE DRAGON

Another retreat, Nathan Bedlam thought with dismay. *Another costly retreat...*

To the wizard, that cost had nothing to do with gold, but with blood and lives. In the five months since Nathan had freed every spellcaster from the influence of the Purple Dragon's magical array, the mages had done everything they could to aid the Gryphon's ragtag army of rebels. There had been some small victories, but mostly the Gryphon and the spellcasters had spent more time trying to find new places to hide than they had attempting to overthrow the Dragon Kings. That had to change...and Nathan knew just how it had to be done.

The only problem was...doing so meant attacking Penacles itself.

The chill wind shrieking through the remotest mountains of the Northern Wastes did not touch Nathan as he stared south. There was little to see other than more mountains and more wasteland. Perpetually covered as they were by ice and snow, they had few distinguishing features. Nathan only cared that he and Yalak had tried to find a location so obscure that even the lord of the Northern Wastes—the Ice Dragon—would not think to look here.

But we can't stay too long, he thought bitterly. *We can never stay anywhere too long...*

Yalak and Dayn were already seeking potential locations to move the rebels. Gwendolyn was assisting in trying to treat the Gryphon's not insubstantial injuries. Those injuries were the result of a surprise attack surely coordinated by Nathan's former master, Lord Purple, and nearly successfully executed by assassins from Lord Brown's clan. Combined with a secondary assault on the rebels by other elements of Brown's military forces, the plot had nearly achieved what the much more massive attack by Brown, Iron, and Bronze months before had not.

Worse, Nathan was certain that the second plan had nearly succeeded in part due to a traitor in the spellcasters' midst...a traitor he was growing more and more concerned might be his oft-absent younger son, Azran.

No one had seen Azran since two days before the Gryphon's near fatal encounter with the drake assassins and that last time, the youngest Bedlam had been acting even more erratic than previous. He had spent most of his time seated alone from the others, and when he had interacted with someone, it had more often than not been Gwendolyn.

Nathan and Dayn both knew that, in general, the enchantress felt uncomfortable around Azran and so they had always tried to make certain that the two had not been alone long. However, with Nathan forced into a leadership role, the task now more often fell to Dayn.

Nathan did not like the change he saw coming over his second son. Azran looked much older than his relative age despite spell-casters tending to look young for most of their three hundred or more year lifespans. More curious, the silver streak in Azran's black hair had spread to encompass all of one side, even down to the short beard he now sported.

The lead wizard shook his head. He refused to believe that Azran was the traitor despite all evidence to the contrary. Besides, one thing in Azran's favor was his almost manic eagerness to enter the fray when there were confrontations with the servants of the Dragon Kings. At times, Azran acted positively suicidal and both the Gryphon and Nathan had been forced to drag him out of danger.

And then there was that sword of his—

"Nathan?"

He turned to find Gwendolyn behind him. She had clearly been there for more than a moment and that made him fear the worst. "Gryphon! Is he—?"

The crimson-tressed enchantress immediately raised her hands to stop his fearful thoughts. "He's better...in fact, he's finally letting himself be healed..."

They had discovered a strange and concerning thing about the rebel leader once they had brought him back. Despite their best efforts, neither of the female spellcasters—not even Salicia, who was skilled in that particular calling—had been able to actually heal the lionbird's wounds. She and Gwendolyn had been forced to be satisfied with using mundane methods to bind his injuries and give him water as needed.

"He is fighting our efforts," the slim, flaxen-haired woman had informed Nathan. *"He or his body..."*

"Could it be some drake trick? Something Lord Purple gleaned from the Libraries? That seems more possible than what you're saying."

Yalak's lover had laughed harshly. "One would think so, but I have delved deeply. This is a choice by some part of the Gryphon's subconscious, perhaps the same part that made him babble those things when you first rescued him."

Nathan had been unable to make out much of what the Gryphon had uttered as they had dragged him to safety. The vague memory had evidently involved some battle aboard a ship and the discovery of a betrayal, but that was all the wizard had divined at the time.

He now took in the news from Gwendolyn with much relief. Without another word, Nathan seized her hand and transported both of them into the caverns below. He and Yalak had uncovered the underground system two months ago, and after determining that the Ice Dragon was unaware of their existence, had worked to make them livable. Three spellcasters also constantly maintained the shields that prevented the lord of the Northern Wastes from noticing the activity in his own domain.

Spheres of golden light illuminated the cavern chamber in which they materialized. Salicia, dressed in a dark brown robes that shimmered slightly as they adjusted to the temperature of the cavern, looked up as the pair closed. One brow arched in what Nathan realized was amusement.

Nathan saw that she was staring at his hand, which he only now recalled still held Gwendolyn's. Feeling his cheeks flush, the veteran wizard immediately released his grip. It took Gwendolyn a breath more to do the same.

"How is he?" Nathan asked, pretending nothing had happened.

Salicia's expression lost its humor. "He will be well soon, thankfully. I am still at a loss as to what we fought against. He is in some ways as unique a creature of magic as the demon Darkhorse is supposed to be..."

"*Darkhorse.*" Gwendolyn shuddered. "That beast—"

"Has the Gryphon said anything?" Nathan interrupted, not wanting the subject of Darkhorse to be continued any longer. He had a complex alliance with the demon steed and the creature's companion, the faceless warlock, Shade, that were not being helped by some incident between Gwendolyn and the ebony stallion. However uncomfortable Nathan himself was around the infamous duo, he knew that they shared the rebels' desire to see the Dragon Kings fall.

"No, nothing more," the older enchantress replied.

At that moment, the inhuman figure groaned. The sharp beak clacked together. The eyes—the almost human eyes—opened, and the Gryphon cocked his head slightly to the side as he viewed his surroundings.

"What happened?" he finally rasped.

"Assassins," Nathan answered. "Drakes from Clan Brown."

"Drakes…" The Gryphon mulled over the word. Despite his beak, he spoke perfectly.

But as fascinating as Nathan Bedlam found that simple ability, he noted an almost questioning note in the lionbird's tone. "Did you think it was someone else?"

"I thought—no. Just my imagination."

The wizard could see that the Gryphon was telling the truth. Nathan chose not to press the rebel leader about his mutterings. He did not want the Gryphon distracted by vague memories from a lost past. Nathan knew that his decision was a cold one in some ways, but he swore that if they survived this struggle, he would then assist the Gryphon in any manner necessary to uncover the truth concerning those fragmented memories.

"WHERE'S TOOS?" the lionbird asked, referring to his second-in-command. The red-haired young man with the vulpine features.

It was Salicia who answered. "He is keeping the others busy. According to him, you said the best way to keep their spirits up was to make certain they continually felt as if they had some direct purpose ahead of them."

"I did say that. Good…" The Gryphon looked far more relieved than Nathan would have expected from Salicia's answer.

He was afraid Toos was dead, the mage finally decided. The young officer was the closest thing the Gryphon had to a true friend here. The rest of the rebels looked at their inhuman commander with awe, and the Gryphon still felt uncomfortable around the spellcasters, even if he himself continued to evince tremendous potential.

That brought Nathan back to his original quandary. He knew that they had to strike back quickly rather than let the Dragon Kings gain the upper hand again, but the thought of trying to take Penacles was unnerving even to him. He had not yet discussed his idea with anyone, but if there was one being that needed to hear it, it would be the Gryphon.

"Are you well enough to talk…alone?" the wizard finally asked.

The lionbird did not hesitate. "If you think I need to be, then I am."

Salicia left the Gryphon's side without a word. She placed a hand on Gwendolyn's arm and guided the other enchantress out of the chamber.

A chuckle escaped the Gryphon. "She greatly admires you."

"Salicia? I admire her, too. She's one of the most skilled among us, not to mention one of the most humble about her abilities—"

"I was referring, as you know very well, to Lady Gwendolyn. You cannot be so blind as to not have noticed—" The Gryphon's eyes widened. "Ah! I do believe you *are*."

Suddenly feeling like a young apprentice, Nathan muttered, "I know she has some admiration for me, but that's all it is…and can be."

"I trust you'll eventually be able to convince her…perhaps…" The rebel leader cautiously started to rise. When Nathan moved to aid him, the Gryphon waved him off. "I just need a moment. I'm feeling quite well. As you said earlier, Salicia is extremely skilled."

The spellcaster finally had to broach a point related not only to the question of Penacles, but also the rebels' hopes in general. "Gryphon, Salicia had less to do with your recovery than you yourself did. In fact, a part of you actually prevented her from attempting certain spells until your body was fit enough for them."

"I don't understand."

Exhaling in frustration, Nathan continued, "Over and over I hear you speak of yourself as a warrior who just happens to have a negligible ability with magic—"

The Gryphon turned away from him. The hair and feathers at the base of the lionbird's neck visibly stood on end as he spoke. "And that's what I am. I'm no great wizard, Master Bedlam. Just a humble fighter."

"Hardly that even. This is important, though. There *is* something in you, some latent or purposely-buried ability, that could mean the difference between victory and disaster—"

Without looking back, the Gryphon snapped, "There is *nothing*! Nothing! Do you think I would let men die if I had the chance to save them?"

Nathan tried to put a comforting hand on the former mercenary's shoulder, but the Gryphon shrugged it off. "No...I've seen you nearly sacrifice yourself over and over to save a single person. You've even saved my younger son, not that he's shown his gratitude much..."

The Gryphon finally looked back. "No one needs to thank me for what is right to do, Master Bedlam."

"Can we please return to calling me 'Nathan', please? And, yes, you do need to be thanked, at least by this father." Before the Gryphon could protest, Nathan said, "And the subject at hand is *you*. You must consider what I'm saying! It's vital that you try to see what lies within you—"

"I know what is in me, Nathan. Nothing like you suggest." The lionbird slapped a fist against his chest. "I am a warrior, plain and simple…and as a warrior, I have a number of other, more important things I need to concern myself with at the moment. Matters I do need to discuss with you right now." The Gryphon met Nathan's gaze. "Matters concerning just exactly what we can do about the *City of Knowledge*…and the true master of the Dragonrealm, Lord Purple…"

THE TWO DRAKE warriors knelt on one knee before the towering figure seated on the tall, jagged throne. Standing, both kneeling figures would have stood some seven feet tall. The intricate dragon head crest atop each helm added another foot to that height. Half-seen in those helms, the blood-red eyes carefully made certain to keep focused on the marble floor at all times. Forked tongues nervously darted from lipless mouths as the pair listened to the commands of the liege. As frightening as a drake could be to those not of their race, they, in turn, had to fight from shivering before the lord of the City of Knowledge.

"You are given one more opportunity," the drake lord hissed, "and if you fail, you had better pray that you will sssuffer the sssame fate as your comrades. I will not reward you so pleasantly as the rebels did them…"

"Yesss, my lord," the senior of the two quickly replied.

"Leave me."

The duo made the greatest haste from the throne room. The Purple Dragon watched them with eyes very different than those of his people. His were of an astonishing pearl and clearly not the result of birth. Lord Purple saw the world as few others did, but how that world looked to him only he knew.

Lord Purple rose from the ivory throne and briefly turned his baleful gaze up to an empty spot on the stone ceiling. Scorch marks decorated the ceiling for several yards. Other scorch marks criss-crossed the marble floor at the same point below.

With a low, angry hiss, the master of Penacles turned to face a blank wall. He raised both gauntleted hands and concentrated.

*No...you will face me in person...*came a dark, reptilian voice in his head.

Before the drake lord could react, his surroundings shifted. The throne room spun around, then faded, to be replaced by a rocky landscape over which loomed snow-capped mountains that made those of the Northern Wastes mere hills. Indeed, directly before Lord Purple stood the most monumental of the giants, the legendary Kivan Grath. Yet, the *Seeker of the Gods* as its name was said to mean, was more than a mere mountain. It was the location of the sanctum of the Dragon Emperor himself.

Lord Purple waited, but the scenery did not change again. The Dragon King considered transforming, but suspected that this would not sit well with Lord Gold. Instead, the master of Penacles started walking.

However, he did not get very far before two riders approached in the distance. Neither rode horses, but rather the bestial cousins of the Dragon Kings, the fearsome lesser drakes. Huge, savage mounts, they lacked the speed of horses but made up for it as useful tools of war. Astride them rode a pair of drake warriors who, like their mounts, had armored hides tinted with gold.

They pulled up before Lord Purple, a third lesser drake led behind them.

"Mount," ordered one rider, purposely ignoring the fact that he addressed the lord of the City of Knowledge. Purple hid his desire to rip out the impudent warrior's throat. All of this unnecessary movement was to remind him just who ruled the lands. Lord Gold did not rest easy on his throne. He had to be aware just how much he relied on Purple to maintain what should have been the emperor's by right of birth alone.

But the realm is changing, despite our best efforts, the drake lord considered as he mounted. *What matters in the end is that I benefit most from those changes...*

He kept those thoughts well-hidden as he neared the huge mountain. Although Lord Gold entrusted Purple with much, the master of the City of Knowledge was aware that the Dragon Emperor had other tools at his disposal. That was why Lord Purple had been forced to tread cautiously since the destruction of the elaborate array that had once been the centerpiece of his throne room. Like his fellow drake lords, Gold did not accept failure on the part of his servants well.

The base of the mountain abruptly shimmered, and the mouth of what was a massive cavern and its guardians materialized before him. The two dragons bore the same hint of gold in their otherwise greenish hide. Each was so gargantuan in size that they could be nothing less than the children of the emperor himself. Lord Purple eyed the pair, but could not identify them. Neither was Kyrg or Toma, the two dukes the Purple Dragon thought the most cunning of the Lord Gold's offspring.

The leviathan on the left let loose with a roar. Lord Purple was undisturbed by the thundering cry; he knew that his arrival was being announced for those inside...as if their liege had not arranged his coming in the first place.

Continuing with the game the emperor was determined to play, the master of Penacles rode with his escort past the sentries. Once inside, the trio reined their mounts to a halt and dismounted.

From out of the shadows slithered a thing that had no features, no details. It took the reins from the three and guided the riding drakes away.

Through the vast passage the drake lord and his escort walked...until at last they entered an even greater chamber ahead. There, the first thing that caught Lord Purple's attention was not the huge throne upon which his supposed master awaited him, but rather the row upon row of magnificent, lifelike effigies representing creatures that included not only those familiar to denizens of the Dragonrealm, but others that astounded even the Dragon King. More important, although he had never uttered such to the emperor, Lord Purple could swear that there was something *living* within each of the statues.

"You are not kneeling before your emperor," rumbled the elegant figure on the throne.

Lord Purple immediately went down. He kept his gaze to the stone floor, waiting.

"You may look upon me..."

Forcing back the sneer he wished to display, the Dragon King presented an expression of obedience as he met the emperor's eyes. "Hail to you, lord of all things! Hail to you!"

The Dragon Emperor was in general shape little different from the other Dragon Kings. Like the rest, he preferred more often than not to utilize the humanoid form. Neither the emperor nor most of Lord Purple's counterparts questioned that preference, but the master of the City of Knowledge had suspicions as to the true reasons. He had gleaned some fascinating tidbits concerning the origins of the drake people, tidbits that explained more than a few things he had witnessed over the span of his reign.

"Let me firssst state as I did when lassst we talked, my sincerest sssympathies on the murder of your son and heir, Duke Vuun. A tragic loss to you, I know, and another matter for which Nathan Bedlam and this creature called the Gryphon shall pay for with more than merely their deathsss!"

"Your Imperial Majesty has made his concern for my son's slaughter well known. I thank you once more for that." Lord Purple cocked his head as if in contemplation of the heinous crime. "They will indeed pay dearly."

"And very sssoon, I trust?" asked the Golden Dragon with sudden fervor. "Thisss little rebellion wasss supposed to come to an end by now..." The Dragon Emperor leaned forward as he spoke, his blazing orbs and forked tongue emphasizing his clear dissatisfaction with the figure before him. The movement also brought better into focus those differences that *did* mark Lord Gold as more than merely another Dragon King. In the ever-shifting light of the cavern—light with naturally no visible source—the gleam of the Dragon Emperor's golden mail armor nearly blinded even Lord Purple. More impressive yet, though, was the crest atop the emperor's helm. It was a dragon head so perfect, so alive, that even among the other drake lords it had been whispered that the head's fearsome eyes *also* watched when Gold held audience.

And though the emperor remained seated for now, Purple also knew that Lord Gold stood nearly a foot taller than his vassals. In every way but one, there was no denying that here was surely the ruler of all there was.

That one thing continued to be the fact that it was *Purple* who plotted the Dragon Kings' strategy. Purple, with an assist from ambitious Brown. The line of Gold was becoming fast an unstable one, with each successive emperor less deserving to rule...at least in the kneeling drake's mind.

"It is merely a matter of time, very short time," Lord Purple replied calmly. Unlike the emperor, the master of Penacles kept his sibilance under control. Loss of that control was a loss of face among the drakes, although none would acknowledge that fact in front of the emperor.

"Ssso...so you said a month ago...and a month before that," remarked Gold with some impatience. "What is a short time to you, my lord? A year? A decade? A lifespan?"

It grated Purple that he had to hear these words from the emperor. Gold knew exactly what the Dragon Kings faced. The human spellcasters were the culmination of century upon century—nay, millennia—of breeding. They were masters of their arts. Indeed, some had these last few months begun to refer to them by just that title. Masters. *Dragon Masters*. Most of the drake lords scoffed at the ambitious title, but Purple knew very well how adept the Bedlams alone were.

And he also had some notions as to the rebel leader called the Gryphon. There was more there than met the eye. Purple's traitorous seneschal Jekrith Terin had been the first to point that out to his liege.

"Six, maybe seven weeks more, and I believe the trouble will be at an end. The plan proceeds on schedule."

He had the emperor's attention. Tongue still darting, Lord Gold leaned back in contemplation. "This new array...there is no doubt that it will be the answer?"

"It will," Purple replied, more than happy to lie to the emperor's face. "It will solve everything."

"Six to seven weeks...you will be held to that promise, my lord."

"Naturally." Six to seven weeks would enable Lord Purple to set into motion his true plan, which would not only bring the human spellcasters back into the fold as the emperor had been told, but also remove all impediments to the master of the City of Knowledge becoming the *new* emperor. "I would expect no less, Your Imperial Majesty."

"You have served well in the past. You are granted the seven weeks."

"The emperor is very generous."

"I am." Gold peered off to the side for a moment. Purple had grown more and more used to these sudden periods of distraction on the part of the emperor. It was yet another sign that the line was no longer fit to rule the rest of their kind. Purple's bloodline was strong, resilient...

Gold abruptly eyed him again. "You will need to show progress, of courssse."

Lord Purple had expected such a suggestion. Even though Gold relied on the other drake lord, the emperor did not trust him. "As you command."

"With that in mind, you will be contacted by a representative of the imperial throne who shall report to me on that progress."

This was *not* something Lord Purple had expected. Still, he doubted that he would have trouble manipulating whichever minor duke Lord Gold foisted upon him. "As you desire—"

"Expect my son Toma to arrive within a few daysss."

It was all Lord Purple could do to fight down his surprise...and dismay. "I had thought that Toma had been appointed emissary to Mito Pica."

The emperor grinned, revealing very, very sharp teeth. "Now, he has been appointed as liaison for this matter. Isss there a problem with that, my lord?"

"None." Lord Purple's mind raced. Toma was *very* crafty. He might not be eligible to inherit the imperial throne, but he was an ardent supporter of his father. Toma would do everything he could to protect Lord Gold's position...which meant that the cunning duke would be keeping a very wary eye on the master of Penacles.

It does not matter! the drake lord defiantly decided. *A hundred Tomas will not prevent me from making the rebels the key to bringing you down, my emperor...*

"I await his arrival with pleasure," he finally declared to the emperor. "When—"

But before he could finish, the cavern vanished. Lord Purple discovered himself back in his own sanctum. Gold had insisted on a last show of power just to remind the master of Penacles that there was only one emperor, and it was *not* Purple.

The drake lord chuckled. Much of his tension faded. The dramatic dismissal had only served to show him just how unstable and anxious Gold was.

Send your hound to sniff at my trail, Your Imperial Majesty, Purple thought with growing satisfaction. *He will not discover anything I do not wish him to discover. None of the others will know the truth until after I am already sitting on the throne...and you are dead at my feet, along with the Bedlams and everyone else who stands in my way...*

The Purple Dragon turned toward the corridor that would lead him directly to the most precious of his resources...the legendary libraries of Penacles. They had given him what he had needed to be first among the Dragon Kings, and soon they would give him what he needed to be master of *all*.

You are in good humor, a voice akin to the grave remarked in his head. *We trust this means that you have agreed to our suggestion?*

Turning to the shadows to his right, Purple beheld the vague shape of what seemed an armored and helmeted human. The drake knew better, though. What had half-materialized before him was far more than that.

"I have given it much thought," Purple responded. "I will agree, so long as you fulfill your part of the bargain exactly as needed. In return, you will afterward have access to the libraries for your search."

The silhouette of the head nodded once. Despite the shadow being of a being shorter than Purple, the Dragon King kept a safe distance between the two of them.

Then the Lords of the Dead will await your word when you wish us to move...

"Asss you say…" The Dragon King tried to walk past his ghostly visitor.

Your son is an interesting addition, it suddenly remarked with a hint of dark mirth. *He wishes you to know that he looks forward to you joining him soon…*

Lord Purple bared his teeth. "Tell my son he can wait for the rest of eternity."

Oh, it will hardly be that long…it never is…

Before Lord Purple could respond, the outline melted into the shadows around it. Only then did the Dragon King sense the warmth returning to his surroundings. He quietly hissed, the only hint that this abrupt encounter had bothered him far more than facing the emperor he intended to overthrow.

But then again, what was standing before even the Dragon Emperor compared to striking a bargain with those who could raise and control the *unliving?*

3

STORM WATERS

Shade frowned, not that anyone, even the warlock himself, could have seen that reaction. The spellcaster shoved his hood back slightly in order to better view the sight below, revealing a lock of dark hair but no other discernible feature. There was a hint of a youthfulness in his general appearance that the legend surrounding him gave the lie to. He who was only known to the world by the one mirky title—that despite the many actual names his various incarnations had given themselves—had walked the Dragonrealm longer than the drakes had ruled the lands.

Of course, *walked* was perhaps the wrong word to use considering that Shade had spent most of his accursed existence being hunted by nearly every other creature. He could not blame them for doing so, either. After all, depending on the incarnation, the warlock had either been trying to help those enslaved by the Dragon Kings...or creating more bloodshed and chaos than all the drake lords combined.

In this particular life—one stretching back a mere five years from his last death—Shade called himself Vadym. He asked anyone who had the bad fortune to meet him to call him by that name, although none of them, not even Darkhorse, did it with much effort. The warlock could hardly blame them, but he still tried. The name gave him some mental—and perhaps *moral*—separation from his previous incarnations and the faint hope that somehow this would be the one that finally escaped the curse.

But considering that his fragmented memory did not include just how that curse had begun, Shade continued with his other efforts. In this case, he did what he could to aid the rebellion. Shade knew that there had been other rebellions in the past and that those had easily been crushed, but he had actual hope that this one might succeed. If it did, it would perhaps make his task of freeing himself easier. All he had to do was make certain that he did not die before that. If not, then he himself might become the rebels' doom.

However, what caught his attention now demanded that he risk himself despite his potential threat to every living being in the Dragonrealm. Shade pulled his hood forward again, then wrapped his voluminous cloak around him just before vanishing.

He reappeared at the northern edge of the Dagora Forest, a place near but not too near where most of the elven tribes lived. Shade liked the elves; they did not immediately try to kill him as most other beings did. Indeed, the warlock sometimes felt that they knew more about him than he did.

It was not elves, though, that he watched, nor was it any of the avian Seekers, who once had dominated this area. Of course, Shade would have been surprised to find Seekers here now; after their ill-fated attack on the City of Knowledge in an attempt to hunt down a renegade of their race, they had all but vanished. The aeries he had visited were empty. Where the creatures had gone, the faceless warlock could not say.

And neither could he say just what Nathan Bedlam's youngest son was doing standing at the forest edge holding his black sword to the south. Azran Bedlam stared without blinking at the dense forest as if seeking something. Shade could sense the other spell-caster's powers at work, and marveled at the sophistication of the youngest Bedlam's abilities.

Azran murmured something. Shade at first thought that the wizard had noticed him, then realized that Nathan's son was talking to himself.

Still, the warlock's presence did not go unnoticed long. The sword suddenly swung Shade's direction, followed belatedly by Azran's gaze.

"You…Shade…"

"Call me 'Vadym'…this time." The warlock frowned. "Are you well, Azran Bedlam?"

The bearded mage's face suddenly came to life. He chuckled. "Oh, I'm more than well! Do you play chess…Vadym?"

For some reason, the question disturbed the warlock. It almost but not quite stirred some ancient memory. "I am certain that I have played several variations over the course of my existence."

"We should play some time," Azran remarked companionably. He sheathed the sword. "I've got this set you'd simply marvel over…"

It took much to disconcert Shade, but the youngest Bedlam was continuing to succeed at doing just that. It no longer had to do with only the odd questions, but something in the wizard's attitude as well. Azran acted like there was no terrible struggle going on, no terrible struggle that had already claimed countless lives and might even take that of Azran's father.

"Perhaps when this is over…" the warlock finally replied.

"'This?' Oh, yes, of course. Is my father with Gwendolyn McArn, do you think?"

"I could not say…" Shade glanced from the Azran to the sword and then to the forest. For once, the fact that no one could make out his face was of use to him. Azran could not see the warlock's observations.

A feminine laugh filled Shade's ears. He stiffened.

"Is something wrong?" Azran asked with a tone of utter innocence.

Ignoring the question, Shade glanced in the direction he had heard the laughter. Despite his considerable skills, he sensed nothing out of the ordinary.

The warlock returned his attention to Azran—and found the point of the black blade barely an inch from his face.

Azran grinned. "Do you think the sword could pierce it? The haze around your face, I mean. Do you think the sword could cut it away? Would I be able to see your face?"

"You would only be likely to slay me," Shade remarked as calmly as he could. For himself, he did not fear death; in fact, often he dreamed of a final peace. However, there was always the knowledge that his demise would be temporary, that he would rise again in some other part of the Dragonrealm with a mind that this time would steer toward darkness. "I would not recommend it...for your sake as well as the sakes of your father and the rest."

"So that part of the legend is actually true?" Azran sheathed the sword once more. "That's fascinating!"

"Not if you live it...or suffer because of it." For one of the few times he could recall, the warlock found himself growing impatient. "For what reason are you—?"

But Azran chose that moment to turn from Shade. "You're absolutely right about my father. I should see how they're doing. Have you any idea where they might be? No, never mind, I know how to find Father. I always do."

And with that, the wizard simply vanished.

Shade swore in a language long dead, a language he had not even realized he knew. The warlock reached out with his senses, but found no trace of the younger spellcaster.

Nathan Bedlam, I think your son has gone quite mad, Shade thought. *Mad…or something worse…*

The hooded spellcaster stiffened. He had no idea why the last thought should occur to him. Yet, as the warlock peered in the direction Azran had been staring, he remembered the feminine laughter…remembered it and felt certain that for some reason it had not only been real, but that he and everyone else should be very, very worried…

YALAK AND DAYN eyed the desolate landscape with less-than-eager expressions. Wenslis was hardly a land conducive to promises of a new, safer site for the rebels, its incessant rains and swampy soil purely the preference of its lord and master, the Storm Dragon. Still, the very nature of Wenslis made it a choice that they had to investigate, for surely none of the Dragon Kings would assume the rebels mad enough to seek it for a hiding place.

"Where do you think we should check?" Dayn finally asked.

In that regard, Yalak glanced at one of the three other spellcasters with them. "Micaya? You grew up in this place. You still think it a choice?"

The sturdy female grinned. "There's more to Wenslis than you think. You're just seeing the surface."

"It is what might lay under the surface that I am concerned about. Recall that entire armies have vanished in these swamplands." Every now and then, disputes would break out between Dragon Kings that could not simply be ended by fear of punishment by the emperor. Wenslis and Lochivar—the latter ruled by the Black Dragon—were often at odds about their borders. More than once, Lord Black had sent his mist-ensorcelled fanatics into the swampy realm, only to have them vanish. On the other hand, Yalak knew that those warriors sent to attack Lochivar naturally

29

ended up becoming slaves of Lord Black due to the mind-numbing mists draping the southern land.

"The plant life here...it's *wrong*," muttered Adam Gudwead. The brown-haired mage frowned as he reached for a blade of grass. Before he could touch it, the blade bent from his fingers. "You see?"

"Is anything normal in any land ruled by the Dragon Kings?" asked a ruddy, squat male with flat, white hair. "We only never paid any attention before because we were their puppets."

"And now we are not, Lucius Moone," Yalak interjected. "Very well, Micaya. Guide us in but be both—-"

"Discreet and swift, I know." Brushing back her short black and silver hair, the enchantress leaned forward...and transformed into a wolf of similar coloring. Despite the swampy landscape, the wolf moved with ease.

"She gets to toy with magic while we're supposed to do nothing more than keep our shields up so that Storm doesn't notice us," grumbled Lucian as the rest followed Micaya.

"She is risking more than any of us," Yalak reminded his fellow mage. "In that form, she cannot transport herself away or cast any strong spells. She relies on *us*. Remember that."

Lucian quietly nodded. They were all aware that exceptional skills such as Micaya displayed now required sacrifice in other areas of the arts.

The wolf picked her way through the swamp, seeking something in particular. Despite the humans having to tread in shin-deep water, their lupine guide barely seemed to get wet at all.

Yalak eyed the horizon. Black clouds covered it, but then, black clouds generally shrouded most of the sky in Wenslis. What the balding wizard sought was any sudden shift in those clouds. That would be a telltale sign that they had been discovered by Lord Storm.

And if that happened, Yalak knew that they had to leave and leave fast. He had already taken it upon himself to see to Micaya's safety, but knew that Dayn would do so if something befell the older mage. Yalak was very high on the Dragon Kings' list of wanted rebels, falling behind only Nathan and the Gryphon.

"This place stinks," Dayn murmured.

"It is a swamp. It—" Yalak froze. To his eyes, it was as if a veil of many colors covered everything.

He had a vision of a water lily casting a spell, followed by a wolf that had to be Micaya chewing on her own tail. Lucian was arguing with a shadow while Dayn cowered before an infant.

The vision faded. Yalak peered at Nathan's son, but neither Dayn nor the others had noticed the change coming over the elder wizard. Yalak's visions often took less than the blink of an eye, even if to him they often seemed to last forever.

Not all visions were so strange, but too many were. When he had worked to make divination his art, Yalak had never expected that it would, in fact, choose to make *him* its tool.

And what a cost it demands, he thought, aware of at least part of it intended for him, aware of things he could not—was not able *permitted to*—tell the others. *But before I pay that cost, I must at least see this war come to the conclusion we need...*

"She's spotted something," Dayn whispered, interrupting Yalak's darkening thoughts.

"Yes, I know." *Part of this new vision is already taking place.* "Dayn...call her back...quickly."

"Why should—?"

"Do it!"

Yalak's rare show of frustration stirred the younger Bedlam to action. Even as Dayn moved to call to Micaya, Yalak quietly stepped to the rear of the party.

Adam was the first to notice his action. "Yalak, what is it?"

The balding mage pointed at the swamp grass. "Bind it, Adam, before it binds you!"

"I don't understand!"

"We have been expected all this time!"

To his credit, the other wizard did not ask any more questions. He eyed the nearest blades—

And froze.

At the same time, Dayn shouted, "Master Yalak! Micaya! She's vanished!"

Too late! Why must so many of these visions come too late! Despite that knowledge, Yalak continued conjuring. "Defend yourself!"

The water from the swamp rose high into the air, leaving a barely muddy landscape. The surrounding grass suddenly wriggled as if dying. At the same time, Adam stirred from the trance the grass had cast upon him.

Dayn set a blaze that coursed along the now-dry swamp bed. Lucian created a bubble of force that shoved aside the rest of the swamp grass and sent the vermin revealed by Yalak's spell scattering.

The nearby swamp grass blossomed, creating fearsome, serpentine heads. The blades pulled themselves out by their roots, and at Adam's silent command, immediately slithered to the east.

And from there, from where the swamp deepened, arose the true threat to the party. A massive reptilian form that bore some resemblance to a dragon, but had even less relation to one than a riding drake.

A Regga... Yalak realized. *A Regga...ten times the size of what it should be...*

Long of jaw and with teeth that remained outside even when the mouth was shut tight on prey, the crocodilian Regga rushed toward the spellcasters with a swiftness its short, muscular legs belied. It opened wide its maw and focused on Dayn and Lucian, the two wizards directly before it.

"Stand away!" warned Yalak.

He saw that Dayn had enough sense to listen, but Lucian acted as far too many mages would have when faced by an overgrown lizard. Lucian only saw a simple beast; Yalak saw the trap.

A golden ring created by Lucian wrapped itself around the charging Regga. It squeezed the jaws together.

Lucian smiled.

The golden ring faded...and another formed around the wizard's arms and torso.

"What by the—?"

Yalak had no choice but to try one thing to save Lucian. The senior wizard released the great volume of water he had raised into the air.

The swamp water struck the Regga with the force of a gargantuan boulder. Crushed under its weight, the Regga sank beneath the surface.

"Find Micaya!" Yalak shouted to Dayn. "Adam! Keep those blades moving to the east!"

"But what about—?" Adam started.

The water roiled. A lengthy, scaled tail thrashed to the surface.

The Regga's head broke above the water again. The narrow, yellow orbs fell upon Yalak. The swamp beast lunged.

But Yalak had foreseen this and had already cast a spell to transport himself to a different location. However, had any of the others read his thoughts at that time, they would have been horrified at his choice of destinations. Yalak sought to send himself to a spot only a few *feet* from the gaping jaws.

Instead, the balding mage materialized far from the Regga... just as he had actually expected. Lucian's near-fatal attack had been the result of what were likely many spells cast in advance upon the Regga. Whatever magical assault was used against the creature— or even within a certain range of it—was turned against its caster. Even simpler spells such as one designed to transport a wizard to safety would be reversed…the last with the intent that the startled victim would end up in the jaws of the Storm Dragon's pet.

There was no sign of Dayn. Yalak had to hope that he had located Micaya, whom the elder mage was certain was not the reason the Storm Dragon had known of their arrival. Yalak and Dayn had only decided to try Wenslis barely an hour before and had only then inquired of Micaya as to the best possible location near this part of the border. The senior spellcaster felt certain that he would have noticed even the most subtle spell on her part had she been the one trying to warn Lord Storm.

The Regga's sudden roar served to remind Yalak that there was a more imminent problem on hand. Worse, beyond the Regga, murky shapes began to rise from the swamp…humanoid shapes.

No, Yalak corrected himself. *Shapes that were* once *human…*

They now knew what had happened to at least some of those who had been lost in the various border wars between Wenslis and Lochivar. Yalak made out matted beards hanging from nearly flesh-less faces and rusting breastplates still with a hint of the ebony color that had marked them as servants of one of the previous Lord Blacks.

It took Yalak only a short glance around to see that the undead rose *everywhere*. There had been no sign of the corpses when he had emptied the swamp, which meant that they had been buried deep in the mud. Considering the consistently foul temperaments of lords of Wenslis, Yalak imagined that those men's deaths had been horrific. He could picture their manic and ultimately futile struggles as the mud had sucked them down, smothering them.

The undead closed on the wizards' locations even as the Regga spun to pursue Yalak. Adam and Lucian stood side-by-side, the former concentrating on the shambling corpses while the latter kept an eye out for any attack on his companion. The wizards had long learned to work together, some so well, in fact, that they were permanently teamed.

And would that we had such as Basil and Tyr here, Yalak thought as he scrambled to a higher location. Ignoring the other prey, the crocodilian monster wended its way after the veteran wizard. Clearly, through Lord Storm, it knew who was in command among the rebels. Yalak supposed he should have been flattered.

As the Regga neared, Yalak used his power to loosen a large fragment of dirt and stone. It tumbled down on the Regga, striking the beast hard on the snout. The force of the blow did not injure the gigantic predator, but it did send the creature sliding back.

Despite the minor victory, Yalak was worried. He would have expected more from Lord Storm than these servants, potent as they were.

Where are your children, master of Wenslis? Yalak silently asked. *Why are there no dragons yet?*

His footing suddenly became unstable. Yalak dropped to his knees rather than fall over the edge. He saw that he had become too complacent; instead of attacking the wizard directly, the Regga was now undermining the low hill. It did not take any guidance from a Dragon King to teach the swamp predator such a tactic. Built low to the ground—even as huge as it was—the Regga knew enough that to reach prey it often had to attack from beneath.

Yalak! Dayn's voice thundered in the other wizard's head. *I've got her! We need to get her help! She—*

You can tell me later! Keep linked to me! Still filled with misgivings for reasons he could not explain, Yalak reached out to the rest. Adam had the first line of ghouls bound to one spot by his animated grass blades, but more and more undead clustered behind them. Yalak doubted that Adam could stem the entire tide.

Lucian and the taller mage quickly joined thoughts with Yalak and Dayn. Yalak then concentrated on a location near the eastern edge of the Dagora Forest.

The five spellcasters vanished—

—And reappeared in the midst of the rotting army.

Yalak could all but hear the Storm Dragon's laughter. The lord of Wenslis intended to play with his enemies before striking the fatal blow.

Yet more rotting corpses erupted from the swamp. Adam and Lucian immediately worked to keep them at bay while Yalak turned to Dayn to see to the unconscious Micaya. The enchantress remained in her lupine form, but where she had been untouched by the swamp before, now she was soaked and mud-covered. Her body shivered and her chest only rose with effort.

"I couldn't find her at first!" Nathan's son quickly explained. "I finally barely sensed her somewhere deep below! She must've been sucked beneath without warning..."

"No doubt..." It verified Yalak's belief that Micaya had not been the traitor.

"They're pressing closer!" Adam shouted.

Not only were the ghouls fighting their way through the other wizards' defensive spells, but the Regga was nearly upon them again. With another roar, the gigantic reptile surged forward.

Yalak tried to foresee the best outcome for the wizards. There were few. Worse, he saw that nearly every path meant death for the majority of the party. Not in one did the group survive unscathed.

Yet, you must pick a path! he ordered himself. *Better one or two perish than all no matter how vile that might seem...*

Only Nathan knew that more than once Yalak had been forced to make a decision that the latter knew would mean certain death for someone. Still, Yalak continued to try to convince himself that he saved other lives of equal value by making such choices. In fact, Nathan had told him just that more than once.

It made his decision now no less easier.

"Lucian! Adam! To me!"

The duo retreated to Yalak. To Dayn, he ordered, "Be prepared to transport her to your father the moment I say so! Understood?"

Dayn nodded. Yalak eyed the other two mages. "Follow my guidance! Trust in me no matter what!"

Both strengthened their links to Yalak. He stared at the Regga, which had finally discovered just where its prey had gone. The crocodilian monster closed on the tiny humans.

Yalak used his spell to help draw the Regga to them even faster.

Despite his assurances, he felt Adam and Lucian immediately struggle to reverse his efforts. Yalak tried to mentally reassure the two. It was the entire party's only hope.

Adam calmed.

Lucian did not. Despite Yalak's efforts, Lucian severed the link with the others and instinctively tried to transport himself to a place of safety.

No! Yalak silent warned him. *You will—*

Lucian paid him no mind. The other wizard completed his spell, vanishing from Yalak's side—

—and landing instead among the thickest gathering of the undead. The magic surrounding the Regga had once again reversed the spellcaster's intention.

Yalak knew that he had only one chance. With Adam still supporting him, the elder mage finished his own effort.

The spellwork around the Regga twisted Yalak's own casting exactly as he planned. Rather than bring the beast to its prey, the spell instead did the opposite. The huge fiend flew backward, heading directly into the mass of undead.

Praying, Yalak focused on Lucian. The other wizard desperately fought to repel the swarming undead. However, with one arm held by a decrepit corpse missing its jaw and the other barely pushing away another ghoul, Lucian was clearly having trouble concentrating.

The Regga crashed into the first ranks of the undead, his bulk so great that he easily crushed all of them and continued on unimpeded. The hulking form headed directly to where Lucian fought to survive.

Yalak cast again, well aware that the Regga's nearby presence would reverse his effort. He concentrated on sending Lucian as far from his comrades as possible.

The other wizard disappeared just as the Regga bowled into the macabre army. The gargantuan beast created a tremendous wave that overwhelmed more undead farther back.

"Yalak," Adam murmured anxiously. "Where'd you send Lucian?"

Instead of replying, Yalak said, "Now, Dayn. Now."

As he spoke, Yalak felt a sinister force he knew to be a new effort to trap the spellcasters form over the area. Of Lucian…of Lucian, Yalak sensed nothing. Absolutely nothing. Yalak had guessed wrong…and proven his premonitions correct in the process.

"Stand with me, Adam!" he commanded, resigned to the choice he had taken. "We need to give Dayn the protection he needs."

Yalak sensed the unseen force begin draping over them. Had he not foreseen exactly this attack, Yalak knew that he and the others would have joined poor Lucian. This new spell was intended to sap their wills, leave them little more coherent than the ghoulish army.

But because he had known what would come, Yalak and Adam were able to shield the remaining party long enough for Dayn to successfully transport Micaya away. Once that was accomplished, Yalak began a departure spell of his own.

The landscape shifted. One of the great chambers from the cavern system hidden beneath the Northern Wastes formed around Yalak and Adam.

To Yalak's relief, Dayn and Micaya could be found only a few yards from them. Even better, Nathan was already rushing toward them—or rather, to his son and the unconscious enchantress.

Before Nathan could speak with Dayn, Yalak called to the father. Nathan joined his old friend without question despite clearly wishing to see to his son.

"Yalak, what—?"

"It's Lucian. Help me, Nathan. Perhaps together we can still do something..."

Nathan did not speak. The binding of their minds together happened with an ease and completeness perhaps only Basil and Tyr could match. Nathan allowed Yalak to guide their efforts, the balding mage better aware of where they needed to search.

Yalak's senses brought the image of Wenslis' border forward. The black clouds still smothered the sky, but other than that, all appeared calm. There was no sign of the Regga, no sign of the undead. Despite their combined abilities, he and Nathan could not sense *any* of the Storm Dragon's insidious defenses.

Unfortunately, nor could they sense any trace of Lucian Moone.

However, another presence suddenly made itself known. Barely had it done so than the two wizards quickly withdrew. They dared not face Wenslis' drake lord just now nor let him discover their whereabouts.

"I'm sorry, Yalak," Nathan whispered as the pair separated minds.

"I could foresee that there was little hope of keeping all of us alive, and then I foresaw that Lucian was most likely to die," the other man answered, his rage at himself barely unchecked. "But I could not even be granted the punishment of knowing just what doom I so cavalierly cast him to! My damned abilities should at least give me *that* if it cannot give me a way to save Lucian or any of the others before him!"

Nathan patted him on the shoulder. "You've saved far more people than you've lost. Few of us can say that."

"What good is foresight when it leads to this?" Yalak gritted his teeth. "We were expected, too, Nathan! Either by someone with better talent than me—and that would not surprise me after this debacle—or because there *is* a traitor."

Nathan shook his head. "Traitor or not, it no longer matters. The Gryphon and I have been talking things over and we've come to an agreement."

"Over what?"

The elder Bedlam guided Yalak farther from the others. "Over just something like this. We'll find this traitor, should they exist. I swear to that, but in some ways, he or she might become a moot point. We've decided to give the Dragon Kings what they want."

Lucian's fate still hung heavy on Yalak, but he could not help becoming caught up in Nathan's words. "My foresight is failing me. You plan to give them what they want?"

"It's very simple." Nathan looked as grim as Yalak had ever seen him. Grim, but very determined. Yalak had seen that expression… and it had always boded ill for those standing against his old friend. "They want to know what we're doing and where we are? We'll give them that. We're not running anymore. We've got to win this war and win it fast."

"You're talking about attacking Penacles." Everything made sense to Yalak now. "About seizing the libraries…"

Nathan's expression grew grimmer. "Yes…Penacles, too. But that's only one half of it. We need to cut off the head, even if in some ways it's a ceremonial one. We need to take Penacles, Yalak, but we also need to take down the symbol of drake dominance. We need to take down the Dragon Emperor, as well."

4

SHADOWS OF THE DEAD

Gwendolyn's relief at the Gryphon's recovery was tempered by a sense of unease that she could not explain. The enchantress felt as if she was constantly being watched, but whenever she looked around, she saw no one eyeing her.

The cavern complex was huge, so huge that the ragtag army had no trouble fitting into a few chambers. Glancing at the walls, Gwendolyn could not help wondering if they were entirely natural. Nathan and the others believed that they were—at least that was how they talked about the place to the rest—but Gwendolyn sometimes felt as if some tremendous power had once existed here—

"You can still feel them, if you're attuned well enough…still feel when this place was one of power…"

Stifling her surprise, the enchantress turned to find Azran. Gwendolyn considered herself a fairly competent spellcaster, but she had not sensed Nathan's son near her. Even if he had just materialized, Gwendolyn was certain that she should have felt *some* hint of his arrival.

She managed to smile despite the fact that something about Azran—something wrong—always disturbed her. She never gave any hint to Nathan or Dayn, but could not understand why they themselves could not sense what she did.

"What do you mean?" Gwendolyn finally asked as pleasantly as possible.

His smile far too wide and hungry for her tastes, Azran indicated the walls. "This was one of their great places! They had one in each of what we call the thirteen kingdoms, plus their key cities on the other continents and major islands!"

"Who? And how do you know any of this?"

He chuckled. "I've been studying a lot. Learning much! You should see what I've accomplished—" Azran cut off, suddenly looking thoughtful. "In fact, I'm working on a spell that you should see—"

"Azran! There you are! Father's been looking for you!"

Although Dayn did not see his brother's expression, the brief shift Gwendolyn noticed nearly made her gasp. She bit her lip to keep from doing so, and by that time, Azran wore a companionable expression that he then turned on his older sibling.

"I was just planning on going to him," Azran replied to Dayn. "I just happened to appear near Gwendolyn and thought I should at least say hello..."

Dayn smiled at his brother, then, with one smooth movement, slipped around him to stand near the enchantress. The smile remained, to Gwendolyn as false as that worn by Azran.

"Well, we're glad you're back. I know Father's been really concerned. He wants to talk to you about a few things we're planning, too."

Azran stood silent for a moment. Finally, with a nod, he turned and left the pair.

Once Azran was gone, Dayn exhaled. "I'm sorry about that, Gwendolyn. I know you don't feel comfortable around him. He's not bad…just…I think he's just not well. He's been obsessed with proving himself to Father, although Father's always been as proud of him as he as he is with me. I don't—"

"Please! Don't say anymore, Dayn. Forgive me for reacting so. I worry about Nathan and how Azran might affect his concentration. One hesitation, one mistake, and your father—" She paused. "—and everyone else might die!"

Despite her dire words, Dayn actually gave her a true smile. "You're worried most about Father and I know that. You don't have to pretend with me. I'd like him to see you as you see him. He's been alone too long." The wizard exhaled. "I hardly remember Mother myself and Azran never knew her, but she and Father were deeply in love despite theirs having started out as a political marriage. I know that. It's been far too long, though. I recall her well enough to understand that she'd want him to be with someone else. By the Dragon of the Depths, from what I remember of my grandmother, the Duchess Verlene, I know that she was hellbent on making certain that Father remarried for Azran's and my sake."

Gwendolyn felt her cheeks reddening. "Please, Dayn…"

"I'm sorry. I just wish Father knew how fortunate he is. The more I know you, the more jealous I am."

Before the subject could grow even more embarrassing for Gwendolyn, Nathan's voice suddenly echoed loud in her head. Even if she had not seen Dayn's expression stiffen, she would have known that the message was not for her alone.

I want everyone to join me immediately…

Neither said a word as they both transported themselves to where Nathan stood surrounded by a small but growing audience. Spellcaster after spellcaster popped into existence. Some of them Gwendolyn had not seen for months. Yet, they and the rest all shared one thing in common; a look of weariness that the thus-far fruitless war had cast upon them.

And what bothered the enchantress even more was that when at last no more spellcasters materialized, she knew it was because those missing members had fallen to the Dragon Kings.

That fact was not lost to Nathan, either. He shook his head. To a bald, hawkish wizard, he asked, "Fera?"

"Lost in the hills near Gordag-Ai," murmured the newcomer. "She took two drakes and a dozen soldiers with her."

Although the numbers might have hinted otherwise, the loss of the two drakes well outweighed that of the human fighters serving them. Drakes did not multiply as quickly as humans did and in general served as commanders overseeing scores—even hundreds—of Gwendolyn's race.

"Thirty-eight, then," intoned Yalak, who stood on Nathan's left. "We are thirty-eight, then."

Thirty-eight. Once, when they had been the prize servants of the Dragon Kings, the spellcasters had numbered as great as a hundred. As Gwendolyn carefully watched Nathan's face darken more, she remembered how a third of that hundred had sacrificed themselves in enabling him to free the rest from the magical array the lord of Penacles had used to maintain the spellcasters' utter obedience. And since the human mages had declared their freedom and fought to gain it for the rest of the human race, nearly another third had already perished. Gwendolyn had already been aware of Lucian Moone's death and now here was another. She had not known Fera, but mourned her as if she had.

At this rate, we'll all be dead in less than a year with nothing but our spilled blood to show, she suddenly thought with horror. A chill ran through her, and she tried to refocus her attention on the moment at hand.

No doubt likely well aware of what not only Gwendolyn but the rest were thinking, Nathan defiantly proclaimed, "But we are about to show the Dragon Kings that thirty-eight is *still* a number that they will come to fear…"

The enchantress took heart from his words, then noticed a figure detached itself from the area hidden by Nathan and Yalak's bodies. Azran. In contrast to the tension radiating from the rest of the gathering, he looked bored. In fact, as Nathan continued, the younger son drifted away from the wizards.

Despite knowing that she should continue listening, Gwendolyn quietly stepped back, then followed after Azran. The irony was not lost on her that here she was pursuing the very person whom she had just tried to evade.

Azran abandoned the chamber for an obscure side corridor. Gwendolyn kept a steady pace. She did not try to hide from Azran. He was too powerful a wizard to be fooled by all but the most potent spells and Gwendolyn saw no reason to attempt such. After all, despite his curious behavior, the enchantress was certain that he was not the traitor they all spoke about.

Azran vanished around a turn in the corridor. Gwendolyn hesitated. She imagined following, only to have Azran waiting just out of sight so that he could frighten her. *It would be just like him to play such a childish trick,* the enchantress thought with some frustration.

Deciding that she had been foolish enough to take things this far, Gwendolyn chose instead to abandon following Nathan's son. Hoping that she had not missed anything important in Nathan's speech, she turned—

And found an icy *wall* blocking her path. More unnerving, she immediately thought she saw something *moving* within the wall, a shape almost human…but as pale as snow.

Recovering, the enchantress took a step away from the wall and concentrated. A wall was nothing to a spellcaster. Gwendolyn concentrated on Dayn, imagining herself standing next to him—

Nothing happened. In fact, Gwendolyn quickly realized that she could not sense *any* of the other spellcasters.

The enchantress could only imagine one person responsible for this. "This is not humorous, Azran! Stop this immediately!"

The only response to her demand was the appearance of another vague shape moving about in the wall. It joined the first in alternating back and forth. The enchantress found herself instinctively trying to keep track of both at the same time and thus managing to follow neither successfully.

The two figures abruptly converged, then lunged her direction.

But before she could discover whether they could actually escape the wall and attack her, Azran leapt between her and the murky figures. The black blade darted forward almost as if of its own will and pierced both the wall and the foremost shape.

A horrific squeal escaped the icy wall. The first shape faded.

The second shape immediately receded deep into the wall.

"You will not escape so easily," Azran uttered. He withdrew the sword, then immediately thrust again.

This time, the blade penetrated all the way to the horned hilt. As it did, its dark hue rapidly spread along the wall, engulfing the ice.

Although Azran appeared to have the situation in hand, Gwendolyn still decided to proceed with a spell of her own. She concentrated on the darkened wall—

—And a pair of white, icy hands coming from behind her clamped against the sides of her head.

The enchantress tried to call out, but no sound escaped her. She had not realized that she had stepped near one of the other walls nor that the creatures had spread to there.

The chill radiating from the hands overtook her mind. Her thoughts clouded…and then began to fill with chaotic images of what seemed to be the underground cavern system, but now filled with color and light. Half-seen figures flitted back and forth, and a sense of lost glory touched the enchantress.

Her entire body shook with cold, but Gwendolyn feared more the thoughts creeping into her head. It was as if something from those ancient images sought to *wear* her, become her.

The horror of that happening stirred Gwendolyn to renewed effort. She pulled her thoughts together enough to cast one last spell.

A blazing red aura surrounded the enchantress. Gwendolyn felt the monstrous hands release their hold.

The passage returned to normal. Absolutely normal. As her gaze cleared, the fiery-tressed enchantress saw that not even the blackened wall remained.

And what was even more odd, there was also no sign of Azran.

For the first time, Gwendolyn feared for Dayn's brother. She remembered what the hands had done to her and worried that somehow Azran had fallen prey to a similar trap.

She looked back the direction that she had seen Azran walking. With trepidation, Gwendolyn peered down the darkened passage. Of Azran there was no sign, not even a magical trace.

But from the way she had come there rose another magical trace that grew stronger by the second. It was utterly like no other and so immediately identified the newcomer.

The inhuman figure slowed as he caught sight of the enchantress. "Lady Gwendolyn...what are you doing down this corridor?"

"I was—I saw Azran—"

The lionbird cocked his head. "Azran? But I just left him with Master Nathan a moment ago. In fact, Azran remained with us for the entire time we talked, maybe half an hour by my reckoning."

"'Half an hour'?" Gwendolyn frowned. "Nathan and Yalak were speaking to the rest of the spellcasters just a few moments ago—"

"If I may, that was before." He moved closer. "You look very pale, Lady Gwendolyn. I think perhaps you should speak with Lady

Salicia. You've done much to help us, but I think the effort's worn you out more than you think."

"No—but—"

At that moment, Dayn entered the passage. He immediately looked relieved to see Gwendolyn. "There you are! We wondered what happened to you."

Gwendolyn grew indignant. "Ask your brother! I followed him when he left your father's speech to the rest of the spellcasters, then—"

His frown cut her off. "Azran never left Father. I should know. I had him in sight all the time. I was afraid that he'd leave again before Father could speak with him."

Gwendolyn started to argue with Dayn, but the Gryphon cut her off. "Lady Gwendolyn, I'm certain that you and Dayn can question Azran about whether he was with you or not. It certainly makes more sense than futilely arguing here."

Dayn reached a hand to her. "He's right. We'll ask Azran and I can promise you I'll know if he's lying. What do you say?"

The enchantress strode past him. "I say we find him now."

Dayn wordlessly followed her. Gwendolyn felt bad about the way she had just treated Nathan's older son, but her concern over what had happened to her had been replaced by a growing fury focused on Azran.

It did not take long to locate Dayn's brother, for he was exactly where she had been told he would be. Azran stood by his father's side as the elder Bedlam finished speaking with Wade Arkonsson. The scarred spellcaster nodded at something Nathan said to him, then simply vanished.

Both Nathan and Azran eyed Gwendolyn with what appeared honest curiosity as she approached. For once, the enchantress ignored Nathan.

"Answer me truthfully, Azran," she demanded as she also pointed at the passage from which she had stepped. "Did you not just come from there, and did you not just save me from something lurking in the walls?"

He grinned. "To be your noble knight would be an honor…but, no, I've been here with Father all along. Isn't that so, Father?"

Nathan met Gwendolyn's eyes. "He's been with me since I summoned everyone together. The only ones missing were Salicia, who was with the wounded…and then at some point, you, Gwen."

She knew that Azran was clever. She knew that Azran was talented. Yet, Gwendolyn also knew Nathan. The enchantress could not fathom Nathan being fooled by his son.

"Give me a moment with her," the elder Bedlam requested of his sons.

"As you wish, Father," Dayn replied. "Come, Azran."

Azran clearly wanted to stay, but followed Dayn. Once the two had left Nathan and Gwendolyn, the master wizard leaned close and whispered, "Tell me exactly what happened in the passage."

She told him everything. Nathan did not look at her as if he thought her mad. In fact, his troubled expression told Gwendolyn that he knew more than he had let on when his sons had been near.

"This is an ancient place, you know that," he began the moment she finished. "Older than the Dragon Kings. Older than the Seekers or the Quel. Older than any of the races that have ruled…except one…"

"You're…you're speaking of the founding race…"

He looked surprised. "The Green Dragon was thorough with your education, I see."

"I know that he's studied the past because he believes it the key to the future."

Nathan hesitated. "Indeed? Has he also mentioned the *Vraad?*"

"No…who are they?"

"A race of sorcerers who rose and fell before the Dragon Kings. Wielders of magic such as we cannot even imagine. From my research, often vicious, sometimes noble. They appeared in this land as if from nowhere and vanished just as mysteriously."

"Is this one of their sanctums? I thought you said that this was a place of the founding race. That seems to be what Azran thinks—"

"Does he?" Nathan visibly considered that fact, then went on. "No. This isn't one of the Vraad's sanctums. I've only found one of those, and I can assure you it looks nothing like this."

Gwendolyn was even more puzzled than before. "Then why bring up the Vraad at all? If they no longer exist—" She hesitated, stunned by a subtle change in his expression. "Do they still? Why wouldn't we know of them, then?"

"We do, I think. At least one. I am certain that Shade is one. It would explain much."

Shade. That made perfect sense to her. It explained much about his *otherness*. Still, she failed to see what it had to do with what had happened to her. Unless… "Was what happened to me *Shade's* doing?" Her anger at the faceless warlock stirred. "I swear that he'll—"

He quieted her with a hand over her mouth. "I didn't say he did, but think carefully. You know what it feels like when Shade is near. You've sensed his magical trace. Now, think…do you recall *anything* akin to it from what happened to you?"

She thought of Shade—a distasteful necessity—and then forced herself to recall the horrific events in the passage.

Gwendolyn gaped. Her face paled.

Nathan gripped her arm. "Gwendolyn! Are you all right? I'm sorry! I should have never asked you to do that!"

The enchantress paid no attention. Her mind still reeled at what she had sensed. "It was—" she hesitated. "I mean…whatever was responsible *did* have a similar trace…but…" Gwendolyn shook her head. She now realized something about her attacker that brought with it a fear from her childhood. "No…"

"Tell me, Gwendolyn. Tell me what scares you. I think I know. I think it verifies some evidence I've come across here and there over the past two months."

"The—the trace is similar to Shade's...but his has a vibrancy to it! A *life* to it! This one...this one feels like it came from a thing risen from a grave!"

She expected Nathan to look askance, but instead, he only nodded in confirmation. "'From a grave'. Aptly put. You know the tales. You know the stories from your childhood..."

"*The Lords of the Dead*," she finally blurted. "But they are myth! Ghosts designed to scare children!"

The wizard shook his head. "The Lords of the Dead are not only too real, but I believe they see our struggle against the Dragon Kings for what it will be regardless who triumphs." Nathan peered past Gwendolyn to what she realized was the passage where she had experienced the unsettling attack. "...a bounty for the Lords and the Lords alone."

THE DECAYING CITADEL stood in a grey, still land that was a shadowy reflection of the Dragonrealm. In and around the crumbling edifice, half-seen figures moved furtively about as if trying to avoid being noticed even though there were no visible eyes about.

A huge, batlike form fluttered onto the moss-covered battlements, in the process scattering those phantasms drifting nearby. The fanged beast alighted like a man and, indeed, its form was in some ways humanoid. The pale monster quickly vanished through a passage as if in fear of something even more horrific than itself. Squeezing through one narrow corridor after another, it descended several levels before entering a vast, empty chamber marked only by a single arched window and the heavy bronze door through which the horrific servant had just passed. The Necri, for that was what it was called, glanced furtively at the door, where the stylized insignia of a dragon stood at eye level.

Hissing nervously, the Necri continued inside. It found a location near the edge of an intricate black pentagram etched into the stone floor.

At first, it appeared that the creature was alone, but then, at pre-chosen points on the pattern, ominous figures took shape. Ten cloaked figures clad in heavy, black armor. Their helmets were reminiscent of those of the Dragon Kings, save that the heads that formed the crests were more stylized, like the insignia on the door. In addition, despite their militaristic outfits, it was clear that at least two of the forms were female.

What was also clear—to anyone other than themselves—was that these beings were no more alive than the furtive shadows scattering from their presence. Their grand cloaks were tattered, rotting; their armor hung loose over nearly-fleshless bones. Some lacked even legs and simply floated above their locations. White wisps of hair marked where the once generous locks of one of the female forms had cascaded over her shoulders.

Yet, the Lords of the Dead saw themselves as they had originally been, great and glorious warriors of a powerful clan lost to time. They were the handsome and beautiful sorcerers who had been tasked with a tremendous project by their master…and in the process had instead found *godhood* for themselves.

The Necri crouched in a futile attempt to make itself less noticeable. One of the translucent figures briefly glanced the creature's way, quieting the beast.

In the center of the pattern, an eleventh shape coalesced. Cold, empty eye sockets within the helmet surveyed the other ten, then the cringing Necri.

"The Necri brings news of our cousin?" asked one of the other males in a raspy voice.

"No, this is the servant I sent out for another, more important matter," responded the lead figure in deeper tones. "Our cousin can wait."

One of the female forms straightened. Her voice was still melodious despite lacking part of her jawbone. "But what could be more important than *him*, Ephraim?"

In response, the Lord named Ephraim raised a gauntleted hand toward the chiropteran monster. The Necri immediately froze. Its pupilless white orbs widened.

Ephraim caught its gaze…and through his own empty eyes revealed to the rest what the Necri had learned from the mortal realm. As one, the rest of the Lords stiffened.

The moment his comrades knew all he did, Ephraim released his hold on the Necri. The winged beast returned to its cowering even as Ephraim looked to the rest of the Lords of the Dead.

"And there you have it…" Ephraim declared with triumph. "The renegade thought to keep it hidden after he betrayed the pact he made with us, but what is a century for us who have sought it for so long? Not even our dear cousin could keep it hidden from our sight forever…if he even recalls its existence anymore…"

"What if he does, though?" the same female demanded. "What if at some point his ragged memory recalls its importance, its danger?"

"We will do as we have always done, Kadaria…we will watch him, watch the beast that runs with him, and, if the moment shows itself…eliminate them. In the meantime, we will worry about only one thing. The fool of a Dragon King who rules Penacles *will* give us the access we need to those infernal libraries, and we *will* use it to attain the spellwork that will unlock the intricate matrices the unlamented Dru Zeree created for his special…'prisons'. Then and only then, we will take what he locked away and use it for our own domination of the mortal world…"

Kadaria and most of the other Lords took this declaration to heart—or whatever remained of their hearts—but one of the other males did not appear quite satisfied.

"And what about *her*, Ephraim? What about her? Even our dear cousin Gerrod might be more preferable than accidentally granting her desires..."

The lead necromancer waved off the other's concerns. "She will fall to us just like the rest, Zorane." Ephraim laughed harshly, a grating sound that sent more of the shadows fleeing from the chamber. "She, Dragon Kings, Seekers, Quel, and these upstart things called humans—these bastard gets of our own glorious Vraad lineage—will all fall to us." His black eye sockets stared beyond the crumbling citadel to the mortal world of which the Lords' realm was a perverted likeness. "Each death this war causes makes us stronger! Each death makes us greater!"

He thrust his hand toward the Necri, which immediately straightened. As one, the Lords of the Dead eyed the creature, which had no choice but to look back.

"Find the set! Find the piece! Know this face!" ordered Ephraim to the Necri, for the last creating a vision that was no less than the suspicious countenance of Azran Bedlam. "And above all...make very certain that *none* of what you and the others do slows this war." He slapped his fist against his breastplate, which, to normal ears, echoed hollowly. "*Our* war..."

5

TO THE ENEMY

The Iron Dragon eyed his legions with pride. Brown might be acclaimed as the greatest military commander among the Dragon Kings and Purple the top strategist, but Iron felt that his soldiers could match anything the former could set against them, and his own cunning was surely the equal of that of the master of the City of Knowledge. Iron was certain that if he had had control of the libraries, then he, too, would have been touted by all as the cleverest among them.

*It certainly would not be that fool who sits on the throne and rules us due to his coloring alone...*the Dragon King thought with momentary frustration.

The heavily armored soldiers methodically swept over the hilly landscape near the northeastern edge of the Iron Dragon's domain. His troops searched dangerously close to the thin ribbon of land that extended from the bulk of Lord Silver's domain. Barely two days' march from here would bring Iron's forces across a second border, that of the Dragon Emperor's realm. Iron often looked longingly in that direction and wondered why none of his predecessors had ever dared take cross.

He knew the one reason that he had never done so…and that reason now proved the ineptitude of the current emperor. *Your precious human dogs have turned on you and your vaunted advisor, Brother Purple…perhaps this is a sign that it is time there is a change on the throne…*

The drake lord and his officers passed the high, arching rock known as the Watching Wyvern. That it faced the realms of Iron's rivals had ever made it a symbol of the Dragon King's might. Even the land itself appeared to acknowledge that here Iron was supreme.

A vast shadow spreading over the Dragon King and his staff made Lord Iron glance up. A blue-grey leviathan soared by. Metalian, Iron's second eldest surviving son, surveyed the landscape and the troops ahead. Metalian lacked the birth markings that would have enabled him to vie for the coveted position of heir, but was a capable commander who knew well how to execute his father's wishes. The drake lord wanted to make very certain that there were no rebel scouts ahead. He would brook no incursions into his realm, no matter how small. Metalian had a keen eye, but, more important to his father, his loyalty was beyond reproach. If even commanded to assassinate the emperor, Metalian would have sought to obey without hesitation.

That thought stirred the Dragon King's ambitions in general and he stared harder at the distant border. *Just give the command,* Lord Iron urged himself. *Send them across that sycophant Silver's bit of land and into the Tybers! These human fleas can be dealt with at any time! All they need is to be swatted by a strong iron fist, not a soft golden one—*

A powerful wind assailed the legions. It was so strong that it even buffeted Metalian, sending the huge dragon careening into a smaller scout just returning from the south. The lesser dragon crashed against a hillside and tumbled into a pair of riders and their scouts, sending the mounts into a rage.

Even as he and the others struggled to keep their own mounts under control, Iron sniffed the air with disdain. This had been no normal gale. The fearsome wind was the product of a powerful but simple spell. While Iron knew that Silver certainly watched for even one soldier's foot to cross the border, the other drake lord would hardly have instigated anything before then. That only left one source…

"Prepare for a rebel attack!" he shouted to his officers. At the same time, the drake lord began his own spellwork. The moment that the first wizard showed his fool head within a hundred yards of the Dragon King's army, Lord Iron would have him. Then, he would use that spellcaster to lead him to the rest.

But there came no hint whatsoever as to the physical presence of any rebels. Lord Iron could not even sense the origin point of the wind, which continued to assault his army. The front ranks were already in chaos, and those behind fought what would clearly be a futile struggle to maintain their ranks.

Come and fight, you little vermin! Come and fight! Iron silently demanded. The rebels would accomplish nothing with this gale save to stir the drake lord's wrath further—

The Iron Dragon stood in the saddle as suddenly what seemed *snow* began to pour from the other side of the border. He doubted that it could be ordinary precipitation, though. With a gesture, the Dragon King created a funnel of intense heat to sear away the coming snowfall. Not one drop of melted snow would fall upon his men.

Yet, instead of melting…the 'snow' *blossomed*.

Thousands of odd, blood-colored flowers drifted down over his army before the drake lord could comprehend what was happening. Only too late did he realize that the heat he had created had been just what the flying *seeds* had needed to immediately mature.

And as that happened, the wind abruptly died.

Lord Iron quickly summoned a wind of his own, but the speed with which the crimson flowers dropped made it impossible for him to stop many of them from alighting on his soldiers. The moment they touched, the petals spread over the armored warriors' bodies. Soldiers struggled to peel the tightening flowers from their outfits. Even from his location, the drake lord could hear the rending of metal as the petals tore into the armor.

He was well aware of at least two spellcasters with an aptitude for magic involving flora. He sneered at the devastation taking place within his front lines, the deaths of a few human underlings and a captain or two of his own clan little sacrifice. War always brought death.

The drake lord clenched a fist. The sky above his struggling warriors immediately clouded. A downpour drenched the front lines, but while it only wetted the armored figures, the flowers dissolved under its onslaught.

Iron did not wait to see how well his counterspell worked. He linked to two of his senior officers, binding their innate magical abilities to his own. They did not resist his usurping of their powers; all who served a Dragon King existed to be used as he saw fit.

His own already daunting skills now augmented, Iron at last discovered the location of the spellcasters in question. Five of them. Two were as he had suspected. The enchantress Gwendolyn McArn and the wizard Adam Gudwead. Iron saw the value in Nathan Bedlam's decision to combine the pair's talents, but the drake lord also grinned at the foolhardiness of the action. With one stroke, Iron would be able to eliminate two valued members of what some humans had begun to call the *Dragon Masters*.

The three other spellcasters were the ones responsible for keeping the entire group briefly hidden from Iron's notice. They were only important to the Dragon King in that they were a part of Nathan Bedlam's band of traitors. The drake lords knew which of the so-called Dragon Masters were the key to crushing the rebellion. Eliminate those and the rest of the rabble would fall swiftly.

Lord Iron remained still in the saddle as his spell reached out to the unsuspecting mages. The Dragon King's forked tongue darted in and out in anticipation of the carnage that he was about to inflict—

From just beyond the right and left flanks of the Iron Dragon's army, *another* force materialized. Barely a breath later, a hail of arrows fell upon the drake lord's forces, inflicting heavy damage on both sides.

Glancing from one flank to the other, Lord Iron swore. He had sensed no blink hole, yet, here were two large groups of rebels assaulting his army. The drake lord wasted no time wondering exactly how Nathan Bedlam had managed it; instead, the drake was determined to teach the wizard a lesson in who ruled here.

He thrust a hand to each side. On both flanks, a solid wall of air struck the attackers—

—And immediately passed through the rebels without so much as shaking a single strand of hair.

Lord Iron snarled. What had happened was impossible. He quickly measured the arc of the arrows that continued to rain down. Fiery eyes narrowed in calculation.

"Ssso..." What was seen was not fact, but illusion. The bolts were flying from a location just beyond the supposed enemy force. "A child's trick, good for a brief ressspite, but doing little for you in the end, Bedlam."

He cast again. This time, the walls of air stretched farther back and halted the arrows in mid-flight. Then, with contemptuous gesture, Lord Iron sent the shafts hurtling back—

And at that moment, high above, Metalian *exploded.*

NATHAN BEDLAM REMAINED aware that the Gryphon did not see himself as a spellcaster of much potential, but if not that, than the inhuman rebel certainly at least understood how best to make use of magic as both a weapon and a defense. While the wizard and the warrior had readily agreed that their first step in bringing the war back to the Dragon Kings meant striking near the vicinity of the emperor, it had been the Gryphon who had chosen Lord Iron as the target.

Nathan would have thought Silver a simpler choice, but the Gryphon explained his reasoning. "Silver is powerful—as is Bronze, who also rules near—but the true military might of the Dragon Kings lies especially in three lords…Brown, Black, and Iron. Brown is more calculating and would have been a good target if not so far from the emperor's throne. Attacking Black means dealing with the mind-numbing mists…and an assault that is even farther from the Dragon Emperor's sanctum than an attack on Brown. That leaves Iron. Cunning also, but even more arrogant and impetuous than most of his brethren."

That reasoning, combined with the Gryphon's knowledge of the landscape where he thought it best to spring the trap had made it easy for Nathan to agree with the decision. Even still, both had known that whatever choice they made…too many good souls would die.

Despite that grim understanding, though, Nathan could still not help but cheering at the preliminary success of the rebels' attack. They had played Lord Iron almost perfectly thus far. He had not realized that his adversaries' intention had been two-fold. Wreak havoc among the ground forces…and then strike a mortal blow against one of the drake lord's most prized weapons…and kin.

Dragon Kings chose their successors by one simple method. Speckled bands marked the eggs that promised future rulers. Nathan had never understood why that alone made a drake worthy of the throne, but it was a method unquestioned by the Dragon Kings...even if a few among the drake lords had of late wondered if the right bloodline ruled as emperor.

Metalian had not been born from such an egg, but like Gold's own son, Toma, he had made himself invaluable to his father. While slaying a Dragon King would have been a tremendous boost for the rebels, even Nathan and the Gryphon had known how hard that would be. Lord Iron had a number of defensive spells about his person that would have required too much effort to penetrate under the circumstances.

But the same could not be said for other drakes...

Nathan had felt guilty about using Gwendolyn and Adam as bait, but they had readily agreed to their part, as had the rest. The plan hatched by the Gryphon and Nathan had relied heavily on misdirection to keep the drake lord's forces off-balance, yet although it had worked thus far, the mage and his companions knew that now they had to strike quick once more, then retreat before Lord Iron could reorganize his troops.

Two new waves of arrows filled the sky even as the fiery gobbets of flesh that had been the drake lord's son also spilled over the enemy. Nathan continued to fight the intense exhaustion that had immediately overtaken him after the successful spell he and Yalak had led against Metalian. Already aware of the younger dragon's nature from previous scouting, the Gryphon had pointed out that the moment Lord Iron's son caught sight of the enemy, Metalian would do his best to unleash a plume of fire at them.

The eager dragon had done just as expected. What the behemoth himself had not expected was the intricate spell Nathan and six other mages had created together, a spell that instantly created a blockage in Metalian's long throat. That spell had required perfect concentration and perfect focus. Even then, had he simply been inhaling and exhaling air, the dragon would have easily dislodged the blockage. Nathan had had to make certain that he and his comrades had created it just at the second when Metalian started breathing fire.

And with nowhere to immediately go, the very primal force with which the iron leviathan had intended to scorch to death dozens of men could only rapidly build up until the pressure grew too great. Even Nathan had been startled by the magnitude of the explosion.

His thoughts quickly returning to the struggle, the wizard watched as scores of the Lord Iron's fighters fell under the new barrage. Drake commanders belatedly ordered shields to the sky, finally stemming the tides of blood.

A third wave of arrows fired from a lower spot ahead of the enemy ranks cut down several of those in the front lines, again, just as planned.

This is going too well, Yalak said to Nathan through their thoughts.

I know... Nathan continued to watch for catastrophe, but all proceeded as the rebels had hoped. Even now, the Gryphon himself entered the fray, the inhuman warrior leading a band of fighters into the Iron Dragon's left flank. The lionbird cut down a riding drake, causing the dying animal to spill its rider. Before the drake officer could recover, the Gryphon ran him through the throat.

Lord Iron's own magical attacks struck hard again and again, but with little visible result thanks to the concentrated efforts of the assembled mages. The drake lord had now the top priority of Nathan's fellow spellcasters. Everything Lord Iron sought to throw at the rebels had to be countered.

The Dragon King's growing fury at his impotence swelled to such a point that Nathan could even feel that anger as if Lord Iron and the wizard had linked thoughts. Nathan sensed the drake lord seeking out the cause of his failures. Lord Iron knew that Nathan had to be responsible and that Nathan would have to pay. Once that damned Bedlam was dead—

The wizard stiffened. *Yalak—*

I know! Do not break our link!

That was a task easier said than done, for Nathan knew now that when he had thought that he had imagined the Dragon King touching his mind…it had *not* been the veteran mage's imagination after all.

I have you now, Bedlam!

Nathan felt his insides feeling as if they were tearing apart. He saw in his head that Lord Iron intended to repay Nathan in kind for the death of the Dragon King's son. Only Yalak had thus far prevented a horrific death—

But another mind joined Yalak in his efforts. Dayn's. Behind Dayn's thoughts came Gwendolyn's. Together, the three forced back the Iron Dragon's spell—forced it back, but remained unable to eradicate it.

Nathan dared not move. Even the slightest shift might not only enable the drake lord's spell to consume him, but also allow the bond between Nathan and the others to pass the monstrous attack on to them. It left Nathan with the choice of severing his link to the rest and suffering the Dragon King's wrath or hoping some miracle would free his entire group from the predicament in which they found themselves.

However, instead of a miracle, what the spellcasters got was *Azran.*

Bound as he was to the drake lord, Nathan saw through as his younger son materialized just feet from the Dragon King. Azran wore a grin that disturbed his father nearly as much as the overwhelming danger Azran now blithely confronted. Barely a breath after the black- and silver-haired wizard appeared, two of Lord Iron's mounted officers charged him. Their riding drakes snapped eagerly at Azran, who simply stood waiting.

Run! Nathan urged, not caring that Lord Iron also heard that plea. *Run, Azran!*

But instead his son's ebony sword thrust forward, sliding into the open maw of one riding drake. It pierced the upper side of the mouth, the skull, the tip ending somewhere in the beast's simple brain.

Azran withdrew the magical sword so quickly that he had it aimed at the second monster before the first even understood that it was dead. The first riding drake took two more steps, shook its head, then tumbled to the left.

As that happened, Azran drove the blade into the second creature's closest eye. He laughed as he drew back the sword, then stared directly into the eyes of Lord Iron—and thus his own father's.

Yesss…I will take your ssson from you asss you took mine! the drake lord promised the elder Bedlam.

The Dragon King's magical attack on Nathan lessened. However, despite now able to act without fear for Yalak and the others, Nathan knew that he was already too late. He sensed Lord Iron's spell take shape and strike Azran.

Yet…Azran stood untouched. He now held the blade up before him. Through Lord Iron, Nathan saw the horned handle afire with crimson energy…energy that both wizard and drake understood was the result of Lord Iron's extinguished spell.

"Thank you," Azran cheerfully commented to the scaly monarch.

Tilting the sword level, the young wizard spun in a circle.

The crimson energy faded into the blade. From the tip burst a black radiance that spread as the wizard completed his circle.

The first drake officer had by this time risen from his dead mount. Nathan felt Lord Iron increase his personal shields even as the Dragon King watched his servant try to behead Azran with a jagged sword more than half Azran's height.

But in his determination to slay this potential threat to his sovereign, the drake warrior did not heed the oncoming ring of radiance. The black ring sliced through the drake as if he were nothing. The two halves separated, the officer still gaping in disbelief as the top part tumbled forward.

Nathan's view through Lord Iron immediately changed, becoming one that receded higher and higher above Azran. The wizard felt an incredible surge of magical forces emanating from his adversary and quickly fought to break what link remained between him and the Dragon King. As he suspected, the Iron Dragon's concentration was no longer focused on anything but Azran, which enabled the elder Bedlam's effort to easily overcome what connection still remained.

Unfortunately, once his own view of the battle returned, it was to discover that a gargantuan dragon dwarfing even Metalian hovered above. With a long set of double plates stretching from the giant's neck down to the tip of his thick tail and webbed wings spanning twice the behemoth's length, the Iron Dragon was an imposing sight that should have burned fear into the hearts of the rebels…and would have, if not for the fact that chaos was instead already spreading among Lord Iron's own forces.

The radiance continued to spread from Azran and his sword, creating an ever-expanding circle of death doubling in diameter with each breath. Scores of severed bodies lay sprawled around Nathan's son, and while on the one hand Azran had clearly dealt a terrible blow to the enemy, the manic intensity the elder Bedlam felt coursing through his son disturbed Nathan immensely.

But what bothered him even more was almost instantly echoed in his head by both Yalak and Gwendolyn.

Nathan! the enchantress called. *It's not stopping!*

Azran is not halting his spell! cried Yalak at the same time. *I see it cutting through the rebels without hesitation! You must—*

Already aware of what he had to do, a troubled Nathan vanished from his position and reappeared next to his son. The cries of battle reverberated through his ears, but he paid little mind to them as

Azran turned to him and the younger mage's eyes fell upon the father.

Fell upon the father...and clearly did not recognize him.

"Azran!" His son's name was all Nathan could blurt out before he had to transport himself behind Azran again. The black blade passed exactly through where the elder Bedlam had just stood.

"Azran!" Nathan cried again. "Stop this!"

Above them, the Iron Dragon roared. Nathan glanced up and for the first time beheld the heavy, metallic scales covering the underbelly. Several arrows bounced off the scales without leaving so much as a mark. The unscathed and still very furious behemoth dropped toward father and son.

Turning back to Azran, Nathan called out, "Get—"

There was a *third* figure with the Bedlams, a very startled, very disoriented Gryphon. Still, despite that initial expression of shock, the lionbird immediately wrapped his arms around Azran, bringing the sword's point to the ground at the same time.

The sinister ring faded.

The Iron Dragon let loose with an unsettling gurgling sound.

Nathan felt the drake lord's magic assailing them at the same time. The wizard knew that to try to transport the three of them away was futile. He did the only thing left to him, praying that it would be enough.

A sizzling wave of molten metal washed over the Bedlams and the Gryphon. The heat burned Nathan, but not enough to cause injury. Still, it left him gasping from the searing air filling his lungs.

The plume of liquid iron pressed against the invisible barrier he had created. The effort to keep the shield from collapsing forced Nathan to his knees, but the thought of what would happen to Azran and the Gryphon kept him from entirely surrendering to the stress.

Through his blurring vision, Nathan tried to make out his son and the rebel leader. He saw a murky form, but could not tell which of the pair it was. "A-Azran! Gryphon! I'll hold—hold it as long as I can! The two—the two of you might—"

The relentless assault ceased. Nathan managed to blink his gaze clear enough to see that both Azran and the Gryphon were gone.

Above, the Iron Dragon let loose with another angry bellow. Peering toward the behemoth, Nathan gaped. Astride the dragon's back was a small figure with a sword. The wizard's first thoughts went to his impetuous offspring.

"Father!" Dayn formed next to Nathan. "Come with me!"

Without waiting for an answer, the younger Bedlam seized his father by the wrist and transported both of them away. They reappeared near Yalak—who looked oddly thoughtful—and, much to Nathan's surprise, a somewhat surly *Azran.*

"I had him!" Azran snapped. "I would've had the Dragon King if everyone hadn't interfered, especially *him!*"

Nathan had no idea who 'him' referred to until he realized that one essential figure was missing from the group. He quickly returned his attention to the transformed drake lord.

It was the *Gryphon* astride the dragon. Nathan whirled on Azran. "You sent him there? Just because he stopped your foolishness? I don't care how angry you were, that's murder! Yalak! Why aren't you doing anything?"

The moment his father began reprimanding him, Azran's expression changed. A look of utter disappointment spread across the son's bearded face.

Yalak intervened. "He had nothing to do with it, Nathan! The Gryphon cast himself there, just as he cast himself to you and Azran!"

"He did *what?*"

"I do not think he even knows how he did it! I foresaw it too late to prevent—"

But once again, the Iron Dragon's roar interrupted all else and demanded their absolute attention. The blue-grey behemoth had turned onto his back. That would have sent most undesired riders plummeting to their doom, yet the Gryphon clung tight, in part helped by one clawed hand carefully locked between the huge scales. With his free hand, the lionbird tried to turn his sword around in order to strike at another area where the scales spread apart just enough to reveal the flesh underneath.

Nathan had seen enough. However daring the Gryphon was, this could only end in his death. "We have to work together! With the Dragon King's magical energies flaring about the two of them, our spell could go awry and end up killing the Gryphon!"

But to his surprise, Yalak shook his head. "No...we need to transport our forces away. This combat between the Gryphon and the Iron Dragon actually works to our advantage! Our time here is done. This battle is over. We've struck a blow that will resound. I've seen this!"

"But the Gryphon—"

"We must let this play out. It—it is not clear, but I know it must be done, Nathan."

Nathan wanted to disregard his best friend's advice, but he had heard the certainty in Yalak's voice. Struggling to contain himself, he nodded. "All right. Yalak, you and Dayn know your part in that regard. Azran—"

His younger son was gone.

There was no time for Nathan to concern himself over this latest episode with Azran, not when hundreds of lives were at stake. As the other two wizards faded away, Nathan concentrated on another spellcaster. *Gwendolyn! It's time for you and Adam to join Tyr and Basil over—*

A thundering boom shook the landscape. Hardened soldiers were tossed about as if nothing. If not for the fact that Yalak and the others had wasted not a moment in transporting away those nearest to the fight, Nathan would have expected utter disaster for the rebels. Even still, he despaired, certain that the deafening sound marked the Gryphon's demise and the launching of a new and more vicious assault on the rebels by the enraged Dragon King.

Sure enough, when the wizard gazed up, it was to find the lion-bird no longer there.

But then again, neither was the *dragon*.

6

A GAME BEGINS

Azran slashed at the ancient stone wall making up part of his growing sanctum, but even watching the blade cut neatly and without hesitation through the wall did nothing to cool his fury.

"I was saving all of them!" he snarled at the empty air. "I had everything under control! I would've even slain a Dragon King...if not for that...for that *misfit*."

Still clutching the black blade, he stomped through the half-ruined structure. Piece by piece, Azran had used his growing power to carefully rebuild it to what he imagined its former glory. Each addition had to be done with care and stealth, though, in order to avoid the notice of the lord of the Hell Plains. Of course, it was not as if Azran feared the behemoth anymore. With each passing day, Nathan's son felt more and more certain that if it came to it, he could defeat the Red Dragon. His decision to jump into battle again had proven that the only thing he had needed to win against a Dragon King was their very power. Unlike the first attempt, this time he had gained that necessary magical energy...and has finally been able to let his creation feed as it required.

Azran held up the black sword, *his* sword. As a child, he had heard the stories about the mighty talismans and weapons others had created, but in his mind he was certain that none compared to—to—

"Someone called you the *Horned Blade*, I think," Azran muttered. "I'm sure someone did. It fits, after all…" He brandished the weapon. "The *Horned Blade*…"

What sounded like thunder marked his declaration. Nathan's son grinned. Even though the sound was just that of one of the countless craters in the region erupting, he took its timing as yet another sign of his rising mastery of the arts. How proud his father would be—

Father… Azran's pleasure faded into anger again. His father had shamed him in front of the others, his father who had always been the only reason Azran had pushed himself this far. *How could you, Father? How could you do that to me? You would've never done that to Dayn!*

Thinking of his brother—his exalted brother—Azran turned the blade toward one of the other stone walls. As he pointed the weapon, an ebony streak of energy shot forth.

The thick stone blocks cracked. Part of the reassembled wall crumbled inward. Had Azran already restored the ceiling in this section of the ruins, much of that ceiling—including that above the younger spellcaster—would have collapsed.

Rather than be irritated by the damage he had done, Azran smiled again. He started to laugh, then turned as if hearing something.

"I've a right," the bearded mage insisted to the emptiness. "I've striven harder than anyone to help bring down the Dragon Kings! What has my brother done at all except just follow Father's lead?"

He tilted his head as if listening. Then, with a shrug, Azran gestured at the emptiness.

A gleaming marble table formed, a marble table with two matching chairs set at opposing ends. Atop the table sat the chess set that Azran had taken from the chambers of the Purple Dragon's treacherous seneschal, Jekrith Terin, after Azran had run the shrouded figure through from the back.

Jekrith Terin—in truth a mutilated renegade from the avian race known to most as the Seekers—had been instrumental in enabling Azran to make great strides in his magical research. Of course, the seneschal had done so for his own sinister reasons, including the intended slaughter of his race. He had also had no qualms about manipulating the human spellcasters in whatever manner he had desired to achieve his ends, even including situations resulting in countless deaths.

Azran stepped to the chair on the right. At a flick of his hand, it slid back enough for him to seat himself. Staring intently at the set, he finally placed the Horned Blade on the other side of the table.

"Shall the three of us play a game?" he asked.

One of the pieces on the opposing side slid forward.

HOT DUST FILLED the Gryphon's lungs. That alone gave him some inkling as to where he was, but the moment he opened his eyes— which he then quickly shut again—he knew that he had somehow ended up in Legar.

With more caution, the lionbird opened his eyes a second time. Given the opportunity, his vision adjusted for the blinding light all around him. The rocky landscape glittered with crystalline growths, which, with the sun directly overhead, made for a dizzying display.

Every bone in his body aching, the Gryphon pushed himself up. The last thing that he could recall was wishing that he could take the battle elsewhere in the hopes that the rest would be able to escape while the Iron Dragon's troops remained in utter confusion. He was still not certain how he had ended up atop the dragon, although it had naturally been his desire to do whatever it took to keep the drake lord from attacking the rebels.

The lionbird shook his head. There were too many dark spots in his memory, too many to add to the ones he already had. Someday, the Gryphon hoped to discover just how he had ended up in the Dragonrealm. However, that was a quest for much, much later. He considered this continent his home now and was determined to somehow bring the Dragon Kings down.

And a fine job you are doing, the lionbird thought wryly.

A loud, raspy hiss sent him ducking for cover. He cursed himself for not thinking that perhaps his foe had made this unexpected journey with him.

The hiss died away. Although sounds had a tendency to echo in the Legar Peninsula, the Gryphon's acute hearing enabled him to calculate just where he would best find the source. Without hesitation, he set off in that direction.

Sure enough, a short climb over an unstable hill brought him to the startling sight of the Iron Dragon lying sprawled on his back. The leviathan let out another brief hiss, at the same time which his wings feebly tried to flap. From what the Gryphon could judge by the rubble surrounding the Dragon King, Lord Iron had crashed with far more force than the rebel leader had.

Good fortune for me...but how? The Gryphon was certain that the pair had materialized well above the ground. The distance separating them clearly showed that the lionbird had finally slipped from the dragon's back. The Gryphon *should* have dropped a dangerous height to the hard ground, enough so that when he opened his eyes, it would have been to see the Lords of the Dead waiting to claim his spirit.

Yet, here he was, alive. The rebel leader concentrated. Under his armor, the two nubs on his back twitched. Few knew of his vestigial wings, pathetic things in the Gryphon's view. They could certainly have not saved him even if they had been uncovered.

The Iron Dragon hissed yet again. This time, the eyes briefly opened, albeit without any focus. The Gryphon reached for his sword, only to find it missing. The small dagger he wore at his waist was of no use, nor was one other item he kept secure in a pouch on the opposite side.

As he anxiously shifted, a slight tinkling sound arose from just over his heart. The Gryphon seized hold of the thin chain that his fur and feathers helped hide from the view of others and considered pulling what hung from the chain free. He knew that somehow one of the items would be able to help him, yet hesitated.

The harsh ground near his right abruptly shook. A mound roughly two yards in diameter steadily grew at the spot.

Quickly slipping around a small hill, the Gryphon cautiously watched as the top of the mound broke away and a hulking brown shape emerged. It had a long, tapering snout and pointed ears, and as it rose from the hole, it revealed that most of its body, especially the backs and sides, was covered in layered scales, much like the tiny armadillos found in most of the southern kingdoms. In fact, if not for the creature's more ferocious aspect, the lionbird might have mistaken the newcomer for some magically mutated version of the simple beast.

But this was no mere animal grown gigantic. As the creature fully emerged, the Gryphon saw that it stood at least another head taller than him and was nearly twice as wide at the shoulders. It was very muscular—no surprise to the Gryphon considering how hard burrowing through the rocky ground here had to be—and had paws that ended in sharp, curved claws. One paw held a small metallic rod about two feet long.

The Gryphon had crossed paths with the Quel before and knew that their appearance belied their swiftness. As he watched, the creature sniffed the air.

Tensing, the Quel flicked its wrist. The small rod instantly expanded, the top becoming a sharp point. The burrowers favored axes and maces, but also utilized spears and lances. While an ax could be strapped to the body, a spear's length could make it ungainly when digging through rock. Hence, the Quel had apparently developed a weapon that they could shorten or lengthen as needed.

The shelled creature carefully moved toward the stunned dragon. As the Quel moved, its scaly shell glittered even more than the landscape. While little was known about the Quel, it was said by some that at a point early in their lives, when their shells were still soft, elder members placed carefully chosen crystals between the segments. The swift growth of the creatures guaranteed that the crystals soon became permanently embedded.

At the moment, one apparent use of the crystals was that they enabled the Quel to blend in to their surroundings here, but the Gryphon was certain that they did more. Still, he had no plans to discover just what else. While it was rare to see more than one or two Quel at any given time—which made some scholars believe only a handful had survived their ancient war against the Seekers— the rebel leader had no desire to see if this encounter would prove the exception to the rule. A semi-conscious Dragon King might bring every Quel in existence out in the open.

The Legar Peninsula's own drake lord—the Crystal Dragon— surely knew of his counterpart's abrupt and painful materialization, but thus far appeared not to have taken measures. The Quel were not known to willingly serve the hermitic Dragon King, but the Gryphon supposed that if he so desired, then the drake lord could command them to do whatever he desired. Still, the lionbird thought this Quel did not move with the confidence of one who had a Dragon King's power behind it.

The Gryphon silently retreated. While he might be able to take on the shelled creature, he preferred to find some means of returning swiftly to his companions. The Gryphon had no idea which of the mages had cast him atop the dragon, but guessed that it had probably been Azran. Certainly, it seemed to the Gryphon something Nathan's unstable son would do. That it had also been the lionbird's desire made no difference, especially since he was confident that it had also been Azran who had sent both to this forsaken place.

His foot sank into the ground.

Try as he might, the Gryphon could not maintain his balance. Worse, more of the ground gave way.

He fell through.

Heavy fragments of rock and earth cascaded down with the Gryphon, battering him even as he finally landed. Despite the pain, he forced himself to the side.

As the lionbird hoped, doing so kept him from being struck by much more of the collapse. Still, he hardly felt safe. He had not fallen into any random hole. This was part of the Quel burrow system running through much of Legar.

Movement in the darkness warned him just as a shadowy figure—a Quel, naturally—tried to skewer him. As swift as the huge creatures might be, the Gryphon knew that this could not be the same Quel that he had just observed. That meant that the Gryphon had to hurry and deal with his current opponent before he had two to face.

The armored monster tried again to impale him. The spear came within inches of the rebel leader's chest.

Swinging around, the Gryphon seized the spear and tugged. Unfortunately, he had miscalculated the Quel's strength. With unnerving ease, the Gryphon's adversary raised the spear...and the Gryphon along with it.

Tightening his grip, the lionbird swung both feet at the Quel. The hard boots slammed into the long snout.

The Quel stumbled back. The Gryphon had been trying for the unprotected throat, but the results still enabled him to twist the spear free. He landed on all fours, the weapon beneath him. Spinning like a cat, the Gryphon seized up the spear and turned to face his much larger foe.

The Quel was gone. A pile of rubble to the left revealed just exactly where the Quel had gone. The Gryphon immediately stepped back, his gaze flickering from the floor to the walls and even to the ceiling.

The attack came from behind. The floor burst open, the Quel trying to rake the Gryphon's legs with its long, sharp claws.

Without turning, the rebel leader thrust the back end of the stolen spear into the Quel. As he hoped, this time he caught the throat.

An odd combination of gasping and hooting escaped the Quel's mouth. The burrower clutched at its throat.

Without hesitation, the Gryphon used the moment to swing the spear around and run it through both the paw and the throat.

The Quel let out a raspy hoot and stilled. The Gryphon tried to pull the spear free, but could not remove it from the half-buried corpse.

The sides of the passage shook with what the lionbird now recognized as the telltale sign of burrowing. He had no idea how many other Quel were near, but even one more was too much for him at the moment.

It took him but a glance to see that he could not reach the hole through which he had fallen. With no other choice, the Gryphon started down the passage. He quickly left what light had shone through the gap...and only discovered then that something on *him* now glowed.

Unable to smother its illumination, the Gryphon quickly undid the pouch and pulled out the item in question. The intricate scrollwork on the handle aside, the small silver key still looked as unremarkable as it had the day it had been given to him by a thing resembling a dragon made of mist. The ethereal figure had not told him for what purpose the key was to be used, only that it did not open *anything*. As far as the Gryphon was still concerned, such a key was useless, but the inherent magic he sensed in it had been reason enough to hold onto it...until now.

No matter how hard he tried, the Gryphon could not smother the light. All the while, he heard the walls and floor rumble as one or more Quel maneuvered around him. He knew that he had only seconds before he was attacked, yet—

The key snapped in half.

Something even tinier slipped out of it. The Gryphon thrust a hand toward it.

Both walls shattered as a pair of Quel came at him.

Lunging, the lionbird seized whatever had fallen free. Tossing it into the pouch, he threw himself forward.

Behind him, an angry hoot warned just how close he had been to being taken by at least one of the beastmen. The Gryphon stumbled forward, hoping that he could find a place to make a better stand.

A thick mist suddenly filled the passage, so thick that the Gryphon nearly collided with one wall when the path shifted to his left. As it was, he still tripped over something, and while he did not fall, he knew that the delay would cost him.

But the Quel the Gryphon had sensed at his heels instead blundered past him as if blind to the intruder's presence. The shelled creature thrust at the empty air ahead of him, then vanished into the mist and darkness.

The Gryphon remained still. Moments later, a second Quel stomped past. This one hefted a heavy ax. It sniffed the air and even paused near the lionbird, but then followed after its comrade.

With the utmost caution, the Gryphon stepped from the wall.

"Ssso…it mussst be you again…"

The voice made the fur and feathers at the base of the Gryphon's neck stand on end for two reasons. The first was that the voice echoed so loud in the passage that he was certain the Quel would come running back. The second was that he had not heard that voice since he had been given the now-shattered key.

Despite the shadows, the Gryphon had no difficulty making out the reptilian head forming in the mist. The dragon peered at him with what he thought frustration or disdain, then faded into the mist again.

An echoing hoot warned that the Quel were on their way back. The Gryphon started in the opposite direction—

—And found himself running across a shrouded landscape.

He came to a halt, a sense of dread that briefly stirred old, buried memories to life overcoming him. In the dank world around him, the Gryphon thought he saw a huge, canine monster half-real, half-shadow.

Barely had he caught sight of this new phantasm than an invisible force dragged him back to the real world. Now, the rebel leader stood crouched in what he believed some obscure part of Esedi, Lord Bronze's domain. That put him southwest of Iron's realm and near the human kingdom of Gordag-Ai. Like most human cities, Gordag-Ai had expressed very vocal opposition to the Dragon Masters and the rebellion, but in secret had supplied the Gryphon and his allies with food and other supplies. Among the rebels themselves could be counted several from the human kingdom.

"You have brought me back here," came the dragon's voice abruptly. "For what reasssson?"

With growing impatience, the Gryphon looked around. Not at all to his relief, the ethereal being finally coalesced before him.

"What by the Sons of the Wolf do you mean?" demanded the lionbird. Hardly had he uttered the question than he wondered just who the *Sons of the Wolf* even were. Unfortunately, before the Gryphon could seize on the vague memory, it locked itself away.

"*You* should know! You have sssummoned *me*, chimera!" the dragon of the mists retorted angrily. "From one demanding ssslave masster to another!"

"I did not summon you!" The Gryphon recalled the key. "That damned thing you left with me…it snapped in two just before you appeared…"

"Ah! Not you…but him…" The half-seen reptilian visage glowered. "And so even now he reaches out to steal away the freedom he so casually promised time and time again…"

"He? Who do you mean?"

"That foul thing that ssserved the lord of the City of Knowledge! You knew him as Jekrith Terin—"

"Jekrith Terin?" The Gryphon instinctively touched the pouch. "The seneschal is dead…or so say rumors…"

The dragon's misty form swirled around the uneasy rebel. "Yesss, dead he isss…and he isss no less dangerousss being so."

"That's not possible!"

"And that isss Jekrith Terin…" The face faded into the rest of the mist.

At first, the lionbird feared that the creature would vanish without further explanation, but then the reptilian countenance reformed. Still, the ethereal creature's peculiar expression did not bode well to the Gryphon.

"I sssenssse nothing! Whatever he hasss done isss hidden even from me…"

"Maybe this will help." The Gryphon reached into the pouch and removed what had fallen out of the broken key. The dragon's head dipped lower as both it and the lionbird gazed upon Jekrith Terin's 'gift'.

To the Gryphon, it was just one more question added to the many he had. He held what was to his eye a *chess* piece. True, it had been fashioned with such mastery that the bear it appeared to be looked almost real, but it was still a chess piece. Even the hint of magic he sensed around it seemed so meager that he doubted it could mean anything significant to the situation.

Yet, the piece drew a reaction from the dragon that startled the Gryphon. The apparition drew back as if afraid to be bitten by it.

"The ssset...it would be the ssset...he would bind me to that abomination, of courssse..."

Peering with more suspicion at the chess piece, the lionbird asked, "What set does this belong to? What are you babbling about?"

"I—" Without warning, the dragon of the mists froze. Its eyes flared bright. "I mussst sssend you *there*. I am sssorry. Thisss isss not my desssire...I am sssorry..."

Slipping the chess piece back in the pouch, the Gryphon backed away. "You'll be sending me nowhere—"

Yet, even as the lionbird spoke, he knew it was too late. The landscape rippled. He felt a sense of displacement far more severe than he had experienced from any teleportation spell in which he had been involved.

A white emptiness surrounded him. The Gryphon felt no substance beneath his feet. He simply floated in the middle of nowhere.

Would that I could leave you here, rather than where he demandsss I sssend you, came the dragon's voice in his head. *Thisss isss but the midpoint in the path I mussst create for you to reach your—or rather, his—dessstination.*

And with that, the emptiness gave way to shadow. A chill immediately ran down the Gryphon's spine, a chill that had nothing to do with the cold and everything with the sense of death and decay he felt from surroundings. Spectral figures darted at the edge of his vision. The landscape seemed to ebb and flow. A dark sphere hanging above might have been the sun or the moon, but either way, it radiated no illumination that he could notice.

The shadows of ancient structures shimmered on the horizon. One in the distance stood taller and more foreboding than the rest, and when the Gryphon chose to turn away, it was to find that sinister edifice again before him. He needed no more than that to verify that he was in a place to where only spirits journeyed...and they very reluctantly.

The dragon had deposited him in the netherworld ruled by the Lords of the Dead...

7

THE GREY LANDS

Nathan exhaled. "All right...that's enough."

Basil shook his head. The imposing mage, even larger than Adam Gudwead, growled, "We can't give in! The Gryphon's what binds this struggle even more than we in some ways! He has a bond with the men in the ranks, even if he's not human."

"I know that as well as you." Nathan looked around at the other ten spellcasters. They were among the best, but even their combined efforts had failed to locate the Gryphon. To Nathan, it was almost as if the Gryphon had ceased to exist.

Or maybe was just slain. In truth, if the lionbird was dead, it would have been just as difficult to pinpoint the location of his body. No one here had a deep enough tie. None of them were blood kin or even knew the rebel leader that well—

"Don't like leaving a man behind," Basil continued, absently rubbing his fingers against some of the scars of war decorating his face. He had been a soldier before he had been a wizard. "Not then, not now."

"*Toos.*" Nathan tried to recall where he had last seen the vulpine man. The rebels had returned from their questionable victory to the temporary security of the icy caverns, whereupon the Gryphon's second-in-command had immediately worked to keep the fighters from thinking too much about the fact that the Gryphon was missing and very possibly dead. "Where's Toos?"

"I think I know where he is," Gwendolyn replied. "I can't sense him…he almost invisible to me all the time…but I think I know which chamber he headed to."

The young officer made for a fine complement to his commander. Toos seemed to have even less magical ability than the lionbird claimed, but Nathan had sensed that the lad had some latent power. Not enough to make him a true spellcaster, but enough that more than once Toos had avoided injury or death due to curious 'fortune'. Something would block a bolt aimed for his heart, a foe's sword would shatter at just the critical moment in combat…Nathan had seen several incidents that he felt backed his suspicions as to the officer's untapped abilities.

But what the master wizard was more interested in at the moment was that Toos appeared to be the nearest thing to a friend to the Gryphon. If Nathan could manipulate whatever power Toos possessed, then perhaps the wizard could use that link to find their missing comrade.

"Basil, Tyr, Gwendolyn, come with me." He considered for a moment, then added, "Samir, I think you should come, too. I need to ask you about something I want to try, assuming Toos agrees."

The studious, olive-skinned mage solemnly nodded. Nathan thought that for a wizard more at home surrounded by his books, Samir had adapted well to the adverse conditions of war. Nathan had not realized until some time after Samir had magically slain a drake officer that the slim spellcaster had only killed one other foe in all his two hundred years.

"I shall draw upon what knowledge I remember, Nathan." Samir had spent his life gathering together the chronicles of nearly every wizard or enchantress' activities. What had begun as a continuation of his father's and grandfather's work had become as much a part of Samir's existence as breathing. He had also been one of the few other than Nathan ever granted permission to enter and use the legendary libraries of Penacles. There, a wizard could learn how to manipulate magic as never before…if he was clever enough to figure out the puzzling clues that were what passed for the contents of each of the seemingly endless corridors of mystical tomes.

Of course, it had also been Samir's unquenchable thirst for learning that had in great part eventually gotten him barred from the libraries by Lord Purple.

A wizard with long golden hair bound in a tail—golden hair save for the silver streak running from front to back that all human spellcasters had—anxiously stepped up to Nathan. "If we're not needed for anything at the moment, I'd really like to see how Staia is faring."

Putting a comforting hand on the other's shoulder, Nathan nodded. "Go to your bride, Wade." To the rest of the dozen, "Go to whoever you have who's important in your life. We won't get even this much respite in the future."

A grateful Wade immediately vanished. Nathan lowered his hand, then indicated Gwendolyn should lead the way to Toos. As he and his small party moved on, the other spellcasters left behind followed Wade Arkonsson's lead. Nathan and Yalak had done everything they could to see to it that the non-talented loved ones of the mages and enchantresses involved in the war were kept safe and hidden from the Dragon Kings. Still, Nathan worried about how long they could continue to do that. There were over three hundred such souls to protect, all of them actively sought out by the drake lords' agents. What better way could there be to break the spellcasters' resolve than by using their families and friends as hostages?

Nathan shuddered. While he had no relatives near enough in bloodline to be in danger because of him, he did worry about his sons, and in particular, more and more about Azran. As dangerous as Dayn's life had become, Azran's increasingly erratic personality threatened to lead everyone to disaster.

I have to find him when I have the chance, Nathan swore not for the first time. *I have to make him understand that I wasn't angry with him, just concerned.*

But, as always seemed the way when Nathan thought about his children, other matters demanded precedence. In this case, it came in the need to save the rebel cause from collapsing by trying to convince a man as obstinate as the Gryphon when it came to shunning his own potential abilities that there was no other choice but to accept them immediately.

Toos spotted them just as they entered the cavern chamber. He took one look at Nathan's expression and scowled. "I'm not going to like this, am I?"

"We need you to help us locate the Gryphon."

Toos eyed the party. "That means me at the center of some spell, doesn't it?"

"Yes, and it means reaching inside yourself and—"

The crimson-haired officer held up a hand to quiet Nathan. Young Toos might have been, but his eyes held a maturity Nathan would have wished on Azran. "I believe that Gryphon could be what you say he is. As for me, there's not much there. I'm sure of that. Still, if it's enough to save him, do what you have to."

The wizard was both surprised and pleased by the swift decision. That Toos did not savor what he would have to do but was willing to put himself in the hands of the spellcasters regardless spoke of the rebel's deep allegiance. Nathan admired the young man more and more.

Quickly directing the spellcasters to circle the rebel officer, Nathan then asked, "Samir, you understand what I want here?"

"Yes. This is very much akin to what Farin Bedlam attempted with the Lochivarite."

Neither Nathan nor anyone else knew to what Samir referred. Nathan only knew the female spellcaster's name. Even if they married, female members of powerful bloodlines such as the Bedlams continued to carry their surnames, and if their children showed promise, then they, too, were called by their mother's line as opposed to their father's. Only if the father came from an even stronger bloodline did that change.

Of course, there was no bloodline stronger than that of the Bedlams.

He waited for Samir to say more, but the swarthy wizard stood silent. Unable to resist, Nathan pressed, "And that went well, I imagine."

"It accomplished what it needed to," Samir replied solemnly.

Hoping that the rest did not wonder as much as Nathan did at the other mage's choice of words, the elder Bedlam had Samir coordinate the rest as needed. When Samir nodded, Nathan steeled himself, then directed the young officer's eyes to his.

"Don't break your gaze with me for the next minute, Toos."

"And after that?"

"You won't be able to break it at all, then."

To his credit, the fiery-haired rebel again did not flinch. "If it finds Gryphon, just do it."

A surreptitious glance at Samir did nothing to assuage Nathan's concerns that he might be risking Toos. Yet, they all knew that the Gryphon remained the heart of the rebel cause.

Nathan matched gazes with Toos again. As he did, he reached out with his power to the vulpine man. The moment the wizard's mind touched that of Toos, an extremely subtle silver aura formed around the figure before Nathan. The mage nearly disobeyed his own order not to break gazes at that critical juncture. The aura was not due to Nathan's efforts, but rather the rebel's curious innate magic. Nathan had never seen anything like it, and from what he could sense from Samir and the rest as they linked their minds to his for the overall spell, neither had they.

Something else to investigate…assuming we survive this war, Nathan Bedlam decided.

With the others properly linked to the spell matrix, Nathan guaranteed that Toos could now not free himself from what was to come. Nathan hoped that he had not overestimated the man. Toos would need every ounce of his wit and strength for this effort. It was clear to the master wizard that wherever the Gryphon and the Iron Dragon had ended, it was even farther away than Nathan had first imagined. If they only—

Father! came Dayn's anxious voice.

Not now, Dayn! It's critical that—

Please! Listen to me! There's word of him!

Nathan hesitated. *You've heard news of the Gryphon?*

The wizard's misgivings concerning his use of the young rebel had not only not abated, but they had increased as the spellwork had begun. If there was a chance of avoiding this—

No…not the Gryphon…Lord Iron…

Nathan felt everyone linked to him—Toos included—tense at the news. The elder Bedlam berated himself for not having kept the communications between his son and himself private. Nathan had been too anxious about everything else to pay attention to that one vital point. *They've found the Iron Dragon?*

Wade Arkonsson discovered the news just a few moments ago.

That bothered Nathan. If Wade, who had just departed, had learned so quickly about the Dragon King, then Iron could not have been found too far away from where not only Wade's bride had been hidden, but the rest of the spellcasters' loved ones.

Tell me. Nathan considered cutting off his companions from what Dayn had to say, but knew that there was no point to doing so. They would just interrogate him afterward.

Four dragons from Clan Iron are carrying him back to his domain. They flew near where Wade materialized. He reported to me immediately. Wade thought that Lord Iron was dead at first, but then sensed his life force. Lord Iron's badly wounded, but Wade thinks he'll live…

And Gryphon? demanded another voice that intruded where no one should have been able to intrude. *Where's Gryphon?*

That Toos had the power to interact with the Bedlams in such a manner revealed again the man's curious abilities. That, in turn, made Nathan think just how unique the rebel's missing commander was. While Toos had many limits, from what Nathan had seen of the lionbird, the only thing holding the Gryphon back was self-imposed.

No news of the Gryphon, Dayn replied apologetically. *None.*

Before Toos could interject himself again, Nathan asked, *Where exactly did they discover Lord Iron? Do you know?*

Wade guesses that from the dust and glittering rock on the Dragon King's back he was found in Legar…

Legar. It both encouraged and disturbed Nathan to know that they had a potential location for the Gryphon. It gave the spell he intended more focus, but being Legar, it also meant interference from the many crystal deposits spread throughout the peninsula.

It also meant potentially bringing into the war a drake lord who in general did nothing if not disturbed. The rebels already had far too many active foes…

There was no choice, though. Without hesitation, Nathan cut the link with Dayn and concentrated on Toos. The officer mentally welcomed the wizard's intrusion, even urged Nathan to hurry.

The rest of the group gave of themselves as asked. Nathan felt himself see the world through the eyes of Toos. Then, he and Toos began to see beyond the mortal plain. Nathan felt the rebel's rare amazement at what he was experiencing.

The wizard concentrated on Legar. The world flew beneath Nathan/Toos. Nathan felt a sudden tug and knew that the officer's bond with the Gryphon was beginning to steer them the proper direction. The rest of the spellcasters fed their efforts as Nathan/Toos neared where both believed they would at last find their quarry—

And then the world *vanished.*

The link to the other spellcasters ceased.

Pain shook Nathan. Physical pain. He opened up his eyes, which he did not even remember shutting.

Toos still stared back at him...but that was the only thing that had not changed.

"Where the hell are we?" the rebel demanded.

Nathan looked around...at nothing. A few small fragments of rock appeared to float around them, but otherwise, the two men drifted in emptiness. A white emptiness.

"By the Dragon of the Depths..." muttered Nathan, trying to come to terms with how he and Toos had ended up in this forsaken place. "The *Void*..."

THE WIND IS *the mourning of the souls, the black river formed by the tears of their laments...*

It was not a line the Gryphon desired to recall as he carefully wended his way through the shadowlands. He had heard the entire poem at the funeral of a comrade during his earliest years as a mercenary working *for* the Dragon Kings. Never had the Gryphon heard anyone recite the poem after that, and not once had he thought about it since that tragic event. Yet, now the one verse continually stirred in his imagination.

He could hardly be blamed for recalling it now, though. His senses were sharp enough to detect the flittering shapes, the half-seen forms gathering around him. They had been but a handful in the beginning. Now, their numbers were legion. Only the fact that they had no substance kept them from filling the area for as far as the eye could see.

Worse, being of no substance, they did not hesitate to move *through* him. Each time that happened, he shuddered from the cold they left in their wake. Yet, the Gryphon sensed no malignant intent. Indeed, he was certain that the spirits were simply drawn to his life force, something that stirred up vague recollections of their own pasts.

But as the specters abruptly scattered, the lionbird was reminded that *other*, less savory creatures might also sense his presence.

He ducked behind the hazy skeleton of an oak as the first of the winged monsters landed nearby. They stood at least as tall as him and yet that despite seemingly being permanently hunched over. They had milky white orbs and appeared to be some mix of a gigantic bat and a human corpse.

Necri... The Gryphon had never seen the fiends before, but he had heard of them from the tales surrounding the Lords of the Dead and had never forgotten the descriptions given of the beasts. The Necri were said to be soul hunters, although the Gryphon suspected that last part was the product of some bard's imagination. Nevertheless, what little the rebel commander *had* gleaned from the stories was that, at the very least, the Necri were vicious and dangerous servants of the Lords.

The second creature alighted a few yards north of the first. They were followed by a third. Moving as if in a running crouch, the three demonic figures spread out. It was evident to the Gryphon that they knew something was amiss. They just did not appear to understand exactly what.

The Gryphon grabbed again for the sword he no longer had. With no other weapon to choose from, he finally drew the small dagger and shifted his position by the dead tree so that the nearest Necri could not see him. To the Gryphon's eye, the three sentinels appeared to be flesh and blood, but there was only one way to find out—

A rough tendril circled his throat.

Barely managing to maintain hold of his dagger, the Gryphon grasped at the tendril as it dragged him from the ground. He managed to eke out a breath before what he realized was one of the limbs from the *tree* further tightened its suffocating hold.

Two more limbs darted toward his legs. The Gryphon twisted, managing to keep his legs free for the moment. With the dagger, he cut into the strangling branch.

Most blades would have taken far too long to cut through the wood, but the lionbird kept his dagger extremely sharp. It also had the added benefit of having been crafted at his special request by the one of the dwarves' best smiths.

The blade severed enough of the limb to cause the latter to crack. The Gryphon dropped.

Another branch seized his waist. Before the limb could tighten, the Gryphon twisted around. Managing to remove the piece still around his throat, the lionbird kicked at the other branches trying to seize him.

Clawed appendages seized his shoulders, squeezing so hard that the top of the breastplate pressed against his flesh. The Gryphon suddenly found himself hoisted high above the outstretched branches of the sinister tree. He did not have to guess just what had seized him and knew that his odds would have been better with the skeletal oak.

The Necri's leathery wings beat hard as the monster flew higher and higher. Whether it intended to drop the Gryphon to his doom, the rebel did not know. He grabbed hold of one of the ankles with his free hand, then slammed the dagger into the leg.

The Necri continued on unabated.

Cursing, the Gryphon started swinging his legs. The Necri ignored what likely seemed a futile attempt by its prey to shake free.

Swinging harder, the Gryphon brought his feet up. However, where before he had used them to knock away the threat, this time the rebel leader managed to wrap his legs around the fiend's stocky neck.

The Necri tried to shake its head free, but the lionbird managed to keep hold. Seeing that the chiropteran creature could not escape the Gryphon's hold, the lionbird pulled with his legs as hard as he could, forcing the head down.

The winged servant instinctively descended. Nearly upside down, the Gryphon watched as the ground neared.

An angry shriek warned him of the approach of the other pair. The Gryphon pulled harder, forcing the Necri's gaze directly below.

Tugging the dagger free, the lionbird thrust for the closest eye.

The tip sliced open the pale orb. The Necri let out a guttural sound and dropped more. The ground rushed up at the Gryphon even as one of the other fiends neared.

Straining, the rebel pulled harder with his legs. So near the earth, the Necri's wings caught.

The fiend whirled onto its back. The Gryphon released his hold. Unable to control its flight, the Necri crashed hard. As it did, it lost its grip on its captive.

Rolling free, the Gryphon turned to face the second Necri. The rebel had no delusions as to his chances against the remaining creatures. Had he had the power that Nathan claimed the lionbird had, matters might have been different. At the very least, the Gryphon would have tried to summon to him a portal or some other force by which he could escape this infernal place—

"Well! This is unexpected, and by no means a pleasure!" boomed a voice both appropriate to the dead lands and yet welcome to the desperate fighter.

The shadow of a great black stallion formed between the Gryphon and the second Necri. Ice blue eyes peered contemptuously at the oncoming monster.

"Your masters should really teach you better!" Darkhorse sneered, turning his body to the side.

The Necri seized hold of the stallion's exposed flank...and before the Gryphon's startled gaze suddenly shrank. The batlike beast tried to pull free, but it was as if Darkhorse was made of some sticky substance. Try as it might, the Necri only succeeded in becoming more mired.

And as it struggled, it continued to shrink. It also began *sinking* into the shadow steed's body. Now, rather than seeming to be stuck, the Necri appeared to be falling into some black abyss within Darkhorse's very torso. The Necri grew smaller and smaller and smaller...

The fiend let out one last shriek before dwindling to nothing. Darkhorse laughed, then turned his baleful gaze on the third attacker.

This Necri proved to the Gryphon that it had some intelligence, for it not only quickly ceased its dive, but even made sure to hover well out of Darkhorse's reach. It opened its mouth and started to utter a keening sound—

"That will not do," added the second voice that the lionbird always expected when Darkhorse appeared.

The Necri's wings wrapped around its body. The creature tried to open them, but failed. The Lords' hideous servant dropped like a rock to the ground, where, despite the harsh fall, it continued to feebly struggle against its own wings.

Shade stepped up behind the monster. With a pose of indifference, he inspected the Necri, then gestured.

The wings immediately tightened more. The sounds of bones cracking echoed through the silent realm.

The Necri lay still.

"My—my thanks," the Gryphon managed. "How did you—how did you know I was here?"

Shade tilted his head. The murky face revealed nothing, but the warlock's tone indicated mild surprise. "*You* reached out to us, Gryphon."

"*I* did?"

"Do you think we would come to this of all places if you had not?" asked Darkhorse, gaze constantly sweeping the grey realm. "Here, in the Lords' own domain?"

Before the Gryphon could answer, Shade raised a gloved hand. "We've been idle here too long! They—"

A grotesque armored specter formed before the Gryphon and his rescuers. The lionbird beheld a nearly fleshless skull within a once-majestic helmet topped with a dragon's head crest reminiscent of those worn by the drake lords. Yet, even though little remained of this phantasm save loose armor and a tattered cloak over scarred bones, the Gryphon knew that that this being had once been more human in form.

Human in form, but much more in power...

Even as he noted all this, the Gryphon acted. He lunged for the throat, assuming that even an undead would find it hard to do battle without its head. Out of the corner of his eye, the Gryphon saw Darkhorse rear up as if to kick at the skeletal menace...while Shade remained oddly still.

"Hello, cousin," the specter said to the warlock.

The Gryphon managed to get one hand on the ghoul—and suddenly sensed through touching the sinister necromancer the presence of the rest of the Lords of the Dead.

They, in turn, focused their dread, cold power on the rebel leader.

"You are one of us now," the grinning skull told him.

The chill of death swirled through the Gryphon.

The hand that touched the skeleton began to *decay*.

8

HANDS OUT OF THE PAST

"Is there something amiss, your majesty?"

Lord Purple quickly banished the subtle spell, hoping that the emperor's emissary had not detected its true purpose. This progeny of Gold's was proving more of a nuisance than the master of Penacles liked. If Lord Purple could have eliminated the young duke without repercussions, he would have.

"Nothing whatsoever, Toma," the Dragon King replied as he rose from his throne. "I have merely been receiving reports from my scouts concerning their missions."

"Your 'scouts'? You mean your assassins?"

"They are one and the same if they serve me."

The younger drake grinned. Toma had sharper fangs, a more forked tongue, than most drakes with whom Lord Purple dealt. He made the Dragon King's own sharp teeth seem blunt by comparison. That made Toma even more of an oddity, for the newest generation of drakes had more blunt teeth and nearly human tongues. Why those changes had come about, Lord Purple had a suspicion, but that was a matter for after Nathan Bedlam and the rebels were crushed...and Toma was back spying on someone else.

"You have sssomething you wish to ask?" the drake lord finally blurted when Toma simply stood in silence before him. The moment Lord Purple uttered the question, he mentally berated himself for letting sibilance slip into his words. It only served to reveal to Toma just how much the duke's presence disturbed the Dragon King.

A flick of his tongue was hint enough of the younger drake's pleasure at seeing how he affected Lord Purple. Nearly as tall as the Dragon King, the duke stared his host in the eye. "I am to report to my father your progress, as you recall. *Is* there any progress to report, your majesty?"

The drake lord waved him off. "Come back to me this time tomorrow. You will get your progress report for the emperor."

Lord Purple started off, only to have Toma dog the Dragon King's heels. However, where Lord Purple intended to go, Toma was a most unwelcome companion.

"Your majesty—"

Whirling, the Dragon King glared at the duke. For one of the few times, the drake lord gave an outsider a glimpse of what lay behind his odd eyes.

It was enough to make even Toma recoil. The younger drake remained absolutely still as Lord Purple quietly turned away.

Free of the duke, the Dragon King journeyed to the chamber where the tapestry hung. Two metallic figures flanked the outer doors, statues resembling what the Gryphon would have recognized as Necri. They were more than mere works of art, though, as anyone who attempted to enter without the Dragon King's permission would have found out much to their regret.

Only Nathan Bedlam had once managed to pass the statues untouched, but had he attempted a second time, he would have found them far deadlier adversaries. Lord Purple had enhanced the chamber's guardians with his former servant in mind.

The iron doors beyond swung open as the drake lord approached them. It immediately became evident what the focus of the chamber was, for the elaborate tapestry filled the far wall.

Its intricate detail showed a skill far beyond mortal ability. Even more amazing, as Lord Purple stepped up to the tapestry, small elements of the image—the City of Knowledge itself—changed before the Dragon King's eyes. Whenever some part of Penacles altered, the tapestry corrected itself. It did not matter how tiny the change might be; the tapestry would always show the city as it was at that moment.

But even this ability meant nothing to Lord Purple. Instead, he located a small symbol in the middle of the image, the symbol of an open book.

Rubbing the book with his index finger, the Dragon King concentrated.

His surroundings vanished, the plain chamber replaced by the intersection of a several corridors. Down each corridor, endless shelves of thick tomes lined the walls from top to bottom. Although the books appeared uniform in size and shape, no two consecutive corridors contained volumes of the same coloring.

The libraries of Penacles remained within the boundaries of the city, but ever shifted their exact position. That they were underground was obvious, but no one had ever been able to detect their location without the tapestry. Indeed, the only known entrance into the legendary libraries was by the method the Dragon King had utilized.

Lord Purple turned in a circle. He did not bother trying to count the corridors, aware from long experience that he would end with a different number each time. Instead, he awaited a familiar figure.

And just as he completed his turn, he found the short, squat form quietly waiting as if standing before the imposing drake all along. Utterly bald, humanoid in appearance, and wearing a long, flowing robe that trailed over the floor, the librarian bowed his head.

"Welcome, current master of the libraries."

From anyone else, such a peculiar greeting would have been rewarded with a harsh slap to the face, harsh enough to break a jaw. The Dragon King knew better than to strike the librarian, though. Not only would it have no effect, but the gnomish figure did not mean any insult. He or they—it had never been clear to Lord Purple or any of his predecessors whether there was one gnome or several—never aged. They quietly served whoever controlled the libraries, thus the choice of words.

"How may I serve you?" the gnome asked innocently.

The drake lord suddenly found himself impatient with the libraries' games. "You know—the libraries *know*—what I want! Bring it to me and spare us both this charade!"

The pinched features shifted to an expression of mild dismay. "If I may, your majesty, you are aware that calm reaps more concise answers from the libraries."

The Dragon King hissed. Taking a deep breath, he continued as quietly as he could, "The book. The right one."

The librarian turned and not at all to Lord Purple's surprise walked down a different corridor than the one the drake lord expected him to choose. Then, the necessary volume had been bound in a cover crimson in color. This time, it appeared the knowledge would come in a dark blue tome. It did not matter if the Dragon King desired the same exact information; the books seemed to exchange their contents with one another at whim.

The bald gnome held up a hand. One of the books flew from an upper shelf and landed lightly in his grip. Clutching the hefty tome under one arm, the robed figure returned to Lord Purple.

Without a word, the drake lord opened the book. Had he attempted to retrieve the information himself, he would have been left with a book whose pages were blank. The libraries did not give up their secrets easily.

But when they did, they served their master very, very well.

The pages flew by of their own doing, pausing a third of the way through the book. At first, only a peculiar black squiggle of ink decorated the left side, but the ink immediately spread throughout both pages, swiftly becoming words, diagrams, and illustrations.

The drake lord studied the contents. The ancient script was just barely legible. In addition, each corner of the page was decorated with stylized dragon heads that reminded Lord Purple more of the one atop the helmet of the specter who called himself Ephraim rather than the drake lord's own crest. Lord Purple thought he knew the reason for that, but cared little about it at the moment as with his eyes he devoured the long-sought spellwork.

His lipless mouth widened. "Yesss. It makesss perfect sense! I should have known! There will be no mistake, no escape, this time..."

Long practice enabled him to swiftly memorize the complex details. Only rarely did the libraries permit written notes to leave. There seemed no rhyme or reason to when that happened, so Lord Purple had made it a practice not to rely on anything but his own wits.

Finally slamming the huge book shut, the drake lord returned it to the librarian. The gnome bowed his head again. "You found that for which you wished?"

"More than that! More than—"

A *second* tome suddenly flew from one of the shelves in the nearest corridor to the Dragon King's left. Lord Purple barely had time to stretch his gauntleted hand to catch it.

"What isss thisss?" he demanded of the robed figure. "Why thisss second volume?"

The librarian gaped, then, "I...I do not know...it...I have never seen it do that, your majesty..."

"'Never'?" With growing curiosity, Lord Purple opened the book. The last time the libraries had given him a mysterious answer, it had turned out to be a warning that Nathan Bedlam would be the cause of much grief to the Dragon Kings. Unfortunately, Lord Purple had not understood that warning then.

The pages flipped by. Where with the previous tome they had halted before the midway point, this time they continued on until well into the back of the book. In fact, the pages did not cease moving until there were but two left.

And on those two pages, Lord Purple beheld a secret for which he had been searching for a very, very long time.

"Sssoo. *Thisss* isss the truth…" He looked up at the librarian, who continued to appear very perturbed by the entire incident. "You knew…you *knew*…"

Before the gnomish figure could answer, the drake lord thrust the second tome at him. As the librarian worked to maintain his hold on both massive volumes, the Dragon King vanished.

The books under control, the short, robed figure glared at the silent corridors. "What have you done? *What have you done?*"

DAYN EXHALED, THEN looked from Gwendolyn to Yalak and back again. They shook their heads. The three remained in the cavern where Nathan had coordinated the spell on Toos. Yalak had sent Samir and the rest to deal with other vital situations concerning the rebellion while he, Dayn, and the enchantress had sought out the senior wizard using methods Yalak believed better suited where Nathan was concerned. Dayn had wanted the others to stay, but Yalak had finally convinced the younger Bedlam that the war could not come to a halt for very long for anyone, even the most powerful wizard known.

"But how can they completely disappear from us?" Dayn demanded of the other wizard as they paused to regain their strength. "How—unless they're both—they're both—"

"No...please don't say it!" Gwendolyn pleaded, eyes as wide and fearful as Dayn's.

Yalak intervened. "Your father is not dead! I have foreseen him in events beyond this moment. Where he is...I do not know...but he is alive." The balding man frowned. "As to the fate of Toos and his commander, those remain question marks."

"This has gone from bad to worse." Dayn grimaced. "I've rarely been unable to feel some presence of my father, even if I had no idea exactly where he was..."

"We will find him. As I said, I have foreseen him at other points in the future—"

"And are your visions completely accurate, Yalak?"

The older mage shook his head. "No...there is that element of uncertainty, but my visions are grounded in truth, which to me means he *lives*."

Dayn opened his mouth to argue when suddenly they were joined by a leather- and fur-clad wizard with shoulder-length brown hair and a lush beard. He stood an inch or so shorter than Dayn, but was of a similar girth. Like Yalak, the newcomer had an older—even middle-aged—cast to him. The look of experience was by choice, as Solomon Rhine was more than two decades younger than Nathan Bedlam and could have retained as youthful an appearance as Dayn. Of course, Solomon Rhine's past contained many reasons why he would choose to let the years touch his appearance, not the least of which was the death of both his children and his wife from illness while he had been away on a mission for the Dragon Kings.

A small raven perched on the bearded spellcaster's shoulder cawed at the other spellcasters. Solomon Rhine tilted his head slightly to shush the bird, in doing so turning his eye patch toward Dayn. He had lost his right eye while still in training, the result of another young wizard's fatal error. The magic inherent in the accident prevented the eye from ever being repaired, but Solomon had compensated with other methods to replace the lost sight. One of those methods included the raven.

His arrival only increased the trio's consternation. Solomon Rhine was one of those set with a very specific task. The most vital task.

"Tell me you found what Nathan sent you for," Yalak murmured.

"No..." The bearded wizard softly petted the raven. "Someone else found it first...I think."

"The Dragon Kings?"

Solomon cleared his throat. "Could be...maybe not." He peered around. "No one else near?"

Despite his concern for his father, Dayn could not help but be caught up in the newcomer's agitation. He knew that Nathan Bedlam had put much stock in the mission on which he had sent Solomon Rhine and four others, even if no one knew just exactly *what* they were looking for. "But you *did* find where it had been?"

"I think so, lad. Your father would've known for certain. I came back to get his verification—"

"We can't—" Gwen began.

"We can't disturb Nathan right now," Yalak interjected without a glance at her. "Dayn...you know nearly as much as your father about this. Let Solomon take you there. Gwen and I will see to that other matter. I promise."

Dayn swallowed, then nodded. There was no one he could trust more with his father's safety than Yalak. Besides, Nathan would have expected his son to press on, especially where this secret quest was concerned.

A second nod to Solomon was all the one-eyed wizard needed. Solomon Rhine gritted his teeth...and Dayn's surroundings melted.

He was greeted by the sight of another cavern, but with a reddish tinge to the rock that marked the location as near or within the Hell Plains. Dayn was suddenly reminded of his father's encounter with Shade, one of the events that would lead to the elder Bedlam's break from his drake masters.

"Don't know how much Nathan told you about what he sent us to find," Solomon muttered as he led the other spellcaster through the warm cavern. "Your father could come up with no trace of Ethas in the official records kept by Penacles nor could Samir locate the man in his own collection, but he wondered just what brought Ethas to the area, evidently more than once."

"More than once?" Dayn could not recall having been told that fact by his father. "How do you know?"

"Just before he had to abandon his quarters in Penacles, Samir noticed a peculiar *absence* in part of the records from that time. He wanted to bring the records in question with him, but had to leave them behind. Your father didn't mention that?"

"No."

Solomon shrugged, then suddenly paused. "Stand back."

Before Dayn could ask why, some of the rocks grew even redder. At the same time, the surrounding temperature greatly increased.

Something long and sinewy burst from the reddest rock. Solomon reached forward and grabbed the serpentine beast just under the long, pointed head. The creature glowed a bright red, as if on fire.

"Got you this time, friend!" Grinning, the bearded wizard held the hissing creature before him. At the same time, the other rocks began to lose some of their fiery glow.

"*Tircoth*," Solomon explained unhelpfully. "Better known as volcano snakes, though they're more like lizards without legs." The tircoth hissed and spat, but clearly was not poisonous or Dayn's companion would have been dead from the spray he received. Still, it had a wicked set of sharp, curved fangs that made Nathan's son instinctively step back. "They can generate so much heat inside themselves that they can melt a path through the toughest rock. The nose also acts like digging tool, I think, though no one's seen it in action."

"Are there many?" Dayn finally asked.

"Hundreds that I've detected. Don't know what they all live on, but so long as it's not us, I'm fine."

Then, to Dayn's surprise, Solomon squeezed hard. With a simple crack of bone, he killed the tircoth. The other mage was known for his interest in animals, but where the tircoth was concerned there was obviously no love lost.

Solomon held the limp body up to his raven's beak. He whispered something to the bird.

The beak opened...and widened beyond what should have been its physical limitations. With one gulp, the raven swallowed the *entire* body, yet appeared no different in size and shape once the beak shut again.

"He's been having quite the feast since we got here," the other man commented blithely. Then, suddenly serious again, Solomon indicated that they should move on.

Strengthening his personal shields, Dayn carefully followed. His gaze shifted from one rock wall to the other, watching for the telltale sign of reddening stone. Solomon had said nothing about magic being able to keep the legless lizards from biting them. There were far too many creatures in the Dragonrealm with the ability to mute a spellcaster's defensive abilities. Many of those had been the creations of earlier Dragon Kings and other great wielders of magic that had for one reason or another been set loose by their masters to spawn. Mostly designed as hunters or guardians, such creatures had a variety of lethal weapons. Indeed, compared to some of those

Dayn had studied while apprenticed, the tircoth was a minor if still potentially deadly annoyance.

"Nathan's gone missing, hasn't he?" Solomon asked without looking back.

Dayn saw no reason to lie. "Yes. Just a short time ago. Yalak thinks we'll find him, though."

"Well, that's all right, then."

The younger spellcaster wished he shared his companion's optimism. Dayn also wished he knew how much deeper into this ever warmer cavern they had to journey. He was constantly adjusting the spell that protected him from the blistering heat of the Hell Plains.

At the next turn, Solomon Rhine suddenly halted again. He looked at Dayn. "What do you know about the founding race?"

Aware of some aspects of the search, Dayn was not entirely surprised by the question. "I know some things my father told me."

"Did you ever see an image of one?"

The younger Bedlam's brow wrinkled. "I don't think I know *anyone* who has, not even father..."

"Well, that's about to change for *you*, at least."

And with that, Solomon stepped out of sight around the corner.

Dayn blinked, then continued after. He expected to confront some grand and glorious spectacle—the golden tomb of some majestic leader of the founders—but instead, only the faint glow of a blue sphere summoned by Solomon Rhine initially greeted him.

"It's over here," the bearded spellcaster muttered from Dayn's right.

Nathan's son peered past Solomon...and beheld at first only more steaming rock. Then, he realized that there was a formation in the rock that had no natural origin, a formation that in its center held a twisted, very dead form.

Half-buried within the black rock lay a translucent shell of onyx. Encased inside that onyx was a corpse. A *founder's* corpse. The shell draped so perfectly around the body that even small details of the dead founder's features could be made out. The most evident of those details and one that initially made even the founder's general appearance a secondary shock was the look of *horror* forever sealed on the face.

This being had been encased alive.

Only after his initial astonishment passed did Dayn gaze upon the corpse and see the grandness that had once been the land's first and most powerful people. Despite the dark shell, the skin appeared very pale, perhaps ivory. The long lush hair had a hint of what Dayn believed emerald. That emerald hue seemed to match the color of the wide, pupilless eyes. The nose was upturned and much slighter than that of a human and the delicate ears were pointed, giving some resemblance to an elf.

The lipless mouth with the perfect teeth might have completed the image of an exotic but handsome face if not for the terrible contortions death and the onyx shell had left them in forever.

Only the right side was visible to the wizards and not all of that, either. The founder's voluminous robe draped down to at least the ankle. Whether the figure wore boots or sandals or went barefoot was hidden by the rock wall that time had formed over the body. One gloved hand with the normal five digits lay flattened against the corpse's chest.

"Amazing..." Dayn finally murmured.

"Disturbing, don't you mean?" his companion remarked.

"His death? Of course! But it's still amazing to see one of them after hearing all the tales."

Solomon's raven cawed again, a sound that for some reason made Nathan's son feel as if the bird mocked him. The bearded mage shushed the avian, then pointed at the corpse's chest near the hand. "Take another look there, won't you? You'll maybe see then what I wanted only your father to know about…if he hadn't gone and vanished."

Dayn leaned close. Two things suddenly struck him about what he saw. "There's the *impression* of something on his robes…it's about a foot long, no more. I can't make out what it might've been…"

"Nor I. Good eye you have, lad. Now, think about the fact that something made its mark on him and look at the shell again."

Dayn stiffened. "Just exactly *what* was my father hoping to find?"

"Whatever it was Ethas Bedlam came to this sweltering region for," the second wizard responded unhelpfully. "Ethas thought it important enough to risk coming here more than once…much to his regret." Solomon looked uneasy. "You haven't remarked about the fact that whatever this poor soul carried was taken from him after death."

Dayn no longer cared. "The murderer took it with him. That was millennia ago. I'm sorry that Father sent you on a futile hunt, but—"

The older wizard exhaled. His raven squawked once more. This time, Solomon did not shush the bird. "Sharp eye, but not sharp enough. Look again. This time with more than your eye."

His thoughts returning more and more to his missing parent and his own desire to return to that more pressing search, Dayn quickly obeyed…and immediately saw what he had missed. The knowledge shook him even more than he let on to Solomon. "This…this was resealed…"

"Yes, but that's the obvious thing. You know what I'm talking about. Tell me I'm wrong, Bedlam. I'd like to be."

"It was resealed…*recently*…and by—" Dayn shook his head, scarcely able to believe what he sensed. "And by…one of *us*."

Solomon Rhine rewarded him with a grim smile. "And *that's* what I need you to keep between us…and Nathan, if—when he's found." The bearded mage shook his head. "Nathan thought there was a traitor telling the Dragon Kings some of what we planned... now we know there *must* be..."

Dayn vacantly nodded as he digested the facts. Only magic could have resealed the founder's casing after someone had removed the unknown artifact, yet, not all magic was the same. The way one race cast its spells remained unique when compared with those cast by other races. A Seeker spell would leave a different trace than either a drake or human spell, just as the latter two would differ from one another.

This spell had been cast by a *human*.

The ground abruptly rumbled. Solomon looked up as bits of rock dropped around the duo. If not for their personal shields, both would have been hit more than once by pieces large enough to cause injury.

"Time to leave this place," Solomon Rhine declared. "If that's not an eruption about to start nearby, then it's the lord of the land himself getting much too close. Either way, it's not safe here. Better a pack of tircoth—or I guess *slither* is the right term for a bunch of those foul serpents—than those two choices."

"You're right!" Indeed, Dayn had already begun casting a spell to transport both of them to safety. However, he did it only in part due to the potential danger now rearing its head. He also did it to prevent any chance, however slight, that Solomon Rhine might just make one last study of the trace the previous spellcaster had left behind. Thus far, Dayn's companion had uncovered only what most would have...that one of the rebellion's own had been here before them and had stolen something that might help salvage the war.

But Dayn had sensed more. He was aware that he had possibly done so due to his superior abilities. That was no slight against Solomon Rhine. The simple fact was that Dayn was a Bedlam and therefore had inherited great innate power.

However, as the two vanished, Dayn could not help thinking that perhaps there was a simpler, if more foreboding, reason for him having discerned more than Solomon about just who had preceded them here.

After all, who other than perhaps Dayn's father would recognize better than Dayn the purposely masked trace of *Azran?*

9

SKALN

The Gryphon's hand began to decay...and then just as swiftly *healed*. At the same time, the lionbird felt his strength return in a rush.

But the sudden reversal of fortune did not go unnoticed by the ghoulish figures before him, especially the one with whom the Gryphon struggled. One rusting gauntlet seized the rebel leader's wrist, reinforcing the contact between the two adversaries.

"You have *her* taint..." the necromancer angrily rasped.

"He has much, much more than that!"

Darkhorse appeared among the Lords of the Dead. The ebony stallion reared. Heavy hooves kicked out at one of the armored shapes.

That Lord immediately vanished, only to reappear behind the shadow steed.

Maintaining his death grip, the Gryphon's foe twisted his skeletal head around. "Fool! He dares not touch you at this moment! He only wants to break—"

"Too late," Shade quietly remarked, materializing next to the leader of the necromancers. The warlock thrust a hand at the rusted breastplate. "Goodbye, Ephraim."

A hollow growl escaped the necromancer. He vanished, but the Gryphon sensed Ephraim had done so of his own accord, not due to anything Shade had attempted. Indeed, as far as the lionbird could sense, the faceless spellcaster had done *nothing*.

"Sometimes, you have to judge your target and how they think," Shade commented wryly, wrapping his expanding cloak around the Gryphon. "Let him—*them*—assume they know exactly what you're doing."

"They are regrouping!" Darkhorse roared from his position. "I would suggest we depart!"

On the one hand, the Gryphon was more than happy with the thought of leaving the Lords' dank domain, but on the other, he was still trying to ascertain just why the dragon spirit had sent him here in the first place.

But as the seemingly living cloak surrounded him, the Gryphon recalled something the ghoul Ephraim had uttered. *You have her taint...*

Before he could ask Shade just who the necromancer might have been referring to, something clutched the lionbird's ankle. Whatever it was also apparently prevented Shade from completing their escape, for suddenly the cloak unfolded again.

Only then did the lionbird see that what not only held his ankle but those of the warlock were skeletal hands. In fact, even as the Gryphon and Shade struggled against those, more and more hands burst from the parched soil, their grasping fingers seeking the intruders.

Shade drew his cloak back about him. "I would say how unoriginal, but effective is still effective..."

Beyond them, Darkhorse raged as other fleshless fingers grasped at his legs. Unlike the warlock and the lionbird, though, the eternal proved untouchable. The skeletal digits clutched only air.

But what caused Darkhorse to rage despite his advantage was a grey haze swirling around him. The shadow steed seemed to want to return to his comrades, but neither ran through the haze nor leapt over it, both quite reasonable choices as far as the Gryphon could tell.

To his side, Shade bent down and swept one gloved hand across the ground. An arc of blue energy followed in the hand's wake and where it passed it cut through the unliving limbs.

The Gryphon did not remain idle, either. While he lacked Shade's abilities, he was not without raw strength. Seizing one of the severed appendages left by the warlock's initial effort, the lionbird shattered the nearest grasping hands before they could add to the party's troubles.

But although he also managed to quickly free himself, the Gryphon had barely taken a step before Shade commanded, "Remain where you are!"

As he spoke, the hooded warlock charged toward Darkhorse, who had started an unsettling transformation. His body twisted and turned, stretched and tore. Any mortal creature would have already perished from the horrendous damage done to him, but Darkhorse only seemed discomforted and angry. Yet, the Gryphon suspected that if something was not done quickly, the ebony stallion still might perish.

Shade clearly thought the same, for the moment he reached the haze, he thrust his hand into it. The gloved hand turned icy as it entered, but whether due to the haze or the warlock's spellwork was not initially clear to the rebel leader.

Where Shade held his hand the haze separated. Yet, instead of simply bits of mist, the elements of the haze became half-seen figures.

Ghosts, the lionbird realized. *It's not a haze or mist...it's a legion of fettered spirits circling Darkhorse...*

There were those who believed the Lords of the Dead dark gods who collected the souls of all those who passed away. The Gryphon's own opinion painted the Lords as just as dark as others thought, but lessened their fearsome powers somewhat. He believed the tales that hinted that they had once been human—or something near that—and that despite their sinister might, they had their limits. Shade's familiarity with them verified much of what the Gryphon believed, but there still remained the fact that they held sway over many dead. Worse, the lionbird was certain that those ghosts were not only part of the Lords' power…they *amplified* it.

Adding his second hand, Shade created a gap. He shoved aside scores of shifting specters as he widened the opening.

"Now, Darkhorse! Now!"

Without hesitation, the ghastly shape that had once been the stallion *poured* through. In the process, Darkhorse passed into the warlock's body. The faceless spellcaster shivered, but held his place.

A sense of unease filled the Gryphon. He looked over his shoulder and saw the landscape behind him shifting. He also felt the presence of something more substantial than the ghosts.

The Lords…

The Gryphon suddenly lunged to his left. He acted on the same instinct that had kept him alive through one battle after another.

His clawed hand tore through something thicker than air. He had a brief glimpse of an armored form, a Lord. It vanished as his hand finished ripping past. The Gryphon had no illusions as to whether he had slain or even as much as injured the necromancer. All he had likely done was distract the ghoul from whatever plan the Lords had intended.

Barely had he dealt the one blow than he spun in the opposite direction. The outline of another helmeted form—this one with long, weathered strands of hair that he realized marked the figure as once female—barely started to form before the Gryphon fell upon it.

It vanished exactly like the first. Still, despite twice having set the necromancers' plans back, the Gryphon knew that he could not continue on like this forever.

A short distance away, Darkhorse reformed. Meanwhile, Shade pulled back from the gathered specters. At first, they immediately flowed after him, but Shade raised a hand and a barrier of silver came between him and the undead.

Yet again, a feeling overcame the Gryphon. This time, however, he felt the menace nearer to Darkhorse than himself.

Another Lord of the Dead materialized behind the shadow steed. Despite the helmets, despite the fleshless faces, the lionbird knew that he once again beheld the leader, Ephraim.

A long, pale blade formed in the necromancer's left hand. The Gryphon saw in an instant that it had not been forged, but rather *carved*. Carved from bone.

There was no time to warn Darkhorse. The distance was also too great for the Gryphon to cross. The lionbird stared at Ephraim, trying in that last second to think of some way to prevent the necromancer from striking.

A burst of light—*sunlight*—erupted in front of the Gryphon. It burned away the grey to reveal a dank, colorless landscape devoid of any life save a few rotted plants and leafless trees. Here was the true realm of the Lords of the Dead, a place even more desolate, more lifeless, than their shrouded world generally appeared.

The searing illumination spread quicker than the blink of an eye. It touched Darkhorse, but naturally did not affect him.

But when it reached Ephraim, the necromancer reared back as if struck through the chest by a lance. He cried out in both agony and anger. The sinister sword fell from his grip.

In the sunlight, he was also better revealed. As decayed as he had seemed before, the Lords' leader now showed himself as little more than rusted, crumbling armor and a few floating fragments of bone bound by a monstrous swirl of energy the color of dying moss. It was this energy that held Ephraim—and the others, the Gryphon reasoned—together.

Ephraim vanished in the next instant. The other Lords followed suit.

Darkhorse returned to Shade, who had just managed to stand straight. The warlock's chest heaved rapidly, whether from his efforts or having the stallion pass through him, the lionbird could not say.

The sunlight began to fade. The Gryphon knew that when it disappeared the Lords of the Dead would return with a vengeance. The spell had caught them by surprise, but they would surely be ready for a second such attack.

Shade grabbed hold of Darkhorse, who once again had the solidity of a living animal. The Gryphon moved to help the stricken spellcaster, but suddenly the shadow steed's flank rippled. The ripples pulled Shade up to the stallion's back, where he wearily mounted.

"Hurry!" thundered Darkhorse to the rebel leader. "Climb behind him!"

Leaping atop, the Gryphon helped Shade remain seated. Around them, the last vestiges of sunlight dwindled away.

Directly ahead, the landscape swirled into the shape of a gaping *mouth*. The Gryphon expected it to inhale, but instead, the mouth did the opposite.

From the dark maw emerged thousands of tiny black shapes that immediately swarmed toward the trio.

"Hold tight!" the shadowy stallion commanded.

His body suddenly reshaped itself again. A transparent black shell formed around Shade and the lionbird just as the first of the swarm reached them.

Tiny skulls with multiple eye sockets and sharp mandibles filled the rebel leader's view. From between the mandibles, a sharp needle darted in and out. The tip dripped with some thick liquid. The monstrous insects had webbed wings and dozens of tiny, pointed claws that opened and closed continuously.

Some of them attempted to reach the warlock and the Gryphon. As they struck the sphere, they melted. However, with each strike, the lionbird felt Darkhorse jolt as if in pain.

Despite that, the ebony stallion charged into the swarm. The shell grew dark with the crush of tiny bodies against it.

Then…only the mouth remained.

Shade stirred. "Keep…keep me stable…"

As the Gryphon tightened his hold on the hooded figure, the warlock planted both hands against Darkhorse.

The gloved hands flared blue…and a moment later, so did Darkhorse.

The shadow steed and his riders burst through the mouth.

The still lands faded around them, in moments replaced by a fog-enshrouded realm.

Shade shook his head. "This is not—this is not where I intended us to reenter…"

"Nor I!" came Darkhorse's voice from all around them.

The Gryphon noted that although the shadow steed had resumed his normal coloring, he had not removed the protective shell. "Where are we? Is this—?"

"Yes, we are in Lochivar." Shade exhaled. "Near its capital, to be precise."

And as the faceless warlock verified the lionbird's suspicions, the mists thinned just enough to reveal the silhouette of a walled city that might very well have been found in the dread domain from which they had just escaped. Savage spikes rose high above the wall and on those spikes hung impaled what the Gryphon knew had once been men.

"Skaln…" he muttered. "Skaln…"

Capital of Lochivar…and citadel of the Black Dragon.

"WHAT THE HELL is a void?" Toos demanded of Nathan as he tried to maneuver in the emptiness.

"Not 'a void'. *The* Void. It's a place known to some wizards, but as far as I know, none of us have ever seen it. I wasn't sure it even actually existed."

"Well, there's not much to see." The rebel officer growled as he took in their surroundings—or lack thereof—again. "So, how long before you get us out of here?"

The wizard frowned. "Understand, Toos, that we barely know *of* the Void, much less how it works. It's said to be where Darkhorse originated, although he's not spoken of it in the short time I've known him."

"What is there to talk about? You're hesitating, Master Bedlam…*can* you get us out of here?"

"I've been trying. I think I may have sensed a link back to our world, but it's tenuous. I'm trying to—" Nathan frowned as something came to his notice.

Toos did not miss the subtle change in his expression. "What's the matter?"

"There's—for a moment, I thought I sensed *Darkhorse*, but it must have just been my imagination. I doubt he would just happen to be in this—"

Yet, the feeling that the shadow steed drew nearer only grew for the spellcaster. However, at the same time, Nathan's unease also grew. It was and was *not* Darkhorse as the wizard knew him.

"We don't want to be here," Nathan announced, reaching for Toos. "Keep a physical hold. Otherwise, I can't promise we'll travel together."

"You found the way back?"

"Let us hope so." Whatever neared them, Nathan now knew that it was definitely not the shadow steed. There was a sinister aspect to it that Nathan wanted no part of.

A black spot formed in the white emptiness, a black spot clearly moving toward the duo.

Toos had also finally noticed they were no longer alone. "Master Bedlam...is that something we should be avoiding?"

In response, Nathan concentrated on the vague link he had sensed. *Let this work...*

I want to play... a chilling voice that yet sounded like Darkhorse's whispered in the wizard's head.

"Please get us out of here now," Toos requested, a slight quiver in his voice confirming to Nathan that the young officer had also heard the voice.

Nathan cast.

Where normally his surroundings immediately changed after such a spell, this time the mage watched with growing anxiousness as the Void faded much too slowly. The black spot drew nearer and nearer and began to take on a shape.

At that point, the Void disappeared...and Nathan let out an exhalation of relief—

An exhalation that he cut off as he took in their new location.

"Hold your breath!" Nathan ordered, already aware of just how futile a command he gave.

Toos was already coughing. Praying that it was not too late, Nathan cast an invisible sphere around his companion's head. The sphere did more than simply seal off the mist from Toos. It filtered the air so that the rebel could continue to breathe without fear.

Quickly doing the same for himself, the wizard watched cautiously as Toos at last managed catch his breath. As the younger man straightened, Nathan caught his gaze. "Who am I, Toos?"

"You're—" A cough. "—Master Bedlam."

Nathan did not relax. "What cause do you serve?"

The vulpine man frowned. "I serve—I serve—" Toos put a hand to his head. The sphere, designed only to keep the threat of the mists away, let his hand pass. "I serve—" With a strong shake of his head, Toos finished, "Damn it! I serve any cause that sees the fall of the Dragon Kings!"

The answer came as a great relief to Nathan, but it did not mean that he relaxed much. "How does your head feel now?"

"Like some poison is slowly leaking out of it." The rebel finally took stock of the landscape. "We're in—"

"Lochivar, yes." Now that he had verified that the officer's mind was still intact, Nathan's instinct was to quickly take both of them from this benighted realm. They were in a place barely better than that which they had left and much of it had to do with the cloying fog enshrouding everything. The mists of Lochivar sapped men's will quickly and made them the fanatical servants of the Black Dragon. While nearly everyone in the Dragonrealm had heard of the mists, few knew the truth about them and even among those, believing that truth was often difficult.

The mists were the exhalations of the Black Dragon himself. Each day, he breathed them anew, reinforcing his will upon all those he ruled. So many generations had grown up under the sway of not only the current drake lord but that of his predecessors that Nathan wondered what would happen if the mists ceased. Would the populace rise against their cruel lord if given the chance? The question had been brought up more than once in council, but no one could say for certain, and at present, the theaters of war had barely included Lord Black's domain. The Gryphon had reasoned that the master of Lochivar would bide his time, preferring to keep utter control of his kingdom while letting others deal with the renegade spellcasters.

Thus far, that strategy had worked, but Nathan wondered how the drake lord would react if he knew that there were intruders unaffected by the mists roaming around.

Yet, Nathan did not cast a spell of teleportation. The tenuous link that he had followed had been related to the Gryphon. If it had led the wizard and the soldier to Lochivar, that meant that the odds were that the Gryphon had at least passed this way.

Exactly why the Gryphon had ended up here, Nathan still did not know. He hoped that the lionbird would be able to answer that question.

The faint trail that had enabled Nathan to follow the rebel leader this far continued on deeper into Lochivar. Unfortunately, it led in the same direction in which the wizard knew that the capital, Skaln, lay. Little was known about Skaln other than its name, for even the other Dragon Kings rarely visited the region. It was not that they were susceptible to the mists; Skaln was simply a place that anyone with sense shunned.

He informed Toos of what lay ahead. To his credit, the young rebel was unperturbed.

"If you say Gryphon's that way, Master Bedlam, then that's the way we go...assuming you're going with me."

Nathan knew that the officer's comment was meant as no slight. If the mage felt that he could not continue on, then Toos was willing to do so by himself. The fact that he thus far could only survive the mists due to Nathan's spell meant nothing to the rebel. So long as he had that one gift from the wizard, he would push on even if it meant trying to reach the heart—if it could be called such—of Skaln itself.

"We go together," Nathan quietly answered, "but I lead."

Toos reluctantly conceded. Nathan carefully probed the path ahead and, finding no hint that the Black Dragon had set any traps, started forward.

However, they had barely been walking for a quarter hour when the rebel—not the mage—signaled for a halt. Toos cocked his head to the side in a manner Nathan thought reminiscent of the Gryphon and listened.

Straining, the wizard finally heard what had caused Toos to stop. The slight clink of metal against metal in a rhythmic manner that bespoke of an armored figure on horseback.

That clink was soon accompanied by other similar sounds. As both men dropped to the ground, the outlines of four riders and their mounts formed on the nearby horizon.

Unlike the well-groomed, polished soldiers of Lord Brown, these four had the look of beasts attempting human shapes. Long hair draped loosely and unkempt melded into thick, bushy beards. Two of the riders held axes ready for use; the other pair broadswords whose points looked well-honed even from a distance. They rode thickly muscled warhorses with shaggy manes who looked every bit as savage as the men astride them.

Although it was impossible to see their eyes from where Nathan hid, he knew the burning fanaticism that those eyes held. That they were in some ways victims of the Black Dragon's power made them no less deadly enemies.

Toos and Nathan kept as still as possible until the patrol vanished back into the mists. All the while, Nathan kept a subtle masking spell over the pair's location. The patrol was far from the worst of Lochivar's threats. The land itself was saturated with Lord Black's magic.

After a reasonable time, Nathan decided that they should move on. He and Toos wended their way along the lightly wooded land.

All the while, Nathan sensed the growing presence of Lochivar's drake lord, a sign that Skaln was not that far away.

And, in fact, as they stepped to the top of a low hill, the wizard spotted the ungodly outline of what could only be Lochivar's ominous capital. The faint vision both disturbed and encouraged him, the former for what the silhouette obviously represented, the latter because as Nathan concentrated, he sensed that the Gryphon could be found somewhere near its walls.

Yet, with that trace Nathan also believed he now sensed two other unique traces. Darkhorse and Shade. While on the one hand their presence meant that the Gryphon had allies nearby, it also occurred to the wizard that the odds of Lord Black not noticing the trio near his capital were faint.

"Stand ready," he warned Toos. "I'm going to take us to the Gryphon."

"You've found him?" The rebel's hopeful expression quickly vanished, though. "In Skaln?"

"No...but very near. No time to say more. We need to get him out of here as soon as possible." Nathan did not bother to tell Toos about Darkhorse and the warlock. Toos knew that they were allies. What mattered was the Black Dragon.

Strengthening the cloaking spell around them, Nathan cast his teleport spell. To his dismay, they materialized far nearer to Skaln's walls than the mage liked. He wondered why the Gryphon and the others would risk such closeness to the Dragon King's sanctum.

A moment later...Nathan realized that they had *not*.

He said nothing to Toos, instead immediately casting the vulpine man away with another spell and praying that it would deliver the rebel to Yalak and the others.

But just as Nathan managed that, the mists closed around him. A pair of triumphant reptilian orbs formed just above him.

The Bedlam... Lord Black mocked in his head. *The great Dragon Hunter...*

The title was one that Nathan had picked up in the months since becoming one of the leaders of the rebellion. He made no claims to it and would have preferred not to have others think of him so, but Yalak and the Gryphon had seen it as a rallying point. Nathan had slain drakes, yes, but so had the Gryphon and the other wizards. Yet, as the most powerful of the mages, the name had fallen on the elder Bedlam.

Nathan drew a line in front of him. The mists gathered around as if tethered to the line. They draped over the region where the eyes floated, blinding the Dragon King.

Concentrating, the wizard vanished—

—and reappeared in the same location.

Fool of a human... the drake lord rumbled in his head. Then, *Breathe...breathe and sssee your true path...*

The protective spell around Nathan faded despite his best attempt to keep it whole. He instinctively held his breath, although he knew that he could not do so for very long.

You will ssserve me and ssserve no other...

Suddenly, Darkhorse materialized out of the mists. As he charged toward Nathan, a *fifth* appendage—an arm ending in a thick hand with three digits—formed.

With the hand, the shadow steed plucked the mage up.

"Darkhorse! Where's—?"

"No time! Hold tight! I think—"

The Black Dragon laughed.

An inky gap—a blink hole—opened up just in front of Nathan and the shadow steed. Darkhorse tried to maneuver around it, but could not stop his momentum. He and the wizard entered—

Stark, black towers surrounded them. Wary eyes fell upon the duo from every direction, eyes from not only men as dour and deadly as those in the patrol, but also women and even *children*. Nathan stared at the throng with horror, seeing the people of Lochivar anew. As a servant of the Dragon Kings, he had thought little of what life under the various drake lords might be like. Humans were meant to serve—that was how he had been raised.

But to see this...

You will fight dragons, came Lord Black's mocking voice yet again, *but now let us see how you fight children...*

As the drake lord's laughter echoed in Nathan's skull, the citizens of Skaln—young and old—converged with swords, sticks, teeth, and nails upon the mage and his mount. Soldiers stood side-by-side with shopkeepers, shopkeepers with servants, and servants with children. They closed on the wizard with the obvious intention of trying to rip him and the ebony stallion to shreds. With perhaps the exception of the soldiers, the throng consisted entirely of *innocents*.

Innocents that Nathan was well aware he might just be forced to kill...

10

WOLVES

An unsettling tingle coursed down Hadeen's spine. The half-elf's hand casually slipped toward the knife at his left.

"Uncle Hadeen...it's been a long time!"

The voice should have cheered Hadeen, but instead it only made him want the knife even more. Still, as he turned and rose—leaving the blade on the table—the half-elf wore the smile he knew his 'guest' no doubt expected.

"Azran! Yes, it's been a long time..." He met the young wizard halfway. The pair shook hands, Hadeen noticing a coldness to the younger Bedlam's flesh. "Is your father on the way, too?"

"I wouldn't know," the bearded mage replied indifferently. He peered around the cabin. "This place looks almost like the last one you lived in. Very quaint."

"I've few needs. Would you like something to drink or eat? What brings you to me?"

Azran continued to look about. As he did, his own left hand slipped down to the side of his hip. Fighting back a frown, Hadeen used Azran's distraction to study the hip area.

For just a moment, something familiar partially faded into view. A scabbard hung at the mage's side. A scabbard in which had been sheathed—

The image faded. Hadeen barely had time to look up before Azran returned his gaze to the half-elf.

"Father wants us all working to find different weapons and spells to use against the Dragon Kings. I know you're supposed to be 'loyal', but the truth is you're one of them, aren't you?"

"One of what?"

Nathan's son chuckled. "A rebel, of course!"

"I think you know the answer," Hadeen responded, still considering the weapon Azran sought to keep hidden. Against just about anyone else—even Nathan—the spell would have been fully effective. Against someone like Hadeen, though—

Suddenly, the outcast had a suspicion why Azran had sought him out. Yet, he said nothing, hoping that he was wrong.

With another chuckle, Azran propped himself against a chair. He was careful to avoid letting the unseen scabbard swing against anything, although Hadeen believed him a capable enough spellcaster to have also muffled any noise the sheath might have made.

"Always tight-lipped, Uncle," Nathan's son finally remarked. Only he had ever called Hadeen by that title, even though in some ways the half-elf had acted just like an uncle to the two boys. "You're good at keeping secrets, I can appreciate that. I know you'll do the same for me, won't you?"

"What secret do you have?"

An earnest look abruptly spread across Azran's face as he leaned toward Hadeen. "You don't use your abilities much, do you...I mean the *other* magical abilities, not the ones you learned to hide your birthright?"

Hadeen did *not* bother to hide his anger. "You know this is a subject of which we are never to speak. I have put that time behind me—"

"But you can't just shrug off those powers! You're still an elemental, regardless of what you wish!"

It was a term Hadeen had not heard in some years. He and his brother never spoke of it during the few times they visited with one another. Hadrea had no idea of her legacy and both males wanted it to remain that way.

"There is a reason that elves are permitted the use of magic unfettered, Azran. It is because our normal level of skill is nothing to the Dragon Kings. We are linked to the land, yes, but in subtle ways...worthless ways for what I imagine you must desire."

His explanation earned another chuckle from Azran. "That's almost word for word what old Hadferus said."

Mention of the name startled Hadeen. "You've spoken with the Guide?"

"I've spoken to your grandfather, yes." The bearded mage shook his head. "Not a very useful title, Uncle. What exactly is he guiding? The elves never do anything, and if you have a problem with that or veer from their strict rules, they throw you out!"

"What did you ask of him?"

"Just to show me how the elemental magic works. He's the same blood as you and he's the elven Guide. He should be able to use it as you do..." Azran's brow furrowed. "...but he said he couldn't... right before he demanded I leave. You know...I actually believed him, too."

And if you had not, what would you have done then? the half-elf wondered. This was an Azran Hadeen did not know. Nathan had warned his old friend about the change his younger son was going through, but at the time Hadeen had not believed the depths the elder Bedlam had described. Now, though, Hadeen thought that Azran seemed even more transformed than Nathan had indicated and not merely in appearance, although the half-silver, half-black hair and beard were in themselves unsettling.

"But you, on the other hand," the younger spellcaster continued, "can still command those powers. Am I right?"

Before Hadeen could deny anything, a dark red aura surrounded Azran. The half-elf knew exactly what that aura presaged and was shocked that Azran would unleash such a spell.

Falling to one knee, Hadeen murmured.

The aura around Nathan's son instantly dissipated.

A furious Hadeen rose. "Do not *ever* attempt that spell again! Do you—?"

Rather than looking troubled, Azran grinned wide. "You *did* it! You actually did it! You completely rerouted the lines of force so that there was nothing with which I could feed the spell! It was amazing! I almost felt like one of the unTalented!"

The term was one some spellcasters used for those with no magical ability. Hadeen had always found the word demeaning.

He stepped up to Azran and while the younger Bedlam was still grinning...*struck* him across the face.

The grin remained, but the eyes flashed with anger.

Hadeen growled, "To be an elemental is to bear both a blessing and a curse! The Guide should have mentioned that, at least."

"I think he did just that as he was demanding I leave."

For a moment, the two silently stood facing one another. Azran's expression remained unchanged.

Reminding himself that this was Nathan's son, Asrilla's child, Hadeen tried again. "Azran. I will tell you this just once. I choose not to use the power of an elemental for one very good reason. Each time that ability is used, it permanently alters the lines of force."

"Can you teach me to do it? Is that possible? Your grandfather wouldn't say if it was possible, but I think it is."

"You are not listening! Each time the lines of force shift like that, it causes the entire arrangement to grow a little less stable—"

He stopped as he noted a subtle change in Azran's gaze. "—but you *know* that, don't you?"

In reply, the wizard answered, "Yes, but think what a weapon that could be against the drakes, Uncle…stripped of their power, they'd fall like leaves from a dead tree!"

"And the rest of the Dragonrealm might do so soon after." Hadeen finally turned from Azran. Reaching for a mug, he prepared to pour some wine for his now-undesired guest. "We elves have tales we keep among ourselves, but that maybe you should hear. They concern what we think caused in great part the downfall of the founding race. Those tales are also why we, although we revere these powers, know they must be used with the utmost care—"

He turned to hand the mug to Azran…but Nathan's son had already vanished.

Hadeen withdrew the mug, his eyes narrowing. After a pause, he drank the contents himself, then returned his gaze to the spot where Azran had stood.

The half-elf suddenly shuddered, although for exactly what reason, he could not say.

"HE IS HERE," Shade had suddenly remarked to the Gryphon.

The Gryphon had at first assumed that the warlock meant the Black Dragon, but then had noticed Shade looking away from Skaln's walls in the direction from which the trio had come. "Who?"

"Nathan Bedlam. The Bedlam trace is very unique. It reminds me of someone I once knew…" The hooded spellcaster rubbed his chin and in a less confident voice, concluded, "at least…someone I think I once knew…"

Darkhorse had chosen that moment to return to them. At the Gryphon's reluctant request, the shadow steed had gone on ahead to investigate a sound only the lionbird had heard.

"You were not mistaken!" the stallion had declared loudly, seeming to forget just where they were. "In the water—"

But then Shade had interrupted with, "Darkhorse! Nathan Bedlam! See to him now!"

Without hesitation, the shadow steed had reared, then raced off to where the warlock had pointed.

Even as that had happened, Shade had once more taken his cloak and wrapped it around the two of them. Barely had he done so than the clatter of many hooves had echoed in the Gryphon's ears.

And although at least two or three minutes had passed, both the warlock and the rebel remained frozen within the cloak. Around them, more than a dozen dark riders including a black drake, scoured the vicinity.

"No one!" they heard a gruff human voice bellow. "No one, lord duke!"

"His majesssty sssays they are here and ssso they are, fool! Leave no patch of earth uncombed! The accursssed one is no doubt hiding them both right before our eyesss..."

Next to the Gryphon, Shade grunted. The drakes were especially interested in capturing him. The Gryphon suspected that Shade's fate would be even worse than the rebel's, for the immortal warlock's checkered past had made him a villain to nearly all creatures. Trapped in a curse that caused him to alternate between personalities following darkness or light, he spent much of his existence either causing mayhem or trying to make amends for it. Most of the drake lords now knew better than to simply slay the hooded figure, though, and so the Gryphon believed that instead Shade would face endless torture designed to put him at the *edge* of death, but not allow him to cross it.

Despite the thick lining of the cloak, the lionbird could still make out the hunting party. It was as much magic as Shade dared cast. Even the Gryphon could sense the Black Dragon's foul power sweeping over the region. If they did anything to draw notice, their hopes of escape would dwindle to nothing.

Another ursine face strode right up to the shrouded pair. Like the previous hunters, this guard suddenly turned to the side and headed *around* the Gryphon and his companion.

They have to give up soon, the lionbird told himself. *They've been over this area several times already.*

The drake officer suddenly urged his reptilian mount toward them. More than one of the guards had called him by the title of duke, which meant that the Black Dragon was his sire. That he was out here was indication that the drake was not Lord Black's heir, though. Still, the magical skills of any high-ranking drake could not be ignored.

Closer and closer trudged the duke's mount. The Gryphon could smell the beast's horrific breath. Even Shade had to stifle a gasp as the monster came within striking distance.

Then, just like the guards, the riding drake turned to the side. The Gryphon quietly exhaled.

The drake warrior pulled tight on the reins.

With his mount still facing away from the hidden duo, the armored figure slowly dismounted. Not once did his gaze leave the location where the warlock and the rebel stood.

The Gryphon flexed his claws, but Shade used his free hand to push the claws down.

Edging nearer, the scaled warrior studied the spot. With his next step, he involuntarily turned aside. Unlike his mount, though, the drake did not move on. Instead, he very slowly reached back to where the two hid, while at the same time keeping his gaze focused just to the right of the pair.

The gauntleted hand touched the cloak. The fingers stiffened as realization struck the duke.

Before Shade could stop him, the Gryphon lunged forward. With a single swipe of his claws, he ripped through the drake's throat.

"Not a move I would have suggested," the warlock remarked as he swung back his cloak.

The stricken drake staggered back. His hand went to his torn throat. A raspy cough escaped him just before he toppled.

One of the guards let out a wild howl, a manic cry picked up by several of the others in the nearby vicinity.

The Gryphon had hoped to steal the drake's sword, but the corpse had fallen away from him. He dodged the swing of an ax, then threw himself at his attacker's midsection.

As the rebel and the guard fell together, the Gryphon heard Shade mutter something. A fearsome wind arose, one that kept both the lionbird and his foe planted against the ground. Out of the corner of his eye, the Gryphon saw two of the other shaggy warriors futilely fighting against the gale. With each step they tried to take forward, they ended up two back.

Another unnatural gust tore the Gryphon from his opponent and sent him back to Shade's side.

"It would be best if we quickly departed, but there is something we apparently need to see first," the faceless warlock muttered cryptically.

Their surroundings—and the furious warriors—disappeared. A new landscape shaped itself around the duo.

And there the Gryphon beheld just what Darkhorse had planned to warn them about until Shade had sent him after Nathan Bedlam.

Southeast of the city, the sea beckoned. Yet, it was not the vast expanse of water that so ensnared the lionbird's attention, but rather the ten black ships anchored in the harbor. Even though he knew little about Lochivar, the Gryphon was absolutely certain that these vessels did not belong to the Black Dragon's domain.

"Plots within plots within plots," muttered Shade. "Even as they fight us, the Dragon Kings cannot help but continue their intrigues against one another."

"Are you saying that those...those ships are not meant to be used against the rebellion?"

"Not directly, but that is another matter." The warlock pointed at the nearest vessel. Figures aboard the ship were unloading something into longboats positioned next to the hull. "Do you see that? A curious manner of work."

The Gryphon grunted in agreement. "Why go through so much trouble? Why not dock first?"

"Perhaps because these are allies that even the Black Dragon does not trust enough just yet. Perhaps another reason. Unfortunately, we do not have the luxury of time to discover the truth."

"There's no markings. Do you know them, Shade?"

The hooded figure shrugged. "Perhaps I did once. Not in this incarnation, though—"

The fur and feathers on the back of the Gryphon's neck suddenly stiffened. At the same time, he heard a sharp intake of breath from the warlock.

Shade turned his gaze back to Skaln. His features might have been unreadable, but not so his tone, which was full of frustration. "He's forced our hand." The warlock looked again to the Gryphon. "I will do my best to send you back to your men first."

"What about you?" The rebel leader suddenly realized where Shade intended to travel. "No! If Master Nathan needs help, then I'll go with—"

The Gryphon hesitated as something else caught his attention. From the direction of the black ships, he felt a familiar but ominous force arising...a force he knew instantly was directed at *him*.

"No...you must be kept safe," Shade replied to the lionbird, the warlock clearly ignorant of the unsettling power reaching out from the ships.

Before the Gryphon could do anything to stop Shade, the spell-caster gestured.

The dank land of Lochivar faded. The cavern where the rebellion hid shaped around the Gryphon...and then just as swiftly *also* vanished.

And suddenly the lionbird stood in the midst of what, from the dire appearance of the people around him, could only be Lochivar's capital.

Exactly why Shade had brought him back, the Gryphon could not say. He did not care. All he knew was that just a few yards from him Nathan Bedlam and Darkhorse stood surrounded by a mob intent on their blood. The Gryphon could not understand why the pair did not simply leave or, if not that, sweep away their enemies, but had to assume that there was some reason that prevented them from doing either.

"You should not be here!" Shade snarled with uncharacteristic anger from the Gryphon's left. "How did you—?"

At that moment, the maddened crowd surged forward. However, they had barely taken a step closer before the foremost of them went flying over their comrades. As the Gryphon watched, the soaring figures landed *safely*—thanks in great part to Nathan Bedlam's sense of mercy—in various spots at the outer edges of the city square.

In the Gryphon's head, a mocking laugh echoed. He knew without a doubt the source of that laughter. He also at last sensed the reason why the wizard and Darkhorse had not simply left. The Black Dragon's spell permeated the city, a spell designed to allow others to enter...but not to leave unless permitted. One aspect of the odd unloading of the mysterious ships made more sense. Out in the harbor, they were untouched by the spell. Had they entered any part of the city, though…

The Gryphon silently cursed. The ships no longer mattered. What did was that he and his companions were all now trapped in Skaln.

All asss planned…a masssterful ssstroke on hisss part…

The lionbird ignored the comment, more concerned with what to do against the mob. True, they were Lochivarites, but they were not, for the most part, members of the Black Dragon's fighting legions. Like the wizard and Darkhorse—and even evidently Shade, from the care the warlock was taking—the Gryphon had no desire to harm innocents.

Nathan Bedlam was clearly guiding the party's tactics, the wizard directing the magical forces used against the maddened throng. However, something in the wizard's expression made the lionbird believe that Nathan fought a second struggle, one that none of his companions could sense.

Not for the first time, the Gryphon acted on some innate instinct. Rather than join in defense of the party, he placed a hand on the mage's shoulder.

…will ssserve me utterly and absssolutely! came a voice that was *not* the Black Dragon's. Rather, the Gryphon knew it for only one other drake lord…the Dragon Emperor himself. Through Lochivar's master, Lord Gold himself reached out to take Nathan's will and bend it to his own. *You will ssslay your children if I ssso command! You will turn on your comradesss, willingly flaying them alive if I ssso desssire…*

The intensity with which those words hammered Nathan Bedlam stunned the Gryphon. The Dragon Kings knew that the wizard remained the key to tearing the rebellion apart. If Nathan fell under their sway again, then it would demoralize the other mages…and in turn the Gryphon's men. Until Nathan had led the spellcasters to the rebels, the best the Gryphon had hoped for was a miracle.

Thus far, the wizard was holding his own against both the Dragon Emperor's tremendous will and the sinister mists, but with Nathan also trying to keep from harming the mob, it was only a matter of time before the mage's mental defenses collapsed. That surely was the Dragon Emperor's plan—or rather the plan the lion-bird believed had been set into motion for Lord Gold by another. The Gryphon sensed Lord Purple's claws in this, but could not say for certain.

He felt Nathan shiver. The Gryphon wished that he could give some of his strength to the wizard. If his meager abilities counted for anything, they were welcome to the human—

Nathan jolted straight. The lionbird felt the mage's will reassert itself as if completely refreshed.

From far away, a harsh cracking sound filled the air.

Pulling back from Nathan, the Gryphon had a brief flash of memory that faded before he could grasp it. All that briefly remained was the image of a monstrous, ghostly wolf.

Something soared over the city walls from the direction of the harbor. The fiery missile arced down toward the square, followed almost immediately by a second...and a third.

Fanatic as the mists made the people of Skaln, they also retained the presence of mind to flee utter destruction from the sky. The throng scattered as the first missile crashed into a stable on the north side of the square.

The Gryphon was familiar with catapults and ballistas aboard ships, but was still amazed at the distance and accuracy of the weapons. He also wondered who would have the audacity to fire upon the city. The only ships nearby were those of Lochivar...and the mysterious black vessels he and Shade had noted.

But as the lionbird pondered why the drake lord's allies might choose to attack the city, a large, monstrous shape stirred from the ruined stable. Shoving aside the wreckage with one massive paw, the fiendish beast sniffed the air. The creature burned with the same fire with which the missile had…and after a moment, the Gryphon finally understood that this demonic beast *was* the missile.

As the second fiery ball crashed into the emptied square, the demon the rebel had been watching let out a lupine howl. Within the flickering flames, the outline of a wolf's head formed.

A wolf's head that then turned in the Gryphon's direction.

The lionbird did not need anyone to tell him that the monster was after him in particular, especially when the second beast that rose *also* focused its attention on the rebel leader.

Even as he heard the third missile collide behind him, the Gryphon sought for a weapon. Unfortunately, the only thing available to him was a fallen lance. Despite the awkwardness of it, the Gryphon seized up the weapon as the initial wolf leapt at him.

Aware that death was imminent, the lionbird nevertheless propped the back end of the lance against the ground and raised the point. There was nothing substantial about the fiend, nothing that the lance could stop. It was a creature of magic, a thing sent by those in the ships to slay him.

Wishing he could die at least knowing more, the Gryphon braced himself.

The huge, burning wolf dropped upon the lance…and howled in stunned pain as the weapon, suddenly silver and glowing, *pierced* the lupine demon as if it were flesh and blood. The beast writhed, snapped its searing teeth at the sweating Gryphon…and then faded like smoke.

But the rebel had no time to cheer at this astounding escape, for behind him he heard the second approaching. Unable to turn the lance around, the Gryphon chose flight. Leaping over the discarded weapon, he ducked into an open door.

The savage growl that greeted him came from no demon, but rather a wild-eyed figure in the armor of a Lochivarite guard. The ursine fighter nearly decapitated the Gryphon with a well-worn ax larger than the lionbird's head.

As the Gryphon ducked, the front of the building exploded inward. Fire in the form of the second wolf demon filled the room and a moment later engulfed the guard. The Lochivarite shrieked as his entire body erupted in flames.

The shriek ended abruptly as the wolf's jaws clamped down over the man's scorched head. The demon worried the body for a moment, then contemptuously through the blazing carcass to the side.

As it twisted around to renew the chase, the Gryphon abandoned the building for the square again. He saw now why the third beast had not followed the second. Darkhorse and Shade held it at bay even as Nathan Bedlam stood like a statue facing the empty air to the east.

And a moment later, the Gryphon beheld the reason for the wizard's peculiar posture. To the rebel, the thing that rose over the city dwarfed the threat of a *dozen* fire wolves, if not more. The vast leathery wings spread *across* the city, in the Gryphon's thoughts surely reaching from one outer wall to the opposite. The shadow it cast dimmed even the demons' bright flames. The eyes that fell upon the spectacle below burned great than those flames, burned with fury at *all* below.

Lochivar's master loomed over Skaln.

II

SHADES OF MAGIC

The Gryphon believed Nathan fought on two fronts, but in truth, the veteran wizard fought on at least *four*. Not only did he face the mental onslaught by none other than the Dragon Emperor and the obvious physical one represented by the black leviathan now hovering above, the mage also had to concentrate on keeping both the Gryphon and himself from succumbing to the effects of the mists. Nathan had found out too late that the magical nature of the mists meant that spells designed to combat them soon weakened. Without constant reinforcement, the pair would lose their protection.

Finally, and most mysterious, was the odd mystical attack the wizard felt originating from the waters beyond the city. He had never experienced a magic akin to it and that meant combating the attacks proved more difficult...which in turn made it harder for Nathan to deal with the other threats.

One of those threats peered down in growing rage at the burning, ruined square. The Black Dragon opened his jaws and exhaled.

The fires doused. Even the demons faded.

But as soon as the dragon finished breathing...the fires burst to new life and the monstrous wolves reformed.

And as the lord of Lochivar snarled angrily, two more blazing missiles descended toward the already-ruined square.

"We must find a path of escape!" Darkhorse called.

"Easier said than done," Shade countered as he seized one end of his cloak and wrapped it over the head of the demon closing on him. The cloak swelled, not only draping the skull, but the creature's entire front half.

The demon struggled to find its way to the warlock, but somehow managed to only move in a tiny circle. Still, Nathan knew that Shade could only hope for a stalemate. Only the Gryphon had thus far effectively dealt one of the demons.

His failure to smother the flames only incensed the Dragon King. With a swipe of one paw, he sent those soldiers remaining in the vicinity fleeing from the square, leaving only Nathan and his companions.

The Dragon Emperor's foul whispers continued to assail the wizard's thoughts. They dug deeper and deeper into his mind, stripping away his defiance. Yet, curiously, Nathan did not see the Gold Dragon in his head, but rather the more familiar visage of Lord Purple. This all wreaked of Lord Purple's cunning...and yet the wizard could not understand how the master of Penacles had been able to keep track of his wayward servant so thoroughly. No spy among the spellcasters would have been privy enough to Nathan's activities to enable the Purple Dragon to formulate such a thorough plan—

Before Nathan could take his thoughts that one step more, he sensed Lord Black's attention now concentrate on him. Every Dragon King saw Nathan Bedlam as the key to their victory. The veteran mage knew that he could not continue to stand against so many foes at once. His head already throbbed and his concentration was weakening.

The square had become an inferno, but the Black Dragon seemed not to care if his entire capital burned to ground. Instead, the dark leviathan saw only the wizard. With a huff of air, he sent a fire wolf that had just formed in front of Nathan tumbling away. That done, the Black Dragon reached with his huge, curved claws for Nathan. The behemoth's jaws opened wider.

Whether the drake lord intended to take the human prisoner or simply swallow him whole and be done with it, Nathan did not know. He was saved from discovering which by Shade's sudden presence at his side. The warlock thrust both gloved hands forward.

The massive teeth collided with an invisible barrier only a few yards from the two spellcasters. Yet, despite Shade's sudden interference, Nathan knew that the barrier would not last long.

"There is a familiar taint, if I can say such," the faceless warlock muttered as he strained against the drake lord's assault. "The Lords of the Dead have contributed greatly to this trap, although I doubt the Dragon Emperor knows that…"

"But Lord Purple does, I'm certain!" Nathan quickly added as he fought another mental attack by the Dragon Emperor. "Somehow they knew they could lure me here!"

"You in particular?" After a moment's consideration—and a visible struggle to strengthen the shield between the dragon and them—the hooded figure nodded. "Yes…that would make sense… although how they could be certain you would end up here is still a question—"

An explosion shook the square and sent Nathan and Shade sprawling. Above them, the Black Dragon laughed.

"The sons of the wolf may have their birdman," he rumbled, "but *we* finally have you, Bed—"

Two of the fire wolves abruptly leapt at the Dragon King.

The behemoth reared back in surprise as the creatures sought his eyes. Although they had no wings, the demons followed the dragon into the sky above the city. Behind them leapt two more.

The four beasts momentarily kept the Dragon King at bay. Seeking an answer as to the unexpected change, Nathan dared glance over his shoulder. There, he beheld the Gryphon standing almost as if a statue. The lionbird's gaze remained veiled, as if he looked *inward* instead of out.

From above, there came a horrific sizzling sound. Glancing up, Nathan saw one of the wolves melting away as if its flames had been doused by a heavy rainstorm. Undaunted, the rest of the ethereal pack continued to the drake lord as best they could.

Returning his attention to the Gryphon, the wizard sensed something taking place on a level normal sight did not reveal. Adjusting his perceptions, Nathan beheld the world as it truly was, a place not just crisscrossed by lines of force, but *filled* with magical energy of all types and intensities.

And nothing radiated more distinctly than the Gryphon.

A *rainbow* of energies swirled around the inhuman figure. Nathan could not say whether those energies implied a potential greater than his own—just that again the wizard had been shown that the Gryphon was definitely far more powerful than the rebel himself insisted.

Yet, with every other pulsation, that fantastic rainbow dulled. When that happened, Nathan felt the Gryphon's power dwindle to nearly nothing. If not for the fact that in the next second the rainbow brightened again, it would have been impossible for the Gryphon to have done what he thus far had.

But the lionbird had not merely seized control of the demon wolves, he had also begun building a shining barrier of emerald energy around himself, a barrier that steadily expanded to encompass more and more of the square. It crossed through an unsuspecting Darkhorse, then reached the still-rising Shade. The warlock glanced back at the lionbird just as the energies enveloped him.

"Fascinating," Shade calmly remarked as he watched it pass beyond him.

A moment later, the barrier reached Nathan...and there at last it faltered. The wizard did not have to ask why. He felt the combined force of more than one Dragon King pressing back at this unexpected challenge, and the one reason that the Gryphon's shield still held at all was because only Lochivar's master was physically near.

Even still, the Gryphon's unusual abilities had clearly reached their limits. The muted look to the energies surrounding him dominated more and more. As that happened, the barrier began to fade.

His gaze still empty, the Gryphon dropped to one knee. The strain began to show in his inhuman countenance.

Without thinking, the wizard jumped to help the lionbird. He seized the Gryphon by the arms just before the latter would have fallen face first.

The moment Nathan and the Gryphon touched, something *else* happened. The veteran mage felt a surge of power flow through him and into the Gryphon. The drain was so strong that Nathan, too, dropped to his knee, yet the wizard did not struggle against what was happening. Some part of the Gryphon needed all that the human could give. For what reason, Nathan could only guess, but he saw little hope for the four otherwise.

The Gryphon looked up. Even though his gaze was directed toward Nathan, it was obvious that he did not see the robed figure. The lionbird blinked once.

Behind Nathan, the Black Dragon roared. A savage wind swept through the square, buffeting the defenders despite the Gryphon's barrier.

Nathan groaned as the demand on him multiplied. Despite the strain on him, the wizard saw that the Gryphon suffered more. The lionbird's body shivered harder and harder, yet his effort did not lessen. If anything, whatever that mysterious part of the Gryphon sought to do, it did so with more determination than ever.

The Black Dragon exhaled yet again. The remaining wolves faded away. With a brief glare in the direction of the harbor, the drake lord stretched his vast wings and dove toward the square.

The Gryphon's body shook one more time.

Nathan gasped. It was all he could do to keep from blacking out as what seemed his very life force poured from him into the catatonic rebel leader.

A wave of pure force burst from the Gryphon, spreading in the blink of an eye throughout the square and then racing beyond. Buildings flattened. The sky filled with wreckage swept along by the growing wave, wreckage that assailed the Dragon King as even the demons had not.

Although barely conscious, Nathan still had the wits to notice that not only had avoided being been touched by this second, more intense wave, but so had Darkhorse and Shade. The same could not be said for anything else in the vicinity. Nathan wondered about the populace, but knew that there was nothing he could do. The decision lay in that part of the Gryphon controlling the moment.

More and more wreckage from the city flew into the sky, swarming around the Black Dragon like maddened wasps. Despite the leviathan's best efforts, he was soon enveloped by the remains of his own capital.

"It is time to leave now," the Gryphon tonelessly informed Nathan.

At first, the wizard expected his companion to transport them away, but all the lionbird did was stare at Nathan with the same blank eyes. The mage finally understood that their actual escape was up to *him*.

Still aiding in the other spell, Nathan nevertheless concentrated on the rebel stronghold. He had no idea from where he would draw the strength, but he knew that if the Gryphon said that they had to leave...they had to leave.

A desperate thought occurred to him. Nathan imagined the cavern...and then his son. If Dayn sensed him—

Nathan?

The feminine voice filling his head momentarily surprised him. Gwendolyn's relief nearly overwhelmed the exhausted wizard, but fortunately, she immediately realized that he needed more than just her help. A second later, Dayn joined the pair.

We understand what you want, Father! We have you!

Even as they combined their efforts with his, Nathan felt the mind of the Dragon Emperor try to stifle their spellwork. Yet, the same force guiding the Gryphon's astounding spell also kept the Gold Dragon at bay enough for the three humans to finish casting.

A new rush of wood, stone, and twisted metal collided with the Black Dragon, a last effort by the Gryphon's subconscious to aid the trio.

The ruins of Skaln faded away.

A blink later, the underground cavern greeted Nathan's tired gaze. Dayn, Gwendolyn, Yalak, and others surrounded the wizard and the Gryphon.

Forcing himself to look around, Nathan searched for Shade and Darkhorse. When he saw no sign of them, he looked to Dayn. "Where—?"

But Nathan got no farther. The strain finally overtook him... and he collapsed.

SHADE GROANED AS he collided with the dead tree. The faceless warlock swore, wondering if his curse had added a new factor, the insistence that he strike one hard surface after another when materializing. As he tried to rise, the hooded spellcaster also attempted to figure out just what happened.

The warlock had felt himself plucked from his location by the same magic that he knew had taken Nathan Bedlam, the Gryphon, and Darkhorse. After that, though, things had somehow gone awry. Someone involved in the spell had tried to separate Darkhorse and the faceless warlock from the other pair. Shade had his suspicions. The enchantress Gwendolyn saw the two outsiders as monsters. A simple reflex action by her during the casting would have been enough to toss Shade—and perhaps the black stallion as well—to other parts of the Dragonrealm.

He was far from Skaln, far from Lochivar. The dead tree was one of several ancient giants on the border between the Dagora Forest and the southeastern edge of Lord Silver's domain. The ruined trunks were the remnants of a dispute from a hundred years before between the current Dragon Kings ruling the two lands.

Shade immediately probed the region, but found no hint of any activity by either side. Still reeling from the unsettling events in Lochivar, the warlock finally managed to straighten.

Truly, there is more to this Gryphon than even meets the eye, Shade considered as he waited for his equilibrium to return. The struggle in Skaln stirred vague memories that surely some of Shade's earlier incarnations would have readily recalled. The faceless spellcaster cursed his fragmented mind.

I am missing something important, Shade knew. *Something that the Lord of the Dead are aware of. What did Ephraim say?*

It was ironic that he knew the lead necromancer's name. Indeed, Shade knew the names of each and every Lord. He also knew enough to be aware that once he and they had shared the same bloodline...when the necromancers had actually *had* blood, that is.

But of myself...why so little...why? Shade had no doubt that his previous incarnations had asked much the same question. Like him, they had also probably sought out an answer to that question...all apparently without success.

But now this sudden revelation concerning the Gryphon stirred anew the warlock's curiosity concerning the lionbird. Something about what the rebel leader had accomplished continued to touch the dark recesses of Shade's mind. Still, one thought grew stronger with each breath the hooded figure took.

The key...he may hold the key to all I have been seeking...

The Dragonrealm contained many legends concerning Shade's continual and very fruitless quest to free himself of the endless cycle of life after ill-fated life. Too many of those legends concerned the horrors Shade had inflicted upon countless innocents while callously pursuing his own freedom. That other incarnations had done their best to atone for those foul acts made no difference to either the people or to Shade himself.

But if the Gryphon held the answer...

The impulse to immediately seek out the lionbird and wring the truth from him proved almost too much for Shade to combat. Yet, this version of the warlock also knew the need to free the human race from the talons of the Dragon Kings and, despite his own desires, that need meant more to Shade than his own escape.

There will be time, he promised himself. *Free the land, then free yourself...*

It was enough to give him hope. More hope than he generally had. If he—

A feminine visage flashed before his eyes, a beautiful, exotic visage that he knew instantly masked great evil.

And with that face came the light laugh that Shade recalled hearing before.

"Ah, here you are!"

The warlock spun about to discover a smiling Azran. Every fiber of Shade's being warned him to stand clear of Nathan's son.

Yet, Azran stood with hands empty and no hint of a spell about to be cast. Shade considered his own abilities capable enough to keep him alert to anything the younger Bedlam might try... assuming that Azran intended *any* trouble.

"You've been seeking me?" Shade asked with some amusement. "Most seek the best path *from* me."

Azran chuckled. "I know! I grew up with all the stories! To actually meet you was fascinating, the dream of a lifetime!"

"A nightmare for anyone else, I assure you." The warlock remained cautious. "For what reason do you hunt for me?"

"You're my only other chance!" A look of such utter earnestness spread across Azran's bearded face that Shade was even able to overlook the curious half and half coloring of the mage's hair. "I tried the one person I thought would understand, but he refused out of some ridiculous concern about possibly disturbing the lines of force—"

"You spoke with an elf."

"How did you know?"

Shade shrugged. "You describe an elemental's effect on the energies of our world. His concern is understandable...if a little frustrating." Shade had in his current life sought out one of the rare elementals, only to be rebuffed and told that a previous incarnation had slaughtered a dozen such elementals in a mad plot to bind their rare powers to his own and reverse the curse.

"Frustrating! That's exactly it! I knew you'd understand!" The eager wizard stepped closer—

Shade extended a hand and Azran stopped dead in his tracks. The faceless warlock surveyed his visitor closely. "Where is the sword?"

"I don't have it on me. I thought you might be easier to approach that way."

"A wise move." The sword intrigued Shade far more than he let on. When last the warlock had confronted Azran's creation, he had noted forces within it that even a gifted mage such as Nathan's younger son should *not* have wielded. Indeed, some of those forces were very ancient and if Shade had not known better, he might have assumed that Azran had been communing with the Lords of the Dead.

Which led Shade to why Azran had come to him. "You wish to learn about my power...for what exact purpose, young Bedlam?"

Azran hesitated, then, in a quieter voice, replied, "It would be better if I could show you something first."

While he did not entirely trust Nathan's son, Shade was confident enough to nod his agreement. Looking more relieved, Azran cast a spell. When the warlock sensed it to be nothing other the teleport spell it appeared to be, he allowed the mage to continue.

The ruined grove became a cavern that Shade knew to be within the domain of Lord Red. The sweltering heat of the Hell Plains even touched this underground realm. If not for their spells, both men would have been quickly overcome.

Several spots in the reddened walls took on a darker, more crimson appearance. Azran immediately put a warning arm in front of Shade.

"Beware! Those are—"

"I am familiar with the tircoth." Shade glared at one of the rocky walls. Despite the intense heat, the wall glazed over with thick frost. The warlock then looked at the opposite wall, repeating the process. "That will keep them at bay for awhile."

Azran only answered with another grin. The bearded wizard guided Shade on.

Even before they reached the chamber in question, Shade felt the first traces of a magical force far older than his own power. It was not one unfamiliar to him, though, for he had come across it now and then during his countless lifetimes. It was one of the few things that, no matter how murky his memories, always remained with him.

And the sight that greeted Shade when they entered the chamber verified exactly what the warlock thought.

"You've found one of them...one of the founders..."

Many would have been startled by the ancient figure's appearance, but Shade took the corpse in stride. He could not recall if he had ever seen its like before, but that hardly mattered. To Shade, what did matter was what might have been left behind with the body. Even the clearly tragic way in which the dead founder had perished meant nothing to the warlock, who had suffered many horrific ends himself. The onyx shell was of mild interest to him, but only in the spellwork designed to create it. Indeed, other than one thing, what intrigued Shade the most concerned the object obviously removed from the corpse's grip.

"What did you take from him, Azran?"

The wizard opened his empty left hand...and a small silver staff formed in it. Shade was pleased that Azran could not see the warlock's features. Somehow, Nathan's son had managed to summon forth the artifact without *any* hint of disruption in the world's natural magical energies. That could be done, but not utilizing the method by which human and drake spellcasters worked.

But such considerations paled before the staff. Shade seized the artifact without asking. He knew the work of the founders, and while this had their touch to it, it was like none of the pieces that he himself had come across.

The top ended in the head of a fantastical bird, a mythic creature even for the Dragonrealm. Shade had come across the symbol of the phoenix once before and believed that he had done so in some of his previous lives. He knew that somehow this bird was significant to the founders' ultimate plans, which had revolved around trying to salvage what was left of their dying civilization. Those plans included the races that would succeed them, but exactly how was at this moment to Shade a vague memory...like so much more.

"Do you have any idea what it's for?" Azran eagerly asked.

Shade turned it over. The bottom bore three marks in what he recognized as the script used by the founders, a script that the hooded spellcaster was aware he had discovered quite frustrating during more than one incarnation.

Still, the simple act of moving the staff around gave him more answers than he could have imagined. A glance at Azran revealed that either the younger Bedlam was a master at keeping his expression masked or he did not sense what Shade did.

"It is..." Shade forced his voice to remain even. A feeling of excitement such as he experienced only once in a lifetime filled him as he thought of the potential uses he could make of the artifact. "It is...a switch, you might say."

"A switch?" Utter surprise tinged Azran's voice. "For what?"

His own eagerness growing as great as that of his young associate, Shade returned his attention to the dead founder. A part of him considered removing Azran from the equation, but such a heinous act was not a part of 'Vadym's' kinder personality... fortunately for Nathan's son. Besides, Shade pondered the possibility that he might even need the obviously adaptable mage's assistance.

"For this," he finally answered, gesturing in the direction of the entombed body. "For this..."

And with that gesture, Shade transformed the volcanic wall. It was a simple transformation, altering the substance from one opaque in nature to transparent.

Azran gaped. "I sensed *nothing*."

"They could not destroy it, evidently, but they did their best to hide it."

Beyond the initial body were *three* more. They had perished no less terribly than the first. Whoever had chosen the onyx shell had found it a favored punishment. The two males and one female had also suffocated, their expression forever a ghastly reminder that the first race had not only been astoundingly powerful…but it had also been, at times, very ruthless.

Yet, it was not the bodies that so interested either spellcaster. What did was a three-sided construction more than twice the size of the dead figures. The side most in view to the onlookers was of a silver and gold surface upon which had been etched symbols identical to those on the bottom of the staff. What was visible of the second surface hinted at a covering perhaps made of pure diamond.

Shade had no idea what the third looked like, but was eager to find out. Still, he knew that seeing the ruins and reaching them were two different matters. In fact, it surprised him that Azran had even been able to break through enough to remove the staff from the outermost corpse.

That particular success intrigued him. He turned back to Azran. "By what method—?"

The staff fell from his shaking hand. The blurriness that ever kept his features hidden could not smother his ragged gasp of pain.

Azran's hand now held something else. The same black sword that Shade had seen him wield the last time the pair had met. As with the staff, there had been no hint of spellwork when the wizard had summoned the foul weapon. Yet, no human spell could have tricked the warlock so—

No human trick, the warlock managed to think as his legs lost their battle to keep him standing. Shade fell back, his head striking the ground hard. *No human trick…*

"She said you could get too caught up in puzzles for your own good," Azran remarked as he inspected his weapon. What few drops of Shade's blood still remained on it quickly sank into the shaft as if swallowed.

Evidently satisfied as to the state of his sword, Azran sheathed it, then bent down to the trembling warlock. Shade reached up in an attempt to rip Azran's throat out, but even so simple a spell as that failed him now.

I am dying! Shade realized. *May the powers that be help this land…I am dying…*

"I wasn't eager to do this, but it's only temporary, after all. You always return, don't you?" Nathan's son actually looked slightly apologetic. "And it was the best way to make certain that the sword took all it could."

"You…are a fool, Azran Bedlam…" The wizard's last name came out as more of a gasp. Shade convulsed and knew that he had only seconds left. "This will not gain you…entrance to the artifact behind this onyx wall…"

Azran's brow arched in respect for the effort the warlock had clearly put him through to say so much. "That thing? I've no idea what it does. Still, as interesting as it looks, it can wait. This was actually all about you. We knew this would keep you distracted for just the right moment. I needed your unique essence. You *are* magic, in some ways even more than that creature, Darkhorse. And besides, if you vanished for awhile, no one would know why, not even you. Really, it was all very convenient, don't you see?"

"Darkhorse…"

"I may need him still. We don't know. We can feel that the sword is stronger, thanks to you." The bearded mage tilted the blade so that it faced the ceiling. The black metal shimmered. "Few would miss him…it depends what needs to be done, I guess. So long as we win this war against the Dragon Kings, isn't that right? That's what this is all about. That's why I created this sword…and that's why I had to do this. Please understand, won't you?"

Shade could no longer answer. He wished that Azran could see his furious glare. It was not for his own sake, but for the sake of *everyone* else.

He managed to raise one hand toward Azran with the intention of still trying to warn Nathan's son about the powers he thought he controlled.

The gloved hand snapped off, the bony appendage dropping next to the shivering warlock.

*I am…*Shade forced the last thought out. *…dead…*

He felt his body collapse within itself. Azran was a hazy, whirling image that vanished as the hooded spellcaster's head tipped to one side, then tumbled free of his shoulders.

Dead…for now…

12

THE COST OF REBELLION

Nathan awoke a day later filled with a sense of foreboding. Despite his best efforts, though, he could not put his finger on the reason for that unsettling feeling. It had nothing to do with the fact that no one could tell him what had befallen Shade and Darkhorse, although their absence naturally disturbed him. Nathan had to assume that they were all right until he learned otherwise.

Nor was the news that greeted him once Yalak and Dayn discovered he was conscious of the cause, although it was itself certainly worthy of much, much concern. That especially amazed the wizard, considering that what he and the others loomed over was a Gryphon *still* staring ahead with empty eyes. The rebel leader sat cross-legged facing one of the icy walls as if something there was of the utmost importance to him.

Nathan peered that direction, but saw nothing.

"He chose that direction himself," Yalak murmured. "We turned him twice, only to find him facing it again later on."

"Has he eaten?"

"No."

Nathan knelt before the prone figure. The eyes looked exactly as they had in Skaln. He gently tapped the Gryphon on the shoulder. There was no reaction. The only sign that the lionbird was alive was his breathing. That it was steady encouraged Nathan somewhat, but not nearly enough.

Standing, he asked, "Where's Toos?"

"Keeping the fighters busy, as usual. I cannot imagine where this struggle would be without that young man, Nathan. The Gryphon may inspire them, but Toos keeps them grounded in a way few could. It is almost as if they were destined to come together for this..."

Nathan considered his friend's words, then replied, "We have to let this play out. It started of its own accord in Lochivar to our advantage. I have to think that when it's finished, the Gryphon will be himself again."

The balding mage nodded. "Let us hope so."

Nathan forced himself to push aside the subject of the Gryphon. "Have we lost anyone else?"

It was Dayn who reluctantly answered. "We are down to thirty-four, Father."

Thirty-four...the great Dragon Masters...see how great we are, Nathan thought with much cynicism. "What happened?"

"Assassins."

The elder Bedlam's thoughts immediately turned to his former mentor, Lord Purple. "From Penacles?"

"Yes. They surprised the party near the town of Anteri."

"Anteri." Nathan knew why the spellcasters had been there. They had been setting up a secondary location for the rebellion. The fact that they had been attacked there meant that the area was compromised. The council would have to discuss other options in that regard.

Other options...more of our own dead and my concern is 'other options'. Of course, those options meant the likely salvation of hundreds of other lives. The fact that they were not spellcasters did not make them any less worthwhile.

"They will be honored...and missed." With regret, Nathan changed the subject. "Who among us is currently here?"

Yalak indicated Dayn. "Other than my Salicia, who is continuing to aid with the wounded, you see the grand total of magical might available before you...unless you wish to count our friend seated here or Toos."

The answer did not surprise Nathan. The spellcasters were, by necessity, at the forefront when it came to keeping the magic of the Dragon Kings from crushing the rebels. Unfortunately, that was why so many, these four now included, were dead.

"We have to focus on Penacles, damn it!" he blurted. Realizing his son and Yalak had heard him, Nathan decided to press the point further. "No more delay. One final distraction to draw the Dragon Kings away from that area, and then we assault the City of Knowledge itself. It has to be done."

Dayn looked concerned. "It's too soon, Father—"

"It's far too late, you mean. I delayed this too much. Yalak?"

In response, the other veteran wizard closed his eyes. A few breaths later, he opened them again. "Three paths reveal themselves to me. One leads to the destruction of all things. I cannot foresee its reason—"

"Then we avoid following that path. Can you guide us that far?"

"I have before, haven't I?"

Dayn gasped at this revelation. Nathan and Yalak exchanged uneasy glances. There were things that they had kept secret from the other spellcasters and even from those closest to them.

"How often—?" Dayn managed, before suddenly shutting his mouth. He shook his head, then added, "Never mind. I understand."

"And you understand not to tell anyone else," Nathan pointed out. "Not your brother, not Gwendolyn..."

"Even Salicia does not know," Yalak quietly added. "Although with her I believe there might be some suspicions."

"I won't tell anyone," Dayn promised, setting a hand over his heart.

With a nod, Nathan looked again to Yalak. "And the other paths?"

"The second would be best. It means waiting until Lord Brown's next harvest is ready. That in itself offers two more options, one involving the burning of the crops, the other sabotaging the shipments at the most critical point in their delivery."

"That's more than three weeks." Despite his concerns, though, Nathan saw the usefulness in following such a course of action. Lord Brown was a wary foe and would be expecting renewed attacks on his bountiful food supply, but Nathan believed that the rebels could still make use of him as a distraction, providing the assault on Penacles occurred shortly after. "Very well. That will be our choice, if you think it the right one. Now, who knows Brown's domain best?"

Yalak rubbed his chin. "Micaya. Wade Arkonsson...they would probably be the most knowledgeable."

"Micaya is with Tragaro, Samir, and some of the others investigating an obscure port north of Irillian's main harbor. Samir's people come from that region, and he thinks that it might be of some use in keeping the Gryphon's men supplied," Dayn interjected. Despite their abilities, the spellcasters had to watch out that they did not rely on magic for everything. Summoning enough rations for the rebellion was indeed possible, but such an effort was likely to attract unnecessary attention. As it was, even simply casting teleport spells for themselves required caution and extra masking spells beforehand.

Which, Nathan again thought with tremendous regret, still did not keep them from becoming the victims of assassins. "Wade, it is, then. Is he still with his bride?"

"Yes, Father. He wasn't needed immediately for anything and I thought since he's scarcely seen her, another day or two wouldn't be out of the—"

Nathan waved off Dayn's explanation. "He certainly deserved the extra time, considering what we're about to ask of him." The elder Bedlam immediately concentrated on the wizard in question. *Wade...Wade, hear me...*

There was no response. Nathan pressed, but after nearly half a minute—a long, long time for such a means of contact—the other mage had still not replied.

"Yalak. Dayn. Join with me."

The pair quickly obeyed, yet, even with their efforts combined, the most that Nathan was finally able to sense was that Wade Arkonsson was *alive*. That was all.

Yalak's expression darkened. "Nathan...I foresaw nothing... if he—"

Nathan had no time for Yalak's apology. None of them— certainly not Nathan himself—was incapable of mistakes. "Never mind, Yalak! I need you to alert everyone! Dayn! Where's your brother?"

"I don't know, Father. I think he's safe, though."

"We'll have to worry about him later." It was a cold thing to say, but Nathan could not hold his younger son's life above those of so many others. Nathan pointed at the Gryphon. "I've sent word to Salicia to let her know we're leaving. She'll keep watch over him."

Yalak, who had been staring at the ceiling with eyes nearly as blank as the Gryphon's, stirred again. "Everyone knows. All who can will move at your signal."

Nathan did not wait. *The camp!* he directed the others. *Be prepared for battle!*

The word given, he, Dayn, and Yalak vanished—

—only to materialize a moment later in the worst of Nathan's many constant nightmares.

Hiding some three hundred innocents from the eyes of the Dragon Kings had been no simple feat. The group had included women, men, children, and the elderly. The Dragon Masters had done what they could to eliminate *all* trace of their loved ones and then masked the location with more than a dozen intricate spells.

*And all that…*Nathan swallowed as he beheld the carnage. *And all that…for nothing…*

The initial temptation had been to keep the spellcasters' loved ones near the rebel base itself, but with the constant need to be on guard or move everything quickly, the Gryphon and Nathan had agreed that the refugees should be hidden far from fighters in a more stable location. Both the lionbird and the senior wizard had thought long and hard about where the safest spot might be and had finally settled on an obscure valley in the central part of the great Dagora Forest.

That the master of that vast realm—Lord Green—was one of the more sympathetic of the Dragon Kings had played a role in the choice, but that did not mean that Nathan thought the drake lord friendly to their cause. Indeed, when Gwendolyn had offered the Manor as a possible choice early on, it had been swiftly rejected. At the time, the valley had seemed the perfect—and perhaps *only*—choice.

But in the end…*someone* had overcome all those spells, all those safeguards, all those hopes.

"Search the area thoroughly but quickly!" Nathan bitterly ordered. "See who's alive! Find Wade Arkonsson if you can!" The missing wizard's presence could be felt, but always as if he were far away…and yet not.

The stunned spellcasters spread out. Nathan Bedlam was aware that many of them struggled not to fall to their knees and cry out in horror. For many, these were their families, the focuses of their personal lives.

He stumbled to a halt before the body of a young boy no more than ten years old. Nathan knew the dirty face, although neither the name nor to which spellcaster the hapless youth had been related. A sword had cut the child open in the chest. Death had been swift…but it had still been terrible.

Steeling himself, Nathan pushed on. None of the simple wooden and leather tents in which the refugees had been living remained standing. The drakes had been horrifically thorough, sweeping through this supposed sanctum like a powerful storm. Even several of the trees in the vicinity had not been spared, which made Nathan wonder how much Lord Green knew about what had happened here. Surely, the horrified mage thought, the master of the Dagora Forest *had* to have knowledge of the monstrous event, if only even after the fact.

And then, while he was still pondering that…it *came*. The first scream. The first futile protest. It was followed by another and another as hardened wizards and enchantresses began to make personal discoveries among the dead.

Yalak immediately joined Nathan. Although he also had no family among the refugees, the other mage looked drained by the decimation around them. Nathan knew that he still blamed himself for not having been able to predict and thus somehow stop this tragedy.

"We…we must leave this place soon, Nathan. I feel it. I propose we take the dead with us. We can give them a proper burial then."

Solomon Rhine's gruff voice briefly rose above the others. The epithet he hurled at the absent drakes shook Nathan. Solomon's curse was accented by another wail, one that the elder Bedlam thought sounded as if it originated from Micaya. Nathan had forgotten that while she had no children or husband of her own, she had taken her mother under her wing. Micaya's father had been the spellcaster; her mother had been a merchant's daughter—and a clever merchant in her own right—hailing from Irillian.

The raven-haired enchantress materialized in front of Nathan. Face streaked with tears, Micaya managed to stare directly in his eyes even though she was shorter than either Gwendolyn or Salicia. Nathan had always known Micaya to have a strong, determined character, but that had now given way to a face filled with rage.

"We need to find them, Nathan!" she demanded. "I can smell their trail! Give me a few minutes, and I'll tell you where they are even if they used a blink hole to travel!" She flexed one hand, the nails briefly growing to resemble those of the wolf whose form she often favored. "We'll rip their throats out and then—"

Nathan took her by the shoulders. "Micaya, calm yourself—"

"Calm myself?" The fury she had built up against the drakes in part shifted to the wizard. "You have your sons! What do I have now?" She suddenly gestured past Nathan. "Or what does he have? Or her?"

Peering over his shoulder, Nathan saw Solomon and one of the enchantresses coming toward him. Their expressions were no less pained than Micaya's. A few other spellcasters, Basil among them, followed.

But when Basil spoke, it turned out not to be the condemnation for which Nathan braced himself. Rather, with a hint of hope but also more than a touch of fear, he immediately blurted, "Tyr can't find his brother. Hymir's not among the dead."

"My husband...my sons..." muttered a gaunt, blonde enchantress named Brili. "I found their tent, but no one...no bodies..."

Nathan quickly looked around. A few other faces wore the same combination of emotions that Basil did. The former soldier had no loved ones. Nathan knew only that the woman Basil had wanted to marry had died of some illness when they were both young. He had later taken on not only Tyr as a sort of sibling, but also Tyr's older brother, who had lost his most of his wits long ago due to a spell that had backfired. Hymir meant nearly as much to Basil as he did to his actual sibling.

"Take a count," Nathan ordered, aware how difficult that might be. "Find out who's missing. We need to do it in short order, too." Thus far, there had been no sign that the drakes still kept an eye on the area, but Nathan trusted in Yalak's recommendation.

The others obeyed with surprising speed, all things considered. When they gathered again, the total missing did not at all surprise Nathan.

"Half...almost exactly half..." Dayn muttered.

Nodding, the elder Bedlam looked to the gathering. "Has *anyone* found a sign of Wade Arkonsson?"

Adam Gudwead finally raised a reluctant hand. "I thought I felt something...as if the trees called his name...but when I tried to listen, I didn't hear anything more."

Nathan did not hesitate. "Show me. Dayn you come with. Yalak...can you—?"

"We shall take care of the dead. You go."

The two Bedlams followed Adam as he headed toward a twisted tree near the eastern edge of the camp. Like the Bedlams, he had no family, but also like the Bedlams, he had many friends among the spellcasters who had entrusted their loved ones' lives to this effort. Tears streaked the gruff wizard's face, tears mixed with the same dread determination that Nathan had noted spreading across the features of the rest of the spellcasters.

Another body lay half buried under the collapsed tent. This one was an adult female. Her head was obscured by parts of the cloth, but unfortunately, the savage rip along her spine was not.

With a feeling of trepidation, Nathan leaned down and carefully lifted the cloth.

He grimaced. It was not Wade's young wife, whom Nathan had met at the wedding. Still, there was some similarity in what was left of the features that the wizard wondered if she were a relative, perhaps a sister.

Does it matter? he asked himself as he gently let the cloth drop again. *Death is death. None of these people deserved this…* Nathan's hands curled into fists and he felt himself instinctively summon the wilder, darker energies that most wizards and enchantresses shunned. There were aspects of the forces at a spellcaster's command that could, in turn, command the spellcaster if he was not cautious. Despite his swelling anger, Nathan forced the energies away again.

And as he did that, he thought he heard a faint voice in his head. Wade's voice.

Nathan…

It was almost imperceptible, so much so that initially the veteran mage wondered if he had imagined it. He turned in a circle, eyeing the ruined camp, the dead, twisted trees, and the churned up ground.

His attention returned to the most twisted of the trees. He stared at it for a moment, wondering why it looked familiar. The branches were bent in odd directions, forming what looked like a letter or symbol—

"Dayn! Adam! Form a triangle around this tree!"

As the others obeyed, Nathan stood before the widest section of the trunk. As soon as his son and Adam had positioned themselves and linked their power to his, Nathan stretched his hands toward the tree and cast.

A sliver of gold formed along the trunk, rising from the roots to several feet above Nathan's head. Brow wrinkled from effort, the veteran wizard spread his hands farther apart.

The tree trunk ripped open.

Two pale bodies tumbled from its cramped interior. Expecting—or rather, *hoping*—for just this to happen, Nathan ceased his initial spell and quickly softened the pair's landing.

The two bodies tumbled away from each other as they landed. Wade Arkonsson rolled onto his back, the stricken wizard's chest rapidly rising and falling as he tried to inhale all the air in the vicinity.

Even before Nathan could move, Wade managed to gasp, "S-Staia...please..."

Signaling for the others to see to their comrade, Nathan rushed to the woman's side. Staia lay half on her right side, her skin even paler than that of her husband. Nathan could not see if she breathed and grew more worried as he touched her shoulder.

Staia fell onto her back, her soulful brown eyes staring sightlessly at the sky.

"Nathan—" Wade called. "Nathan! Is—is she all—all right?"

Softly shutting Staia's eyes, Nathan joined the other wizards. He did not try to hide his expression.

Wade's mouth opened wide in a soundless cry. He shook his head. No tears streaked his face, but his anguish was clear nevertheless.

"Staia...Staia..." As he repeated her name, Wade's expression altered. A stoniness gradually overtook the wizard.

"What happened here, Wade?" Nathan asked, as much interested in the answer as he was in distracting the other mage from his grief and anger.

"There—there was no hint, not even the slightest shifting of the lines of energy. Suddenly, I couldn't *move* no matter how much I tried and the drakes were *everywhere*. They wasted—wasted no time..." Wade managed to sit up. To Nathan's surprise, the other mage did not look in the direction of his wife. "They gave no quarter. They started the killing right away...right away..."

Nathan wanted to hear everything, but realized that there was one important point that could not wait. "Wade...there are several missing. Do you know where they are?"

The stricken mage chuckled, a hollow sound without mirth. "That's—that's why they—he—sealed us in the tree! I was supposed to be—to be the messenger—if you arrived in time. I'm sorry...I forgot all about that and I shouldn't have! He said—" Now, at last, Wade glanced at his lost bride. "Nathan—he said that if we were truly Dragon Masters, it would be a simple thing for you to come and save us before we perished. I tried—I tried to give us enough air, but the spell he sealed the tree with wouldn't let me do it. She was—I knew when she fell asleep..."

"Wade—"

The scarred wizard managed to nod. "The others. Of course. He took them *with*, Nathan. As hostages! Said that was the plan!"

"Who took them? Which of the Dragon Kings?"

"Lord Brown took them, of course." Wade struggled to his feet. He finally stumbled toward Staia. Kneeling, he cradled her head before adding, "Lord Brown's warriors did the bloody work, did it very well...but the master of the Adajian Fields wasn't the one behind all of this."

"No..." Nathan interjected. "It was Lord Purple, wasn't it?"

The pale wizard looked up from his dead bride. "Yes...Lord Brown told me two things as he sealed the trunk. One was that if you and the others wanted to save the remaining family members... you knew where to find them."

Penacles... Nathan knew without asking. *So much for our glorious plan to surprise Lord Purple. He's known all along that we would have to come to him and now he's setting the agenda...*

"Penacles," he said out loud, Wade's slow nod affirming the fact.

"He's expecting us," Dayn growled. "So much for any chance of surprise—"

"Nathan."

The elder Bedlam glanced down to discover Wade eyeing him oddly. The mage's gaze shifted from Nathan to the others and quickly back, clearly signaling that he wanted to tell the veteran spellcaster something more, but without the other two nearby.

Respecting Wade's judgment, Nathan said, "Dayn. Adam. Help Yalak finish up. We've spent far too much time here already."

Wade Arkonsson continued to hold Staia tight as he watched the pair depart. The moment they were far enough away, he finally spoke. "Nathan...Lord Brown's second message was also from Lord Purple. It was specifically for you. I thought—I thought it best to tell it to you alone."

Nathan tensed. He could not imagine what personal message his former mentor had for him, but he knew that it would not be one to his liking. "Go ahead."

Despite Nathan's urging, Wade hesitated a moment more. Then, with another brief look at his beloved, he whispered, "He said you were to be *thanked*, Nathan. Thanked for all you provided."

"'Thanked for all—'" Nathan's heart pounded. He stepped back from Wade without at first realizing it. Nathan's eyes fell upon Staia, but he saw more than simply her limp body. He also saw *every* death on the rebel side since he had become part of the cause. Every death, whether that of a simple soldier or one of the other spellcasters.

Nathan saw that Wade had come to the same conclusion as him. After all, what *else* could the lord of Penacles had meant? It made absolute sense. Explained so very much.

And despite Nathan's desire to deny the truth, the same condemning words echoed continuously in his head.

I am the traitor...

13

CHOICES AND REPERCUSSIONS

Gwendolyn had not wanted to leave Nathan's side while he lay unconscious, but she had also feared facing his wrath once he *did* wake up. Surely, the enchantress had thought, he would know that she was responsible for both Shade and the demon steed not arriving alongside Nathan and the Gryphon. It had been an instinctive reaction, one that she did not regret save for the wizard's anger. In her eyes, the rebellion played with fire every time they dealt with the accursed warlock and his monstrous companion.

When Dayn had returned after a brief absence to attend to his father again, she had used his coming as an excuse to step into the background. Then, when no one had been paying attention, the fiery-tressed enchantress had quietly vanished from the rebels' base.

Her instincts had naturally brought her back to the Manor. She drew comfort from the ancient edifice despite the 'ghosts' that haunted it. Gwendolyn actually enjoyed their occasional presence, making her feel as if she were not alone. Often, the enchantress felt as if the Manor was seeking to speak with her through them, although just exactly what it hoped to tell her she had thus far not discovered.

Sooner or later, Gwendolyn knew, she would have to return to the caverns. In fact, at one point, she had almost imagined that Nathan had called to her, but when she had listened, the enchantress had heard nothing.

The Manor provided her with some simple food, a bowl of fruit and some wine. If she desired more, then she would have to summon it herself, something she did not wish to attempt. Gwendolyn wanted to keep Lord Green from sensing her presence. The enchantress had already risked the rebellion by coming here; while she believed in Dagora's master, she had already learned that not all his servants—or even those of his blood—could be trusted.

Finishing the meal, Gwendolyn determined that she had no choice but to return to Nathan and the others before they grew concerned about her absence. If they chose to punish her for what she had done to Shade and Darkhorse, then she would accept that punishment. Gwendolyn would do anything to make amends.

The voices of the Manor whispered to her as she walked through the Manor. The enchantress listened for a moment, but heard nothing distinct. Whatever reason the Manor had for allowing these 'ghosts' and memories to exist, it did not always have to do with those who inhabited the magical edifice.

As Gwendolyn strode toward the front doors of the Manor, she passed through a building where marble melded with living wood. Roughly half of the Manor had been shaped from a towering tree, possibly the *oldest* tree in all the Dragonrealm. The spellwork needed to not only create such cooperation between plant and stone but also maintain it for countless centuries—or rather, millennia—had staggered the enchantress the first time she had seen the astounding citadel. No one knew who had actually created the building, although the safest guess was some powerful wizard from the mysterious founding race. Still, at times, Gwendolyn wondered if, while safe, that guess might very well also be *wrong*.

The grounds surrounding the Manor were also magical and had a tendency to change of their own accord. A high hedge now lined the boundaries of the pocket world within which the venerable structure sat. The hedge was so thick that it might as well have been a wall of stone. Indeed, Gwendolyn had already tested the hedge and discovered that the greenery likely would hold against a foe *better* than any such artificial barrier.

Her mind swirling with misgivings, Gwendolyn focused on Nathan and the cavern chamber. It was simple to imagine his face in sharp detail; Gwendolyn found herself too often thinking of Nathan Bedlam the man and not Nathan Bedlam the great wizard. In truth, she feared for him more than she feared for the rebellion.

Sighing, the enchantress cast—

—and too late felt the second spell pulling her another direction. The Manor faded...to become the underground sanctum of the lord of the Dagora Forest.

Like so many drake lords, the Green Dragon greeted her in the guise of a towering armored knight. He sat upon a throne created from jagged stalagmites. A pair of armed warriors flanked the throne, but both they and their master were not the most surprising sight to the enchantress.

"Gwendolyn McArn," greeted Hadeen somewhat reluctantly. Next to him, his brother Hadaryn—also seeming uncomfortable—bowed his head to her.

She gaped as she looked from the half-elves to the drake lord.

"Do not make assumptions you may regret," Lord Green quietly remarked as he rose.

Gwendolyn instinctively curtsied as she answered. "I would do no such thing..."

"Thisss…confrontation…hasss grown more complicated. My loyalty is to my emperor, but there are matters that I must deal with for the sake of my own domain."

"Yes, my lord."

Hadeen stepped between them. "Your majesty, if I could explain to her—"

"You may not." Lord Green gestured in the direction of Hadeen's brother even as his gaze remained on Nathan's old friend. "The two of you will proceed as planned. Your tale concerning—" The drake lord paused in thought, then continued, "—sssee to it that you follow through asss we dissscusssed."

There was a finality in the Green Dragon's tone that not only utterly silenced Hadeen, but caused both half-elves to immediately vanish. Gwendolyn wished that she could follow suit; this was a Lord Green that she did not wish to stand before. It was not only his tone, but his bearing. The enchantress sensed a tension in the Dragon King that caused her to take a step back when the drake lord turned his full attention to her.

Her reaction made the armored figure pause. The Green Dragon looked away for a moment. After emitting a low hiss, the master of the Dagora Forest once more shifted his gaze to the enchantress.

"Young Gwendolyn McArn…I had sssuch high hopes for you. Ssso many seasons observing and being informed of your progress. To think that just before you could achieve everything…"

Much of the enchantress's fear faded, to be replaced by confusion and curiosity. "I do not understand, your majesty…"

The Dragon King returned to his throne. As he seated himself, he said to the guards, "Leave us."

The two sentries retreated without a sound. Gwendolyn said nothing, knowing that Lord Green would speak.

"My ssson hasss made a claim against you."

"I did nothing that was not demanded of me by his actions! I am not responsible—"

The drake lord bared his teeth. "I am aware just who isss responsible. Still, Ssilan is my son and heir and you are human..."

"You cannot trust Ssilan! He worked hand in hand with Lord Vuun against your interests!"

"It would not be the firssst time my ssson hasss gone against my wishes, young Gwendolyn. I will deal with that matter. Yet, the incident forcesss my hand at a time when I would prefer not to. That isss why I prepared the ssspell that brought you here. Nothing happens at the Manor that I do not sense, you know."

That fact suddenly disturbed the enchantress more than she could ever have imagined, and for the first time, Gwendolyn considered some step to keep her former mentor from being able to sense everything that went on in that ancient edifice. Yet, to the Green Dragon, she answered, "Naturally, your majesty."

He continued to bare his long, sharp teeth, and for a moment, Gwendolyn feared that he had read her traitorous thoughts. Instead, though, the drake lord gestured toward the floor. From there, a tendril burst above the surface, a thick, thorny tendril that grew to the enchantress's height, then curled at the top. The top of the green tendril circled until it created a window.

In that gap, an image formed.

And in that image, Gwendolyn beheld the reason that Lord Green had very much desired her presence.

The black cloud swirled amid the trees, flowing this way and that with what at first appeared utter randomness. Each time it touched one of the mighty oaks near it, that tree shriveled...no... *melted*. The cloud would retreat a different direction, but always with the same results. Slowly but surely, it created a dead region ever growing.

Lord Green stood. He stared at the enchantress, who, despite his powerful gaze, could not help but keep glancing at the monstrous cloud and its steady wave of destruction.

"The matter between my son and you—and the reassson for which I originally ensured you would find yoursssself here—remains...but thisss new ssssituation demandsss precedence. What you sssee before usss is happening not more than ten miles from where we ssstand. I have tried a number of spells, but nothing affects the damage. Therefore, I musssst turn to you, Gwendolyn McArn. *You*, of courssse."

Gwendolyn wanted to tell him that he was wrong, that he needed someone far more powerful than herself, but she knew that she and she alone had the best chance of putting an end to the devastation overtaking the central part of the forest. After all, the enchantress could sense even from here how her spellwork permeated what was only *visually* a black cloud...but was actually, thanks to her earlier actions, all that was left of the demon, *Darkhorse*.

THE PURPLE DRAGON watched as his counterpart from the west made a highly visible display of marching the ragtag group of prisoners through the main gates of Penacles and into the city. Escorted by a contingent of Purple's finest guards, the Brown Dragon's soldiers marched with heads held high and armored chests puffed out...almost as if they came as victors of some epic battle rather than marauders who had just slaughtered mostly unarmed foes. Lord Purple's plan had included confrontation with at least half a dozen mages, but even that possible resistance had not materialized. Only the one wizard had been discovered at the location, a simple problem simply dealt with and perfect for delivering the message Lord Purple wanted his primary target to receive.

And now…I await you, Nathan Bedlam… The master of the City of Knowledge continued to watch the ranks of brown warriors marching through his city, but his mind raced ahead to the next step in his plan. Nathan Bedlam would have no choice but to forget any further distractions and attack Penacles now, despite knowing that doing so would be exactly what his former master desired. The wizard, at last aware of the part he had played in the various setbacks the rebellion had faced, would confront the conundrum of not being certain what, if anything, he could hide from the drake lord's mind.

"Such pomp and circumstance," remarked Toma from behind him. Chuckling, the younger drake stepped up next to his host. "I almost feel as if I am in my father's court."

Lord Purple did not take the bait. Toma might talk on occasion as if he mocked the emperor, but the drake lord knew that the emissary was deathly loyal to Gold…and why not? Toma had no power beyond that granted him by his blood ties. He would do everything he could to see to it that he kept his father's favor, including discovering any evidence, however slight, of dissension among the other Dragon Kings.

"There is nothing grander than the emperor's court and nothing more glorious than the emperor himself, as you know," the master of Penacles calmly replied. He had Toma's measure now. "Besides, this 'pomp and circumstance', as you call it, has its purpose. A visual display is essential. The news will quickly get to the renegades and further stir them to action."

Toma cocked his head. He smiled, displaying his much sharper teeth. "If I may say so, you are a knowledgeable student of the human mind, your majesty. Although I am here in an official capacity for the emperor, I must admit that this has become a learning experience. I will never underestimate humans again."

"Soon, that will not matter. Once this plan has reached fruition, there will never again be a human problem."

Toma hissed. "You have to admit, they are very adaptable. You yourself have benefited from their versatility."

Lord Purple leaned over the railing. The soldiers and their prisoners had reached the palace gates. "Any beast, if trained properly, will benefit its master." Before Toma could possibly reply, the drake lord straightened, then added, "Still, if you wish to learn how best to deal with humans, you should accompany me now."

"I am honored."

Without another word, Lord Purple transported the pair to the inner yard where even now Brown entered with his capture. The mounted Dragon King acknowledged the master of the City of Knowledge with a triumphant grin that well-matched Toma's earlier one. Traces of blood still spattered the other drake lord's breastplate. Brown could have wiped it off at any point during his journey here, even barring the fact that the blink hole had shortened it to hours rather than days.

"You are exactly on time," Lord Purple complimented. Whatever rivalry existed between the two Dragon Kings, Purple did appreciate his counterpart's propensity for fulfilling his duties exactly to the letter.

"And your plan has succeeded thus far exactly as you said." Lord Brown shifted in the saddle. His riding drake growled, but remained still. "A sorry lot, but the number you requested. Are they satisfactory?"

Lord Purple surveyed the prisoners who, to his eyes, consisted of sobbing children, frightened women, and a few wary men. Some of the men had the appearances of former fighters, but as a whole, the band looked as if they could not have put up much of a fight. Most of the captives were dirty, bloody, and nearly ready to collapse. They huddled together, not certain of just what to expect.

"You followed the path I requested?" he asked of Lord Brown.

"Naturally. I am certain that we were seen exactly as you wished."

Purple nodded satisfaction. Any scouts sent by the rebels, especially from among the surviving spellcasters, would come across ample evidence of the survivors and the belief that they would be found in Penacles. While always a 'knowledgeable student of the human mind', as Duke Toma had put it, Lord Purple had made a special effort to see deeply into the minds of the rebels...and especially Nathan Bedlam. The fact that for some time he had had a steady link to his former servant's thoughts had indeed helped. The drake lord almost felt sorry for what the wizard and his kind faced...but then to *actually* feel sorry for them would have made him more *human* than drake.

How ironic that would certainly be, Purple thought as Brown prattled on about his 'tremendous victory'. He let his counterpart regale him with details of the massacre for a few moments, then finally decided to cut the other drake lord off. "You have also arranged for the security of the fields, yes?"

A slight hiss was the only indication of Brown's irritation at being interrupted. "Of course! There is now no place more secure in all the land than the Adajian Fields!"

"I would perhaps differ on that," interjected Duke Toma.

Lord Brown was quick to agree. "With the exclusssion of the emperor's domain, naturally! I left that asss assssumed."

"Of course."

Turning to one of his officers, Lord Purple gestured at the prisoners. A contingent of the Dragon King's finest spread around the humans. At the same time, Brown's troops retreated...albeit with some reluctance. These captives were their prize; it was difficult to give them up to those who had stood waiting.

"You will want to begin your journey back immediately," the master of Penacles said to his duskier counterpart.

It was not meant as an acknowledgement of a choice earlier agreed upon, but rather a suggestion Brown needed to take to heart. Servants of the emperor and 'brothers' of the imperial court all Dragon Kings might be, but no drake lord savored the presence of another in his own domain for very long.

Brown tilted his head to the side. His smile was as false as that of any drake lord to another. "Yes, of course. It will be necessary to open a blink hole—"

"There is a clearing two miles to the northwest that will more than suffice. You will find a stream there more than ample enough to provide your troops with water."

The false smile remained as Brown briefly eyed the prisoners again. "I look forward to hearing how things proceed."

"You will be kept informed."

The mounted drake lord bowed his head to Toma. "May the emperor rule forever..."

"He shall," replied the duke, answering with something other than the formulaic response. Nevertheless, no one questioned his choice of words. So long as his father *did* rule, Toma had the power to bring down either one of them.

Turning his beast about, Lord Brown wasted no time in getting his troops headed toward the palace gates. There was no hesitation, no protest by the armored soldiers; if their master had ordered them to march out of Penacles, march back in again, and march out a second time, they would have obeyed. No one truly questioned a Dragon King other than the emperor.

"He must be terribly frustrated," Toma blithely remarked as the Brown Dragon led his followers from the palace.

"It is a small enough matter, soon forgotten." However, they both knew that no drake of high caste ever forgot a slight. They might never be able to act upon it, but they did not forget.

The last of the soldiers exited the palace grounds. Purple's servants immediately shut the gates behind them. The same escort that had guided the foreigners in would see to assisting them in swiftly departing the City of Knowledge itself.

His fellow Dragon King dealt with, Lord Purple turned to the matter of the prisoners.

"There must be over a hundred of them," Toma commented. "Room enough in your dungeons for them, though, I imagine."

"There will be no need for dungeons." The lord of Penacles gestured to the drake officer in charge of the guards. "All that mattered was that they be seen reaching here alive and in fair health."

The drake officer drew his sword.

A woman among the prisoners cried out. Two of the males suddenly tried to charge the nearest guard. Unfortunately, their efforts were hobbled by the chains they wore.

With an eager smile, the guard ran one of the men through. The second prisoner grabbed the guard's arm. The duo briefly fought to a stalemate.

At that point, several of the other prisoners moved.

Toma chuckled. "Their tenacity *is* admirable."

Lord Purple paid no attention. He curled one hand into a fist, then let the fist drop.

Weapons ready, the rest of the guards moved in.

Toma stiffened. "Are you—? But why?"

"Again, all that mattered was that they be seen reaching here. The palace is surrounded by spells, one of which will keep any cries from escaping beyond these walls, so there is no need to worry about that."

Toma swallowed. "I undersssstand…completely…"

The second slaughter began…

14

VOICES

Returning to the caverns, they gave the dead the best burial they could under the circumstances, those spellcasters related to each of the victims creating pyres that burned but did not spread their flames or smoke beyond the bodies. Words were spoken before each group. Nathan spoke much himself, although what he said he quickly forgot. All that lingered with him throughout the long funeral was that these people had perished in great part due to *him*.

"He's lying!" Dayn insisted when they were alone, referring to Lord Purple's sinister declaration. "He has to be!"

Nathan had told himself the very same thing more than once, with equally futile results. He knew that the master of the City of Knowledge had not left a false message with Wade Arkonsson. No, the revelation only confirmed the unsettling thoughts the wizard had already had. Too many things now fell into place.

I am the traitor in our midst... Nathan could not stop himself from thinking such things no matter how he tried. Every death he could definitely lay at his feet. The entire rebellion lived and suffered because of his choices...or rather, the Purple Dragon's use of those choices.

"We still have to proceed with your plan to attack Penacles, Nathan," Yalak had told him earlier after being informed of the truth. "Regardless of whether Lord Purple knows what we plan, I have foreseen that this struggle *must* turn to there." Before Nathan could possibly argue, the other mage tapped the crystalline ovoid in the crook of his arm. "The Egg verifies it. Indeed, it *emphasizes* that all our paths must lead to Penacles."

Nathan had known that all along, but had still held out some meager hope that Yalak might have found another way. Now, speaking with Dayn, Nathan could only repeat what his friend had told him.

"We can find another path. I don't care what Yalak or that damned Egg say!" Dayn glared at far off Penacles. "Any path but one leading to there! It only plays into Lord Purple's hand! I—"

The elder Bedlam cut him off. "Penacles is besides the point and you know it. You also know that we've no choice but to attack shortly. I delayed long enough, hoping for something to change, I suppose…but I should have known better."

Nathan and his son peered to where some of the other mages huddled in conversation. The grim cast generally seen on the features of most spellcasters now had an added aspect to it, a hollowness that warned the older Bedlam that if he did not act soon, several of his counterparts might attempt something on their own. The last thing the rebellion needed was for the spellcasters to cease working together.

As soon as he thought that, Nathan berated himself. He continued to think of this struggle, this war, in terms of only him and his kind. The Gryphon had already lost more men than the wizard could count and yet others continued to find their way to the rebellion. Those fighters—men *and* women without the slightest ability to cast magic—were the true backbone of the opposition to the Dragon Kings.

And the Gryphon is their inspiration, Nathan thought. *Something must be done to bring him back from wherever his mind has taken him.*

His attention still focused on the rebel leader, Nathan did not at first notice that two other figures had suddenly materialized nearby. Only then did Nathan realize that among the few spellcasters not at the site of the massacre had been Killian Blackfeather. With the emerald-haired figure came another wizard named Lynus Owan, a swarthy, studious figure with a magically sculptured face akin to the princes in fairy tales. Lynus was a capable spellcaster, but had a habit of reveling in his power, an all-too-common problem among their kind.

Floating beside Killian was a sphere of ice in which something dark could just barely be made out. Nathan immediately headed toward the pair.

Killian saw him approaching. The pale mage stared unblinking for a moment as if silently assessing something, then moved to meet Nathan.

"Killian, where—?"

The icy sphere rose up between them. Killian, his gaze still unblinking, interjected, "Before you say anything, let me show you what I've brought."

He did not give Nathan a chance to decide, instead causing the icy sphere to vaporize. The grisly object within dropped to the cavern floor, hitting with an unceremonious splat.

The slack-mouthed face of a helmed drake warrior stared up at Nathan. The mauve shading did not surprise the veteran wizard.

"We were beset by assassins near Gordag-Ai," Lynus added. "A skilled, worthy pair...but not enough to slay a couple of wizards, eh, Killian?"

"No, not enough."

Nathan knelt down to study the features. When he had served Lord Purple, he had known most of the Dragon King's special assassins. It took a few seconds, but the name finally to Nathan.

"Vasssan…" The elder Bedlam recalled him as a lesser son of Lord Purple, whose only value to his father had been his abilities as an assassin. Straightening, something else came to mind. "Vasssan usually worked with another drake, an older one named Vemo."

Killian slowly nodded. "The other drake seemed more experienced. He lasted longer than Vasssan and nearly killed me."

"It took both of us to slay him," Lynus added. "A fearsome fighter, that one."

"Well, praise the Dragon of the Depths that you both survived." Nathan welcomed the news. Of all the assassins sent out, those of Lord Purple had worried the veteran mage even more than any the emperor himself might have ordered after the spellcasters. The master of Penacles knew the Nathan and the rest better than any of the other drake lords did. The Purple Dragon had seen to the training of each wizard and enchantress. His assassins would have been better informed as to the weaknesses of their targets. "Can't say I'll mourn either drake, but the head wasn't really necessary to bring, Killian. You can dispose of it as you will."

"Yes, Nathan." Killian snapped his fingers and the icy sphere reformed around the severed head. The sphere then rose up to take a place next to the wizard's shoulder.

Lynus eyed some of the other spellcasters. "A tragedy for so many. Would that we could have been with to help."

"There was nothing that could be done." Although grateful the pair had survived, Nathan had too many other matters with which to deal. "I'll be speaking to everyone concerning the attack on Penacles. Stay near."

"We'll be very near," Lynus replied. He glanced at the Gryphon. "We heard about him. Is he still unconscious?"

"I'm not sure what he is. We can only hope he stirs soon."

Killian slowly frowned. "Let me look at him. I may have an idea."

At this point, Nathan welcomed *any* possible hope of awakening the Gryphon. He also had faith in Killian's abilities. "See what you can do."

Without another word, the other mage turned to the prone figure. Lynus followed. Nathan frowned, then concentrated on the subject of Penacles. Whatever course of action he and Yalak chose would still end up in the deaths of many good people.

Watch...beware...

Stiffening, Nathan listened. Yet, the words he thought he had heard in his head did not repeat. The wizard exhaled as it occurred to him just whose voice it had reminded him of. The Gryphon's.

I need rest, the spellcaster decided. *But when will I get that chance unless I get knocked unconscious again or—*

Watch...beware...

This time, Nathan could not deny the voice's existence nor that it definitely sounded like the Gryphon's. He could not help looking over his shoulder at the still form. Killian leaned close to the lionbird's face. The other wizard had one hand in a pouch at his side and the other on the Gryphon's left arm. Lynus stood to the right of both, his intent gaze on Killian.

Watch...beware...

Certain that there had to be a reason for the unsettling warning, Nathan turned to the trio.

Lynus stiffened. He met Nathan's eyes.

Understanding at last what was wrong, Nathan started to cast.

At the same time, Killian pulled a silver blade from a pouch. He thrust the dagger at the lionbird's throat. Nathan, meanwhile, felt another spell seeking to counter the one he was casting.

The Gryphon's hand suddenly shot out. It caught Killian's weapon hand by the wrist. Still staring at the wall, the rebel leader twisted with such force that Killian's wrist cracked audibly.

As Nathan fought to overcome the other spell, he also noticed that despite the severe injury, Killian acted unconcerned. The hand on the Gryphon's arm rose to the lionbird's throat even as a scowling Lynus shifted to face Nathan.

The icy sphere containing Vasssan's head shot toward the elder Bedlam.

Nathan, though, had already prepared for such a possible attack. The sphere only made it as far as midway before it suddenly arced around and flew with even greater speed back at the treacherous spellcaster.

Lynus brought up a hand. The sphere shattered, the severed head splattering to pieces.

Smiling darkly, Nathan sent the icy fragments on. Where Lynus had only had one large projectile with which to deal, now he had scores coming at him from several directions.

Realizing his mistake, Lynus sought to compensate. Some of the fragments melted in front of him.

More than a few did not.

The traitor stumbled back as his face and form were struck. As he did, his shape suddenly altered. The image of Lynus Owan vanished, replaced by another drake in the color of a servant of Penacles.

Vemo. Nathan was not surprised by that. Nathan had no idea how it had happened, but somehow at least the older assassin had survived to take both wizards. The real Lynus was obviously dead, but Nathan could not tell in just what state Killian was.

It was not a promising one, for even despite his injury, the pale mage continued to seek the Gryphon's death. Nathan knew Killian was capable of throttling a man with only a single hand, but before he could try, the Gryphon again fought back. His other hand swung around, slapping hard at Killian's arm and forcing him to release the lionbird's throat.

Leaping to his feet, the Gryphon thrust his open beak at Killian's own throat.

Nathan's fear for the possibly innocent wizard nearly left him open to Vemo's counterassault. Eschewing magic, the drake threw a silver dagger of his own at Nathan.

The wizard moved to deflect it as he had the sphere, only to realize that his spell had no effect on the weapon. With barely a moment to think, Nathan ripped up part of the cavern floor in front of him.

The dagger crashed into the frozen earth just inches from Nathan's chest. This close, the mage could finally sense the subtle spellwork enhancing the weapon and preventing most magical defenses used directly on it from working.

Vemo drew another dagger—and suddenly screamed as his arms and legs ripped free of his body. Blood and gobbets of flesh spilled around the mutilated drake as his twitching torso and head tumbled to the ground.

More than a dozen spellcasters materialized around Vemo. Nathan recognized each of them as having lost loved ones in the massacre. Vemo now represented the forces that had slaughtered those helpless men, women, and children.

No! Nathan futilely ordered the outraged group. He had sought only to incapacitate Vemo. The assassin had knowledge that they needed. *Listen to me! We have to—*

But the drake vanished behind the growing crowd of maddened spellcasters. Nathan felt a rush of frighteningly potent spells strike where last he had seen Vemo.

The blood-curdling howl that followed was mercifully short.

Killian collapsed the second the howl cut off. As he closed on the wizard and the rebel leader, Nathan saw that there was no mark from the Gryphon's beak. Instead, Killian Blackfeather lay like a marionette without strings. His glassy eyes informed the elder

Bedlam as to the fruitlessness of hoping that the other mage still lived.

Kneeling by the body, Nathan felt the man's throat. The coldness of Killian's skin shocked him.

"He has the smell of the animated dead on him," the Gryphon's voice interrupted. "This man was no more before he entered this cavern. All his actions here belonged to his companion's will."

"Poor Killian..." It was a phrase Nathan had found himself repeating too many times, with only the name changed. Yet, Killian's death touched him a bit more than some because Nathan had known the other mage. Solitary and sometimes dour, Killian could still be a loyal friend. He had never been ambitious, although his talent had set him in the upper ranks of the calling.

Near them, the rest of the gathering had begun to move away from where Nathan had last seen the drake. The elder Bedlam glanced there, but saw no sign of Vemo, not even a trace of blood.

Nathan shuddered.

Then, he suddenly thought of the Gryphon. "Thank the Dragon of the Depths that at least all this madness finally woke you—"

The rebel leader had already begun sitting down again, his view once more the blank wall. Nathan saw that the glassiness still remained in the lionbird's eyes.

"No!" Coming around to the Gryphon's front, the wizard tried desperately seize his attention. "Gryphon—whatever you are! Stop! What are doing? We need you—him—now—"

The rebel leader finished sitting. The eyes vaguely focused on Nathan. "No...not now...soon...we will be well again soon..."

Refusing to let matters return to what they had been before the attempted assassination, Nathan seized the Gryphon by the shoulders—

One furred and feathered hand easily shoved the wizard's away. "No," repeated the voice coming from the Gryphon. The emotionless declaration was accompanied by a transformation. The rebel's avian features melted, stretched…and became those of another. "Not yet…Nathan Bedlam…"

The wizard fell back in shock at what he beheld. The lionbird's countenance reverted to its normal state…and the rebel once more looked to the icy wall.

This time, Nathan made no protest. The wizard could only stare as he tried to come to grips with just what—or who—had briefly confronted him.

The Gryphon's face had transformed into what Nathan knew could only be that of a *founder*.

THE WIND HOWLED through the Tyber Mountains with an intensity that made even those creatures born to the rocky realm uneasy. A black-crested wyvern, a smaller cousin of dragons, scurried into its cloud-enshrouded hole in the side of a peak miles northwest of Kivan Grath as the wind picked up more. The growing gale shook loose ice long sealed to cold mountainsides, creating small avalanches throughout this part of the immense chain.

One of those avalanches tumbled into a shadowed crevice between two sharp peaks born from the ancient severing of a once-mighty rival of the Tyber's greatest mountain. The crash of rock vied with the howling wind before gradually dying down.

But as the avalanche quieted, a new, barely audible sound arose in its place, one which seemed to cause even the howling wind to recede in fear. The *whisper* of many voices. Voices without mouths to speak them. Their words remained unintelligible, but the intensity with which those words were repeated over and over grew with each passing second.

As the intensity magnified, in the midst of the rubble something stirred. It began with a handful of pebbles that shifted as if a tiny creature crawled from beneath them. Yet, when the pebbles fell away, what emerged was not a beast, but rather a thing of emerald magical energy barely the size of a fingernail.

The tiny ball of energy flared bright...and then doubled in size. As it did, its coloring altered to a dark blue.

The whispering became more and more urgent. The ball of energy reacted to each repetition, swelling until it reached the size of a dragon's egg.

And though it had no discernible mouth, it *screamed*.

The cry was one of pure pain, unfettered agony. It echoed throughout the crevice, sparking new fear into whatever creature heard it. The scream renewed again and again, yet never seemed to completely drown out the constant whispers. They, in turn, sounded more determined, more *controlling*.

Still shrieking, the ball of energy began a new transformation. As it crashed against one side of the crevice, a primitive appendage burst into existence.

This only seemed to add to the ball's pain, for the shriek grew louder yet and now the ball writhed. Its wild movements only served it ill, though, for barely had it survived the first collision than it struck a heavy pile of rubble.

A second appendage sprouted on the opposite side of the first. The energy sphere's radiance also faded, revealing something of substance within.

With each impact by the sphere, more rocks and ice tumbled into the crevice. Several pieces hit the writhing form. Those strikes, too, had an effect. The radiance continued to decrease, giving way to the solidifying shape inside.

A third limb sprouted farther from the other two. A fourth developed near the third. The scream continued unabated, but a pair of huge, winged sentinels perched on peaks not all that far away seemed the only living creatures that did not hear the horrific cry. The two gold dragons instead kept their focus as their orders demanded...on the south and the north, where could be found the twelve lesser realms and the most obvious threats to the Dragon Emperor.

Yet, if their lord and master had known what took place so near, he would have ordered every drake and dragon to the dark crevice without care how many perished once they reached there...

A fifth, much smaller appendage thrust up, giving the nearly solid form a vaguely humanoid appearance. The mouthless thing then attempted to crawl using the four larger limbs. The fifth twisted and reshaped, becoming akin to a head.

The initial attempts to crawl failed miserably. The uneven ground and the weak appendages meant that the unsettling shape moved only inches. All along the thing screamed and writhed... and grew. It was now more than triple the size it had been barely a minute before and continued to increase with each passing second. Its limbs finally stretched long enough that they could at least drag it better across the harsh ground, yet, the path indicated no particular direction in mind, only some need to move, perhaps in a futile attempt merely to escape its agony.

Now the size of a dog, the pale, indistinct shape suddenly tried to stand. It fell more than a dozen times before managing to balance on two limbs that then thickened and formed at their bases rounded 'feet'. From the appendages at last designated arms, 'hands' with two digits shaped.

But standing proved only a temporary success. The constant whispering reached a new crescendo and with it came a doubling over by the creature, as if the whispering pained it even more. The creature stumbled against one wall—and with a flash of escaping magical energy, suddenly stretched taller and thinner.

For a brief moment, the screaming stopped. The narrow chest began expanding and shrinking, as if breathing occurred.

The macabre being reached out with its primitive hands, clearly beseeching someone.

But if it was to the unseen speakers, that beseeching went unanswered. Indeed, if anything, the whispering only multiplied.

The thing shrieked anew. Clutching itself, it rushed forward. More energy scattered from its body as it continued to add to its height and width. The awkward run ended after only a few steps, though, the creature finally falling to its 'knees'.

At this point, the scream became a moan that finally died away. The thing let one hand drop to the ground to better support its weight…and five fingers shaped from the original pair. The other hand joined the first, with the same results.

Chest heaving, the featureless figure rose. With obvious determination, it continued on its chosen path. However, if it thought to escape the crevice, it was sadly mistaken. Barely had it taken three steps than the whispers rose higher yet, causing the creature to suddenly seize its head and renew its moan.

The lingering traces of energy flickering around its body abruptly flared bright. A fiery aura surrounded the stick figure. The moan shifted back to a scream and as it did, a gap ripped open in the lower part of the empty 'face'. With at last a mouth, the struggling form unleashed a wail that made even the previous cries seem tame by comparison. Falling against one rocky mountainside, the figure shook and shivered as the resurrected energies overwhelmed it. The magical fire seared the thing black, but the continued violent shaking first cracked the charred coating, then sent the burning fragments to the figure's feet.

Silence reigned, then, even the disembodied whispers finally ceasing.

From the broken shell, a human shape—a male with dark shoulder-length hair—slowly emerged. A human shape with one glaring difference.

Where there should have been a face...there was only a hazy hint of a mouth, a nose, and eyes.

Breath coming in rapid gasps, the male figure started on his trek again. As he did, dark garments formed over his body and boots covered his bare feet. He held out a hand and black gloves engulfed it and its twin. From the air, a voluminous cloak wrapped around his shoulders. The hood that sprouted from the neck of the cloak draped over the dark hair and further obscured the murky features.

The breathing slowed to normal. *Shade* peered down at his gloved hands, which shook despite his seemingly calm demeanor. The memory of his resurrection remained with him, if few other memories did. Nothing—not even death—could ever make him forget the grueling punishment he suffered each time he came back to life.

Yet, one thing finally at least enabled him to push the foul memories to the back of his mind. There was one thing that still had to be done before he could consider himself whole—or at least as whole as he could ever be.

It did not take him long to think of the answer. There always seemed to be an answer waiting at this point, almost as if the actual choice was *not* the warlock's.

"Wulfrin..." Shade murmured, tasting the name. "Wulfrin..." The hooded spellcaster nodded to himself. "Yes. I shall call myself Wulfrin...*this time*."

15

HALDIS

Wiln set the sealed missive his master's contact in Pagras had sent by bird on Hadaryn's desk. The hooded half-elf stared at the precious document he had so casually placed in the open, waiting.

The small scroll faded away. It was still there, but the masking spell the master of the Vale had placed on the desk made it all but certain that no one other than Hadaryn would know the document was there.

Not entirely satisfied with the arrangement but having to trust in his master's judgement, Wiln turned away.

Something suddenly made him tense. He quickly pulled the hood further over his head—and then vanished himself.

Barely had he done so than Azran appeared but a few feet away.

Nathan's son eyed Master Hadaryn's personal chamber with a mix of mild interest and impatience. As usual, he gripped the black sword tightly.

"You said he'd be here," Azran murmured seemingly to himself. "Well, he's not."

His gaze fell upon the desk…and then to the spot where the missive lay hidden. At the same time, the wizard cocked his head as if listening to someone.

"I'm *being* patient!" Azran growled. He raised the sword before him. "You—"

Wiln, a dagger in one hand, formed behind the bearded spellcaster. He wrapped his other arm around the side Azran held his own weapon, forcing the wizard's blade down in the process. The dagger went to the human's throat.

A crackle of black energy surrounding the wizard threw Wiln across the room. The hooded half-elf collided with the far wall next to the door.

Turning toward his attacker, Azran muttered, "I assume you must serve the master of the Vale or you'd be in worse shape right now—"

Already on his feet, Wiln threw his dagger. As he did, he pulled the hood forward again.

The black blade deflected the dagger. Azran smiled as he noted his adversary's disappearance. He brought the sword forward. "If you're wise, you'll stop this foolishness now. I'm not here to do anything to your master—"

Another dagger shot toward him from out of thin air. Once more, the black blade moved almost as if it defended Azran of his own accord.

A *third* dagger followed the second, then veered to the mage's opposite side.

Despite Wiln's attempt to catch Azran by surprise, the wizard's sword had no trouble first blocking on sharp missile, then the other. Few trained fighters would have been able to move so swiftly and with such certainty.

"This really needs to end." Azran pointed the blade in the direction from which the daggers had flown. The black sword crackled darkly.

An angry Wiln reappeared. For the first time, the wizard noticed the cropped ears. He wondered what Wiln had done to deserve the maiming.

The crouched half-elf already had his hand at his side, but whether he intended to draw yet a fourth dagger, Azran would never learn, for at that moment, another figure burst through the doorway into the elegant chamber.

"Wiln! No!"

Azran's attacker hesitated. The mage felt tempted to teach him a very painful lesson, but decided against it. He had come here to seek knowledge and power. The master of the Vale was not likely to assist in that request if the wizard left his servants injured or worse.

Azran also did not want to anger the female before him. While the half-elf was not Gwendolyn McArn, she was certainly beautiful, even if only a servant.

"I seek your lord, the master of the Vale," he declared in his most commanding tones. "Where is Hadaryn?"

"You—" Wiln started.

"I will take it from here, Wiln," the newcomer calmly interrupted. She curtsied before Azran. "Our lord is away and I fear I cannot say exactly when he plans to return...Master..."

"Azran! Azran Bedlam!"

Her eyes widened in clear recognition. "The son of Nathan Bedlam!"

"Youngest," the wizard corrected her before silently cursing himself for doing so. Even *he* had gotten into the habit of setting his brother before him.

"But clearly as much your father as your brother must be, if not more."

Azran preened. For the moment, he ignored the two voices in his head, both of whom seemed to also find interest in this servant.

Few people acknowledged Azran's might; he wished to savor it. "I've learned a few things even my father hasn't."

"I've no doubt about that." She gestured to the door. "Will you come with me downstairs? There is a more fitting place for you to wait while I see if I can discover some word about Master Hadaryn."

Wiln took all of this in with more and more distrust of the spellcaster. "Ha—"

"Haldis is my name," the female informed Azran as she guided him from the chamber and the dour Wiln. "I oversee the household for Hadaryn."

Azran concentrated.

He and Haldis materialized downstairs. She looked suitably impressed.

She gestured toward another chamber that was clearly Hadaryn's library. For the first time, something other than his hostess stirred Azran from his disappointment at not finding Hadeen's brother at home.

"It would be best if you waited in here," Haldis informed him. "While I am certain my lord will be pleased with your visit, he's kept his link to the rebellion hidden from the Dragon Kings and even King Paulin."

"I know that, of course." Azran had kept his personal spells fresh, but he could see where Haldis would be concerned about any possible hint of disobedience by her master being noted by the drakes. His estimation of Haldis increased again. He suspected that she did more than just oversee the household. From what little he knew of Hadeen's brother, the master of the Vale surrounded himself with only the most trustworthy followers...Wiln aside, perhaps.

She smiled. "Of course. Is there anything I can bring to you? Some wine?"

"That will be just fine," the wizard said with what he thought his most charming smile. "Thank you."

Haldis curtsied again, then left Azran to the temptations of Hadaryn's library. Grinning, Nathan's son finally sheathed the black sword. He did so with some effort, the weapon seeming to want to resist his attempt.

Then, hands free, he eagerly started to pick through the ancient tomes.

Wiln seized hold of her arm the moment she left the library. She shushed him until they were far enough not to be heard by the Vale's unexpected 'guest'. "Hadrea! What kind of game are you playing? You know the message your father got from your uncle! Master Nathan's son is dangerous, unhinged—"

"*You* were the one who attacked him, Wiln."

"He intruded in the master's chamber! I have my orders, Hadrea—"

"You take your orders from my father, true," she agreed, "but you also take your orders from me, isn't that so?"

He did not hide his frustration with that point. "So long as they do not contradict your father's."

Hadrea planted her hands on her hips. "Well, for now, you've nothing to show that what I decide contradicts his commands."

"Just what're you getting at?" the maimed male asked with clear trepidation.

"Master Nathan and Uncle are worried about Azran and with good reason. I admit that." She peered over her shoulder. "Yet, perhaps there's something that can be done for him. Right now, he appears utterly reckless, nothing more. I'm going to see what I can learn—"

Wiln's face only grew darker. "So why play the role of a servant, my lady? Why not be yourself?"

"It lets Azran feel that the advantage of encounters between us will always be his. In that manner, I might learn what we need and then we can decide what must be done—"

"My lady...you're talking about this going beyond his current visit."

Hadrea smiled solemnly. "I'm going to encourage him to return...but you have to make sure no one tells him who I am!"

The other half-elf looked incredulous. "Your father will hardly agree to that!"

"Leave convincing him to me. Wiln, I have a feeling...a premonition, call it."

He paused, then, "You're barely into adulthood, Hadrea. I know you as if you were my own—you're much like she would've been, I think. I know the powers of an elemental run rich in your line, but premonitions are not part of those powers."

"Nevertheless, somehow I think I have to do this. For his sake, if nothing else."

"That one's sake? His father would be better if Azran had never—"

"Hush, Wiln!" Hadrea briefly peered back. "He'll hear you. Now do as I say. I *order* it."

The sullen male finally acquiesced. "I'll see to it that the others do as you desire...until your father hears about this and puts an end to such foolishness."

"Father will see my way. I promise you that." Satisfied, Hadrea moved on. "Now, I need to get his wine before he grows restive."

Watching his master's daughter hurry away, Wiln shook his head. Under his breath, he added what he knew he could not say to her face-to-face. "Father will see your way? That is exactly what I am afraid of, Hadrea. Exactly what I am afraid of."

THE IMAGES CONTINUED to race through his mind. The bearded man in the black armor. The vague image of a horrendous wolf. A veiled figure. The catman from the ship. An utterly empty face. An actual gryphon.

A dragon with every color of the rainbow represented in his scales.

The time is not now...

The Gryphon vaguely realized that it was not the dragon that spoke, but some other distant voice.

To his surprise, a voice that was and was not his own replied. *No...but this time is important also...*

A pause. Finally, the first voice reluctantly replied, *Let it be done, then.*

Something began to take shape before the Gryphon. It was a thing of smoke, yet also a thing alive. Still, although he knew it to be barely beyond his reach, it seemed so far, far away at the same time.

A definite shape began to coalesce...and even in his trancelike state, the rebel leader recognized the mist dragon.

"I thought it wasss the accursed ssseneschal who bound me to thisss creature..." the dragon said in a surprisingly subdued tone. "I did not know it wasss you..."

The unsettling voice that was in part the Gryphon's replied, *You were presented. You were to serve...*

"I have alwaysss ssserved faithfully." Still, there was what the lionbird thought just a hint of resentment.

Some have not.

The dragon actually shivered upon hearing this short declaration. "I have alwaysss ssserved faithfully!" he insisted. "Alwaysss..."

And you shall serve now. The way is lost. The direction is argued. And pieces are playing their own game...which is where you must move.

The dragon looked no happier. "Then, it isss ssstill his game... and hersss."

It is.

"And thisss changes all?"

It may.

The dragon of the mists brooded. "I have alwaysss ssserved faithfully."

And I, only, thank you, concluded the voice.

Despite the wording, the response stirred a visible change in the ethereal beast. The dragon dipped his head in what was acknowledgement of a tremendous reward given him.

A great weariness overtook the Gryphon, a weariness he knew originated from that other part of him that spoke to the dragon. *It cost this much to preserve the change. He is now more than me. Others might speak with you, but I give myself to his fiery spirit now. He is more than we imagine...and more than he can himself imagine...*

"Thisss chimera? He isss ssso?"

I give the last of my existence for him...and you would be served well if you had to do the same, gserian.

The last word meant nothing to the Gryphon, but it made the dragon bow his head in respect. Then, the misty creature murmured, "Would that I were of sssuch a level. I am but of the mossst minor of ssservants."

No...you are not.

And suddenly, there was only the Gryphon. Curiously, it was not as if the source of the voice had departed. Rather, the lionbird felt *whole* for the first time.

He also realized that he now sat staring at an icy wall in the underground cavern that served the rebels. There was no sign of the dragon, either.

Just as the Gryphon began to wonder if he had imagined everything, he heard a slight hiss. In the wall there briefly appeared the murky outline of a reptilian form. It hovered above and around the lionbird's own indistinct reflection, but when the Gryphon glanced up, there was nothing to be seen.

Someone called his name. As the Gryphon pushed himself to his feet, he saw Dayn Bedlam quickly approaching.

"Praise be! You're finally awake!"

Rather than risk having the wizard start asking any questions that might bring uncomfortable answers, the lionbird quickly said, "We need to move our forces. This place is no longer secure."

The younger Bedlam looked startled. "I was going to tell you that! After the horrific slaughter of the families—"

The Gryphon stiffened. "What did you say?"

Dayn swallowed. "I'm sorry. You were already unconscious then..."

He went on to tell the monstrous details of what had happened. All the fears the Gryphon had had for not only his own men but those important to them came crashing down on him. He silently cursed the forces that had held him immobile all this time, whether or not they had good reason to do so. A part of him was certain that if he had just been conscious, he could have done *something*.

Fighting back his guilt, the rebel leader pursued his earlier decision. "Pagras. It was the best of the choices we had last I heard... unless there's somewhere else now?"

"No. Yalak is still trying, but he says there's a lot of questionable paths and—"

"We've no time for anymore searching." What the Gryphon wanted to say but did not was that while Yalak's foresight—and that of the Egg—had proven helpful in the past, too often it took the wizard too much time to decipher the answers he received, time the rebels did not have. "Where's your father?"

"I don't really know." Dayn glanced around the cavern. "He told me he had to do something and then just vanished. It's been more than two hours since..."

Already familiar with Nathan Bedlam's habit of vanishing and returning as he saw fit, the Gryphon decided to push ahead. The master wizard would show up when he felt it was necessary to do so.

"And Toos?"

"He should be with the fighters."

Of course, the Gryphon thought with grim amusement. No matter what else happened, Toos could always be counted on to do his duty. *Someday, I fear it will kill him...*

Dayn followed the rebel leader as he searched for his second in command. They found Toos just as the wizard said, Toos taking a personal hand in getting the men—and women—to keep active. The Gryphon suspected that Toos had been pushing himself hard to keep the fighters from thinking about their commander.

They still rely too much on me, he thought bitterly. *This war must not be won or lost based on mine being the guiding hand. They must believe that they can win with or without me.*

The vulpine officer looked very relieved to see him. "I was beginning to run out of orders to give everyone."

"Well, I have one more for you to relay. We move to the Pagras site."

He did not surprise Toos. The young officer simply nodded, then asked, "Timeline?"

"As soon as possible. We need to be ready to attack the City of Knowledge the moment we're settled."

"It'll happen this time?"

"It will...and do not look forward so much to it, Toos. When it does happen, I promise you it will seem all too soon."

The officer grimaced. "Yes, Gryphon."

As Toos turned to inform the other officers, the lionbird looked back to Dayn. "What did you say?"

The wizard shrugged. "I didn't speak. Gryphon, if we're to move to the Pagras site now, I'd better talk with Yalak and see how we can help mobilize things faster."

"That would be appreciated."

Barely had he spoken than Dayn vanished. The Gryphon rubbed the underside of his beak in thought. The move would require enough effort that the rebels would need three days to reorganize and recuperate—

Again, he heard a voice. Just what it said, he could not make out, yet it seeped not only into his ears, but into his mind...and soul.

He suddenly realized that his hand had slipped into the pouch at his belt. More unsettling, his fingers gripped the object within, an object he had somehow forgotten about.

The new voice grew stronger...and more seductive. It had a definite feminine quality. It teased him, drew on his most basic feelings.

He pulled out the chess piece. The growling bear stared back at him. Again, the Gryphon marveled at how lifelike the piece appeared. Even the elves, with their artistic skills, or the dwarves, with their own mastery of metals, would have been hard put to match its detail.

The bear's savage jaws widened.

Despite the shock of seeing it happen, the lionbird could not pull back. Instead, he found himself leaning *closer*.

As he did, the jaws continued to widen. They now encompassed his entire view. The Gryphon imagined them stretching so wide that they would engulf him—

But the jaws abruptly drew back as something else came between them and the Gryphon. A familiar, misty form swirled before the jaws.

"You will not take him..." the dragon declared. "He isss not yoursss to play with!"

The bear roared. One paw swiped at the dragon, cutting through the tail. The dragon scoffed, his tail reforming.

"Your power isss not enough, not here!" The guardian dove forward.

Instead of recoiling, the bear suddenly laughed...laughed with the same dark, feminine tones the Gryphon had noted in the voice.

The chess piece opened its jaws again...and inhaled.

The dragon sought to retreat, but the inhalation was too strong. First the tail, then the lower half of the creature disappeared into the bottomless maw.

With a struggle, the Gryphon forced his other hand up. He planted it against the seemingly gargantuan jaws and discovered that he was still able to cover them.

The half of the dragon still free immediately retreated.

A sharp pain wracked the rebel leader's hand as what felt like teeth tore into his flesh. He stifled a cry as he fought to free both hands from the chess piece.

The bear fell. The Gryphon heard it clatter on the cavern floor. Moving his hands away, he quickly searched for the malevolent piece.

The tiny bear ran across the floor, heading for the nearest wall. The Gryphon lunged after it.

A tendril of mist snared his outstretched fingers before he could reach the animated figure.

The bear neared the wall.

A hand thrust forth from the icy barrier. It clutched the bear and immediately withdrew into the wall.

The tendril receded. The Gryphon twisted around to confront the dragon...only to find his would-be rescuer gone.

At that moment, the lionbird also became aware of several figures quickly approaching. Toos and a number of rebels rushed up, their expression filled with concern.

"Gryphon! Are you all right? Is it happening again?"

The lionbird realized that Toos feared his commander was falling into another mysterious trance. "No...nothing like that." The Gryphon's thoughts raced. No one had mentioned the dragon, much less the animated chess piece.

He made a quick decision. "No, it was...a spell, but a short one."

They took his meaning as he desired, believing his wits had just momentarily left him. It would have hardly been surprising, considering what had happened to him previous to this attack. *Best that this be kept from them...*

But the Gryphon swore that he would not keep this from Nathan Bedlam. He needed the veteran wizard's invaluable guidance. Nathan would better understand all this. Surely, *he* would. A simple soldier himself—despite what others claimed—the Gryphon had little idea just what had occurred. He only understood that there had been a battle of wills focusing on him, a battle of wills in which he could not even consider himself one of the players...but rather a piece moved at the whim of *far* too many unseen masters.

16

A PIECE MOVES

Gwendolyn approached the swirling mass with unease. She had already tried twice to put an end to whatever spell she had inadvertently cast upon Darkhorse, tried twice and failed. Then, the enchantress had attempted to stop the eternal's wild thrashing from the safety of Lord Green's sanctum. However, when that had failed, there had been no choice but to journey to the ravaged section of forest and see what might then be done.

Although she stood physically alone, Gwendolyn was hardly on her own. The drake lord observed every action she took from his lair and stood ready to assist should something go awry. His decision to remain behind had nothing to do with cowardice on his part; in his sanctum, the Green Dragon had methods by which he could boost his power even more. With Darkhorse a part of the equation, Gwendolyn knew that they might need every bit of ability they had. The demon steed was just as likely to turn on them once he was restored to his normal state. After all, he very likely knew just *who* had been responsible for his torture in the first place.

Gwen wished that they could leave the creature as he was, but seal him somewhere he would cause no more trouble. Lord Green seemed to think it necessary to free the thing, though, which meant that the enchantress had *no* choice but to keep trying.

The oddly melted trees surrounding Gwendolyn sent a shiver through her. She could sense the wrongness of the magical energies Darkhorse had unleashed when he had so easily destroyed them. Again, she marveled that Nathan had dared traffic with such a monster...

The swirling cloud paused.

The enchantress immediately strengthened her defensive spells. She knew without a doubt that Darkhorse now sensed her presence.

The cloud churned violently within, yet Darkhorse did nothing. It was almost as if he waited for her to make the first move.

She decided not to let him wait any longer. Drawing forth from the lines of energy around her, she struck at the cloud from four critical points.

Just as her spell was about to culminate, *another* seized control of it.

Gwendolyn fought to regain mastery. There was a brief struggle, but the surprise with which the second caster had entered the situation prevented the enchantress from succeeding.

Worse, Gwendolyn knew exactly *who* had taken over.

He formed on the other side of the ruined area, a shadow within a shadowy cloak. The warlock had both gloved hands raised toward the cloud, but Gwendolyn knew that Shade also kept his senses attuned to whatever the enchantress might next attempt.

She felt no hint of the Green Dragon's presence. *He can surely not be ignorant of what's happening!* Gwendolyn thought with growing horror. *Not even Shade could be that powerful...*

But the lord of the Dagora Forest did not intercede as the warlock continued his own work on Darkhorse. The spell he had stolen from the enchantress had become something she no longer recognized.

Yet, whatever he had done to it finally appeared to have some effect on the transformed demon steed. Darkhorse looked less and less like a mass of smoke and more like the black ink with which Gwendolyn was already too familiar. In fact, within seconds of that observation, crude limbs and what she knew had to be a head also formed.

The enchantress tried to contact Lord Green, but a barrier blocked her mental probe. Worse, when she then attempted to escape the vicinity, her transport spell also failed.

Shade's low chuckle echoed in her head.

Darkhorse now had full legs and even a tail. His body was round, but smoothing out. The head grew two gleaming orbs, icy blue in color.

Gwendolyn braced herself. She had been concerned enough when aware that she might have to face the demon steed's power— and that with the drake lord supposedly prepare to back her—but now she had *both* sinister legends before her.

Darkhorse's shape refined. He blinked. His terrible gaze fell upon the enchantress—

His hind legs kicked out...at Shade.

Had he been a true stallion, his attempt would have hardly been sufficient to reach his target. Not only did Darkhorse still float above the area, but he was several yards from the warlock. However, physical laws did not apply to the eternal; his legs simply *stretched*.

But before the hooves could strike, Shade vanished. He reappeared the next breath, his mocking laughter now audible.

"Now, now, is that anyway to thank an old friend?"

Snorting, Darkhorse thundered, "And by what name do you go *this time*, old friend?"

A chill ran through Gwendolyn. She knew the faceless spell-caster's story more than many and knew exactly what Darkhorse meant. She had distrusted Shade enough before…

The hooded figure bowed. "Call me—"

The entire region—save for a small patch not coincidently surrounding Gwendolyn—exploded with deadly burs. The prickly missiles expanded in size as they swarmed through the area.

As if clairvoyant, Shade already had his voluminous cloak wrapped around him like a shroud. One bur after another struck the cloak, but rather than pierce the material, the missiles bounced harmlessly away.

Gwendolyn had no question as to the source of the new attack, nor did she think either Shade or Darkhorse remained ignorant. If they did, that was soon corrected by the upheaval on the northern side of the area. There, the ground swelled up, the greenery and ruined earth shaping itself into a very familiar face.

"Damnable warlock!" the Green Dragon roared. "My domain suffers enough without your mad presence unleashed here!"

"I am hardly the reason for your current troubles," the faceless spellcaster mocked as he shook open his cloak. Another barrage of burs went flying toward the drake lord's construct. As they neared, though, they reshaped and darkened, becoming ballista projectiles.

Now iron, the missiles bombarded the Dragon King's earthen shape. Spiked balls ripped through the wings, torso, and head with ease.

This time, though, it was the drake lord's turn to laugh. "Your new incarnation showsss little wit, Shade! You could tear apart a hundred of these constructs and never will you so much as scar a sssingle scale upon me!"

The fingers of the warlock's left hand fold tight, as if he held something small but precious. "Who said that was what I had in mind, lord of the forest?" The cloak wrapped tight again. Shade may have smiled…it was impossible to tell for certain. "And call me Wulfrin…when next you see me…"

"Stop him!" Darkhorse roared.

But Shade simply shrank into himself and disappeared. As that happened, the demon steed cried out in what Gwendolyn thought utter frustration, then raced off in what she supposed was the direction he believed the warlock had gone.

Gwendolyn prepared to follow, only to have Lord Green bellow, "Stay! Only a fool tracks Shade where he desires to go…"

She wondered whether he included Darkhorse in the ranks of fools, but did not ask. Nodding, the enchantress exhaled. At the very least, she had done what had been requested of her. The Dagora Forest was safe…at least for the time being.

"Curssse the warlock and hisss trickery! This cannot be good! Thisss cannot be!"

Spinning around, Gwendolyn found Lord Green himself standing nearby. As he strode toward her, he bared his sharp teeth in a clear sign of unease. The enchantress had studied under the drake lord long enough to read the depths of that unease and found herself shaking. Just what had she missed?

"What will he do with it? It cannot be a good thing! I should have ssseen it!"

"What is it, your majesty? What has he done?"

The Dragon King paid her no mind, though, instead muttering something that to Gwendolyn not only made little sense, but also magnified her own apprehension. "Find him quickly, demon horsssse! Find him quickly…or you yourssssself may be the causssse of even greater disaster than thisss land has ssseen thusss far…"

NATHAN STARED AT the Sea of Andromacus, trying to keep his thoughts as much on the surging waves as he could. Yet, at the same time, a part of his mind he had been taught to keep separate from all else plotted and discarded desperate plan after desperate plan. It did not help that the one most responsible for teaching him this technique of compartmentalizing his thoughts was the very threat to which he sought an answer.

I am the traitor in our midst... Nathan could not stop thinking over and over. Lord Purple had followed each and every step taken by the rebels through the best of sources...Nathan Bedlam himself. At first, the wizard had been unable to figure out just how his former mentor had succeeded in doing that, but soon enough, the obvious answer had presented itself.

We are not as free as we thought...or, at least, I'm not. Nathan put a hand to his chest, but not to feel his heart beat. Rather, the wizard sought to sense the fragment he knew rested there, a crystal and pearl fragment implanted in him long ago when he had first earned the robes of a spellcaster. *Every* wizard or enchantress had such a stone in them, all placed there without their knowledge.

Those stones had in turn been linked to a monstrous magical array hanging in Lord Purple's sanctum in Penacles. With it, the drake lord had kept all the human spellcasters blindly loyal to the Dragon Kings. Nathan thought that with the array's destruction he had freed he and his comrades, but with him, at least, that freedom appeared to have been nothing more than illusion. Even if Lord Purple could not command him outright, through the link that remained the master of the City of Knowledge had known everything the wizard had.

And so, Nathan had given the drakes every bit of knowledge he carried concerning the rebellion the moment that the human himself had known it.

The turbulent sea echoed his heart. Nathan knew what he had to do, but did not want to do it. His instinct was to be with the rest, sharing in the risk. He had never been one to shirk from what had to be done, not even when serving the Dragon Kings. Had things not changed, it would have been very possible that he would have given his life for them, as so many of his ancestors had.

As Ethas Bedlam had?

He remembered again the scorched bones Shade had revealed to him, the bones of one of his own line who had early on discovered the truth about the Dragon Kings. Ethas Bedlam had paid the price, slaughtered by the Red Dragon in an underground passage in the Hell Plains. Ethas had surely known the sacrifices he might have to make to free his kind and he had accepted them. Nathan knew that he could do no less.

It has to be done, then. There's no going back.

He meant that literally. Nathan could *not* return to the rebellion. If he did, Lord Purple would know the rebels' next move. It was terrible enough that the drake lords could already assume that the Gryphon would lead an imminent attack on Penacles, but if they knew the exact strategy involved, there would be no hope whatsoever for the attackers.

Yet, Nathan could not simply sit around and hope that the war would end well for the rebels. If he could not help the Gryphon and Dayn, then he had to focus on a matter of equal concern to him.

Azran.

The decision made, Nathan concentrated on his younger son. Curiously, he felt a barrier arise. For a moment, Azran ceased to exist. The inherent bond Nathan had always had with both his children could no longer be felt where Azran was concerned.

Worried, Nathan pressed. At last, the vaguest shadow of Azran's presence revealed itself. Grasping at it, the veteran wizard finally managed to locate where he believed his son might be. At the very worst, it was certainly a location where Azran had recently stood, which meant that Nathan could then use it to pinpoint his final destination.

He transported himself...and the unwelcome, too familiar sulphuric stench of the Hell Plains quickly seared his nostrils and burned his eyes. Gritting his teeth, Nathan adjusted his senses. The burning ceased.

He was not familiar with this part of the Hell Plains, not that there was any part he cared to know well. Volcanic craters dotted the vicinity, one of them belching ominously. While Nathan trusted in his abilities, like so many realms, the Hell Plains had their inherent magic. The raw power radiating from the craters was not to be ignored, which made Azran's recent presence here somewhat disturbing.

But there was no sign of Azran. Nathan surveyed the area with his heightened senses and finally noted a trace further into the Red Dragon's kingdom. A simple spell brought him to the location.

A feeling of disorientation overtook him. As Nathan tried to focus, he momentarily beheld what seemed a half-ruined, half-rebuilt citadel of black stone. The image faded as quickly as it appeared, quickly enough so that Nathan, aware of the illusions the noxious fumes could make even wizards see, paid it no more mind.

Instead, he suddenly reached to the side and cast.

The blue flash bursting from his palm illuminated the darkly armored figure once invisible to him. The decaying figure had one gauntleted hand stretched toward the wizard. A black energy cut into the emerald aura, eradicating it.

With Nathan's spell countered, the ghoulish figure also vanished again. Still, the mage knew that not only did the one Lord still remain near, but others also surrounded him.

How they had been able to plan so readily for his abrupt appearance, Nathan could not say. What did matter more to him than even the threat to himself was that they might have Azran already.

That thought stirred Nathan on. While with some wizards it might have caused them to act recklessly, with Nathan it only made him focus more. His sons were his world, despite what they might think at times. They were also all he had left of his wife, gone so long but ever with him in spirit.

Nathan let his instincts take command. While he did not exactly sense the Lords of the Dead themselves, he did feel their use of magic.

When the spell struck, he was ready. Nathan no longer stood between the two casters. Instead, he appeared behind where he was certain one of them had positioned himself. He was rewarded for his efforts by a flash of black energy exploding just a few feet ahead of him.

Whether or not one Lord had injured another did not matter to Nathan, only that the group as whole might be thrown into turmoil long enough for him to find out whether or not they had Azran. He quickly cast about for his son and found a faint trace in the direction that he had thought he had glimpsed a ruined structure.

A simple thought sent him that direction. He knew that the Lords of the Dead would be right behind him. Still, all Nathan wanted was one moment to ascertain whether Azran's trace was recent enough to have relevance.

Instead, what he faced was another of the ghoulish necromancers. "Hold!" the armored figure rasped. "Hold, Nathan Bedlam..."

Despite the odds being that this was some deadly trick, Nathan held back. He kept a powerful spell ready, though. "What do you want?"

"We are here because of your son." Although the words flowed evenly, there continued that gasping sound that almost made it appear that the necromancer rarely spoke audibly.

"And so am I. Where is he?" Even as he spoke, Nathan sensed the other Lords converging. He concentrated on his spell—

"Away, you fools!" snarled the figure with him to the others. "Bad enough you started this encounter with violence!"

The wizard did not know whether to laugh at the declaration or simply finish casting. "Peace-making? From your kind?"

Within the helmet, twin flames the color of night flared. "No peace-making, Nathan Bedlam. A truce. A necessary truce. There are *concerns* about your son...your Azran..."

"Just why are you so interested in him?"

Behind the leader, four other Lords vaguely formed. One was female...at least if the mage was any judge of the long, brittle hair and adjustment in the rusting armor. They kept their hands at their sides and faded into and out of sight at random.

Do not include him in this, Ephraim! a voice that belonged to the lone female insisted in Nathan's head. *He will side with his son!*

"Of course, he would," Ephraim replied, "and that is what we should both hope and expect."

A sense of harsh disagreement filled the wizard's mind. Ephraim might be leader, but he treaded dangerously close to stirring a rebellion among his kind for speaking with Nathan.

One of the craters rumbled. As it did, the veteran mage suddenly found himself in the shadow of the sinister edifice he thought he had imagined. The image lasted but a breath, though, disappearing with the next volcanic tremor.

"Welcome to Azran's new abode." The Lord made a mocking, sweeping gesture toward where the structure had stood. "Your son is very attuned. Even we did not note this place until he opened the way...and that with a portal to our domain so very near..."

His focus remaining on the necromancers, Nathan commented, "It's from the founders, isn't it?"

"Of course! Is that not what we all constantly seek? Is that not always the greatest of prizes to we who follow the calling?"

It bothered the elder Bedlam more that Ephraim seemed to be trying to sound as if they were fellow students of the arts. Legend always hinted of a desire by the Lords of the Dead for a godlike status…a status many were willing to give them. Few knew that while they seemed immortal, they were still only spellcasters, albeit very, very powerful ones.

"And is this place the prize you want in exchange for my son?"

Ephraim chuckled. "Once, it might have been, Nathan Bedlam, but now it means little compared to the monstrous thing your Azran thinks he controls…"

If not for his own recent experiences with Azran, Nathan would have shrugged off the necromancer's words. "What sort of monster puts fear in the—" He had been about to say 'hearts,' but then doubted that such still remained in the cadaverous bodies. "—minds of the Lords of the Dead?"

This brought renewed anger from the ghostly forms behind Ephraim, but the leader continued to ignore his comrades. "You would be surprised at the monsters in your own bloodline, Nathan Bedlam…indeed, 'tis a shame we never snared the first or else this might have all been unnecessary—"

You tell him too much! the female voice insisted. She manifested stronger, becoming almost solid. One gauntleted hand stretched toward Nathan.

Without looking back, Ephraim shoved aside her hand. "I tell him what he must know, Kadaria…"

I disagree, she replied strongly. Nevertheless, Kadaria faded back among the others.

It said much to Nathan that there remained clear disagreement between the Lords of the Dead on this subject. It also made him more concerned than ever about Azran. "If we can stop this bickering, I want to know what danger my son is in."

For the first time, Ephraim showed some reluctance. Then, visibly steeling himself, the fleshless figure said, "Your son has acquired a chess set."

At mention of this innocuous item, the agitation the wizard noted among the other Lords increased at least tenfold. "But more than a chess set, I assume…"

"More than a chess set…we never knew until it was too late, Nathan Bedlam…never wondered what exactly he did with them…"

Ephraim—Kadaria began again.

The lead necromancer started to wave off her latest objection—

—And the ground around Nathan and his dark companions erupted.

Yet, if there was any question as to whether the catastrophe was the result of an underground eruption, that was quickly answered by the horrific form taking shape in front of Nathan from the earth itself. The gigantic figure had a vaguely ursine look to it and seemed particularly interested in the wizard.

Zeree…

The giant defined. It still resembled something akin to a savage bear, but also something nearly human.

How long I've waited for this, Zeree! it roared maniacally in Nathan's head. *All I had to think about for all those centuries, all those lifetimes trapped in darkness! Thinking of tearing you apart, Zeree!*

One huge paw thrust at where Nathan stood, but the wizard had already vanished. Yet, instead of materializing far away, Nathan discovered himself only a few yards from where the giant stood.

They said you wouldn't be able to get far! gloated the monstrous figure as he tore his paw free from the burning earth. *They said that if I was patient and waited, you'd come and I'd have you! Finally!*

Who 'they' were was a question Nathan would have liked the answer to, but first he knew that he had to survive this—he was not exactly certain *what* the creature was. It had human traits, but the magical energies surrounding did not feel like those of any wizard or enchantress Nathan knew. In fact, the only spellcaster whose power bore some resemblance to this fiend…was *Shade*.

Before he had the chance to delve deeper into the possible link, the beast attacked once more. This time, though, the attack came on two fronts. Even as the giant grabbed at Nathan, a dark green shell formed behind the wizard. Nathan felt the spell he had been about to cast twist against him. He barely canceled it in time, but now that left him open to the giant's physical assault.

The beast's laughter echoed in his head. *Forget how to duel, Zeree? I've played this one over and over and over…*

The huge fist slammed against him. Nathan's personal shield barely held against the powerful blow. Fragments of sizzling rock spilled over the mage, but did not touch him.

Only then did Nathan understand the extent to which his foe had augmented his true form with the natural forces of the Hell Plains. It gave him a better idea as to the monster's powers and limits. What it did not do was explain again just who this mad creature was and who he thought Nathan was.

Does that matter? the wizard reprimanded himself. Nathan tried an indirect spell, ripping up the ground beneath his adversary. To his relief, the giant fell through the gap created, disappearing into the burning depths.

Of the Lords of the Dead, there was no sign. Nathan found that both curious and disturbing. If he had not known any better, he would have sworn that they had fled rather than face this behemoth.

An idea came to the mage. He glanced toward the ancient citadel, but could no longer locate it by any means. Indeed, Nathan could not even swear which direction the edifice actually lay. It was as if the building had shifted location—

Suddenly, Nathan once again felt the unsettling presence of the Lords of the Dead. Yet, now he sensed not only Ephraim and the three from earlier, but *more*.

He knew then that he had made a mistake. The necromancers had not fled, but rather simply regrouped.

Barely had they done so than the entire area shook as the ursine behemoth rose back into view. He laughed at Nathan.

Foolish Zeree! I will—

You will come with us, Yoran Jakaree…we have been waiting much too long for you…

The giant hesitated. He peered down at an empty spot to his left. *The children of the dragon…*

The faint images of the Lords of the Dead formed around the thing they called Yoran Jakaree. For the first time, Nathan felt an uneasiness arise within the giant. He knew the necromancers, knew them far better than the wizard did.

It is time you were collected, Ephraim's voice echoed.

Yoran Jakaree turned from Nathan. Molten earth washed over the Lords of the Dead even as the behemoth grabbed for the ghostly shape the mage believed to be the lead necromancer.

You are not her, Yoran Jakaree, Ephraim continued to mock. *Indeed, you are the least of the Zeree's collection and she knew it…*

I am Vraad! the monster silently roared. *I am—*

You are ours… The Lords of the Dead raised their hands toward Yoran Jakaree.

Nathan suddenly felt as if a part of the world ripped apart. The chill of the grave touched the wizard. He instinctively backed away, aware that what he felt was the encroachment of the necromancers' foul domain on the living world.

And with that encroachment came shapes, shadows. They swirled around the Lords of the Dead, then moved with purpose toward the behemoth.

Yoran Jakaree laughed at the phantoms. He swung one fiery fist at the foremost, scattering them. However, as soon as the fist passed, the stream of shadows reformed and pressed forward.

A low mutter arose from the Lords of the Dead. As it grew in intensity, the flow of shadows—of ghosts—grew stronger in number. They swirled around the giant, who now looked less amused and more vexed.

No swords? No axes? he taunted the necromancers. *The Dragon would be so disappointed in you!*

Nathan did not know of whom Yoran Jakaree spoke, but noted that the necromancers' efforts momentarily faltered. Then, as if shrugging aside a hated memory, the Lords renewed their attack. The swirling river of shadows washed over the giant.

Yoran Jakaree roared again, but the cry came out muted. Flames burst from his hide, in their brilliance revealing individual phantoms. Nathan beheld men, women, and children and even beings of other races, such as Seekers and Quel. All were thin, drawn, and clearly with little desire to be where they were. Yet, they continued to assail Yoran Jakaree because the Lords of the Dead demanded it.

The ursine leviathan tried in vain to shake them off. However, when he finally succeeded in doing so, with each specter appeared to fall a piece of *Yoran Jakaree.* He did not seem to notice this at first, his flailing only increasing.

Then, the fact of what was happening to him finally dawned upon Nathan's former adversary. Yoran Jakaree glared at the Lords of the Dead.

She warned me of your tricks…and gave me one in turn just for this moment…

The giant glowed a bright emerald.

Nathan tried again to cast a teleport spell. At the same time, he saw the Lords of the Dead adjust their attack as they, too, registered just what Yoran Jakaree attempted.

A rupture in the very fabric of reality opened where the giant stood. Through it rushed a storm like none Nathan could have ever imagined, a storm filled with the same foul energies he associated with the necromancers, the giant...and Shade.

Nimth—Ephraim's voice declared before being cut off.

The storm enveloped the area...and all within it.

LORD PURPLE JERKED to his feet. He stared toward the ceiling, seeing beyond the confines of the palace, beyond the confines of the City of Knowledge. The drake lord gestured and a circle of silver formed before him.

He peered through the circle, then dismissed it with a negligent wave of his hand. As he did, the Dragon King hissed.

"Ssso. Two birdsss with one stone, asss they sssay," Lord Purple murmured with satisfaction. "Two with one ssstone."

The drake lord concentrated. A moment later, the image of Lord Brown formed in his mind.

Well? the other Dragon King asked with clear impatience.

They should be on the move, now, the master of Penacles remarked with confidence. *If even one of them sensed as I just did, they will realize that they have no choice, no more time to wait...they will make the move with the assumption that immediately after they must attack here...*

Brown was pleased. *My legions will begin to move, then...and the emperor?*

He will be alerted as necessary.

Purple severed the contact, then returned to his throne. His own forces were already in place. All he had to do now was watch as Brown dealt with his end of the bargain. Then, at last, he could finish this farce and take the crown that belonged to *him*, not Gold.

"And all thanksss to you, my bessst and most predictable student..." the Dragon King murmured to the empty air, "and all thanksss to you doing exactly asss needed, Nathan Bedlam..."

17

BEDLAMS

"Any word from him?" the Gryphon asked impatiently.

Yalak shook his head. "No. And before you ask, I've looked into the Egg as well. It is as if Nathan..." The balding wizard glanced past the rebel leader. "Dayn approaches."

The Gryphon's beak shut with a brief clacking sound, the only sign of his frustration. He turned to greet Nathan's eldest.

"How fare things, Dayn?"

"Everyone's crossed. Adam, Samir, and I've sealed all the blink holes connecting us to the Northern Wastes."

"And our contacts in Pagras?"

The younger mage rubbed his chin. "I'm about to go meet Hadeen about it. Only he and his brother know who our allies in Pagras are."

The Gryphon nodded. With security so difficult to maintain, minimizing the knowledge of any one senior member of the rebellion was the only path left. Even the lionbird did not know most of their outside contacts. "The sooner you're back the better. We need their information before we strike."

"I'm already gone," Dayn replied...and then was.

Yalak exhaled as soon as Nathan's son vanished. "That was an awkward moment avoided. I foresaw several paths in which the first thing he did was ask about his father...and then went and did something very foolish."

"We need him focused on the attack. If anything *has* happened to Nathan, Dayn will be of more importance to us than ever." The Gryphon mulled over the last comment. "Can you foresee anything with Dayn in that regard?"

Yalak shut his eyes for a moment. When he opened them again, he looked troubled. "That's...odd. I've never looked into future paths concerning Dayn beyond the near future, a couple of weeks at best..."

"What did you see now? Would there trouble?"

"I don't know...I wish Nathan was here..." Yalak's hand touched the Egg. "I looked through a dozen possible paths to see where Dayn's added importance to the rebellion might take matters...I looked as far ahead as my abilities give me, which for this would mean two, three months..."

"And what did you *see?*"

The wizard's brow wrinkled in confusion. "Each time, I saw nothing but *Azran.*"

DAYN MATERIALIZED ON a wooded hillside north of which stood the eastern Tyber Mountains in the presence of not only Hadeen and Hadaryn, but also a thin, dark-skinned figure who had some traits reminiscent of the wizard Samir. Pagras was a kingdom on the edge of the regions from which Samir's people came, so the look did not surprise Dayn, even if the name did.

"This is Duke Adric Gura-Ai," Hadaryn said to the wizard after introducing Dayn to the stranger. "He speaks for forces in Pagras that are sympathetic to our cause."

"Which is more than can be said for those of your own Mito Pica," muttered the contact.

Hadeen's brother exhaled. "I have told you again and again, King Paulin's position is tenuous. We always have the eyes of the drake lords peering down on us."

Adric did not look satisfied with the answer, but finally nodded. To Dayn, the Pagrisian said, "My name, since your eyes show your curiosity so well, comes from my father, once the ambassador of Gordag-Ai before he chose to retire to Pagras after marrying my mother."

"I'm sorry. I didn't mean to—"

The swarthy man waved off his apology. "I tell you so that we can move on to matters of importance. Your father is well-respected in Pagras."

Well-respected... The words were said as if in compliment, but Dayn sensed something else behind them. The duke spoke of the elder Bedlam as someone respected in much the same manner as most humans respected—or rather *feared*—the Dragon Kings.

He served them well for many years, Dayn thought with a shudder. *How many suffered...how many—?*

"Dayn?" Hadeen murmured. "Shall we proceed?"

Dayn realized that Hadeen had known exactly what the young wizard had been thinking. Nathan Bedlam had blood on his hands, the blood of those whose only crimes had been that they had stood against the drake lords.

And so, for that matter, did Dayn.

"Yes," he finally replied. "We'd better. The Gryphon's waiting."

However, as Lord Adric turned to retrieve a large pouch, Hadeen leaned close to Dayn and whispered, "Ignore any tone from the duke. None of you had a choice. Lord Purple made puppets of you all."

But we were the great Bedlams! The most powerful wizards in the world! Dayn wanted to shout out the words, but held back. What his uncle said true...and yet...

"We have the charts you asked for, showing the linked blink hole sites most utilized by the drakes when moving large contingents quickly," Duke Adric commented. "They are very much creatures of habit, even more so than humans at times."

"Utter mastery over all else can do that to one," Hadeen replied. "Let us hope that it proves their downfall."

Trying to shake off his regrets, Dayn peered at the charts. "This covers the entire continent. How long have you been gathering this information?"

The Pagrasian's expression darkened. The bitterness in his voice was very evident. "Long enough. Did you think this rebellion sprang up just for you mages? Or even this opportunistic creature they call the Gryphon?"

"I meant nothing wrong by that! If you—"

Hadaryn came between them. "Enough of this! We've no time for past differences." To the duke, he added, "The mages have given their lives for this struggle, Adric. And they had little choice in their past decisions."

Their contact grudgingly nodded. He tapped one of the other charts. "That one there. Best estimates at where the Dragon Kings keep their nesting areas."

Dayn almost dropped the chart in question. Even those of his calling had been prevented from knowing exactly where in the sprawling underground lairs the main nurseries of the various drake lords were located. To be sure, Dayn and his father could make educated guesses, but since the Dragon Kings draped the nesting areas with the most powerful of spells, those would remain guesses.

Before he could ask just how they could trust the accuracy of such information, the duke continued, "Seven generations of men suffered grisly deaths to accumulate the last. Make certain that this chart in particular finally proves worth their lives...and everyone in Pagras, for that matter."

"There are many who've worked hard and long for this day," Hadeen replied with more than a hint of sadness. "The sacrifices of Pagras and its children will certainly be honored among the greatest."

"But only if we win," the Pagrisian countered. "Never mind. My time is short. Duke Kyrg is arriving in two days. We're not certain as to the reason for his visit, but he must be met with the proper pomp."

"Be wary of Kyrg. He is not so cunning as his younger brother Toma, but he is more vicious."

"We always remain wary. It is how Pagras survives while it waits."

Duke Adric pulled a small emerald pendant from beneath his shirt. He rubbed the emerald twice...and disappeared.

Dayn sensed nothing when the spell took place. He glanced quizzically at Hadeen.

"A gift to the duke from my brother here. A combination of basic elven magic and a touch of the powers of an elemental," his father's friend explained.

It made the human consider again a subject the Bedlams had discussed more than once. "I still can't fathom why the elves have always been overlooked by the Dragon Kings. Despite what you keep telling me, your powers—especially those of an elemental—should've drawn their attention long ago."

It was Hadaryn who answered...although what he said Dayn hardly considered an answer. "Yes, it should have. Try not to think about it."

The wizard was about to argue that he *should* think about such things, but suddenly both half-elves stiffened as if hearing something. Dayn concentrated, but instead of a sound, he felt a familiar presence, but one that had nothing to do with his concerns, but those of Hadeen's family. Out of respect, Dayn severed the tentative mental link he had already formed and stood back.

"What could possibly be so important—?" Hadeen's brother began, only to cut off abruptly. His eyes shifted to Dayn, who suddenly felt uncomfortable for reasons he did not understood.

"The Gryphon will want these as soon as possible," Hadeen reminded Dayn. "You'd best get them to him."

Seeing he would fathom no secrets from the pair, Dayn reluctantly nodded. Still, he had to ask one more question, a question that had been secretly disturbing him since before he had even met with Yalak and the Gryphon. Here now was perhaps the best person he could ask. "Hadeen...can you sense where my father is? It's as if he ceased—"

Before the younger Bedlam could finish the awful thought, Hadeen interjected, "Nathan's talents are great. If your father feels the need to mask himself from even you, assume that he had good reason...and have faith."

It was no better a reply than Hadaryn's previous one, but Dayn let the matter rest, at least where Hadeen was concerned. It was true that Dayn should have had faith in his father. The alternative would be to think that—

No. Don't go down that path. Gathering the charts together, Dayn tried to focus on his mission. Yet, despite Hadeen's reassurances, the mage knew that the moment the Gryphon did not need him, he would begin to seek his father in earnest. *Perhaps Azran knows where he is...if anyone can sense Father's location, he can. Yes, I'll turn to him. Who else better?*

Satisfied that he had an idea of how to begin his search, Dayn faded away. Azran and he might have their personal problems, but they were still brothers and Nathan their only surviving parent. Even if Azran did not know where their father was, he would surely offer his abilities, which, between the two of them, would all but guarantee that they found the veteran wizard.

Nothing else mattered to Dayn as much as finding his father. Family was the only constant he had, and that family consisted of the elder Bedlam and Azran. For either of them, Dayn would give his life.

And he was certain that both felt exactly the same.

"THAT WAS AN uncomfortable moment," Hadeen muttered.

"Just the latest in too many," his brother returned.

"He's not satisfied. He'll go hunting for Nathan."

"Let him. If he finds him, so much the better..." Hadaryn's brow furrowed. "She's coming *here*."

"Are you serious? Does she not know the risk simply leaping near Pagras!"

"Have no fear. I'll soon remedy this." Hadeen's brother concentrated...and both half-elves departed.

They reappeared a breath later in Hadaryn's home at the center of the Vale. Before them stood a startled Hadrea.

"I was just about to—"

Her father confronted her, his face filled with an unusual anger. "We know what you were about to do! Did you not think for a moment that the Dragon Kings' agents are constantly scrying for any peculiar magical activity? You know we've kept the extent of your abilities hidden from them. They'd detect the difference in your casting from that of a true human spellcaster and at the very least wonder—"

"But—"

Hadaryn made a cutting motion with his hand. "Enough. I have done my best to protect you since your mother passed...which brings me to the vague message you sent when you first touched our minds. Azran Bedlam was *here* and you confronted him?"

"Yes..." Hadrea swallowed, then added, "And let me tell you everything before you judge..."

"What does that mean? What did *happen* between you and Nathan's son?"

His daughter paled, but remained firm. "Please! Let me tell you—both of you—and let me make you see what I'm doing makes sense..."

Hadaryn sighed. "We are definitely *not* going to like this, are we, brother?"

Hadeen peered at his niece, trying to read her intentions from her face. In the end, all he could do was shake his head in response and hope that the rebellion was not about to get more complicated than he—or Nathan—could have ever believed it could.

CHAOTIC MAGICAL ENERGIES swirled around Nathan. He could not tell what was up or down or even if he still remained in the Dragonrealm. Distorted images of nearly human creatures flew past his gaze and an ominous name echoed through his head.

Nimth...Nimth...Nimth...

But just as suddenly, the world became a torrent of frothing earth that enveloped the wizard and tossed him about. Nathan tried to cast a spell, but his thoughts would not collect long enough to allow him to do anything.

He waited to die.

But then a darkness blacker than a moonless night swallowed him whole. The mage's surroundings calmed. Nathan knew that he should have taken that moment to finally cast *something*, but was too exhausted.

In the end, he fainted.

When Nathan did wake, it was not of his own doing. Instead, a voice he thought he recognized burrowed its way into his subconscious until he could no longer ignore it.

And not at all to the wizard's surprise, when he opened his eyes, it was to find darkness still surrounding him...darkness that stared back at him with icy blue orbs.

"At last!" came the stentorian voice from all around Nathan. "Really, Master Bedlam! I do as you request at the risk of both of us and at the cost of losing his trail! You could at least remain awake!"

"Darkhorse...how did you...where are...?"

The eternal's tone softened. "You are not well...forgive me! Even after so long among your kind, I sometimes forget your fragility!"

As Darkhorse spoke, the inkiness that was the eternal receded. It immediately condensed into the far more recognizable shape of a shadowy stallion.

But as amazing as Nathan always found Darkhorse's transformation, the pair's surroundings still managed to steal the spellcaster's attention.

"Darkhorse...where is this place?"

'This place' was a winding, crystalline cavern that at first Nathan would have placed in the Legar Peninsula. Yet, the incessant heat that washed over the human once he was no longer shielded by the shadow steed was evidence enough that the wizard had not left the Hell Plains behind.

"We are where you demanded I take you when you summoned me!"

Although Nathan's head still pounded, his thoughts had gathered enough so that he *knew* that it had not been he who had called for help from the eternal. Indeed, there were many Nathan would have called on before the demon steed.

But that was a point quickly forgotten by the wizard as he studied the glittering cavern. There was something familiar about it, although he knew that he had never been here before. Yet, that familiarity touched his very being—

"Dragon of the Depths..." Pushing himself to his feet, Nathan stepped toward one wall. As he did, one hand went instinctively to his heart, while the other he stretched forward.

A faint pulse of energy flowed through the wizard the moment he touched the nearest outcropping. Yet, for some reason, he did not withdraw his fingers.

"How do you know this place?" Nathan asked Darkhorse.

The shadow steed snorted impatiently. "I do *not* know it! As I indicated, I simply followed your direction!"

"*I* didn't direct you..." However, the veteran mage had an idea just who might have done so. "*Shade...perhaps...*"

The simple mention of the warlock's name stirred Darkhorse to great anxiety. "Do not speak that one's name, Nathan Bedlam! His accursed existence has taken another tragic turn! At some recent point, the faceless one met his latest death...and now returns a terrible threat that even Dragon Kings fear walks the land!"

The mage shivered at the implications. "Are you saying—?"

But before Nathan could finish, the ground shook violently. The entire floor of the cavern collapsed...taking him with it. The last he saw of Darkhorse was the stallion racing toward him, but even the eternal was not swift enough to seize the mage before he dropped into a deeper cavern.

Shutting his eyes, Nathan concentrated. Barely had he done so, than the wizard landed hard on the rocky floor. Rubble rained down on him, but his defensive spells protected him from harm. Nathan glanced up, but instead of finding a gap through which

Darkhorse should have been descending, huge rocks evidently from above the wizard's previous location now created a plug.

Why that should stop the eternal, Nathan had no time to wonder, for suddenly, the heavy rattle of hammers echoed in his ears. Turning, Nathan saw a glimmer of light to his left.

Both curious and concerned, he cautiously headed toward the glow. As he did, he realized that it was coming from a neighboring cavern, the narrow entrance of which lay directly ahead of him.

Reaching the gap, the mage peeked through.

In a chamber that dwarfed his current location, scores of Jaruu toiled at the rocky walls, digging out what appeared to be the same substance that Nathan had confronted above. The testudinal creatures worked under the wary gazes of a handful of drake warriors, including one that bore the elaborate crest of one of the highborn, perhaps even a son of the Red Dragon himself. Indeed, when one of the shelled workers paused in obvious exhaustion, he was urged to renewed efforts by a lash of silver energy erupting from a small rod carried by the nearest drake. The lash not only left a black scorch mark on the Jaruu's shell, but clearly caused the worker pain as well.

As the Jaruu forced itself back to work, the lead drake whirled Nathan's way. The mage pulled back from the gap and held his breath.

An angry voice hissed an order. Several metal objects clattered against what Nathan suspected the floor. The wizard disliked the thought of casting a spell that would surely catch the notice of the Dragon King, but knew he had little choice. Even one that attempted to transport him back to his companions risked instead being usurped by the master of the Hell Plains. Yet, it appeared to Nathan that he had little choice...

But the sounds of movement instead ceased. At the same time, the illumination vanished. Even then, the human waited a lengthy time before finally daring to glance into the other chamber again.

Darkness greeted Nathan. He let his eyes, already long-ago enhanced by magic, adjust.

The Jaruu and their taskmasters had utterly vanished. Nathan stood stunned, astonished at how swiftly they had left the vicinity. The nearest exit was at the far end of the cavern. The mage had felt no blink hole open, either.

Finally stepping into the chamber, Nathan eyed the work area nearest him. Something bothered the mage about its appearance. He dared a tiny glow sphere.

The spot looked as if it hadn't been touched in generations. Nathan found no sign of any of the axes and other tools with which the Jaruu had toiled. Sending the sphere to other spots ahead of him, Nathan saw only more ancient excavation, nothing new. No tools, no—

Jaruu surrounded him. They materialized with no hint of spell-work and not a sound. With them formed the drake warriors.

Swearing, Nathan started casting—and then halted with the spell all but finished as his foes did an astonishing thing.

They *ignored* him. The Jaruu worked the rocky walls while the drakes urged them on with cracks of their whips or angry hisses.

On a hunch, Nathan reached out to the nearest Jaruu and tapped its shell...or tried to. His hand went *through* the shell, just as he expected.

Memories...they're nothing but memories...like the ghosts of the Manor...

Nathan surveyed the Jaruu and drakes, trying to understand why and how such an event would become so burned into the fabric of reality that it would replay itself over and over. The ghosts of the Manor appeared to be tied to certain events, at least that was his personal theory, but what event could have taken place out here that it would create this massive image?

The Jaruu he had tried to touch turned his direction. The leathery features looked even more grotesque up close, a truly ugly parody of those of the turtles and tortoises the race most resembled. What was worse, though, was that mixed in with those features were traces that looked akin to human traits.

The underdweller strode forward…walking through Nathan. The wizard turned to watch the creature, then heard a warning hiss.

He looked just in time to see a repeat of the one drake's whipping of the slow worker. The wizard frowned, aware that this meant that the memory would soon end, then likely repeat as it already had. Nathan still had no idea why such a rather mundane scene should be burned magically into the world.

The crested drake twisted toward the chamber entrance. He hissed an order.

The gathered Jaruu tossed down their tools just as Nathan expected. Scaled hands withdrew into the shells, then immediately thrust out again, this time bearing the wicked daggers with which the human had become familiar.

Nathan tensed again, half-wondering if the ghosts would yet converge on him.

A crimson glow swept across the chamber, coursing over everything and everyone so quickly that even Nathan had no time to react to it. Next to him, the nearest Jaruu raised an arm and screamed with an almost human voice.

The hapless Jaruu crumbled to ash.

Around Nathan, the rest of the underdwellers perished in like fashion, the scene so monstrous that the mage felt great pity for the creatures.

The drakes struggled for a breath more, then suffered the same fate. Only the leader remained. Literally burning, he began to transform. His body swelled in size. Leathery wings sprouted from his back and his arms and legs twisted into the limbs of a reptilian beast. The dragon crest slipped down over the helmed countenance and became his true face.

The dragon reared above Nathan, but his gaze looked beyond the wizard. The leviathan roared...and then, despite his considerable efforts, finally crumbled to ash just like the rest.

Stunned by the vision, Nathan at first continued to stare where the drakes and the Jaruu had stood. Now he could see here and there the faded piles of ash that still remained as testament to several of the victims' last locations.

Then, Nathan felt eyes on him. A spell already forming, the mage spun around.

He discovered himself facing another robed figure—a thinner, more studious male with a slightly older look to him. Although Nathan knew that he had never met this wizard, there was something oddly familiar about him.

Dayn! Nathan realized with a start. *He bears some resemblance to Dayn!*

And then, the other mage said, "My name is Ethas Bedlam..."

18

SHADES OF THE PAST

"*Ethas*..." Nathan murmured. "What—?"

"I have to assume that I'm dead," the other mage said almost nonchalantly. "Else this spell wouldn't take effect. I also have to assume that the Dragon Kings still rule..."

Although Ethas continued to look directly at the living wizard, Nathan knew that the ancient figure did not know exactly who stood before him. After all, Ethas was not really here, but merely another memory...albeit one fueled by some ancient conjuration.

"You must be strong of power to have awakened the spell," the image went on. "Maybe even one of my own line..."

At this point, Ethas paused expectantly. After a moment, Nathan nodded and replied, "Yes. I'm a Bedlam."

"I thought as much," his ancestor said with a sad smile. "They bred our line well...just like prize horses..."

That the figure interacted with him to a point did not surprise Nathan. It was not something beyond his own abilities. Still, that Ethas' casting had lasted so many centuries bespoke of the other wizard's formidable powers.

And yet…Ethas had still perished, his mission a failure.

"For the moment, you are safe here," Ethas finally went on. "The fact that I—" He shrugged. "—this illusion of me, rather, talks with you now is proof of that. I worked hard to make certain that even the lord of the Hell Plains would forget this place, not that he did not have other rich veins from which to draw the raw stones the master of the City of Knowledge requires…"

The figure paused. Not certain as to the extent of the image's adaptability, Nathan hesitated, then started, "Ethas…what are—?"

"So, you are here, too," the image suddenly remarked, looking past Nathan.

"Ethas Bedlam…" rumbled Darkhorse as he formed. "No wonder the spell was so full of cunning twists and turns that even kept me at bay until now."

"You knew him?" asked Nathan with some surprise.

"As did a far better version of Shade."

The image smiled, albeit with more than a hint of regret. "Welcome, Darkhorse. You said you would be there for my children and I see you still are. The Bedlams have no more loyal friend… even if they have not always understood that. Even I did not, until I stumbled into here."

Darkhorse dipped his head in acknowledgement of the compliment while Nathan tried to digest what his ancestor had just said. Even more startling than the shadow steed's apparent long-standing relationship with the wizard's line was the last part of Ethas' comment. If Nathan understood his predecessor, Ethas had been as loyal a servant to the drake lords as any other spellcaster until coming to this cavern.

But what changed him, then? Nathan recalled the veins running through the caverns and the link he felt between the raw rock and the stone he still carried within him.

Could it be?

"The spell covering this cavern was the most complicated and draining of my two hundred and sixty years," Ethas went on. "It cost me my family, who call me traitor and outcast, so firm is the Purple Dragon's hold on them. It cost me physically; even should I succeed in my overall efforts—and if you listen to this, I have not—the stress created by energies I drew through me will destroy my body within two or three years. That's why I cast this vision; should I fail, I can only hope that you will take what I've done and use it toward defeating the Dragon Kings..."

A deep sigh escaped Darkhorse. "That is the Ethas I recall! Lacking the mystic skill of foresight, but more than making up for it with cunning! When he last disappeared into the Hell Plains, he promised me that even if he did not return, he would set in place that which he hoped would still someday help free his family and everyone else from the drakes..."

With a sweep of his left hand, Ethas indicated the cavern. "This is zemonite and can only be found in a few places on the entire continent, all but one of those locations in the Hell Plains. The substance's formation requires fearsome raw magical forces combined with the fiery might of a raging eruption. Even then, creation of the raw stone is unlikely, which is why I feel the hand of Lord Purple and the arcane knowledge of the libraries was involved."

"The libraries," muttered Nathan. "Always the damned libraries..."

"The damned libraries," Ethas echoed coincidentally. "So long as they remain the tool of the drakes, I fear we may never gain our freedom."

"Too true," the younger Bedlam returned without thinking.

The vision suddenly rippled. As it did, the scene with the Jaruu and the drakes began anew.

Ethas continued as if nothing had changed. "I gave up my life, my chance, to protect this secret. I used my abilities to an extent

I never would've believed. I even killed wantonly to make sure no witnesses remained here." He suddenly leaned forward, his expression no longer calm, but rather urging. "Listen close! My time is short! You serve the drake lords because of a spell-fashioned stone implanted here." He indicated his breast where the heart was. "That stone makes you utterly loyal to Lord Purple and, through him, the Dragon Emperor!"

He paused, possibly, so Nathan believed, in order to let his expected audience get over the initial shock of discovering what lay beneath their flesh. However, before Nathan could fear that the silence would continue too long, Ethas pushed on. Nathan's ancestor seemed to grow more agitated with each breath he took.

"Be warned! Do not leave this place before you finish hearing me out! If you leave now, you will only return to your slavish desire to serve the Dragon Kings even if they demand you kill your own—" Ethas abruptly choked back a gasp. "—which you will, oh, yes, you will. It is only that the zemonite veins running through this cavern are by nature so powerful that they negate the damned piece in your chest and give you your right mind…"

"There's no need to fear that," Nathan instinctively responded. He wished that he could have at least somehow let Ethas know that he had discovered the truth and destroyed the array controlling the stones. Nathan hated the thought that Ethas had sacrificed himself for something that now, while still of some value to the spellcasters involved in the rebellion, was not the great weapon with which to utterly defeat Lord Purple and take the libraries.

The ghostly image looked back in the direction of the chamber into which Nathan had fallen. Ethas' countenance darkened considerably. "My intention after leaving here is to head to the second cavern system I know containing these veins. It's nearer to the Red Dragon's sanctum. I've some question as to my source's trustworthiness on this subject and may be heading into a trap. If you're listening to me…then I suppose I did."

Nathan recalled the scorched bones. Even though he knew it was pointless, he wanted to warn his ancestor not to proceed.

"Hmph." Ethas returned his attention to where his audience stood. Once more visually in command of his emotions, the ancient wizard pointed at one of the half-worked veins. "Forgive me. My fate is already sealed…apparently. Yours may not be, if you see the stone within you—and those around us—as weapons *you* can wield against them…"

The living Bedlam frowned. A weapon he could wield? If Nathan could have ripped the stone out of his body without killing himself, he would have done so long ago. The fact that Lord Purple knew every thought of his every second of the day constantly assailed Nathan's mind. Only here, thanks to Ethas' ancient spell, was he apparently hidden from his former master's scrutiny—

Here…

Nathan eyed the rich veins, sensing the latent energies within. A sudden realization came to him—

"You've a quick mind, I think," Ethas said, as if reading his whirling thoughts.

Nathan quickly glanced at the image. Ethas had a grim smile on his face.

"A quick mind…but you may be surprised at what you—*and* even the Dragon Kings—don't know about the very stones they use to help enslave us…things that for you, I hope…will make all the difference." As he concluded, Ethas Bedlam held one hand out. In it, he recreated the stone as Nathan knew it existed in his chest—in *all* spellcasters' chests.

"May she forgive me…" the dead mage whispered to himself without evidently realizing it. Steeling himself, Ethas passed his other hand over the stone.

The two substances that composed the stone as Nathan knew it *separated*. He beheld both the one akin to the veins running through the cavern…and something *else*.

As he stretched his palm forward, Ethas seemed to stare deep into his descendant's eyes. "This is what can be done…this is what may help you succeed where I failed…"

AZRAN MATERIALIZED NEAR his hidden sanctum with a sense of foreboding that erased the moment of pleasure he had experienced being in the presence of Hadris. While she still was not Gwendolyn McArn—no woman could be—she was beautiful and pleasant enough to talk to for the time being. For the first time, Azran had felt important—or perhaps *impressive*—to someone else.

But all that faded as he noted the recent stirring of magical forces from more than one source. It did not surprise him to note that the Lords of the Dead had been in the vicinity, although the evident magnitude of their spellcasting did bother him. It also did not surprise him to sense that *other* presence he himself had released to guard his sanctum…at *her* suggestion, of course.

But what did disturb him was that for a brief moment, he could have sworn he noted his *father's* magical trace. However, before Azran could determine whether or not he had actually sensed the elder Bedlam's earlier presence here, the sword warned him of another figure in the vicinity…the very one Azran both needed to find and yet knew might be the most danger to him.

"Where is he?" the mage asked the sword.

In response, the sword tilted to the northeast…to Azran's citadel.

"Inside?"

"Not at the moment."

The black blade swung toward the voice before Azran himself could completely turn. The wizard eyed the hooded form, especially the ever-vague features.

"What should I call you?" Azran finally asked.

His new companion bowed. "Call me Wulfrin...this time."

The sword remained pointed at Shade's chest. One thrust by Azran—or by the blade itself—and 'Wulfrin' would be yet another of the warlock's incarnations lost to time. Yet, neither the wizard nor his weapon moved. "What do you want here?"

"Not your death..." With an utter lack of concern, Shade put one gloved finger to the tip of the sword and gently pushed the blade aside. The sword gave no resistance.

"No? I killed you."

"You killed an idealistic fool. I'm not him."

Azran was not entirely satisfied, but both voices he now constantly heard in his head told him to bide his time. Shade could be useful, just as had been agreed.

"All right," he muttered to them, not caring if the warlock thought him mad. After all, what right did Shade of all people have to judge what was insanity and what was genius?

"I'm so glad you've all come to an agreement," replied the faceless figure with a touch of mirth in his tone. He pointed at the Horned Blade. "I know that you and he especially have much to do."

Azran blinked. Shade spoke as if he knew that the sword had a mind of its own. While Nathan's son had not gone out of his way to hide that fact, few had seen his creation for long enough to understand the truth.

"Oh, don't play the simpleton with me, Azran Bedlam," Shade went on, the mirth remaining. "I can hear him plain as day, just like you." The warlock tapped the side of his hooded head. "It all has to do with being attuned in a *special* way. You and I are kin in that..."

"What do you want?"

"What *you* want. Why you killed me in the first place."

The blade slid to face Shade again. It was difficult to read someone whose features remained undefined, but Azran thought the spellcaster continued to remain unperturbed.

But while the blade appeared to lose much of what little trust it had in Shade, Azran found himself more and more intrigued by the possibilities the hooded figure now offered to the young Bedlam's experiments. Besides, if things got out of hand, Azran *could* always slay the warlock again. It was not, after all, as if Azran were actually committing murder. All he would be doing would be bringing back a more tolerant incarnation, something that had happened scores, if not *hundreds*, of times before.

Perfectly satisfied with the course of his thoughts, Azran forced the sword down.

Chuckling, Shade indicated the citadel. "Come. I want to show you something you may not know about this place."

Before Azran could reply, the pair suddenly stood in what the wizard had always thought of as the 'ballroom'. A few steps ahead of him, Shade stepped to the center of the roofless chamber.

"It's often said of me that I forget much of my past with each—version—born." The hooded figure paused and stared at the ancient marble tile beneath his feet. "What isn't mentioned—or perhaps just isn't so well-known—is that I do on occasion *recall* memories…"

"You do?" For all the tales Azran had heard about Shade, this was one aspect that had *never* been mentioned.

"Oh, yes…there are those who would be very surprised at what I recall at times…and retained *this time*."

With that said, Shade drew a circle of silver energy before him. He then let it descend to the floor.

The moment the circle touched the ancient stone, a heavy, grating sound erupted. The floor began to shake apart.

Azran watched avidly as from the gap created rose a cylindrical platform the color and look of ivory. Yet, the platform did not hold the wizard's attention long, for what hovered above it *demanded* to be acknowledged.

A storm in miniature raged over the top of the platform, a storm no more than a foot in diameter but radiating such power that Azran marveled that he had not sensed its presence before this. Indeed, even the sword and *she* revealed surprise at this discovery beneath the mage's citadel.

But as Azran attempted to use his powers to probe the storm, he sensed magical energies nothing like those he or his family wielded...and not even quite like Shade did, either. There were definite touches of the warlock's unique abilities, but also others, as if this tiny maelstrom were the result of many hands.

"It still rages," Shade commented with satisfaction. "I planned very well, didn't I?"

He did not seem to be asking Azran, but rather some other part of himself. More important to the wizard, the female presence who had guided his own efforts so much seemed particularly interested in the faceless spellcaster's creation.

Life...substance... she whispered in Azran's head. *So clever as always, Gerrod...*

Azran barely paid attention to the comment, so enthralled was he by what Shade had wrought. The storm actually tied in well with what the mage had been attempting. All this time, a great leap forward in Azran's work had lay hidden under his feet.

The black blade—the *Horned Blade*—pulsated as Azran neared Shade and the storm. Only then did the warlock finally turn his attention back to his companion.

"Sheathe that for a moment, will you? Unless you wish this to all be for nothing."

The sword cared little for the suggestion, and when first Azran tried to sheathe it, he had little success. Scowling, the wizard focused. With reluctance, the Horned Blade acquiesced.

Shade chuckled, but made no remark about the trouble. Instead, he gestured Azran closer.

The mage eagerly went to the warlock's side. This close to the storm, Azran felt other minute energies carefully woven into the overall spell. Again, the thought that many skilled hands had contributed to this remarkable creation occurred to Nathan's son.

"So glad of you to accept my invitation," Shade said.

"Invitation? What do you mean?"

Shade leaned toward the storm. He passed a gloved hand in front of the storm. The churning energies abruptly shifted in the opposite direction. As they did, the center of the storm opened up, revealing a darkness that seemed to go on forever.

Azran leaned close. An intense feeling of vertigo immediately overtook him. He fell forward—

Gloved hands caught him. "No, I need you for now."

Shaking off the effect, Azran took a step back. "It's—it's so—"

"Yes, it is." Stepping away from the wizard, Shade opened his right hand. In it appeared a ball of darkness.

With a start, Azran recognized the energies radiating from it... and, thus, knew the source. "That—that's a piece of—of—"

"Darkhorse, yes. He was quite bothered when I took it. I suspect he understands better this time that my original intention was not something he would care for."

As the last comment sank in, Azran glanced at the gap within the storm. Now he recognized the essence at its core. It came from the same source as the ball of darkness.

"I remember enough to know he thought it would help me. Darkhorse always wanted to help me. It remains one of his greatest flaws."

The sphere rose from Shade's palm. It fluttered over the storm, then, without hesitation, dropped into the bottomless gap.

Azran expected it to simply vanish into the gap, but instead, the moment the ball vanished from sight, the storm flared so bright that the wizard had to briefly shield his eyes. Simultaneously, the shrouded sky above thundered violently, and the wind around the half-ruined citadel grew so fearsome that if he had not already had his defensive spell well in place, Azran knew that he would have been ripped from the ground and thrown high into the air.

Shade's massive cloak swirled around him as he held both hands toward the miniature maelstrom. A dark blue aura surrounded the warlock.

The female presence urged Azran to join in the hooded spellcaster's effort, even usurp it. Yet, Nathan's son held back. It was very possible that he could have done as she desired, but Azran had the suspicion that Shade waited for him to try just such an attack. It was almost as if the warlock *knew* that there was not just one other presence with the mage, but *two*.

"*Now* is the time for you to wield the sword!" Shade abruptly called. "*Now* is the time to draw him and point him toward the center!"

Whether or not Azran wanted to obey became a moot point, for the Horned Blade rose from its sheath of its own accord and clamped itself in his hand. Azran's arm rose without any effort by him, bringing the black sword toward the storm.

"Thrust!" Shade commanded.

The Horned Blade obeyed.

Azran could scarcely believe the swiftness with which everything had so far happened. Shade had barely made his presence known, and now the warlock and Azran were in the midst of a spell of such magnitude that most wizards would have spent weeks merely contemplating all the potential outcomes. The young mage could not help grinning as he watched the casting culminate; he and Shade were truly of like minds, acting boldly and decisively where others dithered forever and ever.

"The Lords of the Dead are quite predictable," Shade remarked as he manipulated the forces before them. "But then, one can usually trust to family to remain consistent." He grunted from effort before continuing, "Just as one can trust certain *others* to remain consistent in their desires no matter how many lifetimes pass...such as *her*..."

No sooner had he said the last than the sword abruptly swung clear of the magical storm, its point seeking the warlock's throat. At the same time, the female presence ever with Azran urged him to add his power to the weapon's treacherous attack.

Nathan's son assumed that Shade now represented some tremendous danger, yet, the wizard's deepening interest in the spell kept him from doing anything but watch.

Shade expertly caught the edge of the black blade just before Azran's creation would have severed his head from his body. The warlock's hand continued to glow, but now with an ominous crimson tinge.

"I showed you the way," the faceless figure calmly said not to the wizard but the weapon, "and just where his chess set lay. I remember that...this time. I remember much." The murky features turned to Azran, but seemed to stare *through* him to someone else, "and, oh, how vividly I remember you..."

Both the Horned Blade and the female presence pushed harder for the wizard to add his might to their attack. Together, they could surely overcome Shade's considerable power.

But Azran continued to hold back...and felt more the master for it. The two had taught him much...but they needed to know their places. *Everyone* needed to know their places.

Even Shade...eventually.

"You retain some of your father's wisdom," the warlock complimented as he forced the Horned Blade back to the storm. "And his patience, it seems. Try to teach it to both of them. It won't be long now. I planned for that."

As he spoke, the Horned Blade burned a fiery red, as if the storm reforged it before their very eyes. Both Azran and his unseen companions sensed the incredible energies—including those stolen from Darkhorse—become a *part* of the wizard's creation. Azran felt the change, and his eagerness to test the Horned Blade's new limits was such that he could barely keep from withdrawing the weapon before the casting was complete.

And then...it was done. The storm simply flickered out of existence. Shade stepped back and the floor resealed itself.

Azran wielded the black sword, marveling at the magnitude of its increased potency. With it, he felt he could now face *any* foe... even the Dragon Emperor himself.

"Not the weapon it was intended for—I think—but a very reasonable substitute," the warlock remarked as he stepped back. He peered at the sword. "And everyone played their necessary roles just as originally planned, even if not all of them the exact players I calculated."

The sense of triumph that not only Azran but also his two 'mentors' had felt faded abruptly. From the sword and from *her* there returned an almost overriding feeling of threat.

Shade must have noted all three's reactions, but all he did was chuckle again. "Calm yourselves. You'll get what you desire...as will I at long last."

The warlock *may* have smiled; Azran could never tell.

"After all," Shade finished with a note of humor in his voice, "I didn't spend more than a dozen lifetimes guiding the Dragonrealm to this very war..."

19

STORM OVER PENACLES

The storm struck Penacles hard just before dawn. The guards on the walls steeled themselves, aware that to show any weakness due to something so simple as the weather was something no soldier—either human *or* drake—dared show or else they risked becoming feed for the ever-hungry reptilian mounts.

In his sanctum, the Purple Dragon sat as if a statue. He quietly stared into the semi-darkness that he himself had summoned and searched beyond mortal sight for one being in particular.

You are not dead, Nathan Bedlam, but where are you then? The drake lord pondered that one question that continued to evade him. All else proceeded as planned, but Purple needed to verify the wizard's fate. It was the one factor that now, surprisingly enough, frustrated his otherwise perfect plan. The drake lord had expected a particular conclusion to the events he witnessed through his link to Nathan, but instead...instead his former servant had utterly vanished.

A shadowy form separated from the nearby darkness, the vague outline of an armored figure enough to identify one of the Lords of the Dead—not that Lord Purple had not already sensed the creature's approach.

"Greetings, master of the libraries," the necromancer Ephraim rasped. As thunder crashed outside, the ghostly figure added, "There is a tempest of tremendous proportions stirring."

Lord Purple hissed. "It is one long awaited...as is an answer to the question posed to you..."

"We have been...preoccupied. You yourself should be able to understand that..."

"Ssspare me such excussses. Do you *have* him?"

"We have added an interesting...catch...but no, Nathan Bedlam is not ours. In curious point of fact, he is nowhere that our power can sense...and that should be impossible..."

A cracking sound arose from under Lord Purple's left hand. With a glance, he noted that he had crushed the end of the armrest. The specter gave no sign that he had noticed the reaction, but Lord Purple was certain that Ephraim had seen everything and made note of it. Allies they might be for the moment, but that did not mean that either trusted one another. Once the question of the rebellion was settled, the lord of Penacles knew that the Dragon Kings would next have to deal with the necromancers.

And I understand more about you than even you imagine, ghoul, the drake thought slyly. *Imagine if you knew what the libraries have given up on you and your cohorts...*

Lord Purple stood. He towered over the necromancer, no mean feat. "I care not what you do with him when he is dead, but he must *be dead...*"

"Nathan Bedlam will be a valued addition to our collection," Ephraim replied, his outline fading out and in at random. "Rest assured, master of the libraries, that we would be pleased to announce such a catch..."

Thunder crashed again, this time with such ferocity that the palace shook violently. The drake lord glanced to his right...to the north.

"I have kept my end of the bargain, necromancer," he commented impatiently. "Asss you can no doubt sssense. The bounty will be great."

"And we will keep our end of the bargain, too," Ephraim grated. "Even though the cost to us has been more than expected."

"Not my concern..."

The palace shook again. Now both glanced to the north.

"You will feed well enough very soon," Lord Purple remarked. "Fulfill your end and you will continue to feed well for a very long time..."

"We shall." Already fading away, the necromancer performed a more elegant bow. "And my best wishes on a successful conclusion to your own efforts, *emperor*..."

The Dragon King did not respond. Instead, now assured that he was alone, Lord Purple dismissed the semi-darkness that had especially kept the ceiling obscured from not only prying eyes, but prying magic. Even the cunning magic of necromancers.

A glistening arrangement of crystals greeted his gaze. The crystals swirled in a complex pattern that constantly shifted. Had Nathan Bedlam seen it, he would have recognized it immediately. It was very much akin to the array with which the Dragon King had controlled every human spellcaster's mind and loyalty...but radiating an intensity of power that even the original had not.

Lord Purple looked to the north once more. He grinned, his sharp teeth completely displayed.

"Let it begin, with or without you, Nathan Bedlam...let it begin...and then end, once and for all..."

Rain bombarded the City of Knowledge. Thunder shook its walls. Lightning flash after lightning flash blinded its wary sentinels.

And as those sentinels were blinded yet again, in the north, the first of the blink holes opened.

Oblivious to the storm, the armored ranks charged through. Guiding them was the foxlike Toos, who immediately organized a row of archers just to the side of the portal. Such a maneuver might have seemed the height of foolishness considering the torrential rain, but although the archers were not spellcasters, they *were* accompanied by a pair. Basil and Tyr, to be precise.

When the initial flight of arrows shot up, they did so protected from the elements. That fact was apparent to the defenders on the wall and they prepared accordingly, crouching with shields raised.

Their attention focused elsewhere—as intended—they failed to notice the next blink hole open up midway between the first and the city walls. Yet out of this emerged not more of the Gryphon's hardened fighters, but rather Yalak and six other spellcasters.

They barely stepped from the portal before casting. However, their focus was not on the men above nor even the wall itself. Instead, they stared at the ground beneath the wall, which immediately softened.

Savage cracks immediately raced up the side of the thick barrier. The now-unstable wall shook as one of the cracks swiftly grew into a massive fissure.

The defenders scattered from the crumbling area...and then the flight of arrows, purposely slowed by magic, struck as shields slipped down.

"Back!" Yalak roared. "Back! Hurry!"

The spellcasters retreated...or tried to. The blink hole faded just as Yalak reached it.

Yet, the balding wizard showed only mild concern. A second, prearranged blink hole opened up exactly where the previous one had stood.

Yalak smiled grimly as he quickly ushered his companions through. One or more of Lord Purple's subordinates would very likely be punished hard for underestimating the human spellcasters.

The Gryphon met him as he and the others stepped out the other side. "You did it!"

"A minor victory. Lord Purple's officers are already compensating for it."

"He hasn't entered the fray himself?"

"You know as well as I that he would not throw himself into the battle so early. He is either observing all and judging strategy or he is involved with the libraries, no doubt in order to find some spell that will wreak havoc on us."

The lionbird sighed. "You are not the most encouraging person, are you?"

Smiling apologetically, the mage replied, "You have no idea how many times Nathan asked the same thing."

"Still no sign?"

"I am afraid we must continue to move as if we assume Nathan will not be with us...perhaps ever."

The sound of thunder erupted through the blink hole. The Gryphon and those not yet committed to battle stood waiting to move in the wilderness west of Pagras. Here, there was no storm. In fact, here, the day was looking idyllic.

The contrast was not lost on either warrior or wizard.

"Dayn doing his part?" the rebel leader asked, his mind constantly calculating odds.

"He is. Of his brother, there is no sign, although I do sense something of him in the direction of the Hell Plains."

That earned a grunt from the Gryphon. "Better for all of us if Azran stays wherever he is. We've enough trouble."

Yalak said nothing.

Summoning one of his officers, the Gryphon concluded, "Time to move on with the next step, eh?"

"Now that we are committed, yes."

"I had no choice, wizard. With Nathan suddenly nowhere, we had to strike at Penacles before the news spread."

"I understand...and agree." Yalak started to fade away, then hesitated. "Watch yourself, Lord Gryphon."

Already starting to give orders to the officer, the lionbird only paid slight attention at first. "I always do—what was that?"

But Yalak had already left, and though the Gryphon could have summoned him back, he knew doing so just to clarify what he thought the wizard had called him made no sense under the dire circumstances.

Still... "Devin, did you hear what he called me at the end?"

"No, sir. Sorry."

"Never mind then. Here's where your men will be going next. Listen closely. Much matters on it."

Although he kept his focus on the battle plan, the lionbird still had mind enough to briefly ponder the wizard's parting words. *'Lord'? Me? Let somebody else rule this land if we manage to free it! By then...by then, I'll just be one more corpse on the field.*

And whether or not Yalak had called him by the high-and-mighty title because of some possible path the spellcaster had foreseen, the Gryphon was well aware that, as with so many of Yalak's visions, hearing them and actually *achieving* them were two very different things.

THE BATTLE RAGED in the north, but that did not mean that those on the other walls relaxed. Only twice in its known history had Penacles ever been attacked, and then by rival Dragon Kings. Both times, those battles had ended as expected, but they were example enough that armies did not have to march for days in view of those within before reaching Penacles's boundaries. In a land where magic was prevalent—too much so in the minds of many—only magic could truly protect a realm.

And if any one realm could wield the magic to defend itself, it was the City of Knowledge.

At the north wall, the fissures resealed and the ground beneath hardened. A second flight of arrows bounced harmlessly off an invisible barrier now strengthened against the wizards' efforts.

But no one other than the master of Penacles himself knew the intricate magicks protecting the city better than the spellcasters who had once blindly served the Dragon King and even aided in the creation of many of the realm's protections. In fact, other than Nathan, no mage knew those spells better than Yalak and Dayn, once among Lord Purple's most favored.

Dayn Bedlam materialized in the west. Nathan's son stood alone, but linked to him were three other spellcasters—Adam, Wade Arkonsson, and Samir. Samir knew the layout of Penacles better than most, no mean feat with the kingdom's ultimate geographic design based on magical calculations continually redrawn by the current Lord Purple.

Adam and Wade had not been chosen for any other reason than their abilities, although the moment Dayn began his casting, he started having concerns about the latter. Wade had seemed to have put his pain and loss aside enough to continue to be part of the overall plan, but now that they were actually involved in the battle, the other mage's immense bitterness could be sensed. If that bitterness spilled over into his concentration, the four risked disaster overtaking them.

Wade! Please! Dayn called. *Focus!*

Nathan's son received only a brief, wordless apology from his fellow wizard, but at least Wade's concentration returned to their effort. With all four now acting as one, Dayn struck above the city.

Penacles' defensive spells blocked his initial casting, just as he expected. However, in doing so, their reaction gave Samir and the others the opportunity to measure the matrices and adjust Dayn's efforts for the next attempt.

Nathan's son struck again. As he did, his comrades worked to undermine the structure of Penacles's shields. Samir and Adam failed...but perhaps fueled in some part because of his loss, Wade forced his efforts through, creating the minute gap the younger Bedlam needed.

Dayn threw everything he could into the small and very temporary hole. He could not actually see his success, but the simple fact that they had pierced the defenses meant that the spell he had unleashed after *would* succeed...at least for as long as they needed.

It was an unorthodox attack that, when first explained to the Gryphon, had left the rebel leader perplexed as to its value.

"You are going to rearrange the streets in random parts of the city center?" the lionbird had asked in disbelief. "Enlighten me as to how that would do anything save confuse several locals?"

It had been Samir, naturally, who had explained. "We told you that Lord Purple adjust the city plan based on his researches in the libraries. The entire city is in effect a spell matrix, multiplying not only his spells, but the shields protecting the city."

Understanding had finally shone in the Gryphon's eyes. "You could undermine their entire defensive structure. Is that really possible?"

"Other than Lord Purple, no one knows the layout of Penacles better than Samir," Dayn had promised.

The swarthy mage had shaken his head at this praise. "There is the t—"

"Samir knows all we need...we just have to make the smallest of penetrations in the current shields," Nathan's son had interjected, not sure whether his father wanted the Gryphon to know just yet about the tapestry connecting the libraries to the city.

And now that odd and audacious plan had succeeded. To what extent, Dayn could not say, for Wade finally had to let the gap seal again.

Even as that happened, the ground beneath Dayn's feet started to churn. Aware that the drakes would be watching for a magical assault from any point on the compass, it did not surprise the wizard when the land tried to swallow him. The effort was so primitive that Dayn kept waiting for another attack until the very moment that he and the others returned to the Gryphon.

"Did you do it?" asked the rebel leader.

"Yes. Now would be a good time for your men to move in closer...and for you and the others to do as planned."

The mage had not even finished before the Gryphon waved to a subordinate to give the signal. Three horns blared. A fourth responded.

"They're on their way," the Gryphon muttered. "And I'm on mine."

"Good luck," Dayn whispered. "Good luck..."

"The same to you. May *one* of us survive this day..."

IN THE SOUTH, east, and west, new blink holes opened up, unleashing the bulk of the lionbird's followers. Rebels rushed through, as ever the archers first to set up. However, with the rebels now also came horse-drawn siege weapons—catapults and ballistas.

A fireball abruptly rose high above the city, then fell toward the foremost catapult. Wary rebels manning the weapon peered up at what should have been their doom.

Tragaro materialized behind them. With a wave of his arm, the grey-eyed wizard sent the fireball circling around toward where it had been launched.

The blazing missile exploded a moment later, the same shield through which it had been cast now defending against it.

Despite the last, Tragaro chuckled. He gestured to the rebels at the catapult. "Well? Do your part!"

As the men put the siege weapon into play, Tragaro sneered at the city walls, then vanished again, just as planned. None of the spellcasters dared remain in one location near Penacles for very long. Any hesitation might enable not only the drake commanders to strike at them, but give the Dragon King himself time to target his former servants.

Tragaro returned to Yalak. As he appeared, a female spellcaster vanished. While those of their calling could not remain too long in any one location, they still needed to protect the fighters against magical counterassaults.

"This is a preposterous plan," the shorter wizard snarled upon seeing Yalak. "It would be better if we attacked as a group immediately and threw our might at undermining the main defensive spell matrix."

"You know what Dayn and the others have done, Tragaro. Let us see how it plays out."

"Hmmph! You mean you don't know? Your vaunted foresight is getting less and less trustworthy."

To Tragaro's surprise, Yalak nodded. "There is a tremendous change coming. It makes most of the paths I see too murky to follow far…and the ones I *can* follow far none of us would care to have prove our ultimate future."

"As bad as that?"

"As bad as that?"

Dayn popped in. "It's nearly time, Yalak! I didn't dare send you a mental summons to let you know."

"No, we do not wish anything so important to be overheard by Lord Purple or any of his underlings. I'll join you in a moment."

Nathan's son vanished again. Tragaro snorted. "So now the son succeeds the father? We're to follow the boy's lead from here on?"

"That's hardly what's happening—"

"Isn't it?" The other mage looked frustrated, but before Yalak could say more to assure him, Tragaro glanced to his left. "Micaya needs my aid. I've got to go." Yet, before he disappeared, the shorter wizard scowled and added, "Think about what I suggested the other day. It makes sense…"

With his piece said, Tragaro vanished. Yalak pursed his lips in thought before finally muttering, "Think about your suggestion? Tragaro, I would not do that even to a *drake*…"

THE GRYPHON COUNTED off. He had to have his own force move in at the precise moment Dayn and Yalak had said. Any sooner or any later, and men would die…more men than if the entire rebellion simply charged the walls.

This must work! If we don't do this just right, this battle will drag on too long and give the drake lords the time they need to crush us once and for all…

It was an audacious plan, a desperate plan. It had the potential to change the entire war…or end it badly in two, three days at most.

And if it succeeded, no Dragon King would dare stand against them.

Even though it had been his own contribution to the plan, the Gryphon could scarcely believe that the rebellion was even attempting it. Curiously, Yalak and Dayn had looked at the lionbird with something akin to admiration when first he had suggested it, Nathan's son finally remarking, "The ultimate misdirection! You think like a spellcaster..."

"I think like someone trying to make certain as many of those who've followed me into this struggle survive to see the land free."

That conversation echoed in his head as he finished the countdown. In other areas near Pagras, the other groups would be waiting their turn.

A wizard abruptly appeared next to him. The Gryphon was not startled, having expected this particular spellcaster at just this moment.

"It's time," Wade Arkonsson muttered.

"It's time."

"Don't hesitate. Slay on sight."

Something in the wizard's tone made the rebel leader stare at the human in the eye. "I know very well what *we* must do. Slay on sight. Seize the prize...and leave. No unnecessary fighting."

Instead of answering, Wade raised his arms. "Brace yourself."

The blink hole opened with a rush of steaming air that made the Gryphon grimace. The fur and feathers on his neck stiffened, but the lionbird held his resolve and gave the signal to move forward.

The fighters streamed through the portal. At the same time, the other selected rebels moved through the blink holes opening elsewhere. Everyone had to move in unison.

His eyes stinging from the sulphuric air, the Gryphon led the way into the fiery cavern. A hundred handpicked men—and women—spread out as previously directed by the rebel leader.

Wade Arkonsson formed beside him. The wizard was sweating, but not due to the incessant heat.

"Make sure your followers do their part," Wade reminded the lionbird. "I've got the blink hole secured."

The Gryphon nodded, his mind already racing. The rebels had had more than minute of surprise on their side. That was more than he had hoped for. The others were already spread out in the formation he, Yalak, and Dayn had agreed on.

But the monstrous roar echoing through the steaming chamber informed everyone that they had finally been noticed. The Gryphon watched as one group broke off from the rest to follow him as he headed *toward* the roar.

The huge reptilian head rose above an oddly perfect arrangement of stalagmites ahead. The dragon that spread its wings and roared a second challenge was perhaps the largest the Gryphon had ever seen other than one of the Dragon Kings themselves... including the Purple Dragon, whose color this leviathan also wore.

And no wonder, for through the slight gaps between the row of stalagmites, the lionbird spotted the true reason for the rebellion's intrusion into this dangerous place. *Eggs.* Five eggs the size of a half-grown child.

Thanks in part to the information they had received from Pagras, the Gryphon and his followers had managed, with the work of Dayn and his fellow wizards, to invade the one location perhaps more precious to Lord Purple than the libraries...the incubation chamber housing the future of the drake lord's clan itself.

20

TO STEAL PEACE

L ord Purple made one final analysis of the rebel attack. There were few surprises. Enough followed his previous assumptions that he felt very comfortable arranging for the final crushing blow.

He reached out to Lord Brown, whose image immediately formed before him.

"Isss it at lassst time?"

"Shortly...they are almost completely committed. I await one more step. Then...we are ready."

"And what says the emperor?"

"What he will say will not matter..."

Brown grinned. "I will begin moving my troops."

The image faded. Lord Purple mulled matters, briefly considering reaching out with his thoughts to the Tyber Mountains after all. Then, with a sneer, the master of the City of Knowledge instead returned his focus to the battle.

AS THE GARGANTUAN female rose above the Gryphon and his followers, the lionbird wondered whether their surprise assault was so much a surprise after all. He feared for the other bands now being transported to the egg chambers of the other various Dragon Kings. Were those men, too, expected? Had the information that the rebellion had received from Duke Adric been part of a trick?

As the dragon lunged over the barrier protecting the drake lord's unborn progeny, the Gryphon immediately waved the fighters to his left to a place of safety behind one of the towering stalagmites. Those on his right he signaled to retreat to the far wall there.

As for the Gryphon himself, he did all he could to make himself the focus of the dragon's wrath. The rebel leader raced forward as if ready to meet her face-to-face.

She reacted just as he hoped, dropping her head in order to try to swallow him whole.

The Gryphon leapt. Most humans would have been unable to make the height he managed. As he hoped, she assumed him similar enough to those he led that she underestimated his jump.

The lionbird landed hard on her snout, then quickly pulled himself forward. The dragon reacted instinctively, shaking her head violently in an attempt to toss him off. Even prepared, the Gryphon struggled to maintain his balance as he pulled himself over the brow ridge and toward the back of the head.

Utterly occupied with the vermin clinging to her skull, the female paid scant attention to the rest of the party. That turned the situation nearly into what the Gryphon had intended originally. Not for a moment had the lionbird hoped that they could avoid one of the guarding females, but the thought had been that the *rebels* would be the ones surprising the dragons and not the opposite.

To his relief, the Gryphon noted that his followers now acted as if the plan had never been upset in the first place. As he twisted around for better purchase, the lionbird saw those he had sent to the stalagmite skirt around it out of the dragon's view. That brought them closer to the eggs, still the ultimate goal.

With the eggs—and particularly the two with the royal markings—the rebels could hold the very future of the drakes for ransom. Most drake lords held their eggs in high value. It was no secret that the ruling caste had never produced a vast number of young. That was why the race had always relied on humans for much of their labor.

Unlike Dayn, the Gryphon had long ago known of Pagras' slow but steady attempt to gain the hidden locations of the egg chambers. Indeed, he had been instrumental in getting that focus renewed more than fifty years ago when first he had come to realize what a fool he had been to ever serve the reptilian race.

But now, in the process of actually making use of those vital bits of information, the Gryphon questioned his sanity. Even if the Dragon Kings had not discovered his plan, he realized that fighting a mother dragon was very different from dueling with a male. This female was a veritable force of nature. Despite being larger than nearly any dragon of Clan Purple other than her mate, she moved abruptly with a fluidity that almost cost the lionbird his life. Her neck twisting in a manner no male could have managed, she brought her head around enough that if not for the Gryphon's own agility, she would have had him.

The huge teeth came within inches. Only by throwing himself toward her back did he manage to evade being decapitated. Even then, her hot breath almost suffocated him.

Aware that not only the success of the mission but the very lives of his companions depended on him, the Gryphon seized hold of one of the sharp plates running down the female's back. The sudden jerk nearly pulled his arm out at the shoulder, but he managed to hold on.

"Vermin! You'll not have them!" the dragon roared. "You'll not!"

While he understood her maternal instinct, the lionbird knew that he could not let such sentimentality turn him. He had every hope of keeping the eggs viable—destroying them did not suit his needs—but promising *her* that was hardly going to make the dragon cease her attack.

Out of the corner of his eye, the rebel leader saw his men moving in from both directions. Thus far, the dragon remained ignorant of their advances, but that could not last much longer. The Gryphon had to do something to keep her focused on him and him alone—

But the choice of just what to do was taken from him as a bolt of emerald lightning struck the leviathan square in the head. The dragon roared in agony and writhed so madly that she almost succeeded in dislodging her rider that way.

As the Gryphon desperately sought to strengthen his handhold, he saw Wade Arkonsson grimly standing just beyond the stalagmite barrier with his palms—still bright emerald—raised toward the female dragon. The Gryphon had only a moment to study the wizard's eyes before the dragon turned and obscured Wade from the lionbird's view, but it was long enough for the rebel leader to note the anguish and fury in that gaze.

Yalak and Dayn had kept a careful eye on those spellcasters who had lost loved ones to the drakes. They had adjusted the tasks of some of them—Micaya included—to prevent as much as possible any rogue activities. The Gryphon was well aware that Wade Arkonsson had been questioned more than once by Nathan's son and had only been entrusted with this part of the mission based on what had seemed Arkonsson's mental recovery from the death of his wife.

Now the lionbird saw that they had all been wrong. Wade took another step toward the barrier. As he did, he clenched both fists. A crackle of black energy shot from those fists and encircled the leviathan.

"Arkonsson, don't!" the Gryphon shouted. However, reprimanding the distraught mage availed the Gryphon little. The lionbird had to compensate for Wade's actions, which had unfortunately brought the movements of the rest of the rebels to the stricken dragon's attention.

"You will not have the eggsss!" she cried, immediately after exhaling.

A plume of flame streamed toward the fighters near the other stalagmites. The fighters there scattered...but two moved too slowly.

The screams filled the cavern, and though the Gryphon had feared that there would be casualties, those deaths still weighed heavily. The Gryphon silently cursed Wade's impetuous behavior while at the same time understanding just why the mage had launched his own attack. The lionbird knew that the wizard had not meant to endanger the rest, but, unfortunately, matters had not turned out that way.

"Die! Damn you! Die!" the furious spellcaster cried in turn as he struck anew. "Die!"

But despite Wade's not inconsiderable attempt to achieve his adversary's demise, the female dragon finally strained forward. Standing before the wizard, she exhaled yet again.

The mage barely strengthened his shield enough to prevent being reduced to ash. Sweating profusely, Wade pushed his own assault, but now it seemed that nothing he did had any effect on his foe. The dragon opened wide for a new, deadly burst.

The Gryphon, his weapon sheathed, reached into one of the pouches at his waist and pulled free a coiled line. Clutching tight, he swung one end free and sent it circling toward the dragon's throat.

The line wound completely around the thick neck, then tightened. As expert with a toss as the Gryphon was, the latter action was not his doing. The rebel leader was not above making use of magical tools and weapons and this sort had served him well, especially against dragons.

With a startled gasp, the giant female pulled up short. She grasped at the line, but when her claws touched it, she received a tremendous shock.

Pulling tighter, the Gryphon shouted, "If you try that again, the line will go right through your neck from front to back, flesh and bone all!"

The dragon hesitated.

Before she could make a decision one way or another, the lionbird continued, "I've no desire to damage the eggs and you will do them no good if I let this line do its grisly work!"

For a moment, there was silence. Quickly peering over the leviathan, the Gryphon cast a wary eye at Wade Arkonsson. Fortunately, the wizard held back from attacking, although from the expression the human wore the Gryphon did not trust that the reprieve would last long. He had seen men suffering as the wizard did, the loss of family often even too much for otherwise strong-hearted fighters. The lionbird still did not blame Wade, but hoped that the spellcaster would manage to refrain this time.

"What—will you do?" the female finally rasped.

"We will keep the eggs safe and secure. Let your lord deal fairly with us and I swear no harm will come of—"

Roaring, the dragon unexpectedly twisted around and tried to snap at the Gryphon. The line immediately tightened.

Blood spewed from the long, deep valley created by the magical line as it sank into the female's flesh. Even then, she continued to seek the Gryphon's death.

The desperate, suicidal act did what the dragon's previous efforts had not. Dislodged, the lionbird slipped down the behemoth's side. Hot blood from the gaping wound spilled over him as he dropped to the ground.

Despite the strength with which the line had been imbued, somehow the female still remained alive and conscious. Her long, tapering tail whipped about, smashing stalactites and stalagmites all around them. Yet, the tail ever avoided the vicinity of the eggs.

The Gryphon was about to order the others to abandon the mission while he kept the dragon at bay, but the wizard already had the fighters on both sides moving in on their goal. Wade himself stood beneath the dragon and the rebel leader, his face filled with concentration. The Gryphon could not see what spell the mage cast, but hoped it would keep anyone else from dying.

The female continued to thrash about. The lionbird remained astounded by her resilience. The line—a variation of the ones he had used on the drake warriors guarding the supply caravan—should have by now beheaded the leviathan or, at the very least, strangled her. Yet, despite everything, she kept moving and, worse, still finally managed to focus blood-shot eyes on what was happening to the eggs.

Letting out a gurgling sound, the dragon sought the men stealing the last egg. To her evident frustration, though, her claws instead grasped air as solid as rock. The dragon scratched at the invisible barrier, her claws causing ear-splitting scrapes that echoed through the chamber.

That no other drake had come thus far was not entirely a stroke of luck. Every bit of evidence the Gryphon had collected on the subject had indicated that the egg chamber was always guarded by the dominant female. All eggs, even those laid by lesser consorts, were considered *hers*.

More to the point, though, the high value of the eggs meant that to the drakes the less who knew the exact locations—including devious and ambitious heirs determined to eradicate any potential rivals—the better.

Still, only because each group had at least one mage to help cover their presence had the Gryphon hoped for any success. The lionbird prayed that the other teams had had better luck. If not...

The female dragon shimmered a bright mauve. At first, the Gryphon thought that it was due to something Wade was attempting, but a short glance at the wizard revealed him taken aback by the scene.

The Gryphon tried to shout to the mage, but now the fierce glow surrounding the behemoth overtook the rebel leader as well. A tremendous heat swept over the Gryphon.

This time, he managed to cry out to his companion. "Wade! Get them all out of here! Hurry! She plans to destroy us all!"

He could not tell whether or not Wade heard him, for again the female's writhing turned the Gryphon's view from the spellcaster. As that happened, the heat became sweltering and the gargantuan dragon shook in a new and even more violent manner.

Releasing his hold on the line, the Gryphon jumped from the behemoth's back.

The great beast *exploded*.

The massive tremor shook apart the chamber, sending tons of stone tumbling from the ceiling.

Dropping to the floor, the Gryphon rolled away. He had no idea why he was still alive considering the intensity of the blast. He also had no idea why the female had chosen such a death when it meant likely endangering the very eggs she wanted so badly to protect.

But those questions evaporated from his thoughts like a single raindrop misdirected into the Hell Plains as more of the ceiling came crashing down. The Gryphon could not make out if everyone else had escaped. He could only hope they had and pray that he found somewhere to shield himself before he was crushed to a pulp—

With that thought—and very much to his surprise—the rebel leader vanished.

BUT IF ANYTHING, his first thought upon seeing where he now stood made the Gryphon wonder if he would have been better off in the collapse.

21

MAGIC RISING

Gwendolyn had been unaware of the Gryphon's decision to move ahead with the attack on the City of Knowledge, but she easily sensed the tremendous powers at play far southwest of the Manor. Even then, despite the tremendous urge to join them, the enchantress remained at the ancient edifice. Gwendolyn had promised the Green Dragon that she would do whatever she could to help him try to locate Shade.

That Darkhorse supposedly pursued the transformed warlock no longer satisfied the drake lord. Through various means, the Dragon King had divined that Shade remained at large. Shade could shield himself well, but Lord Green had a number of methods at his disposal that Gwendolyn finally realized not even the Dragon Emperor had at hand, or rather, paw.

Gwendolyn herself was not at all surprised that Darkhorse had not caught the warlock. In fact, she would not have been surprised to find out that the demon steed and Shade worked together. The enchantress had no trust in the stallion despite the fact that others did.

Curiously, while the drake lord had performed some of his spellwork in his sanctum, much of his more intricate castings he had insisted doing in the Manor. Gwendolyn had some suspicions as to just why, but could not verify—

She suddenly sensed someone desiring entrance onto the Manor grounds. Lord Green needed no permission. Tensing, the fiery-tressed enchantress cautiously exited the ancient edifice.

At first, Gwendolyn saw no one, but as she approached the edge of the grounds, a familiar figure slipped out of the forest. One hand stretched before her, Camilla sought blindly for the hidden grove, unaware that each time she came within reach of the barrier, it directed her away.

Gwendolyn did not want to grant the drake entrance, but then she noticed that in the crook of Camilla's other arm the other female held a cylindrical container that bore the Green Dragon's magical trace. She knew immediately what it was, the master of the Dagora Forest having spoken of it when discussing his next attempt.

Once again, the enchantress felt another mind call out to her in hopes of being allowed into the Manor. This close, it was obvious that it was Camilla. More to the point, the female drake's thoughts were clear enough that now her purpose in being here made more sense.

His majesty wishes me to bring this here…let me in…I bring something at his majesty's command…

Gwendolyn knew that Lord Green still trusted Camilla, although the enchantress thought that in this respect the Dragon King was terribly mistaken. Unfortunately, there was nothing that the human could have said that would have convinced her former mentor otherwise.

With tremendous reluctance, Gwendolyn finally acquiesced. A simple thought and suddenly the Manor grounds lay revealed to Camilla.

The female drake gasped, then quickly recovered. She frowned at the enchantress. "I've been waiting out here some time. His majesty wanted this brought to you as soon as possible."

Camilla thrust the container at her. Gwendolyn remained casual in expression as she received it, even though the drake's natural strength meant that it was all the human could do to keep from being shoved back.

With one graceful movement, Camilla slipped past the enchantress. Gwendolyn hurriedly turned after her.

"His majesty spoke of an old book with a golden spine," the female drake remarked without looking back. "He said it lay on a shelf in some library room. You know it?"

Gwendolyn's mind raced. "Yes. I'll retrieve it for you." She managed to get ahead of Camilla, then turned to not only face the drake, but to block her path. "You can wait here."

Camilla bared her teeth—teeth that instantly grew into fangs—but did not press forward. She finally gave Gwendolyn a curt nod.

Daring to turn her back on the other female, the enchantress rushed back into the Manor. The sooner she could rid herself of Camilla's presence, the better.

But as she entered, Gwendolyn was struck by a new and much more welcome presence. She quickly turned to her left.

Nathan materialized. His physical appearance eradicated any pleasure that Gwendolyn felt at seeing him. Nathan looked extremely drawn, as if he had gone without eating for days. However, as a spellcaster, the enchantress recognized the look for what it actually meant. Had Lord Green been present, he would have exhibited traces of the same exhaustion.

Before she could ask exactly what he had been casting, Nathan stumbled toward her. As Gwendolyn held out her free hand to help steady him, the wizard seized her wrist.

"I'm sorry!" he blurted wearily. "It took more out of me than I thought it would even—even though he warned just that!"

"Nathan, what are you—?"

"No time! We've got to go!" Energies rose around the mage.

Before she could stop him, the Manor vanished...to be replaced by a glittering cavern whose stifling air and oppressive heat took the enchantress's attention from the source of that gleam.

"Nathan...why are we in the Hell Plains?"

"Because he can't sense us in this place. None of them, in fact."

The wizard leaned over a pattern set along the cavern floor. As Nathan put a stone in place, Gwendolyn's focus returned to the source of the cavern's illumination. One glance at the nearest wall was all she needed to understand why there was a sinister familiarity to her surroundings. "Those veins...those stones you're setting in place...are they—?"

"Yes. They're tied to the pieces within us." Nathan adjusted the one he had just placed on the ground, then stood up to look at her. "Help me make certain that these are all aligned properly. The moment I set this into play, Lord Red will definitely notice our presence."

Trusting to Nathan despite her lack of understanding, Gwendolyn joined the wizard as he shifted to the approximate center of the pattern he had created. Only when there did she notice that some of the stones had been altered by magic.

A bit of what Nathan had in mind finally occurred to her. It was enough to make her hesitate again. "Nathan...this will build up a field of energy so potent—"

"Let us hope so. It follows some of what Lord Purple did to create the original array..."

She did not miss the last two words. "Original? Has he actually completed the second you feared? Can—?" Gwendolyn recalled the utter obedience of the human spellcasters before Nathan had freed them by destroying the arcane device. Generation upon generation of wizard and enchantress had willingly sacrificed themselves for the drakes thanks to the diabolical array. "Nathan…"

"He can." Yet, the veteran mage hesitated. "He can…but I can't help feeling that he would have something more in mind than merely repeating the past…" With a shrug, Nathan turned to another stone.

At that moment, the chamber filled with other figures. Gwendolyn quickly formulated a defensive spell the moment she recognized both red drake warriors and their Jaruu servants.

Before the enchantress could cast, Nathan warned, "They're ghosts! Memories! Just like those at the Manor!"

Looking from one drake to another, Gwendolyn saw that he spoke the truth. The scaly warriors continued to disregard the two humans among them. The Jaruu likewise paid no mind, although their focus on their digging could have just as easily been explained by the drakes' brutal whips.

Gwendolyn watched with fascination until Nathan summoned her to him. He indicated a spot to his right.

"Stand exactly there. Don't deviate from your location once we begin. Not even an inch." When she took her place, he stared deep into her eyes. "Pray this works."

"What—what do you hope to do?"

Nathan began casting. "If Ethas was correct, I hope to turn a double-edged weapon to our advantage…providing Lord Purple hasn't already discovered the same flaw in his new array that I think I have."

The enchantress understood little of the explanation, but before she could ask Nathan to clarify, the wizard's spell overtook both of them. As that happened, Gwendolyn also felt him silently ask for her power, which she gladly gave.

The stone pattern flared bright. The veins in the cavern walls did likewise.

And as the chamber filled with a swirl of energy the likes Gwendolyn had never herself summoned—or believed any creature other than a drake lord could—even the ghosts seemed to pause in their endless toil, before their essences, too, became a part of Nathan's desperate plan.

CAMILLA WAS NOT a creature of patience like her lord and master. Indeed, she was much more akin in spirit to his heir whose marriage bond the female drake felt certain that she had nearly gained. With a promise that she would keep him apprised of all that his father did, Camilla had then maneuvered her way back into the good graces of the lord of the Dagora Forest. That had meant having to treat his favored human as if she were an equal, but for the sake of Camilla's own plans, the female drake had considered the play-acting worth it.

But now she wondered just where the damned human was?

With a frustrated hiss, Camilla slipped into the Manor. She had been here a handful of times in the past, but always as part of the personal retinue to Lord Green. Never had she—nor Duke Ssilan for that matter—been allowed to enter the legendary edifice alone. Lord Green did not trust them *that* much. He had assumed, rightfully, that the enchantress's presence would ensure that Camilla behaved herself.

But if Gwendolyn McArn had for some reason vanished from the Manor, then it certainly behooved Camilla to see to the fulfillment of her duties…even if she had to enter previously prohibited areas.

As she peered around the sprawling entrance hall, the female drake smiled dangerously. She had some time before her master wondered where she was. Time enough to investigate the seemingly empty building to her satisfaction.

And time enough to see if she could manipulate its barrier spells so as to make certain that both she *and* Ssilan could come here whenever it pleased them…

THE GRYPHON HAD no idea why he should end up near the damaged port just outside Lochivar's capitol, but he knew that to stay any longer than necessary was to risk not only capture or death, but very possibly a loss of his own will to the Black Dragon's desires. The rebel leader had no interest in becoming one of the drake lord's fanatic warriors.

Trying to keep his breathing as slow and calm as he could, the Gryphon weighed his options. The sea was out of the question, especially since three of the dark ships remained anchored in the harbor. Just seeing their silhouettes made the Gryphon's skin crawl, but why, he could not say. Not even a fragment memory served him now—

A different and far more ominous sensation abruptly coursed over him.

Whirling, he caught the armored figure at the throat before the latter's sword could cut him down. The helmed assassin grabbed at the dripping wound, then fell without a sound.

The Gryphon took no joy in his victory, not that time would have permitted him. Two more armed figures materialized around him, both with swords drawn. Yet, as threatening as the wolfhelmed men were, the lionbird somehow knew that they were only a decoy, that the actual danger lurked a short distance away.

He managed to draw his own blade just as both men attacked. They were highly skilled, not a great surprise for what he was certain was an unauthorized incursion into the Black Dragon's realm. The drake lord suffered the occupants of the dark ships for reasons the Gryphon did not know, but there was clearly no love lost between the 'allies'. These men—men, not drakes—had been willing to risk a volatile Dragon King's wrath more than once simply to strike at the Gryphon.

But why? Before he could delve again into that question, the rebel leader found himself being forced by his two assailants toward the source of the odd magic he sensed. A trap was coming into play, one he had only seconds to avoid.

Twisting in a manner that the armored men could not match, the Gryphon brought his foot under one foe. The assassin instinctively withdrew a step...just as the lionbird wanted. It gave him the chance to focus on his true target, the mysterious figure already casting some spell.

The rebel leader threw his sword with expert aim at the cloaked shadow. At the same time, the Gryphon rolled into his nearest physical foe, bowling him over. Shoving himself on, the Gryphon tumbled past all three figures.

He came up in a crouching position that left him facing the spellcaster. A crimson aura surrounded the bearded man, the only reason that the Gryphon's sword had not struck him squarely in the throat. With his acute senses, the Gryphon had the satisfaction of smelling a hint of nervous sweat on the figure.

The spellcaster closed his fist. Both the aura and he vanished into the night. The lionbird's sword dropped to the ground with a harsh clanging sound.

The Gryphon dove after the sword just as the foremost of his armed opponents tried to stab him through the back of the neck. Retrieving his weapon, the Gryphon spun to meet his foe. He deflected the still high blade, but then twisted his aim so as to sever the man's hand from his wrist despite the protective gauntlet.

That the assassin only grunted as he fell back to clutch his bleeding arm was a sign of the men's dread purpose. These wolf-helmed figures were at least as fanatic as the Black Dragon's warriors, but of their own volition, not because of some cloying mist that sapped their will and made it subservient to another.

That they attacked without fear of falling prey to the mists enshrouding Lochivar also meant that their own leaders had tremendous power upon which to call. Indeed, even now, the Gryphon could feel the returning presence of the spellcaster… along with what were certainly reinforcements.

Time and time again, Nathan and the others had insisted that the Gryphon was some powerful mage in his own right. Perhaps it *had* been his own abilities that had cast him from the egg chamber to Lochivar, but, if so, the lionbird found such abilities of dubious value. He had gone from one tremendous danger into another.

More than a dozen armored shapes abruptly surrounded him. Most wielded weapons, but now there were *two* of the cloaked figures, one in front and the other behind. This time, the assassins were taking no chance with him.

"You should have stayed drowned," muttered a voice that sounded so familiar to the Gryphon that he all but forgot the rest of his foes. "We shall remedy that—"

But suddenly the wind churned, spilling armored figures every-where. Only three of the assassins managed to keep their footing, the two spellcasters and—and someone who was not but was to the rebel leader's higher senses very well shielded against *any* sort of magic.

"Take him before he—" was as far as the last figure got before the swirling form of the mist dragon circled around the Gryphon.

"The ssscavenger cannot have thisss one…" the dragon hissed at the trio. "*You* cannot have thisss one…"

One of the spellcasters stumbled back in obvious fear. The third figure swore at him, adding, "Fool! This is but a shadow of him! The master has sealed him away! Strike!"

But before they could, the mist dragon spun harder. The wind he created pulled the Gryphon into the air.

The remaining spellcaster held forth his palm, where an odd talisman shaped almost like the fang of a large predator lay glowing. A stream of crimson light shot toward the lionbird and his protector.

The mist dragon only laughed. The reason why became apparent a breath later as the scene around the Gryphon vanished.

Barely had it done so than the rebel leader landed hard on a rocky shoreline the Gryphon estimated a short distance from Irillian by the Sea. The mist dragon unwound, then took up a position just above the edge of the water.

"They have too much trussst in you..." The creature snorted. "You should not have gone to that place, not with *him* there."

"Who?"

The mist dragon started to answer, then seemed to be unable to move his mouth. After a second attempt, the ethereal being shook his head. "I am not allowed to ssspeak, evidently. They have their gamesss, they do, even after ssso many millennia..."

The Gryphon no longer cared about whatever situation he had just been a part of. His men were in danger, perhaps even already dead. "I need to return to where I was before Lochivar. Send me back!"

"I never took you from there in the firssst place! That wasss your decision!"

While the lionbird could not exactly argue that point, he clearly did not have control enough of whatever power he had or else he would have never ended up near Skaln and the dark ships. "Can you set me somewhere near Penacles, at least?"

The creature eyed him with sudden curiosity. "You are not what even *they* think you are...or will be. I sssee that now. What you are—remainsss to be ssseen, I think."

Before the Gryphon could grow angrier, the mist dragon again encircled him. The lionbird rose from the sand, lifted into the air again by a means other than his own. Once more, he was reminded of the irony of not only the name someone forgotten had long ago given him, but his very appearance.

A mongrel I am...and hardly a master wizard...

A storm broke out. A storm where but a moment before there had been calm.

The raging wind that came with it ripped the mist dragon from the Gryphon. The creature roared a protest, but could not keep from being carried off out of sight.

Despite the loss of his companion, the lionbird did not fall to the ground. Now the storm carried him, although not in the direction the rebel leader desired. Instead, the fearsome winds sought to take him farther out to see.

And as the wind and storm took him, the Gryphon heard the whispering voices, voices that seemed to come from the very land itself, the very world itself.

Voices that seemed in argument over just what to do with him.

Away...away... some demanded.

To the city...to the city... insisted others.

Too dangerous...to the sea and be done with it... raged more.

The Gryphon knew the many legends of the Dragonrealm, knew of those concerning Shade, Darkhorse, the Dragon Kings, and much more. He also knew what some only whispered, that the very world itself was a thinking thing, a living thing, and all the creatures upon it living at its sufferance.

Whether or not this was that legend now proving itself fact, the Gryphon did not care. He was tired of being other people's pawns.

All he had ever asked was to be given his own chance to face whatever fate life itself had for him.

"*I will be...no one's puppet anymore!*" he roared at the voices. "No more!"

Lightning crackled. A bolt shot down where the Gryphon floated.

But by then, he was once more gone.

This time, when his surroundings came into focus, the Gryphon discovered he had gotten his wish. He had been returned to Penacles.

Returned to Penacles...but deposited in a place of corridor upon corridor of filled bookshelves.

The libraries...I'm in the libraries... he thought, stunned.

From behind him there came a voice. "Welcome...we've been expecting you."

He spun around to find a bald, gnomelike figure clad in robes that dragged on the floor. The Gryphon peered around, but saw no other figures.

Despite certain that he would regret the answer, the lionbird asked, "'We'?"

The gnome indicated the shelves...and especially their contents. Row upon row of thick tomes.

"We."

Books began rising from the shelves, rising until they could turn their opening pages to the Gryphon.

And on those opening pages, he saw his image repeated again and again.

LORD PURPLE GAZED into the scrying sphere he had summoned, noting each swiftly passing image with satisfaction. Some might have questioned his calm demeanor, for many of the images related to rebel strikes at the precious egg chambers...including that of his own clan. Yet, if anything, the master of the City of Knowledge appeared quite satisfied with all that transpired.

"Yesss...you will all fall to your knees in gratitude to me when this is revealed," he murmured, chuckling at the end. Not even Brown knew the extent to which Purple's plans went in guaranteeing both the end of the rebellion and Purple's own ascension to the imperial throne. "Sssavior of the Dragonrealm..."

The palace continued to shake as the so-called Dragon Masters aided the fighters in breaking through Penacles' magical and physical defenses. Both men and drakes had already perished seeking to keep the rebels from winning. That they died for something that would not—could *never*—happen did not bother the Dragon King in the least. Their sacrifices served him...and was not that all that mattered?

Even the destruction in his own clan's egg chamber had been foreseen...foreseen and even, to a point, *intended*. As with many—but not *all*—drake lords, Purple had more than one consort. She who had faced the rebels had once been his favored, but she had also been *Vuun's* mother and that alone had marked an end to her days. In his new empire, Purple intended to start with what the humans called a clean slate. His new favorite had, as if by destiny, already provided him with one egg with the rare markings designating it as a potential heir. *That* egg and its mother had long ago been secreted from everyone else.

As he dismissed the sphere, he paused to admire his own ingenuity. *Do not see the future...form the future.* Those were the words by which he and his predecessors had always ruled, but he believed that even they would have been surprised by the extent with which he had taken those words to heart.

And even they would not have been so audacious as to actually slowly and slyly guide the humans as *they* attempted to locate the egg chambers, feeding the information to generation after generation of researcher until someone made use of it.

"You seem in a good mood."

There was very likely only one being who could surprise the drake lord these days, but even that one did not startle Lord Purple at the moment. Despite all this planning having literally taken centuries, he had known that he could trust his most vital ally—or *puppet*, actually, the Dragon King corrected—to be here *exactly* when needed. "So, the message found you as intended?"

"He did plan well...and you, too, it seems. I am very grateful to benefit from both of you...and more than willing to pay for that benefit..."

Lord Purple turned to face—as best as anyone could—the warlock, Shade. The hooded figure bowed low.

"What shall I call you...this time?" Lord Purple asked.

"Wulfrin...and to what name do I owe all this?"

The drake lord turned from his sudden guest to where the new array slowly and patiently pulsated. "He called himself *Argaes*. One of your more—inventive—incarnations."

Shade straightened. "Not in terms of names, evidently. Argaes. I knew an Argaes once...I think." The warlock shrugged. "No matter." He raised a gloved hand and a golden goblet appeared. "I drink to him...and you."

"You sensed the array reach full alignment?"

"As suggested in the very thorough magical missive that materialized before me only a few minutes after I reformed." As the drake lord glanced up at the array again, Shade shuddered in remembrance of his resurrection. "I must admit to some admiration that you would expect me to be...of my current nature at so timely a moment."

This brought another chuckle from his host. "*Everything* was planned for...even your demise." Purple pointed at one stone in the array. It shifted slightly. Nodding in satisfaction, the towering Dragon King returned his attention to the spellcaster. "Nothing... and no one...acts without my having manipulated their decisions. Not humans, not drakes, not even ambitious, treacherous seneschals..."

Shade dismissed the goblet. "And even me?" Before Lord Purple could answer, the hooded figure waved off the need to do so. "The answer is of no concern. I have both manipulated and been manipulated far more than you can imagine...and usually by my previous lives. Only tell me this, master of the City of Knowledge; do you think that all this will aid me in *escaping* my curse?"

"Very much so. One way or another."

"So, you are saying that I *might* die...permanently?"

"Yes. There is great potential for that."

Shade rubbed his unseen chin. "And either way, whether I survive or not, many might also perish?"

"That is a certainty."

"Seems very reasonable to me." The warlock joined the drake lord, then suddenly laughed.

Despite himself, Lord Purple could not hide a brief sign of annoyance. "What ssso amuses you?"

"Just a thought that occurred to me. Nothing and no one acts without you having manipulated their decisions?"

"Asss I sssaid."

"*Even* this revolt by your precious spellcasters? I find myself doubting that you instigated that."

The Dragon King hissed. "A ssslight miscalculation which we will now correct."

Shade stepped below the center of the array. "I suppose it doesn't really matter so long as I either become the final incarnation of my accursed self through death or otherwise."

"You have my promissse—and yours—to that."

In response, the hooded figure raised his gloved hands.

The array flared a blinding red. Energy coursed down from it into the gloved hands and through Shade.

"Whenever you're ready, your majesty," he calmly spoke. "I'm eager to see—or not see—the results."

The Purple Dragon bared his sharp teeth in anticipation. In a few minutes, all he had dreamed for centuries would come to a head.

He stared at the array, his will becoming its.

The red deepened, changing to the color of blood. It quickly spread from Shade and the array to fill the room, then the rest of the palace.

And then…it washed over *everything*.

YALAK SAID NOTHING as the blood-red wave overtook the rebels and spellcasters before they could even draw a breath. He had foreseen something akin to this and knew what it meant to him and his comrades. He had lived and relived their deaths—*all* of their deaths—but had also seen that this was the one and only path that continued to promise a chance for the rebellion as a whole to succeed.

A pain such as Yalak could not have imagined if he had not already experienced it more than once in his visions ripped apart his insides. He felt the others suffering as well and his guilt deepened. He had placed their lives in the hands of one person. Not Nathan or Dayn, of course. Not Azran either, fortunately, although the visions Yalak had had concerning Nathan's youngest continued to puzzle and concern him. No, the fate of everyone now hinged on the Gryphon making the worst choice of all…to do *nothing* at the critical moment.

To do nothing, in the midst of raging war.

22

CREATURE OF
MANY CHAPTERS

Darkhorse kicked at the ground beneath him as he impatiently waited for the signal the wizard Nathan Bedlam had promised. The eternal sensed the incredible sorceries at work around the City of Knowledge, so much power that it disturbed even him.

Speak to me, wizard! Speak to me! But no word came from the human. Things were reaching a point where there would be no chance to stop what Nathan Bedlam had said the drake lord intended.

The shadowy stallion dug another valley in the dirt...then, with an impatient snort, Darkhorse raced toward the battle.

DRAW IT IN... *draw it in...* Lord Purple silently commanded the warlock as he surveyed the results thus far. With the new array and Shade linked, the Dragon King now had the ability to draw magic through each of the captive spellcasters and then amplify it. The culmination of calculations was now at hand.

A grunt of pain made him glance at Shade. The faceless warlock shook, but held his ground. For a moment, the drake lord thought he noted a strained but triumphant smile materialize. Lord Purple hissed in anticipation; whether the smile had been real or simply his imagination, the fact was still that, in moments, he would literally reshape the Dragonrealm.

First, though, he had to move a few last pieces in position. Reaching out, he touched Lord Brown's mind. *Now.*

Brown said nothing, but his eagerness was evident. Breaking contact, the Purple Dragon extended his gaze beyond the battle, beyond where the human spellcasters doubled over as they reached the edge of death.

There, the forces of Brown began to move...but not toward Penacles. Distracted by what was happening in Purple's domain, the true target would not realize the threat to him until it was too late.

Thinking of that, Lord Purple glanced toward his right. The one possible thorn in his side remained ignorant, his attention also fixed on the battle.

So, all is ready. I have but to take what the warlock devours.

He turned back to Shade. The warlock's entire body glowed brightly. Before the drake's eyes, the blurriness that was Shade's countenance...vanished. The true face of the legendary spellcaster lay revealed to the Dragon King.

How...ordinary... Dismissing the revelation, Lord Purple reached forward. His hand grazed the stiffened warlock's chest, then *sank* in.

The power flowed from Shade into the drake, but in a measured manner based on Lord Purple's desires. With what he intended, both the humans and Shade would literally burn out, but their sacrifices would serve to bring proper order to the Dragonrealm.

My realm will be a perfect one, an orderly one—

And then the voice of Nathan Bedlam echoed in the drake lord's head. *No, my lord…no empire for you today…*

NATHAN'S BODY GLOWED pure white. A heat radiated from him, one so intense that Gwendolyn, who worked to keep his spellwork in balance, had to increase her personal shields more than once.

They stood only inches from each other. The wizard's lips moved as if he spoke, but Gwendolyn heard nothing. She did not expect to hear anything, for any word Nathan had would be for one and one being only.

As for Nathan, he now stood in two places. Physically, he remained before the enchantress, but magically, he occupied a place between worlds, where both his physical location and Lord Purple's sanctum overlapped one another.

To his eyes, Gwendolyn Bedlam was a translucent phantasm through which he could make out an equally transparent Lord Purple. Their expressions were a study in contrasts, hers one of such deep concern for him that it made Nathan uncomfortable in a different manner than the fury the drake lord focused on him did.

Pure force struck the wizard hard, only Nathan's expectation of just that happening enabling him to be prepared enough to shrug it off. Even still, the sight *behind* Lord Purple almost distracted the mage enough that he barely deflected the second and more devious assault on his mind that the Dragon King cast immediately after the first.

What had brought Shade here, Nathan could not say. Clearly, the warlock was an integral part of the Purple Dragon's plot, which raised a number of questions the wizard knew he had no time to digest. In the end, Nathan knew that Shade's presence only meant that the mage had to be more than willing than ever to sacrifice everything and everyone if he hoped to salvage the rebellion.

Praying that he had succeeded in organizing what Ethas had never had the opportunity to do, Nathan concentrated on the array.

The result was both instantaneous and astounding...even more so because the wizard felt no resistance whatsoever from either adversary. Taking mastery of the array proved so simple that for a moment Nathan was taken aback by his success...which is when Shade struck back.

I will live or die by my choice! the warlock declared with such mad emphasis that Nathan's head pounded painfully. *I will not continue this curse!*

The warlock might have succeeded if not for Gwendolyn. Where Nathan faltered, the enchantress filled the gap. No, the wizard felt her more than fill it, sending Shade's mental assault reversing.

Unaware of her presence until her action, the faceless spellcaster reeled as his own monstrous attack overtook him. Shade shrieked as his body spewed acid from what seemed to Nathan every pore of his body. His garments blackened and burned and his flesh sloughed off, revealing seared bone and sinew save where Shade's curse still left his undoubtedly ruined face hidden from the sight of all.

Shade stumbled back, in the process separating from the array. The act further strengthened Nathan's hold on the array's power.

Lord Purple's mind separated from Nathan's. The drake lord reached a hand to the array.

One of the center stones tried to drift toward the Dragon King. Nathan felt the energies begin to pull away from him.

He focused. The stone returned to its place and the array's forces were once again the wizard's to command.

An angry growl arose from Shade's direction. As the warlock straightened, his skin healed and his clothing reformed. Despite his lack of features, the raw power stirring around him more than radiated the outrage the hooded figure felt toward both Nathan and Gwendolyn.

The wizard did nothing despite Gwendolyn's urging. So long as Nathan had control of the array, he could not shirk from his plan.

Shade thrust one gloved hand toward the array, his intent clear. Through it, he could burn Nathan's very mind and soul.

The wizard steeled himself, well aware that even with Gwendolyn's support, this strike by Shade would likely be too much for either of them to stave off.

But help came in the unexpected form of the drake lord, who, with a swing of his hand, threw a glittering rain of emerald spikes at his supposed allies. Shade reacted instinctively, turning his hand toward the Dragon King.

A mist shot forth and enveloped the spikes. Lord Purple's missiles dissolved in the mist with as much swiftness as Nathan suspected that his flesh would have.

The sudden shift in the battle gave Nathan the final breath he needed. He caused the stones in the array to adjust to match the pattern that he had set on the cavern floor.

Lord Purple's creation flared once...then faded away.

It had not ceased to exist, though. Instead, it now floated above the wizard and Gwendolyn, its component stones still creating a three-dimensional match to the pattern on the ground.

Nathan immediately cut all links to the palace. Trusting to the cavern's natural shielding abilities to keep him from Lord Purple's probes—at least for the time the wizard needed—Nathan turned his attention to his fellow spellcasters...and, especially, Yalak and Dayn.

This is our one chance...the Sunlancers must prepare themselves...

YALAK EXHALED WITH relief as the agony he suffered suddenly ceased and instead a sense of rejuvenation filled him. Never in his entire long life had he felt so well, so powerful. Not even when Nathan had coordinated the spellcasters' efforts to free themselves from the original array.

We are ready, he immediately answered. Only twice had he ever called upon the ability that labeled him and select other spellcasters as Sunlancers. Even the drastic needs of the rebellion had only demanded the second of those times and that in a desperate attack in which Yalak had only had himself to depend upon to save more than a hundred souls.

Give thanks to Kylus, then, Nathan answered, *and maybe Lord Purple, too…*

The irony was not lost on Yalak as he stretched out his arms as if holding something. The next second, a bow of *light* formed in his grip.

Yalak glanced at Kylus—the sun—and marveled in its energies. No spellcaster, be they human, drake, or Shade, could long safely touch its energies and make use of them. The primal forces were such that even the energies of the world no more than a shadow in comparison.

Basil, Tyr, Salicia, and a handful of others responded to both Nathan's and Yalak's warnings. Each held their gleaming bows ready.

Take all that you can, Nathan asked.

The array's energies filled the chosen spellcasters, but did not give them what they needed to fulfill their roles as Sunlancers. Rather, Nathan utilized the array's powers to enhance his comrades' abilities to draw from the sun as they never could have before without leaving of themselves nothing but blackened shells.

Aware that they had limited time despite this gift, Yalak pulled back the 'string' of his bow. *Sunlancers* was a misleading term to him, although he understood how it had come to be used by first unTalented humans and others and then by those few special wielders themselves. As Yalak concentrated on Kylus, the fiery arrow formed, already nocked.

Without hesitation, he fired. The other Sunlancers followed suit.

Even despite the power of the sun behind them, the wizards could only have hoped in vain for their bolts to penetrate the shields created through the arcane spells of the libraries by Lord Purple. The Dragon King had also made use of Kylus' power in casting the shields, making them impervious even to the fiery shafts.

But with the array now involved, all that changed. As the magical arrows reached the shields, they passed through without any pause.

Despite having seen this possible outcome among the many less desirable ones, Yalak could not help but shout in relief. Not only did the burning arrows continued their swift flight, but as they passed through the shields, they doubled, then tripled their lengths. Their points grew wider, yet sharper. Now they revealed the reason why so many had come to call those who cast them as *lancers*.

Yalak could no longer physically see the shaft, but through his link to it he followed its route. In its line of sight appeared a row of armored figures. Most of them were human and were thus ignored by the wizard.

The drake leading them, however…

The scaled warrior saw the missile descending and immediately created a steel shield before him that Yalak estimated had to be at least four inches thick. Unfortunately for the drake, it might as well have been woven from straw. Yalak's bolt perforated the barrier and then did the same to the startled drake's armored hide.

The stricken warrior shook, then collapsed. As he fell, the mage's bolt faded away and a new one formed in Yalak's bow.

He wasted no time in firing again. There were many, many targets…too many. Yet now, at least, Yalak actually thought that the rebels had a chance…

That is, *if* the Gryphon still followed the difficult path the veteran wizard hoped he would.

"I DON'T UNDERSTAND this at all," the Gryphon growled as he stared at the open books.

The gnome looked sympathetic. "Yes, it would be confusing. It confused me at first, too."

"Who are you exactly?"

The short figure shrugged. "A librarian."

The lionbird fixed one eye on the robed form. "And before that?"

The librarian gestured at the hovering books. "You would do best to listen to them."

Despite aware that the gnome was trying to distract him, the Gryphon could not help but turn his attention to the fluttering tomes. "Listen?"

"Listen…"

At first, the rebel leader heard only what he expected. The pages of each of the flying books flipped from beginning to end and end to beginning over and over. Despite that, each continued to display the Gryphon's image, as if every page in every book carried the same illustration.

But as the Gryphon concentrated, he began to hear more than the rippling of parchment. Instead, a single word that sounded as if some wind spoke caught his interest. It was followed by another and another…until coherent sentences formed.

Creature of many chapters, creature of many stories, the tale of you is now a part of us…

The voice came from everywhere, its many facets the combination of each fluttering book. The Gryphon cocked his head in astonishment and confusion.

"What by the Dream Lands do you mean?" he asked before realizing that once again he had used some oath whose origins he did not recall.

This tale takes different pages, different volumes...but must have one chapter end here...

The lionbird grunted. "You wouldn't mind being a little clearer, would you?"

As if not hearing him, the books continued. *The chapter relies on a new page, a rewritten page...*

One of the ancient tomes separated from the rest. Its cover a deep azure, it positioned itself arm's length from the rebel at a height equal to the Gryphon's chest. The pages flipped back and forth, and as they did, the lionbird's image faded.

The book's pages ceased moving. Despite that, the book did not fall. Instead, it hung in the air, two pages revealed.

Words filled the left page, words written in a script that the Gryphon could not read yet felt he should know.

The right page was blank.

The Gryphon waited for the other tomes to continue speaking, but rather than do that they also merely hovered.

That left him only the gnome as a source of information. "So what am I supposed to do—?"

Of the librarian there was no sign.

Clacking his beak in frustration, the Gryphon grabbed for the book in front of him. He expected it to move from his reach, but instead it fell into his grip as if waiting just for this moment.

Turning the pages, the lionbird found more of the same indecipherable script. He finally turned back to the blank page.

No...not entirely blank. In the center had been set what appeared to be a dot...a *period.*

Curiosity getting the best of him despite his exasperation, he touched the lone spot with one finger—

The dot swelled. Symbols spilled from it, spreading over the page. Words in the same odd script scattered over the empty parchment, but where the Gryphon expected them to spread across the page, instead, they suddenly swirled toward the hand holding the book.

The Gryphon quickly released his hold…only to find the book remained clutched in his hand. He shook the ancient tome as hard as he could, but his fingers would not let go.

The words touched his fingers, then *crawled* up his hand like an eager swarm of ants.

Cursing, the lionbird tried to brush them off. Unfortunately, that only served to allow the words to scurry up his other arm as well.

The moment the first word touched his face, a sharp pain coursed through the Gryphon's head. He tried in vain to twist away, but the words continued to pour over his beak, his temples…everywhere. Worse, they did not simply crawl over his skin, but rather began to *burrow* under it.

And as they burrowed, not only did the Gryphon's pain magnify…but his face—his entire body, for that matter—began to transform.

His shape became more human. His countenance shifted from avian to that of a stern man with aquiline features. Yet, barely had that face materialized than another took over, this one a more animalistic, more savage. It resembled that of the Gryphon, yet with more feral features and eyes in no manner mistakable as human. Some would have recognized it as the face of the creature after which the rebel leader had named himself.

Even this snarling visage did not last. As the Gryphon howled his agony, his eyes and beak sank out of sight.

Silence momentarily filled the libraries, silence still marked by the futile struggles of the lionbird. Now, though, he had no features whatsoever. In fact, his entire head was devoid of any marking or hint of hair.

And then...the face that Nathan Bedlam had briefly seen, the face of a founder, shrieked into being. It held a few seconds longer than the rest, unleashing all its pain to the endless corridors of books.

The Gryphon dropped to his knees. As he did, the series of faces reversed, shifting from one to the next with twice the speed with which they had first appeared.

When his own visage finally returned, the words abruptly spilled out of his mouth and flowed back to the book. Gasping, the Gryphon glared at the open pages as the script again circulated over the empty side. This time, though, they lined up, soon creating a page of writing akin to the one on the left.

The book fluttered to the librarian, who caught it with ease. The gnomish figure looked slightly ill at ease, but the Gryphon doubted that the other felt anything near the strain that the rebel leader did.

"Now the libraries know you—" the librarian started.

The book blackened.

Gaping, the gnome threw the book away. As the tome hit the floor, it shattered, spilling ash everywhere.

"That is not possible..." the librarian finally managed to declare. "That *cannot* happen! It has *never* happened!"

The Gryphon glared at the robed figure, but before he could utter the scathing epithet on his tongue, a different voice emerged from his beaked mouth. It spoke in a tongue that the Gryphon did not know.

The librarian, on the other hand, seemed to at least recognize it. More significant to the lionbird was the reaction by the libraries itself. The books fled to their shelves, leaving only the gap where the ruined tome should have sat. The Gryphon not only noted the silence that followed the end of the mysterious words he had just spoken, but even *felt* it.

"You are—you are—" the gnome sputtered.

"I am me. No one else..." the lionbird demanded as he straightened. "No one...and no one's puppet..."

His companion shook his head. "You have no idea what you mean by that! The libraries must have—"

A warmth filled the hand with which the rebel leader had first held the book. The Gryphon glanced at his furred palm.

It was glowing.

He looked to the gnome, but the swiftness with which the gnome began backing away from him was evidence enough that this was yet something else not planned by the libraries. Around him, the shelved books shook as if some quake rocked the vicinity...but where the lionbird stood, the ground was as still as death.

"But *they* chose *you*," the librarian murmured to him. "*They* chose *you*..."

"No," responded the Gryphon in a voice that was both his and the same one that Nathan had heard in the icy cavern. "*I* chose *him*...although *many* think they did, including the wolf..."

He left the gnomish figure no time to try to puzzle out what the last statement meant. Instead, the Gryphon and his other self turned to face the wall behind him, the only place in the libraries where there were no books.

And at that spot, a cloud of mist formed before him. The dragon bowed his head.

"I felt your sssummonsss....I did not expect it..."

"They did not expect me to stand with him..." the second voice in the Gryphon responded.

"Who are you?" the lionbird immediately after asked himself. "Who are you?"

"I am you...and we are at our moment to change all."

"I live to ssserve..." the mist dragon murmured.

The Gryphon's head shook. "You will not serve. I need you to stand as an equal."

If the mist dragon could have preened, he would have. "I am honored..."

Once more, the lionbird forced himself into the conversation. "Just what do 'we' plan to do?"

His other self merely replied, "You know."

And the Gryphon suddenly discovered that he *did*.

The fur and feathers on not only his neck but over the rest of his body stiffened in fear...fear for not himself, but for everyone else in or near the City of Knowledge. "No..."

"It must be done," his other self said. "I see it now. They—" One hand swept back toward the books. "—have proven that to me... to us."

Books suddenly began flinging themselves off the shelves toward the Gryphon and the dragon. However, the same hand that had just gestured now made a simple flipping motion.

A fearsome wind threw the books back. They collided with one another, then fell into a great pile.

"Yes," the second voice insisted. "It must be done...even though it may doom the entire City of Knowledge...and all in and those near it."

And with that, the Gryphon and his other self vanished from the libraries.

"No, no, no..." muttered the librarian as he sought to make order. "No, this cannot be..."

"And it will *not* be," promised another.

The gnome glanced at the mist dragon, who had not yet followed. "You obey him! Why say it will not be...?"

The mist dragon sighed. "Becausse in thisss particular regard... my loyalty musssst be to another."

"What will you do, then?"

Reptilian features twisted into an expression of self-loathing. "I will have to ssslay thisss amalgamation of animal, man, and ghossst who has jussst left us..."

The mist dragon faded away. The librarian brooded over the revelation for a moment...and finally smiled grimly.

23

THE HAND
OF THE FOUNDER

Lord Brown's forces surged into the portals as commanded, their eager master at the forefront. The Dragon King wielded no visible weapon, but a surge of magical energy surrounded him as he prepared to cast the integral spell. He would have only a few critical moments at best to achieve his goal. His forked tongue darted out as he anticipated the battle ahead.

The cavern he sought lay open before him. He readied his spell—

And then the drake lord gasped.

SHAME FILLED WADE Arkonsson as he managed to bring the last of the men and their meager prizes back to the wilds near Pagras. His shame did not lessen in the least when he saw some of the others returning from their ventures with even less than his party. The widowed mage doubted that any of his counterparts had acted with such foolishness as he had. Men had perished because of him.

"Kirsa!" he shouted, drawing the attention of a pale, blond enchantress with shoulder-length hair. "Take my charges! I have to leave!"

"But Wade—"

It was too late. Even as the first words escaped her lips, she found herself talking to empty air.

A DEAFENING CACOPHONY accompanied an equally breathtaking display of magical force above and around the walls of Penacles. The golden bolts of the Sunlancers wreaked havoc on previously impregnable shields, and in the wake of that attack, the physical efforts of the rebels under Toos began to show progress. Siege weapons brought in through blink holes at last proved their worth as massive stones shattered one area of the wall after another.

With no word coming from their master, the drake officers were left with the desperate task of defending what had never needed to truly be defended before. However, with the Sunlancers taking their toll on those very same officers, some of the survivors at last chose desperate measures.

Roaring a challenge, the first fearsome dragon rose above the city. His challenge to the rebels was echoed by a second and a third behemoth following in his wake, each scaly leviathan then choosing a different direction to assault.

Yet, before the first dragon could breathe upon the tiny figures below, Yalak directed those Sunlancers nearest to fire on the leviathan. While aware of his vulnerability to the fiery arrows when in a humanoid form, the dragon now laughed at the puny missiles. In addition to his thick, natural armor, the dragon glowed with spells designed to make it impervious to *any* weapon, magical or otherwise.

But to the giant's surprise, the flight of arrows sank readily into his hide. The magical bolts not only pincushioned the gaping leviathan, but hit him with such force that he was shoved all the way back over the city wall.

Hacking briefly, the dragon eyes glazed over and his wings stilled. No longer held aloft, he dropped like the proverbial rock. That he was already dead before he hit the ground was of little comfort to the defenders manning that part of the wall. The huge corpse not only crushed them, but utterly destroyed the high barrier at that point.

The second dragon managed a burst at the attackers coming from the west. Despite the efforts of two mages stationed nearby, several brave men perished. Although Yalak mourned them, he knew with certainty from his visions that it could have been much, much worse. With more Sunlancers able to focus on the second behemoth, a second blast proved impossible for the dragon as another wave of magical bolts targeted him.

The great beast immediately veered off, his effort enabling him to evade the arrows. Yet, as he arced around to face the rebels again, the arrows, rather than dropping, turned as one toward the unwitting dragon.

The flight ripped the behemoth's webbed wings to shreds. Other bolts buried themselves in the struggling dragon's back. Two last shots—one of them Yalak's—bore through the thick skull, finishing the behemoth off.

As the second dragon died, rebel forces moved in on the ruined parts of the wall. Many in the initial ranks fell, but in the process, they bought valuable ground for those behind them, finally enabling the attackers to do what few could have ever thought possible—breach the walls and actually enter Penacles.

DAYN FIRED ANOTHER shot, but before he could prepare a new blazing bolt, something caught his attention. He immediately focused his thoughts on the wizard to his left. *Solomon! I need to separate from the link! Can you compensate?*

I've got it, lad! Do whatever you need to! Not for a moment was there a hint from Solomon Rhine that he wondered why Dayn would break from the battle at this juncture. To most of the other spellcasters, Dayn was Nathan's son not only in blood, but in trustworthiness. If Dayn needed to be elsewhere, then it had to be for reasons essential to the cause.

That knowledge left Nathan's eldest feeling very guilty as he reappeared on a hill to the north of Penacles and well behind where the rest continued their crucial efforts. Rhine and the rest trusted in Dayn. They believed that he was now on some crucial mission, perhaps at the behest of his father.

The last might have had some bit of truth in it, if Dayn dared stretch the definition of the word. Dayn *had* left the battle for a reason that would have been of definite interest to his father...and that reason stood not all that far from where Dayn now hid himself by means of a carefully crafted spell.

A few yards ahead, *Azran* stared at the violent tableau. Dayn could tell that his brother surveyed the struggle for Penacles by both visual and sorcerous means. It was the latter that had alerted Dayn to Azran's sudden presence nearby. The elder brother still recalled Azran's deadly leap into battle the first time he had wielded that unsettling sword still clutched in his hand.

Azran abruptly vanished. Dayn hesitated, caught between concern for what his brother had in mind and the need to tell his father. Then, aware he had no real choice, Dayn, too, vanished.

THE STRAIN WAS beginning to tell on Nathan. Despite that, not for a moment did he think about giving in to his exhaustion. Doing so was not a choice. That direction only meant doom for everyone.

He felt the others continue their relentless assault on Penacles and marveled that the wall he had grown up thinking impervious to any foe now seemed to be crumbling much easier than he could have imagined. The protective barrier had been breached in at least three places, enabling the rebels to begin pushing inside. Even more significant, the greatest defenses the city offered—the drakes and their magical attacks—had been readily countered by the Sunlancers and other spellcasters. Everything pointed to the rebels succeeding in doing the unthinkable…capturing Penacles and thus perhaps tilting the overall war to their favor.

And yet, Nathan continued to fear the worst, fear it because he knew that his former mentor could not be that easily defeated. Lord Purple had something in mind, something that—

But it was not the Dragon King that struck again at Nathan with such force that he nearly lost control of the vital spell.

No, the icy touch in Nathan's soul could only belong to the warlock, Shade.

The attack from within did not startle Nathan. Not for a moment had the wizard forgotten the shrouded figure. In fact, he *needed* a link to the warlock's unsettling magic. Only it would enable him to do what he needed to finish this.

Nathan! Gwendolyn called as he began his final effort. *What are you doing?*

In response, he severed the tie with her. If his plan backfired, Shade's spell would utterly consume him.

The array and its counterpart on the ground shifted, stones swiftly moving into new positions.

Nathan struck—

And to his shock, *everything* stopped. Everything...his spells, the one he felt Shade beginning to cast...even those being shaped by the Dragon Masters and their drake adversaries. Every spell, small or fearsome, had been usurped.

But not by the one he would have expected to do just this. Not Lord Purple. The Dragon King was no more free of what was happening than the wizard or Shade.

Instead, Nathan realized the spellcaster who held all of them in thrall...was none other than the *Gryphon*.

"YOU BROUGHT THIS on yourselves," the Gryphon—or rather that *other* part of him—stated to the darkness surrounding them. The Gryphon himself had only a vague idea where he—*they*—were, that information slowly creeping into his thoughts from his other self. "The attack in the libraries was the final transgression on your parts. This has now gone into realms the likes of which we *never* agreed. This is *betrayal* of our ultimate goal..."

There was no response, although it seemed to the Gryphon that his other side *did* hear something. A mirthless laugh briefly escaped their beak.

"Cease your protests and efforts to resist. You can do nothing. Everything is in check. It did not have to come to this. We had a plan, a future..."

With that, the Gryphon's left hand rose. As it did, the lionbird himself briefly glowed.

The darkness fell away...and through a single pair of eyes they beheld the seated figures.

There were fifteen in all. They sat in chairs that the Gryphon believed were carved from diamond or at least something that glittered as spectacularly. All faced into the center of the engraved pattern upon which their great chairs had been set.

And all had clearly been dead for many, many centuries.

"Many, many millennia," the rebel leader's other half corrected the Gryphon's stunned thought. "Millions of years…"

"How—how is that possible?" The corpses sat as if having just recently fallen asleep. They all had the same look to them, the beautiful yet inhuman cast that the Gryphon now knew marked them as members of the nameless founding race.

"We once had a name…I've forgotten it, though…as have the rest, I believe." The Gryphon's head turned to survey a few of the bodies. Particular features became apparent. No longer were these merely legendary beings to the rebel leader, but rather real individuals.

No gods these, he thought. *Certainly not infallible ones…*

"Yes, we made many mistakes, first in our beliefs about how our world worked, then in what we thought was best for it. A trait, I am sorry to say, passed on to most of our children…"

The other self was not referring to young born of the womb or even the egg, but rather entire *races* created from the imagination of such as these fifteen. That the Gryphon knew this surprised him despite being more and more aware of how his thoughts and those of the other entity within blended together.

"The world was no longer fit for us. We had aged beyond it and it beyond us. If we let things go on, both we and the world would die. We knew that with our great power we could see the world rejuvenated…but not so ourselves. Yet, in our arrogance, we were certain that we could create from our essence that one race that would inherit all and thus, to our conceit, give us the immortality we thought we deserve." Another humorless laugh escaped. "As if we deserved such…"

"What—what is all this?" the Gryphon managed. "What were they doing here under the city?"

"Not under the city...ever under the *libraries*..." The same usurped hand pointed from the dead to the cavern ceiling. "Ever under the libraries, no matter where that structure moves. A nexus of power, arranged like so many around the world, all created to rebirth this world and populated with those who proved sufficient to be our successors...until there came disagreement on the actual path to that supposed triumph..."

Ever under the libraries, the lionbird thought with growing concern.

His head nodded as the other entity used it to agree. "Yes... the Vraad sorcerer thought that *he* had discovered a place where his sanctum would be able to draw upon power and make him the strongest of all. He never suspected that he was purposely drawn to the location and purposely encouraged to create the structure to the specifications that he did."

A vision flashed before the Gryphon's eyes, a vision cast by his other self. He saw a familiar, gnomish figure who could be none other than the librarian with whom he had just spoken. Yet, in the vision, this was no simple servant of the books. Rather, here was a sorcerer on par with Nathan Bedlam or Shade.

Indeed, there was something in the bald sorcerer's countenance that reminded him of the warlock despite the latter having no visible features. It was in the attitude, the sense of superiority that not even the Dragon Kings for the most part radiated.

"Yes, we thought the Vraad most potentially like us," the founder within him remarked, "and that is why, before their sphere could reach maturation and release them into the world...we rejected them. They were supposed to stay sealed inside their little world, but like vermin, they found their way here, this one the first."

As the Gryphon listened—or rather, was forced to—he kept in mind that men still died outside. Each moment here meant that more lives would continue to be lost. The knowledge ate at him more and more with each breath, yet, when he tried to seize control of his own body, everything ignored him but his eyes and mouth.

"It will not be much longer. Soon, this will be corrected."

The rebel leader did not like the sound of that, nor did he like the sense of unease filling the chamber immediately after...unease that he realized originated from the still forms seated before them.

"I am not alone in this," his other self informed the ancient figures. "There must remain unanimity in all this. We have sacrificed too much."

The Gryphon was beginning to realize that the presence that was part of him might not necessarily be an ally after all. Struggling for control of the voice—the *first* time he had been forced to struggle—the Gryphon rasped, "Just what are you intending? How are you going to make this—this *correction?*"

It was with the greatest ease that the other took command of their voice again. "The wizard and the Dragon King have provided the way, with assistance from the necromancers and our prime pawn—your faceless friend."

Had their body belonged solely to the lionbird—as he continued to feel it *should*—the rebel was positive that the hair and feathers on his neck would have stiffened. That the entity could have relied on so much coincidence, on so many unpredictable characters coming together in just the right manner, did not seem possible to the Gryphon.

"Human, drake, Vraad...you all share the same trait we managed to purge from ourselves when we left our mortal forms. *Ego* can help one accomplish astounding things...and it can also make one the perfect puppet." As he spoke, the founder took them toward the center of the pattern. The sense of unease magnified. "Prod them a little bit and each believes he has made this war for his own benefit."

Lightning could not have struck the Gryphon with more force than understanding finally did. He had been correct to assume that too many factors had been involved for all this to come together so timely for the entity.

"Yes," the other answered to the Gryphon's silent fears. "You would do well to continue to remember that *nothing* happens that we do not master. *Nothing* happens that we do not desire."

The rebel's mind whirled. What the spirit indicated was that everyone continued to be pawns of his kind, even down to the decisions that they believed they had made at the last moment. Not even Shade appeared to be immune to their machinations; Shade, often believed a master manipulator in his own right.

The founder glanced at the bodies as he grimly continued, "And no deviation is permitted, not even from among our own."

The reaction to his words shook the Gryphon. From the surrounding seats, robed forms with gaping mouths and empty eyes rose and reached for the rebel leader. Yet, the animated corpses did not try to physically grasp the lionbird. Instead, from their fingertips they unleashed eldritch energies he knew were meant for his other self...not that the undead figures cared a whit that the rebel would also suffer.

But the attack never reached the Gryphon, for some invisible force not only repelled it, but sent the energies darting back at their casters. The fifteen corpses shook and twitched in what the lionbird believed surely had to be intense pain despite their macabre state. One by one, they dropped back into their seats like limp dolls.

It did not end there, though, for the bodies continued to settle, swiftly sinking into the seats.

"There is, after all, one way to ensure death with us," the rebel's other half murmured, "or something so equivalent to it that the differences do not matter."

Some of the bodies attempted to reach forward again, this time as if seeking some hold to prevent themselves from being drawn into the diamond chairs. If that was truly their hope, though, they failed miserably. The chairs engulfed them, sealing them like insects in amber.

"That is settled, then," the entity declared with only a hint of satisfaction. "Now there only remains a final cleansing in order to set everything on its correct course again."

A cleansing? The Gryphon had no question whatsoever as to what his other half meant by that. With every ounce of will that he could muster, the rebel leader tried to regain complete control over his body...tried and failed.

"You are strong...we are stronger..." The founder spread their shared hands wide, as if attempting to take in the entire pattern. "This is what must be done...you will have to accept it—"

"We have accepted too much...far too much..."

The words were not the Gryphon's, but rather did belong to someone who he had come to know too well already. Yet, as distrusting as he was of that speaker, the lionbird knew that here now materialized his only hope.

The mist dragon wrapped himself around the Gryphon, the smoky tendril that was the lower half of his body tightening painfully across the lionbird's chest. The Gryphon suddenly felt as if he were being ripped free from his own body.

And so, too, evidently, was his darker half. For a moment, the lionbird saw the figure of the founder next to him. Between the pair, the rebel noted, was the blank-featured form.

But then the Gryphon felt the entity draw them back together. The mist dragon's hold failed.

"I was wrong about you," the founder murmured at the dragon. "You are nothing...and so shall you be..."

The dragon exhaled. A heavy fog enveloped the lionbird.

The fog faded away. A moment later, with a frustrated hiss, so, too, did the mist dragon. However, the creature did not do so of his own volition.

"We should have dealt with them rather than left them to tend to our legacy," the entity remarked about the vanquished dragon. "They have grown too confident with the power that *we* granted them...like so many others..."

Before the Gryphon could react, his view altered. Not the actual surroundings—for he could still make out the chamber of the dead as a vague background image—but rather what his other half *chose* to see.

The snarling, helmed visage of Lord Purple confronted them. At the same time, the weary but determined face of Nathan Bedlam filled their gaze. The two adversaries appeared to fill the same space, but the Gryphon quickly saw that they were in two different locations.

Then, behind the Dragon King, another being materialized. Unlike the wizard and the drake lord, this one seemed very aware that other eyes observed all.

Shade's expression might have been lost to his curse, but his stance easily betrayed his emotions. The deadly warlock recoiled as if in fear.

"You...no...I will not be taken! I will not!"

Both Lord Purple and Nathan Bedlam reacted to Shade's cry, especially the drake lord, who appeared to be in the same room. The Purple Dragon turned as if to say something to the hooded warlock...but Shade had already disappeared.

"He will serve again, as he has since the beginning," the founder reflected briefly. "He has been an excellent pawn..."

With that cryptic remark, the entity returned his attention to both the other two. The Gryphon felt both fight against the founder's power, fight but fail.

"It is time for your little war to end and for the world to be set right," the entity informed Nathan and the drake lord. "Know that in your own way, you have both served well."

Neither the wizard nor Lord Purple seemed satisfied with such a declaration, both continuing to fight futilely against the entity's power. Without even so much as a flick of the Gryphon's fingers, the founder turned the complex matrices to his benefit.

"The plan will be set right. The world will be set right."

The lionbird's hand rose in what he knew from his other half's thoughts was the next to last step in the monstrous spell not only this founder but the majority of the other ancient spirits had chosen to set the world as they desired. In the Gryphon's mind, a horrific tableau unveiled itself, a world where both humans and drakes simply no longer existed. It was a virgin world open to what race the founders chose to next inhabit their former home.

A virgin *world*. Not simply a continent cleansed of its two major races. To the Gryphon was revealed a glimpse of a staggering arrangement of towers and citadels hidden throughout the world that had enabled the founders to first set into motion their original mad, complex plan—and that still continued to allow them to manipulate one successive species after another.

Stirred by the horror of what was about to take place, the Gryphon made one last, futile effort to stop his other self.

Only…the effort proved *not* so futile. The hand stilled.

A sense of displacement such as the Gryphon had experienced during the mist dragon's failed attack filled the rebel leader. The lionbird wondered if perhaps the dragon had not failed after all.

His head pounded as the founder sought to take control once again. Yet, with a mere shrug, the Gryphon forced the entity deep into the recesses of his mind, where it continued to struggle in vain to reestablish itself as master of their body.

But as the Gryphon sought to come to terms with his sudden victory, he was painfully reminded that there were other players in the game. The fury of the Purple Dragon struck him. The power that the entity had taken began to slip from the lionbird to the drake lord.

And worse, so very worse, only then did the Gryphon sense that the spell the founder had been casting had continued on despite the lionbird's interference. It not only continued on, but a breath later fell under the mastery of a new caster.

The lord of Penacles now held not only the fate of the City of Knowledge in his hands...but, unwittingly, the entire Dragonrealm and beyond, as well.

24

THE GRYPHON CHOOSES

Duke Toma heard the thundering crash outside, and even though he was deep in the palace, he knew exactly what it meant. The wall surrounding the City of Knowledge had been shattered in at least one place. The emperor's son hissed. *Nothing* should have been able to bring down the wall, not with all the power Penacles's master supposedly wielded.

Self-preservation suggested that he immediately depart Penacles, but doing so before being absolutely certain that the city would fall would only remove him from his father's favor. Lacking the damned birth markings that should have rightly made him heir to the imperial throne, Toma had done his best to make himself indispensable to the Gold Dragon. No one had the emperor's ear as much as Toma did, which was why he had been sent here in the first place.

The young drake slipped from the chamber that served as his personal quarters and returned to the nearest window facing the bulk of the battle. The change from when last he had peered out— that barely ten minutes before—was remarkable. Toma had sensed the incredible shift of magical forces, but actually seeing them again made him hiss in consternation. His forked tongue darted out and again the thought of departure teased him with its beauty.

But once more, the auric-tinted drake hesitated. Lord Purple still had some devious plan in mind that Toma needed to ferret out before he dared report to his father. What it was, Toma could only suspect…but those suspicions were enough to keep him here. He was of the opinion that the master of Penacles was as much a threat to the throne as he was to the humans. Just how remained the greatest question…

Toma stepped away from the window—then quickly returned to it as something touched his magical senses. Yet, this time, his gaze went not to the glimpses of the battle, but rather to a nearby rooftop.

No one had to tell him who the shadowy figure only just forming there was. Toma had made it a point to learn all he could about *every* major factor involved in the power struggles of the Dragonrealm. Even if he had not, he would still have had no difficulty identifying something as legendary and as ominous as the demon steed, Darkhorse.

The ebony stallion reared, then vanished again. Yet, Toma sensed that Darkhorse had not left Penacles. Rather, the shadow steed was now somewhere much nearer.

The drake grimaced. He quickly turned his palm up and concentrated.

A faint image began to form—and then vanished just as quickly. Despite two more attempts, the image of the emperor would not form.

Toma swore under his breath. There was no contacting his father. The final decision of what he would have to do would be up to him and him alone.

Which to Toma's mind left the drake but one radical choice…

DARKHORSE SENSED THE strange magical energies arising within the palace, magical energies so reminiscent of how he experienced the world of the Dragonrealm that he knew that their source was something far more ancient than Dragon Kings, Seekers, or even Vraad sorcerers. He had noted those energies inherent in the land itself and had, for so many centuries, assumed it just the way this alien world was.

But through Shade and others, he had come to learn differently. There was, for lack of a better word, a *presence*…a presence that affected the realm and its inhabitants in a conscious manner.

This time, though, the shadowy stallion felt such an active force at work that he knew something terrible had to be happening. Darkhorse was a straightforward creature by nature; he felt certain that the wizard Nathan Bedlam would be in the midst of the worst struggle and, therefore, the eternal needed to be there, too, despite previous instructions contrary. What he would do when he arrived, Darkhorse did not know. He trusted to instinct and to the mage. One or the other would guide him…

At least, so he hoped.

A TREMENDOUS URGE coursed through the Gryphon, an urge to unleash the spell on *all*. He knew where that desire came from; his other half—the spirit of the founder—who still sought to 'correct' matters.

The rebel leader felt other minds pressing at his will as well. Lord Purple continued to seek domination over both the active spell and the energies of his stolen array. The Dragon King's will was extremely strong, enough so that the Gryphon knew that he had to make a decision as to what to do very quickly.

His initial thought was to let Nathan Bedlam take control of everything. After all, there was no spellcaster more skilled, more able, than him.

Yet, hardly had he considered that possibility, than he knew that in Nathan's current situation, turning over what the founder had already cast would very likely overwhelm even the veteran mage. The Gryphon's darker half had subverted the energies, made them into something the lionbird doubted that even Nathan had experienced.

And so it came to him that he had two choices. He either tried to cast the spell in some manner that kept it from fulfilling its dire purpose...or he did nothing, which meant that the spell would turn back on him, utterly devouring him in the process.

In truth, he saw that there was no choice at all. His life was hardly worth those of everyone else. Foes would perish, but so would innocents and friends.

The Gryphon did nothing.

The spell collapsed into him. He felt a rush of pain and incredible heat. Death would not be long in coming, yet, still he chose to do nothing.

And as the pain swallowed him, the Gryphon knew that he had chosen the right course.

NATHAN REALIZED WHAT the Gryphon intended, and while he understood the choice and even would have taken the same path himself, it distressed him that he could do nothing for the rebel. It was all the wizard could do just to make certain that Lord Purple did not gain some advantage that enabled the drake lord to seize the power of the array back.

Then, one slim hope did occur to him, but he knew that to try to reach out to the one he needed would again potentially shift the balance in the Dragon King's direction. If Nathan had only not—

Master Bedlam! Master Bedlam!

At that moment, no other voice, not even those of his sons, would have brought more hope to Nathan. He thanked the fates for the impetuous personality of the creature, even as he also prayed he was not about to willingly sacrifice someone who had become a trusted ally.

Darkhorse, listen! The Gryphon! Can you see what I need you to do with the Gryphon?

I see…but what of you and the rest?

You need not concern yourself with us! We live or die on our own… if you do this…

Nathan expected the shadowy stallion to hesitate, but Dark-horse broke the link without another word. The next second, the eternal materialized in the midst of the chamber where the Gryphon stood like a statue. The agony the lionbird suffered was not visible, but both Nathan and Darkhorse could feel it. Indeed, that the Gryphon managed to stand at all at this point stunned the wizard, who doubted that he could have withstood such an onslaught for so long.

The ebony stallion immediately swelled. His limbs, tail, and even his head quickly sank into his growing form.

Without hesitation, the bloated, nearly unrecognizable form fell upon the Gryphon.

A SILENT DARKNESS surrounded the rebel. The Gryphon floated in nothingness.

You may release it… came Darkhorse's voice.

The torture the lionbird had been suffering had eased some-what the moment the eternal had swallowed him. Yet, the Gryphon was aware that not only was the reprieve a very temporary one.

Release it…

But the Gryphon sensed that if he simply did as commanded, the founder's spirit would have a perfect opportunity to regain mastery. Even now, he could feel the entity probing for weakness.

No... he replied to Darkhorse. *No...but thank you for doing this. Here...here I think I can do what needs to be done...*

What do you—Nathan! He—

Before the shadowy stallion could finish his warning, the Gryphon turned the spell completely to himself...and released it.

The agony he had suffered paled in comparison to what overwhelmed him now. Every fiber of the lionbird's body burned...

...and then a scream filled his ears.

TOMA STOOD BEFORE the tapestry, momentarily awed by its intricate workmanship. He ran one clawed finger over where the city square was depicted, recognizing location after location.

Behind the young drake lay the ruined remains of the chamber's guardians, guardians whose destruction Toma had decided was a risk that he had to take. If Lord Purple did maintain control of his kingdom, things would not go good for the emperor's son. Toma hoped that whatever treasure he brought back would more than mitigate matters where his father was concerned.

Enough admiring, the duke reprimanded himself. *Time to grab a few volumes and then give them to Father as a gift...once I've perused them a bit, of courssse...*

He located the symbol of the library, then started to rub it just as Lord Purple had always done—

A human materialized before him, forcing the drake to retreat. The unexpected newcomer was a human Toma belatedly recognized—

"You're in my way," Azran murmured with a smile.

Toma barely had time to note that the bearded wizard had done just as he had planned. Two thick tomes lay nestled in the crook of the human's right arm, braced there by the hand.

The left hand wielded a disquieting black sword, a sword that somehow suddenly flared even *blacker*.

The drake went flying back, finally crashing into one side of the doorframe. He dropped to the stone floor with a grunt, where he lay unconscious.

Azran grinned. "That was very delicate of you," he said to the open air. "Oh, right, we don't want to take a risk of damaging the books in the process. Well, shall we go?"

As if in answer, the Horned Blade flared again...and Azran vanished.

AS THAT HAPPENED, a third figure briefly formed out of the shadows in one corner. Dayn had struggled hard to keep *anyone* from noting his veiled presence. His success meant little to him considering what he had just witnessed. Shocking enough to discover his brother sneaking into the venerable and generally well-secured libraries—after some force, possibly Azran himself, had torn apart the golems guarding the entrance—but to observe what his sibling had done now shook Dayn to the core. This was not an Azran he knew. In fact, this was an entirely different Azran that the elder sibling in some ways greatly *feared*.

And yet, with one last glance at the unconscious drake, Dayn continued after his brother.

NATHAN FELT THE Gryphon act, but could do nothing. The mage knew that if he did not maintain his vigilance, he might very well still open the way for Lord Purple to attempt to usurp the powers with which the lionbird struggled.

But barely had he thought that, than he sensed a sudden gap as the drake lord vanished. The wizard's first instinct was to take advantage of the cessation of one threat, but he knew that the Purple Dragon would hardly have abandoned the battle for Penacles. Lord Purple had something else in mind, and it behooved Nathan to find out what it was as soon as possible.

Yet, he dared not break away, not even when he felt through Darkhorse the powerful forces begin to consume the Gryphon. Nathan tried in vain to think of some way to save the lionbird, but knew that it was already too late.

That was when Yalak's voice echoed in his head. *Leave him be, Nathan…and prepare to accept what he gives in return…*

Nathan had no idea what his old friend meant and wished that Yalak would not choose now to be so vague…but before he could demand a clearer explanation, the *scream* struck him.

The scream emanating from within Darkhorse.

The scream that was—and was *not*—the Gryphon's.

THE GRYPHON WANTED to double over, but his body did not respond. It was caught in flux between the Gryphon and the founder, the latter of whom was the source of the scream.

However much the lionbird suffered, the entity suffered far, far more. The Gryphon did not understand why until by sheer reflex he caused one of their shared hands to move. Only then did the Gryphon see how his hold on the body grew and that of the founder failed more.

It was the opposite of what the Gryphon would have expected. The entity was a much older, supposedly stronger thing than him.

If the Gryphon understood matters properly, the founder even had greater claim on this body they shared than the lionbird did.

And yet...with each passing moment, the Gryphon felt more securely bound to his body. The founder appeared less distinct, a fading shadow. As that happened, the rebel leader's pain also began to subside slightly.

Feed it into him...came another voice in the blackness that was Darkhorse. *Give the black power he desssired to him asss he would have given it to all othersss...*

The new voice was not unknown to the Gryphon, but its very existence startled him. It was the voice of the mist dragon, the creature the Gryphon was certain that the founder had destroyed.

They made usss resssilient, the unseen dragon murmured to the lionbird. *They forgot jussst how resssilient...*

Even as the elemental spoke, the founder's spirit sought yet again to seize the potent magical forces from the Gryphon. To the lionbird's surprise, the attempt failed miserably. He was no more than a shadow of a shadow now.

The Gryphon did as the dragon suggested, feeding the full force of the spell into what remained of the entity.

Unable to control the flow, the founder was engulfed. The scream rose once more, then quickly faded. The essence that was the ancient entity lost all cohesion, all consciousness.

The Gryphon would have simply let it dissipate, but the mist dragon suddenly encircled him again. In doing so, the creature drew what remained of the founder's spirit back into the rebel leader... something the Gryphon did not care for in the least.

*You mussst...*the dragon insisted. *You cannot live without it...*

Whether that was true or not, the Gryphon had no chance to determine. The dragon brought both parts of the lionbird together...and suddenly the Gryphon felt whole.

He also felt *free*…free for the first time that he could recall. The abilities that had always been *meant* to be his were now at his command. They were powers unique to the Gryphon's astonishing existence, created solely by the amalgamation of elements that had forged what had become the lionbird. He was more than the founder, more than the brute force of the beast he resembled, more than the mysterious shell that housed both his soul and the essence of the ancient entity…

But in discovering that new strength, that new power, the Gryphon also discovered that he still needed to quickly dispose of what remained of the great spell before it next devoured *him*, Darkhorse, and more.

And so, the rebel leader sought an outlet that would not result in the deaths of hundreds, perhaps thousands.

Unfortunately, what he discovered instead was that, even despite all he had done, all he had been willing to sacrifice, the battle for Penacles—and the perhaps the rebellion itself—was still about to be lost.

THE BROWN DRAGON raged. His elite forces surged forward, only to find themselves marching on their own rear flank. They were caught in some magical loop of a complexity the likes of which even the drake lord had never confronted.

He envisioned a thousand intricate tortures he would inflict upon the so-called Dragon Masters for this trick. He was certain that it had to be them, even though the Brown Dragon's destination had not been Penacles. Indeed, the longer he and his soldiers were kept trapped here, the more likely that his original target would discover the treachery he and Lord Purple planned and inflict upon both *worse* tortures.

Suddenly, a ripple coursed through the limited reality of the loop. Out of that ripple stepped his counterpart to the east.

"Matters have changed," Lord Purple solemnly informed him. "Your destination has changed."

Although he was grateful to soon be free of the loop, Lord Brown still had to ask, "And the emperor?"

"He remains ignorant. His demise is only postponed. I require you in Penacles."

Brown could not hold back his grin. "Underestimated the human vermin, did you?"

Lord Purple turned from him. "Have your soldiers follow me right now. The way out will not hold long."

The other drake lord vanished into the ripple.

Lord Brown immediately roared orders. The day still promised blood...and in the end, that mattered more to him than even overthrowing an emperor.

25

THE STRUGGLE

The inky shadow separated itself from the ruined wall, joining another shadow just forming. A dozen rebels eager to enter Penacles through the gap made in the wall raced past the shadows without noticing them.

The first shadow flickered, briefly becoming the silhouette of a feminine form clad in armor, cloak, and high-crested helmet. She watched the rebels vanish into the City of Knowledge.

We are reaping an excellent harvest, the other shadow remarked to her in the voice of the necromancer, Ephraim. As he spoke, he, too, momentarily took some vague form.

What about what happens within? the other voice, that of the one called Kadaria asked with more than a touch of frustration. *What about all that power? When do we take it?*

We do not. That, we let play out. Our task here is to gather from the dead and in that manner build our strength to greater heights...

But—

Ephraim raised one gauntleted hand. *We reap now...and with what we gain, we will sow our ultimate triumph over the living world...*

Kadaria bowed her head in agreement.

The shadows faded. There was much work still left to do. Much *harvesting.*

GWENDOLYN SENSED THE new surge of magic and knew with horror what it presaged. She touched thoughts with Nathan.

I know! he immediately responded. *Don't break your concentration!*

Yalak had foreseen Lord Brown's forces being sent to reinforce Lord Purple's defenders. What had taken them so long to arrive, neither Gwendolyn nor Nathan could say. What mattered was that in moments the first blink holes would open and a fresh army would come pouring out to trap the rebels.

The enchantress was aware that Nathan's original plan had been to utilize the energies he seized from the array and use it to seal the portals the second that they opened. Unfortunately, that choice was no longer available to them.

She sensed the wizard swiftly calculating what options remained to them. There were very few and none of those he clearly cared for. Gwendolyn also tried to think of something, but—

She barely noticed the sudden presence of another in the cavern and knew instantly that Nathan—caught up as he was in so many aspects of the struggle—remained ignorant of the intruder. Worse, Gwendolyn knew exactly just who it was who stood with them even before he became visible next to the unsuspecting wizard.

Lord Purple swept one arm across a startled Nathan's chest.

Gwendolyn acted. The drake lord's arm closed on empty air.

The helmed, reptilian countenance turned to her. Inhuman orbs flared dangerously. "I underestimate little, but I have more than once underessstimated Brother Green'sss little pet human…"

The immediate area surrounding the enchantress solidi-fied, forming a monstrous, mauve prison sealed against her flesh.

Gwendolyn found herself gasping for air as a pressure threatened to crush in her chest. A panic such as she had never felt filled her. She kept trying to breathe, but failed. Worse, her prison had quickly turned opaque, preventing her from seeing what else might be happening beyond her.

The enchantress strained. Claustrophobia overwhelmed her. Gwendolyn *had* to escape. She *had* to be free—

Her frantic will finally proved too strong for her prison. The shell *cracked*, the pieces fading away even as they scattered.

The stricken enchantress fell to her knees as she inhaled lungfuls of air. She looked up, certain that the lord of Penacles was already casting a second, more lethal attack.

Only…the drake lord no longer stood before her. In fact, she could not even sense his presence.

With growing fear, Gwendolyn sought out Nathan. She had sent him to the one place where she was certain he would be safe… the Manor. It had taken tremendous effort on her part, which, in turn, had contributed to her lack of defense against the Dragon King's horrific attack.

Unfortunately, there was no hint of Nathan in the Manor. Gwendolyn feared the worst; either Lord Purple had managed to seize Nathan after all or the wizard had chosen to leave safety and throw himself right back into the battle.

Only then did the enchantress notice something else was missing. There was no sign of Nathan's handiwork; the crystalline pattern—*everything* concerning it—had vanished.

Gwendolyn shivered. Lord Purple not only had the array back under his control…but now he had the wizard's creation at his command, too.

THE PURPLE DRAGON eyed his prize with satisfaction. Not only was the array his again, but so was Nathan Bedlam's impressive handiwork, which now served to enhance the original arrangement.

The Dragon King admitted to himself that he had underestimated the rebels. Specifically, he had underestimated not only his former protégé, but the Gryphon as well. Even the drake lord had missed the link the creature had with the ancients, the ones some called the *founders*. There had been no noticeable hint, no residue marking the Gryphon as a creation of the lost race, yet still the Dragon King felt he should have noticed *something*.

But despite everything that had happened, Lord Purple now saw only a glorious victory ahead. The emperor's overthrow had only been postponed; indeed, the imminent sweeping triumph over the rebels would bring more of Lord Purple's counterparts to his side. Gold would not be able to stand against such an uprising. The imperial throne would soon belong to the master of the City of Knowledge.

Already, he had everything in place. The array and Nathan Bedlam's creation merely awaited the drake lord's slightest casting. The swiftness with which Lord Purple had adjusted to so many unpredictable factors only proved again his superiority.

"Now..." he murmured. "Now we wait for you to do what you mussst do, *mongrel*...and then I will at last put my house—and this entire land—in order."

THE GRYPHON COULD sense the blink holes opening. In his mind, he could see the eager soldiers in their brown armor begin coursing through the holes into the land surrounding Penacles...and behind the lines of the lionbird's still unsuspecting followers.

Toos! I have to warn Toos!

Thought was now evidently action for him. The power he barely kept in check at least allowed the Gryphon to do that one thing. He felt the lanky redhead suddenly stiffen as their minds linked.

Gryph?

The enemy is behind you as well! the lionbird warned. *The enemy is—*

He had to cut off the warning; the manic energies the Gryphon barely kept in check suddenly stirred so strongly that it was all he could do to keep them from escaping his weakening control. As he battled to hold everything in—aware all the time that soon he would *have* to release all of it one way or another—the Gryphon sensed that the abrupt stirring had not been a random event. Someone else sought to take control.

Someone else who could only be Lord Purple.

The Gryphon stood trapped in indecision. His men were caught between foes. The Dragon Masters were doing all they could to stem the looming disaster, but they were at their limits. The lionbird was well aware that if he tried to do anything to help them—even attempt to manipulate the overwhelming energies for the sake of his friends and allies—then he very well risked finishing the founder's task.

Gryphon! Gryphon, can you hear me?

Nathan? What—

The wizard cut him off. *Can you hold everything together for a moment more?*

Although the lionbird indicated he could, he hoped that the human did not make him wait very long. Fortunately, Nathan Bedlam immediately acknowledged his understanding of the Gryphon's desperate situation. The mage then vanished from the rebel's mind...only to thankfully return a breath later.

He has it all arranged...just as I thought he might. This is our one chance.

Who? Who has it all arranged?

The Purple Dragon, of course. I was counting on him.

The Gryphon gaped. *Wizard, are you mad?*

We're about to find out. I took in consideration that he might seize everything I arranged back...and so I took a precaution. My plan should still work even though I never expected...Never mind! Now, it's up to you!

Then tell me what I need to do and tell me fast! Even now, the Gryphon could feel the Dragon King trying to seize the energies from him.

You just have to do one thing! et him have it all, Gryphon! Let him have it now!

He thought at first that he had heard Nathan wrong, then, realizing that he had not, wondered if the mage had gone insane. Yet, some instinct still made him obey even despite those misgivings.

As expected, Lord Purple eagerly took everything. The Dragon King's sense of triumph almost overwhelmed the exhausted Gryphon.

Stay conscious! Nathan warned. *I need you! Gwendolyn! Help us!*

The enchantress's name startled the lionbird for a moment, but then he felt her presence join them. She radiated tremendous relief—and something more private—at being reunited with the wizard, if only through thought.

Yalak has the others ready! Nathan continued, apparently oblivious to what the Gryphon thought much too obvious. *I need you two to do as I say! I need you two to focus the energies back to me just when I say so!*

To you? Gwendolyn asked before the Gryphon could. Her confusion matched his.

To me. To this.

He let them see how he had planned for all of this.

And the truth made the Gryphon and the enchantress shudder.

LORD PURPLE BATHED in the tremendous power now his. All the knowledge that he and his line had painstakingly gathered from the libraries had led to this. Now, he would change the land even as the founders had not been able to do. Now, a new empire would flourish...one with *his* color dominating its banner.

He had the power. Soon, he would also have the eggs he had arranged for the rebels to unwittingly steal for him. The latter would keep any of the other Dragon Kings from attempting something foolish, like stopping him. For that matter, in a few minutes, the rebels would be slaughtered, their destruction so grisly, so thorough, that no one would *ever* think of rising up against him once he ascended the throne. The Purple Dragon would sweep away every obstacle, including the Lords of the Dead. Even the land itself would bend to his will.

All that mattered was how first to show his supremacy. It took the drake lord but a moment to decide just how to do that.

And the thought made him grin.

YALAK AGAIN CURSED the day that he had chosen to pursue the twisted path of foresight. He had been warned by his teachers that the few before him who had done so had learned to regret such choices. Most had gone mad. Worst of all, even seeing the future did not mean that one understood it or could do anything to alter it.

Naturally, Yalak had not listened. How he wished that he had. The Gryphon had played his part as the wizard had hoped, but in doing so had opened up several new possibilities, few of which he found palatable.

And now, Nathan had picked the one that Yalak feared the most.

How I wish I could warn the others...

But it was already too late. He could only hope that Nathan had chosen right.

NATHAN BRACED HIMSELF. Then, aware that Lord Purple was even now making use of the energies and the array, he hurriedly took the stone that he had carefully adjusted and placed it on his chest.

As he did, the one still imbedded beneath his flesh pulsated.

Nathan took a deep breath...and concentrated.

TOOS SHOUTED ORDER after order, not certain if all he did would make any difference where the rebels' chances of survival were concerned. To their credit, even when the word spread that a drake army—Lord Brown's dreaded army, of course—was about to pour through behind them, the men and women simply awaited his orders. He realized how much they believed in him and not just saw him as an extension of the Gryphon. It made him more determined than ever to do anything he could to keep them alive.

The ground shook.

Toos fought to maintain his footing as both humans and drakes around him tumbled like rag dolls. A sound like thunder erupted from deeper within the city.

The vulpine rebel planted himself against the side of a building, aware just how dangerous that might be in the midst of what seemed an earthquake. Still it gave him a moment to gather his wits and try to make sense of what was happening. At first, Toos saw nothing but the shaking buildings, the cracks coursing through the streets...the elements that all pointed to a tremor.

But then he noticed a change in the sky...or rather a *shifting* in the sky.

The city was *rising*. The entire city.

It was more than that, though. A strange, grinding sound accompanied the other noises, as if something massive were being slowing ripped out of the ground *underneath* the city.

Underneath…it's underneath… Toos peered at one of the widening cracks. Although he could see nothing within, he had imagination enough to know what was happening below.

It was not just the city that was rising into the air. It was also the *libraries…*

WADE ARKONSSON MATERIALIZED in the palace, his expression haggard from the incredible effort needed to make it this far with absolutely no one, not even Nathan nor Yalak, knowing where the other wizard had gone.

The vision of his dead, broken bride floated ahead of him. Wade murmured her name, then, steeled by that ghastly image, he started down the grand hallway.

A guard stepped from a side corridor. The drake hissed in surprise, then drew his sword.

Wade glared at the drake. A rapid series of horrific cracking sounds erupted from the guard, who twitched madly. The drake looked as if he wanted to scream, but his mouth was now tightly shut. The wizard wanted no sound alerting others.

The guard ceased moving. His face went slack.

The bitter mage let the body drop. He felt no guilt for having just literally broken every bone in the drake's body, saving the neck for last. His only regret was that he had not been able to do the same to Lord Purple.

Grunting, Wade Arkonsson continued on. If he was lucky, he thought, perhaps he still might have a chance to correct that…

WORK WITH ME! *Work with me!* Nathan asked the Gryphon and Gwendolyn again. *He's already started!*

With Gwendolyn's aid alone, Nathan knew that he would have failed. Even the additional aid of the Gryphon as he had been prior to this battle would not have sufficed. Only now, only with the Gryphon's true abilities apparently unleashed, did this have more than a minimal chance of success. Nathan saw that he needed to do more than what he had originally planned; Lord Purple's grasp of the stolen energies was even stronger than he had imagined.

He continued to press the stone against his chest. Both it and the one inside his body now *burned*, but the wizard knew that he could not relax his hold in the least. The stones needed the physical contact of his flesh to keep the bond between them viable.

As Nathan considered all this, he continued to concentrate. In his thoughts, he saw the array and the pattern that he had created. In particular, he saw the two insignificant fragments that he had matched up in both, additions he had prayed the drake lord would not notice.

And Lord Purple had *not*.

Even as the ground shook, Nathan acted. Through the fragments, he drew everything from both patterns into the stone on his chest—the stone from which the fragments had been taken—and then fed all into the stone the Dragon King had so long ago buried inside his former puppet.

Nathan had now chosen a position to the south of the city. It gave him all too good a physical view of what Lord Purple was doing. The mage understood what the Dragon King had in mind; he intended to raise up both Penacles and the libraries and then seal them off from everything. It was the first step toward creating a new empire of the drake's own. It also was an image that no one in all the Dragonrealm would be able to deny, an image to give the Purple Dragon the semblance of more than a spellcaster.

He would resemble a *god.*

But that won't be happening today, my lord, Nathan thought angrily. *Not at all...*

Had he attempted to hold in the energies as the Gryphon had miraculously able to do, Nathan knew that he would have been burned to a cinder. Fortunately, that was not his plan.

Nathan willed the power to come to him. It did so initially in a rush that daunted the mage, but he held strong. He only needed a few seconds, which, with the aid of the Gryphon and Gwendolyn, he managed.

As Nathan took control, the floating city shook again. The wizard watched as it began to slowly drop to the ground. The fact that Penacles did not plummet, slaying everyone inside and many beyond in the process, was due only to Nathan's constant manipulation.

He passed the energies to the rest of the Dragon Masters. Already made aware by thought of what he had in mind, they readjusted their positions, wizards and enchantresses alternated between facing the city and confronting Brown's forces.

Those that faced Penacles continued to aid the rebels against the city's defenders. There, the battle slowly but surely turned back in the rebels' favor.

The spellcasters who had turned the other way brought their hands to their sides, then stared not at the approaching enemy, but rather the ground before them.

The earth there exploded upward, tons of rock and dirt rising before Lord Brown's startled soldiers. A massive wall formed, a wall that continued to rise higher and higher.

I thank you for the idea, my Lord Purple, Nathan grimly thought. The master of the City of Knowledge had wanted to create a barrier around his floating realm and the libraries. Nathan had merely taken that idea and used it simply, logically.

From the rear of the invading army arose three tawny dragons. Spreading out as they ascended, the behemoths headed directly toward the gargantuan wall. Nathan continued to urge the wall to greater height, but despite the Dragon Masters' best efforts, it was clear the winged terrors would still be able to overcome the barrier.

Before Nathan could decide how to deal with them, the Gryphon interjected.

Let them do just that, the lionbird suggested. *Let them fly over…*

An image of what the lionbird desired filled Nathan's thoughts. Hoping this was not going to be a fatal mistake, the wizard bowed to the rebel leader's choice, then relayed the order to the rest.

The first of the fearsome trio reached the wall. With a contemptuous roar, he beat his wings hard and pushed up the additional height needed to cross over the towering wall.

Nathan would have acted then, but the Gryphon made him hold back. Only when the second behemoth also started to cross over did the lionbird give the order.

The upper part of the wall exploded. Yet, rather than simply scatter every direction, the force of the explosion focused in the directions of the attacking dragons.

Assailed by the savage torrent, the three giants struggled just to stay aloft. Huge chunks of rock ripped wings, battered bodies, and struck heads again and again.

One sharp piece several times the length of a man and shaped almost like a lance veered directly toward the throat of the foremost leviathan. Distracted by the onslaught, he failed to notice the massive projectile until it was upon him.

The dragon attempted to swerve, but the jagged rock, steered by the Gryphon more than Nathan, simply adjusted. It impaled the tawny beast in the throat.

The dying dragon spiraled to the earth. Even as that happened, the other pair began a hasty retreat from the focused carnage.

Brown's at bay, the Gryphon said to Nathan. *How long, I can't say! We've got to secure Penacles now!*

Agreed! But Nathan knew only one way to achieve that goal. They had to bring Lord Purple down. It was not enough that they had managed to thwart the Dragon King; so long as he controlled even part of the City of Knowledge, the rebellion had no hope of success.

Yet, when Nathan now sought his former master...he found no sign of the drake lord. Despite a swift but thorough survey of the palace, the wizard could not note even a hint. With the stones and the array at his command, Nathan was certain that if Lord Purple remained in the palace, then the mage would have found him.

Unless...

Gryphon! I have to—

I understand! Go!

Nathan concentrated—and materialized in the palace. Before him stood the chamber he sought, the chamber leading to the tapestry...and thus, to the libraries.

The view that greeted him worried the wizard greatly. Someone had destroyed the guardians. Lord Purple would have hardly done such a thing.

Strengthening his personal defenses, Nathan entered. Only in the libraries could the Dragon King remain in the palace and yet be invisible to the wizard's array-enhanced search.

But by retreating into the libraries, Lord Purple had cornered himself. Nathan stepped toward the chamber, trying not to think why the entrance had also been torn apart.

That proved all too easy...for what Nathan beheld in the chamber made him forget all else, even the hope for a rebel triumph.

The tapestry was gone.

26

DEATH IN THE LIBRARIES

Caught up as they had been in other events, neither Nathan nor even the Gryphon had paid any attention to Darkhorse's abrupt departure. The eternal had also done all he could to surreptitiously slip away once he saw that the wizard and the rebel leader had the matter of which Darkhorse had been a part well enough in hand.

In truth, Darkhorse knew that he had still taken a chance by leaving the Gryphon when he had, but something else had suddenly caught his attention, something so important that he had felt it demanded immediate investigation. The shadow steed had been filled with guilt over his departure, but where it came to the subject of *Shade*, Darkhorse had ever believed that he was the one best suited to deal with the warlock.

Of course, that was assuming that *anyone* could actually deal with Shade...

LORD PURPLE GRIMLY surveyed the corridors surrounding him, the drake lord sensing something amiss with the libraries but unable to say just what. He finally dismissed the concern, more interested in how best to punish Nathan Bedlam and the rest of the rebels for their continued if eventually fruitless transgressions.

The Dragon King glanced at the large cloth dangling from his right hand. Tossing it into the air, Lord Purple watched as it immediately adhered itself on the blank wall that always marked where one entered some part of the libraries.

The tapestry spread itself out over the entire wall. Yet, where in the palace chamber it revealed the layout of Penacles, here in the libraries, it displayed another something entirely different.

The drake lord hissed in surprise. He had anticipated this, but to see it still amazed him.

Unveiled by the tapestry was the *entire* complex system of corridors called so simply 'the libraries'. For the first time, the drake lord verified that the system existed on several layers, several levels. Indeed, as he peered at the image, he saw that the various levels shifted order. The libraries did not just change position, they changed design.

"Fassscinating..."

"Yes. I was very proud of it."

The Purple Dragon turned to face the gnomish librarian. "So, the truth at lassst! There has always only been one of you. I suspected, but it was difficult to say..."

"I live to serve the libraries," the short, robed figure murmured. A dark look briefly crossed his face. "Although once, so very long ago, it was the other way around."

It was a story that Lord Purple had always desired to know, but at the moment, it was the least of his interests. "And the libraries now live to ssserve me."

"So long as you are master of the city."

The drake lord grinned wide, showing his sharp fangs. "I shall *alwaysss* be master of the City of Knowledge."

Rather than reply to the comment, the bald figure looked to a shelf. "Hmmph. The books must readjust for the losses. This is the most traumatic effect to it since my...since the beginning of my service to the libraries."

For the first time, the Purple Dragon realized just what had bothered him. There were *spaces* on the shelves, just two or three, but still *spaces*.

"I've asssked for nothing yet. Why are there booksss *missing?*"

The librarian looked more aggravated than troubled. "Yes, that is curious, isn't it? I sensed *nothing*. There is no precedence for this. In fact, there is much going on of late that has no precedence. Much too much..."

"What do—?" Lord Purple waved off the question he had started to ask. "No matter! A few missing books mean nothing in the long run! You will ssserve your purpossse now and bring me the tomes *I* need for what I have in mind for my traitorous servants. If I mussst level Penaclesss and build it anew to keep to teach them all their place, then ssso be it!"

The gnome paled. "I am naturally aware, as you know, of what you wish. So work the libraries. I would urge you to another course of action—"

The Purple Dragon let out a low warning hiss.

"As you wish." The short figure turned toward a shelf. One of the heavy tomes leapt into his grip. "You are aware that the secrets you desire might take some time to decipher—"

The librarian gasped as horrific pain shot through his body. He felt moisture on his back and knew it to be his life fluids.

The gnome fell to his knees. As he struggled to peer behind him, the book he had been holding flew from his weakening grip to the Dragon King. Lord Purple's right hand—the claws extended to their fullest—dripped red. The other hand now held the book.

"If I judge correctly, you will regenerate in sssome manner. Consider thisss a lesson in knowing your place." The drake lord bent down and wiped his claws on the bleeding librarian's robes. "The rebels have the city. The city is nothing, though. The librariesss are truly all that mattersss...and I have them."

THE LIBRARIAN FELT the flesh and muscle in his back binding together again. It was not the first time that he had suffered such agony—nor was it even the worst of those times—but for once, the librarian felt great uncertainty. This was not how the libraries worked. This was not how it was supposed to be...

A shadow suddenly moved at the edge of his vision. A shadow whose source the librarian knew. Yet again, another thing that should not have been.

But this time, the very fact that the shadow was there made the gnome smile grimly...and hope that the current lord of Penacles did not notice what was happening behind him until it was too late.

THE IMPASSE BETWEEN the second army and the Dragon Masters remained. The spellcasters kept Brown's forces behind the gargantuan wall of earth, but could not entirely repel them. The Gryphon was aware that this stalemate could not last. If the rebels hoped to take the city, they needed to be certain that there was no threat behind them.

Unaccustomed to fighting so deep in their own city and with several of their drake overlords already targeted successfully, Lord Purple's soldiers appeared to find it difficult to decide just where to make a stand. The lionbird found that intriguing; so confident had those serving Clan Purple over the centuries become that no one had apparently considered defensive strategies involving the deep interior of Penacles as necessary.

Like his commander, Toos led the rebels into the fray. As the Gryphon observed the struggle though newly enhanced senses, he saw the young officer wielding his sword with as much skill as the lionbird believed he himself had. Toos cut down a human defender, then traded blows with a lower caste drake warrior. What the Gryphon could make of the drake's half-seen visage showed a creature very harried. The drake's eyes constantly darted to the sky and back again...which finally proved a fatal mistake as the redheaded rebel chose one of those glances to behead the scaly warrior.

He—all of the drakes left—are afraid to transform, the Gryphon realized. They had seen what had happened to those who had done so, most of them drakes of much greater power, much higher caste. That those had been slaughtered surely daunted the remaining warriors.

We are winning here...but are we winning where it truly matters? The Gryphon suddenly understood that there could be no victory until Lord Purple was captured or dead. There had still been no word from Nathan, which worried the lionbird so much that he finally dared resurrect the link between the wizard and him.

Nathan! Are you—?

Gryphon! Quiet!

The command was not a reprimand. Instead, Nathan needed the rebel leader to see something. The image came full blown, but at first all the Gryphon saw was a blank wall, which made no sense to him.

Then... The tapestry! Is that where it was supposed to be? Where is it?

I don't know...it's just gone! Lord Purple must have it!

And where's he? The Gryphon suspected he knew, but prayed that he was wrong.

I think—I think he must be in the libraries, but without the tapestry, the way is cut off!

The lionbird trusted his comrade's instincts...which meant that the rebellion was in even more trouble that he had believed possible. Lord Purple had the libraries at his beck and call. Worse, with the Dragon King's centuries of practice deciphering the books' powerful spells, it would not take him long to find one that would bring the rebellion to ruins.

Nathan suddenly spoke again, but this time not to the Gryphon. *Gwen! Help Toos and the fighters in the city! It's integral that the rebels don't falter right now!*

I understand! Nathan—be careful! the enchantress severed the link.

Gryphon... the wizard continued. *Come to me! Immediately!*

The Gryphon imagined himself next to the wizard...and a breath later found himself there. "What can we do? Have you found a way to enter without the tapestry?"

Nathan looked to the blank wall again. "There's something. I don't know if it'll work, but perhaps with the two of us, we can *summon* the tapestry to us. It's a desperate gamble, but it might work."

The Gryphon nodded. "I've certainly no better answer. Let's do this. We've little other choice."

"You've really never seen the tapestry yourself. Let me show it to you in better detail."

Neither the glimpse the Gryphon had earlier seen nor the descriptions he had heard in the past prepared him for the intricate work of the actual artifact. He saw Penacles in fine detail and yet knew that while it appeared that an artisan had spent months, perhaps even years, to perfect this image, parts of it were even now changing, adding to the overall display the destruction caused by the battle.

See it, Nathan commanded in the Gryphon's head. *Know it…*

The lionbird did as Nathan said. The image seemed to take on even more of a life of its own in his mind. Now he thought he saw the most subtle changes taking place throughout the illustration. Tiny alterations, all made to keep everything about the picture completely accurate to the moment.

The wizard continued. *We need to try to summon—no!*

Nathan's sudden mental exclamation caught the Gryphon by surprise, but no more so than what suddenly happened to the wall before them. The blank stone *rippled.*

A hand thrust through…a human hand.

LORD PURPLE RAN a finger over the page. The libraries continued their infernal tricks, giving him confusing fragments of poetry and images that hinted at various things. Despite that, the Dragon King was confident that he would not need long to decipher them. Soon, he would—

The slight stirring of magical energies was the only warning the drake lord needed. He glanced up at where the librarian should have been standing, but of course, the gnomish creature was nowhere to be seen.

At the same time, his bones abruptly sought to break of their own accord. The Purple Dragon groaned. The book he had been perusing dropped from his hands. He fell to one knee.

But a moment later, the drake lord rose again, the attack on him easily thrown off. He turned to face the source of his momentary pain.

It took him a moment to recognize the human spellcaster standing near the tapestry. *Wade Arkonsson.* The human wore a harried, bitter expression and did not look at all surprised that his assault had failed against his former master.

"She's dead because of you..." the wizard muttered. "Because of you."

"You are certainly welcome to join her, whoever she wasss." The Dragon King sneered, already formulating a focused spell. The only reason he had not struck down the pitiful human thus far was the mage's very close proximity to the tapestry. In fact, even under the certainty of death, Arkonsson leaned almost casually against the tapestry as if—

No. Lord Purple saw that the wizard was not leaning but rather had thrust his arm *into* the tapestry.

Into the tapestry and through manipulation of its unique magic *out* into the chamber beyond.

"I realized I wasn't strong enough, though I prayed I was," Wade Arkonsson admitted with a sneer of his own. "But fortunately, they've arrived in time. They'll put an end to you and your damned kind..."

Hissing, Lord Purple no longer worried about the tapestry. His spell struck the wizard square.

The dark-haired mage screamed. Only his personal shields prevented him from dying there and then. Now turned gaunt and as pale as the dead, the stricken wizard somehow still managed to keep his arm in the tapestry.

He managed to keep his expression confident. "S-saw the tapestry just—just hanging there in the chamber! It was—it was fate! Someone opened the way for me. Thought—thought I could use the libraries to find a s-spell—but I couldn't read a damned thing!"

"No, it takesss time and practice...and you are out of time."

Wade Arkonsson screamed harder as a second more pointed attack pierced his shields. His body shook violently and bits of his flesh began to fly away as if blown by a strong wind. Yet, he remained where he was, his arm still magically imbedded in the tapestry. Even as the spell ate away at him, he bared his teeth at the drake lord.

"L-long enough now!" he gasped staring past the Dragon King to some unseen figure. "I swore to you I'd last long enough for them, S-Staia—long enough…long—"

The wizard let out a last breath and tumbled forward. Even as he fell, fragments of his body continued to break away. By the time the wounded mage struck the floor, he was not only dead, but much of his body had already been reduced to blackened ash briefly fluttering around his corpse.

The drake lord glanced from the dead mage to the tapestry—

"May his spirit and hers be together once more," the voice of Nathan Bedlam sadly declared.

A sharp pain coursed across the Dragon King's throat. He felt his blood spill from the gaping wound there.

With effort, Lord Purple threw himself forward. As he did, he placed one hand over the wound. The flesh immediately healed.

The drake lord felt another spell strike him, but by this time, he had already enhanced his personal shields. With utter contempt, the Dragon King confronted his would-be slayer.

Or rather, *slayers*.

"You were alwaysss a clever ssstudent, Nathan…but even having thisss mongrel with you will not be enough."

And as he finished this declaration, the Purple Dragon opened his mouth wider…and wider yet.

A deafening sound erupted from the drake lord's ghoulishly wide maw. The sound swept over Nathan and the Gryphon with such force that both were thrown down the corridors in front of which each stood.

The Purple Dragon did not let up. He took a step toward the fallen mage. It was time to teach his wayward protégé a final lesson in loyalty and the punishment for abandoning that loyalty.

"Nathan Bedlam. Bedlam," the drake lord remarked as he suddenly began to swell in size. "A curiousss but appropriate sssurname for your line. A line that ssserved mine well, until recently."

Despite his dire circumstances, Nathan did not look at all afraid. Lord Purple appreciated that his former student had taken his training so to heart, but still intended to make the human shriek for mercy before finally granting him death.

"Let me show you sssomething of the librariesss I think you will find interesting," the drake lord continued. "Let me show you why I am and will remain *massster* of the libraries..."

The Dragon King shifted shape. He laughed as Nathan Bedlam saw what was not only happening to the drake, but also to their *surroundings*. If he had thought that Lord Purple could not change to his true form here in the libraries, the human had been sorely mistaken...for as the scaled warrior quickly transformed into the gargantuan dragon that only one of the Kings with their tremendous power could become, the libraries, too, *adjusted*. The ceiling shot higher and the corridor stretched wider. Shelves rearranged and more materialized, all filled with thick, ancient tomes.

The Purple Dragon stretched his wings—*stretched* them without the least fear of spilling books or battering walls—and laughed again at the pitiful human far below.

"Massster of the librariesss, Penaclesss, and sssoon, *all* the Dragonrealm..."

THE GRYPHON FOUGHT to rise even as his surroundings shifted size and form in what he at first thought a madcap manner. But as the ceiling shot away from him, the lionbird suspected that he knew just why the corridor was growing in both height and breadth. He prayed that he was wrong, but the roar that resounded from the direction the rebel leader knew Nathan had to be destroyed all doubt.

A dragon stalked the libraries, but not just any dragon. A Dragon King. The Purple Dragon. The master of the City of Knowledge.

The corridor in which he lay at last settled. The Gryphon instantly leapt to his feet. He had no idea just what he might be able to do against a fully transformed Dragon King, but could hardly leave Nathan to face the behemoth alone.

Yet, as the Gryphon regained his footing, he could not help look instead to the shelves at his left. Some instinct drove him to reach for one of the hefty books.

Aware that each passing moment might mean the death of the wizard, the lionbird nonetheless felt almost compelled to open the tome.

What he saw on the open pages made his eyes widen.

"It appears they have chosen," the voice of the gnomish librarian whispered from the Gryphon's right.

The rebel glared at the robed form. "But *what* have they chosen?"

"That depends on you. They have given you what you asked for, even if you did so in silence...you must just accept."

The Gryphon returned his gaze to the contents of the book. He could scarcely believe what he was reading. If he understood it, it *did* give Nathan and him a chance. Yet... "And if I accept?"

The librarian shrugged. "If you succeed, you will be master here."

"Will I?"

The bald creature's expression grew veiled...and also, to the Gryphon's opinion, *bitter*. "As much as any can..."

The Purple Dragon's mocking laugh shook the libraries. The Gryphon's gaze narrowed in anger.

"This isn't a real choice. I'm being forced into this decision."

His diminutive companion shrugged.

A surge of magical energy made the lionbird's fur and feathers stir. Someone was casting a very powerful, likely very dangerous spell.

The Gryphon quickly looked over the contents of the book again, then seized four other volumes at random from the shelves. The five books propped awkwardly in his arms, the rebel leader rushed down the corridor.

The librarian watched him for a moment, then stared grimly at the shelves where the empty spaces stood. "You really plan to do that to him, do you?

In answer, the remaining books silently began shifting position...

27

MASTER OF THE LIBRARIES

The savage forces of the Brown Dragon pounded at the barrier maintained by several of the Dragon Masters. Samir and Solomon Rhine led the effort in that direction, while Yalak oversaw the struggle against the city's dwindling army of defenders, both military and magical.

Yalak coordinated matters in Penacles with Gwendolyn and found her a clever and resourceful comrade. He had known that she was capable—had known even more than Nathan had—but her adaptability in the midst of chaos truly impressed him.

She would be your perfect complement, Nathan, the veteran wizard thought as he directed another spell. *If the fates permit that…*

Trying to shake off another host of mental images hinting at potential futures, Yalak organized those under him for the next attack. There were still too many possible endings remaining for this battle for him to concern himself with what might happen afterward. If he let his mind wander beyond the moment, he risked steering things to paths leading only to greater disaster.

And there were far too many such paths already. Far too many…

NATHAN KNEW THAT Lord Purple had not transformed simply because he thought his true shape would so terrorize the mage that he would surrender and plead for a mercy that would never come. The Dragon King had another reason for shapeshifting, one that Nathan feared he would discover to his regret much too soon.

The drake lord beat his wings, sending a gust of wind that threw the wizard further down the endless corridor. As Nathan rolled to a halt, he saw the behemoth barreling down on him.

Reacting instinctively, Nathan cast. The spell he chose was a simple one, a burst of pure force. However, even as the wizard acted, the drake lord stopped and inhaled.

To Nathan's horror, the leviathan drew in the magical forces the mage had unleashed as if merely breathing air. As that happened, Nathan felt his strength suddenly flag. The mage tried to break free, but the Dragon King kept the bond between them strong. Gasping, the wizard slipped to all fours. With each passing second, he felt weaker and weaker.

In desperation, he planted his palms on the floor and tried a different spell, a much more indirect one. A crackle of crimson energy coursed from his palms along the floor to the Dragon King. As it reached the giant, it flared brighter.

The Dragon King roared as if burned. His hold on the link weakened.

Nathan used the moment to break the link. Some but not all of his strength returned. It was enough to barely save him in time from the Purple Dragon's attempt to reestablish the accursed bond. The wizard strengthened his shields as much as he could, but attempted no other spell. Even an additional defensive one might have given the drake lord the opening he needed to absorb the last of his foe's power and life essence.

Unfortunately, that left Nathan with no manner by which to directly strike. Anything Nathan cast would be seized and used by the Dragon King to finish off the human.

"Yesss. You understand. You were alwaysss a quick learner, Nathan Bedlam," the drake lord jested. "More like your mother than your father...she realized what wasss about to happen to the pair of them before he did...not that she learned sssoon enough to sssave either."

Try as he might, Nathan could not even use this monstrous revelation to draw forth even the slightest memory of his parents. It enraged him to think that they had been so easily eradicated from his mind. Whenever he thought about them, he only did so in regard to their years of loyal service to the Dragon Kings.

Years of unwitting *slavery*.

"They perished here, just asss you will, though the circumstances leading to their deathsss were different. They thought they were being given the honor of asssisssting in a new disscovery in the librariesss...but in truth, they were no longer needed sssince you were ready to take their place at my right hand..."

While aware that the Dragon King was seeking to goad him enough so that the wizard made a fatal mistake, Nathan could still not keep his grief and fury completely checked. He fought to keep his concentration focused on finding some new avenue of attack against his former master, but tiny fragments of memory at last began to intrude on his thoughts, fragments of memory that included personal moments with his parents that the wizard could not even recall having *happened*.

He realized only then that his father bore a great resemblance to him, the differences mainly in the elder Bedlam's light brown hair and narrower chin. Nathan's mother, on the other hand, reminded him of Dayn, and for the first time—or perhaps not the first—Nathan saw that his oldest son favored both women and not the male Bedlam line much at all. That then brought his thoughts to Azran and—

Curiously, it was Azran that stirred Nathan from his reverie... and just in time. As darkness surrounded the human, he realized that his drifting into memories had been one more deadly trick on the part of the drake lord.

The dragon's jaws closed on the mage's location, but Nathan was no longer there. As the drake lord's sharp teeth closed on empty air, the wizard reappeared further down the corridor.

Nathan swore under his breath as he took in his new surroundings. He had tried to teleport himself to a different corridor. His current location bought him a few seconds, nothing more.

Lord Purple raised his head. The reptilian mouth stretched into another knowing smile.

"It takesss yearsss to master the unique nature of the librariesss. Yearsss you do not have, Nathan Bedlam..."

At that moment, a figure appeared well behind the huge dragon. Nathan's hopes rose slightly when he saw that it was the Gryphon, but then the wizard saw the odd burden in the rebel's arms. Rather than a sword, the Gryphon carried *books*. That they were books from the magical libraries did not encourage the wizard in the least; the lionbird had no experience with the legendary depository and so any knowledge the books might offer would likely be so complex to decipher that it would not help.

Still, whatever the Gryphon had in mind, it behooved Nathan not to alert the Purple Dragon to the rebel leader's presence. That in mind, the veteran spellcaster steeled himself and cast. He directed his spell not at the gigantic creature, but rather at the rows of books to the drake lord's left.

The entire wall of heavy tomes tumbled toward the dragon. Lord Purple glanced at the rain of books and did just as Nathan hoped, the Dragon King trying to keep the precious artifacts from striking him.

Yet, when the Purple Dragon grabbed at the first of the ancient tomes, his paws slipped *through* them. Nathan had known better than to try to actually move the true books. Not only would the libraries likely not permit that, but it also would have again risked binding the wizard's power to the drake lord.

Behind the dragon, the Gryphon opened one book and set it down face up against one wall. Nathan saw that a second book already lay in an identical position on the opposing wall.

The Gryphon still had two more books in his grasp, but now he signaled to Nathan that he needed to bring them toward the wizard.

As that happened, the Purple Dragon turned back to Nathan. The Dragon King looked more amused than furious at being fooled by the simple illusion. "Clever! Ussseless, but clever!"

Nathan did not reply. Instead, summoning the energies for a powerful assault, Nathan lunged toward the dragon.

The drake lord emitted a sound that might have been one of astonishment...or perhaps merely humor. Glancing up, Nathan watched as the head dropped toward him again. Simultaneously, the wizard could feel his former master strengthening the spell that would enable Lord Purple to seize control of Nathan's magic again.

But instead of casting, Nathan let his own spell fade away. The action did what he hoped; Lord Purple hesitated, certain that the human had some other weapon ready to put in play against him.

The hesitation gave the Gryphon the opportunity to leap ahead of the battling duo. He immediately dropped the third book on the floor. Then, bending low, the Gryphon slid the last book toward the other wall. As it coursed along the floor, the rebel leader jumped in front of the behemoth.

"This is your one chance to surrender!" the Gryphon cried. "Best take it, my lord!"

The dragon looked incredulous, then laughed. "A buffoon asss well asss a mongrel! You could have bought yourself a little more life by trying to hide deeper in the librariesss, but so be it! If you wish to be first, I will certainly grant your requessst!"

The Purple Dragon's right paw swept across the spot where the Gryphon stood. The rebel jumped over the paw, only to have the drake lord's left one strike him while he was still in mid-air. Spinning, the Gryphon crashed into the nearest shelves, sending books tumbling.

Nathan eyed the fourth book. He had no idea whether it lay where the Gryphon wanted it to be. The wizard had to give the lionbird a chance to get back to the book. The Gryphon seemed to think the tomes their best hope against the Dragon King, although in just what manner Nathan still could not guess.

Even as the mage concerned himself with the last books, he saw the dragon's tail sweep over the second. Nathan expected the tome to be bowled aside, but as the tail moved on, he saw that the artifact remained exactly as the Gryphon had set it. The wizard frowned, but before he could consider the ramifications of what he had seen, the Purple Dragon chose that moment to return his attention to the human.

"One more thing you mussst learn about the librariesss," the giant bellowed. "It can be ssset in disarray, but it *cannot* be destroyed!"

The drake lord exhaled.

The plume of fire not only enveloped Nathan, but washed over row upon row of books. The flames did not touch the wizard, but the heat was such that he could scarcely breathe. So used to Lord Purple relying on mental and magical machinations to achieve his desires, Nathan found himself unprepared for so simple, so raw, an onslaught. He found himself gasping for air and sweating profusely.

The flames did not let up. The wizard managed to keep his shields strong, but knew that soon the heat would overtake him. When that happened, his shields would begin to fail…and after that…

Then, it occurred to him that he had added protection at hand. Backing up, Nathan seized one of the books. As Lord Purple had promised, neither it nor any of the others looked even slightly scorched. Indeed, they were not even hot to the touch.

With a struggle, Nathan brought the book in front of him. Opening the pages toward his face, he created a shield protecting his head.

To his relief and astonishment, the area protected cooled. Again able to breathe, Nathan pushed forward again. As he moved, he began to formulate a spell to counter the flames…

But suddenly, the fire ceased. The wizard stumbled, then peered over the book to discover the Gryphon *atop* the dragon's head. The rebel had one clawed hand keeping him in place while with the other he threatened the drake lord's eye.

Though the Purple Dragon could feel the attacker above, he could not, of course, *see* the Gryphon. Thus it was that the drake lord did not notice the lionbird's desperate glance to the fourth book, then to the third.

Nathan thought he understood. The Gryphon needed him to steer the Dragon King's focus to the direction of the third tome so that the lionbird could finish arranging the fourth.

The wizard used the most convenient distraction he had. He tossed the book in his hand at the leviathan, using just enough magic to send it directly toward the right eye—the same one the Gryphon had been attacking.

The book did what the lionbird's claws could not. Lord Purple's gaze followed the flight of the artifact. At the same time, he shook his head hard in a clear attempt to free himself of the gnat swarming over his skull.

The Gryphon obliged the dragon by releasing his hold. Letting out what sounded like a cry of dismay, he threw himself off the behemoth.

"And now, let usss finish with you..." the drake lord announced cheerfully to Nathan. With one paw, he caught the wizard's book, then gently set it down near the third one placed by the Gryphon.

Nathan restrengthened his shields. He tried not to look the lionbird's direction. Whatever the rebel hoped to achieve, the mage prayed that it did not require more than simply adjusting the final book.

Power gathered swiftly around the Purple Dragon. Whatever he intended would not wreak havoc on their surroundings, but Nathan was not so certain about himself. The wizard felt the drake lord's spell coalesce—

"Your majesty!" called the Gryphon.

Ignoring him, the drake lord unleashed his power against Nathan.

The spell broke apart, the energies torn in not four directions, as the wizard might have thought, but *five*.

"Your majesty!" the lionbird shouted again.

Both dragon and man looked to the rebel. The Gryphon held a *fifth* tome, one that Nathan had not seen him carrying earlier. The wizard had to assume that his companion had slid the book in earlier, before beginning to set up the other four.

Still, exactly when the Gryphon had tossed the fifth artifact into the corridor mattered much less than what he did with it now. The lionbird held it with the pages open toward the Dragon King.

The pages he revealed glowed a bright gold that increased with each passing moment.

"Another little trick, mongrel?" mocked the drake lord. "What have you found—?"

Without warning, the dragon shook uncontrollably. As he did, he shrank slightly in size.

"I've *found* the libraries have an opinion of their own as to who should be master here," the Gryphon replied flatly, "and it appears they don't believe it should be you any longer."

The Gryphon flipped a page. As he did, the Purple Dragon shrank a bit more.

Nathan blinked. No, not just shrank. Some of the reptilian features had become slightly muted, almost as if...

"Fool!" The dragon managed despite his violent shaking. His size increased again and his features returned to their reptilian sharpness. "The librariesss will and mussst obey me! Alwaysss it hasss been and alwaysss it shall—aaaaaaaaa!"

Along with the unexpected scream came another shifting of size and shape by the behemoth. He shrink smaller yet, and his features became less reptilian.

The Gryphon turned another page. For the first time, Nathan saw that the nearest book on the floor glowed in an identical fashion. Quickly looking from one tome to another, the wizard discovered that the other three did the same.

The Dragon King let loose with another angry roar. He drew power to him, preparing to cast what was surely a spell meant to overwhelm the one the Gryphon had unleashed.

However, hardly had the energies begun to gather than they scattered, spreading to the five tomes. As Nathan watched, stunned, some of the essence of the *drake lord* did as well. The behemoth shriveled to barely half his once-imposing size. Lord Purple *was* shifting to his mortal form, albeit very unwillingly. His wings became wrinkled remnants and his snout grew blunt. His limbs even bore some vague resemblance to those of a human now, although the elbow and knee joints still bent as they had when he had been a full-grown dragon.

Nathan could scarcely believe what he was seeing. They had Lord Purple at *bay*. The spell that the libraries had given to the lionbird were actually working. The master of the City of Knowledge struggled in vain and the Gryphon—

The Gryphon... The wizard stiffened. A faint dark green aura surrounded the rebel. Nathan saw that the lionbird was obviously unaware of the change. The aura had a subtle touch to it, one that even the wizard could barely sense. Trying to probe it, Nathan met with incredible resistance.

The Gryphon turned another page. The books glowed brighter. Lord Purple shrank yet again, his shape now shifting to something midway between dragon and warrior. The Dragon King raged, but his efforts continued to go for naught. He now glowed with the same color and intensity as the pages.

Yet, as the glow increased, so, too, did the aura surrounding the Gryphon. Even more to Nathan's horror, the lionbird *flickered*, briefly vanishing and then reappearing. The wizard might have thought that he had imagined it save for the fact that a moment later it happened again.

Nathan swore as the awful truth dawned on him. *The spell! It's not just meant to deal with Lord Purple—it's meant to take the Gryphon, too!*

The wizard knew that he dared not call out for fear of the libraries reacting against them. Instead, Nathan did the only thing he could think might save the Gryphon, even if it also meant likely freeing the Dragon King in the process.

He struck at the book the lionbird held, trying to seize it in magical claws forged to be as strong as steel.

Claws, much to his horror, that melted the second that they tried to touch the book. Worse yet, Nathan saw that the Gryphon did not even notice what the wizard had just attempted.

No longer caring anymore about secrecy, Nathan shouted, "Gryphon! Beware the books!"

However, even though the distance was not great, neither the rebel nor even the drake lord paid any attention. Both remained enveloped in the treacherous spell.

Gritting his teeth, Nathan started for the Gryphon.

A book struck him solidly in the chest.

As he tried to keep his balance, a second and third hit him from opposing walls. Despite his shields, the heavy tomes had no trouble reaching their target. Nathan managed to deflect one aiming for his face, but in doing so missed seeing another flying toward the right side of his head.

The book caught him square on the temple.

Dazed, the wizard toppled over.

THE GRYPHON TURNED another page. Lord Purple had been reduced to a creature more Dragon King than dragon. Another page or two and the last vestiges of the monstrous behemoth would disappear. Then, the Gryphon could deal with the drake lord himself.

A shiver ran through the rebel. It was not the first one. The Gryphon paid them little heed, certain that they were just due to the stress on him. He reached for another page…

Nathan? The lionbird hesitated. For just a breath, he thought that he had heard some cry from the wizard. However, when the Gryphon listened further, he heard nothing.

His fingers touched the page…and again he paused. Even though the cry had not repeated, something made the Gryphon finally tear his concentration from the spell just long enough to see to the wizard.

Only then did the rebel leader see the half-buried form under the growing pile of books.

Simultaneously, another chill ran through him. This time, the Gryphon sensed something amiss. He glanced at his hand…and saw with a shudder that it was partially translucent.

He also watched as his hand moved on its own to the page for he had been reaching. Despite his attempts to prevent it from doing so, the hand succeeded in turning the page.

Lord Purple lost all trace of dragon. Now fully the armored warrior, he grabbed at the Gryphon with gauntleted hands. To the drake lord's frustration, though, he could not move from beyond the location where he stood.

Nor, the Gryphon discovered as he tried to throw away the book, could he.

The truth finally dawned on him. *The libraries are trying to destroy both of us!*

It made terrible sense. The libraries were in truth infused with the essence of the founders. They wanted nothing to do with the Gryphon, whose other half had worked against them. The lionbird had thought them destroyed, but some trace of them still apparently remained active in the libraries. They had seen their chance to remove both dangers to them, although for what ultimate reason the libraries wanted *both* dead remained unclear. The Gryphon would have assumed that they would have at least sided with one or the other…which was exactly the thinking that had enabled the libraries to use him as their puppet.

Again, his hand sought a page. Despite his failure to stop the hand before, the Gryphon renewed his fight for control.

His fingers tightened on the corner of the page. The Gryphon clamped his beak tight. Once, he would have thought his chances against such magic minimal at best. Yet, since then, he had survived one fantastic threat after another, one insidious spell after another. He had even overcome his powerful other half, who had, in turn, tamed those guiding the libraries' magic.

The Gryphon let loose with a leonine growl. As his fingers turned the page, he used every ounce of effort he could to take command of the hand, if at least for a moment.

With more ease than he could have imagined possible, the Gryphon *tore* the page out.

He was instantly struck by another chill, but this one faded almost before it began. Both the book and page shook violently, as if living creatures now badly wounded.

A raspy sound erupted from the direction of Lord Purple. The Gryphon looked up to find the spell surrounding the Dragon King beginning to fade.

"Firssst I will rip you apart while you beg for mercy," the Dragon King taunted as he managed a step toward the rebel, "and then, once the city isss under proper control again, I will very ssslowly teach my former ssservant how many typesss of pain I have alssso learned of through the librariessss!"

Visions of the men and women who had already perished for the cause along with those who still might do so even if the rebels ultimately triumphed was too much for the lionbird. Fueled by his awareness of so much sacrifice by others, he brought the ruined book forward and in his head *demanded* that the libraries continue what they had begun.

The books flared brighter than before, their illumination sweeping over the Dragon King.

Lord Purple covered his eyes and hissed. The Gryphon watched in worry as energies surrounded the drake lord, energies the lionbird first thought were those being summoned by the Dragon King for a counterspell. Instead, though, the energies swiftly enveloped

Lord Purple. His movement toward the Gryphon came to a jerking halt. The drake lord hissed angrily, but was unable to push on.

But without warning, the glow from the books lessened again. The Gryphon felt resistance rising from *two* sources. Both the Dragon King and the libraries again worked against him. This time, it was more than the lionbird could withstand. He felt his effort failing—

"A-Allow me to lend a hand," Nathan murmured at his side. The wizard clamped his fingers on the Gryphon's shoulder.

A new surge of strength filled the rebel leader. With it, the Gryphon was able to push back both the libraries' resistance and Lord Purple's attack.

"We h-have to end this quickly," Nathan added. "Very quickly..."

The lionbird nodded. Once more, the libraries surrendered to his will. Holding the fifth book as far as he could toward the drake lord, the Gryphon turned one last page.

Lord Purple hissed. "Fools! I am master of Penacles, master of the City of Knowledge! I *am* and always will *be* the libraries!"

He struck harder than either the Gryphon or Nathan expected him to still be able to do. For a moment, the two faltered—and then the spell of the books at last seized utter control of the Dragon King.

The Gryphon instinctively shut the fifth book. As he did, the glow from the other four intensified. The pages of the books began to flip madly.

Lord Purple shrieked. His limbs stretched, one to a book. The Dragon King hissed and struggled, but to no avail.

"I am—" he managed one last time.

And then, as if also suddenly parchment, the Purple Dragon literally *ripped* into four pieces, each centered on a limb. The mad hissing continued as the four segments of the drake lord flew toward the glowing books. As each piece neared a tome, it shrank, becoming no larger than one of the pages within.

The four parts of Lord Purple sank into the books. The hissing ceased. The glow immediately ceased.

As one, the four books shut.

Silence reigned in the libraries.

A silence broken by Nathan Bedlam's astounded whisper. "B-By the Dragon of the Depths…I think we've taken Penacles…"

The Gryphon shook his head. "Not just yet…we've one more thing to do…"

SOMETHING WAS WRONG. Lord Brown could feel it. Something was very wrong. No matter how hard he tried, he could not reestablish his mental link with Lord Purple.

The earthen wall remained an obstacle, too, another troubling sign. By now, it should have fallen, yet, the human spellcasters still managed to maintain it. What should have been a glorious, bloody victory was turning into a—

A thundering noise that shook the very ground beneath the Dragon King and his mount made Lord Brown and his aides look up at the towering wall. The Dragon King leaned forward, peering at something in the humongous barrier.

There were *cracks*. Long, sinewy cracks that spread even as he watched.

Lord Brown concentrated…and his eyes suddenly widened. An uninvited image formed, an image of the Gryphon holding a thick book.

The Gryphon winked. He opened the book and revealed to the drake lord the contents.

The Dragon King gasped. For one of the few times in his existence, Lord Brown was taken aback.

The vision vanished. Lord Brown hissed. He seized the nearest aide, nearly tearing the other drake from his mount.

"Sound the retreat! Sssound the retreat!"

Barely had the officer managed to do that than more thundering took place. This time, the thundering was low and long, too long for Lord Brown's taste.

The wall began to teeter toward the Dragon King's army.

There were spells the Dragon King might have cast, powerful spells that might have worked well under normal circumstances, but the vision that the rebel leader had shown to Lord Brown had been enough to let the drake lord know that the day—and the city—were lost.

Shuddering, Lord Brown summoned the first of the blink holes. At various areas behind the lines, other portals began forming.

The first ranks started toward the blink holes.

The top of the wall collapsed, followed by the mid-section, and then the rest.

As the Brown Dragon raced his reptilian mount through his own portal, he wondered just how many soldiers would actually make it through…

NATHAN AND THE Gryphon watched through a sphere the wizard had cast as Lord Brown's forces fled through the blink holes. As the last of the army disappeared, the pair exhaled.

The wizard adjusted the view, revealing to both that the wall still *stood*.

"A cunning maneuver," Nathan commented.

"I merely borrowed your own trick in the libraries. Why waste the wall—which we may need later—when an illusion will do… well, an illusion backed up by a very precise vision granted to Lord Brown."

Nathan grimaced. The pair stood near the tapestry. The Gryphon still held the book in his arms, the book he had taken from the floor. The book that held part of what had once been the former master of Penacles...a fact that the lionbird had momentarily shared with the Brown Dragon.

It had been more than enough. With it, they had placed sufficient doubt in the second Dragon King's mind to make the illusion of the wall work.

The wizard glanced down at the floor. He had already transported Wade Arkonsson's remains to Salicia. Once the city was secure, there would be many funerals, some of them other spellcasters, many of them brave souls with only a sword to protect themselves.

"A victory nonetheless..." he muttered.

"A victory," agreed the Gryphon, tossing the book into the air. It flew unerringly for one of the shelves. "A temporary respite..."

Nathan nodded.

Making certain that he held onto the tapestry, the lionbird touched the exit mark on the image of the libraries.

The pair vanished, the tapestry with them.

28

AFTERMATH

The remaining defenders soon surrendered. The Gryphon wanted to let the matter of their fates be in the hands of the Dragon Masters, but Nathan proclaimed that since the libraries had given in to the rebel leader, he was not only their master, but the new ruler of Penacles.

Although refusing to be called a king, the Gryphon at last saw the futility of denying his control of the City of Knowledge. Besides, the rebellion needed a secure location, and where was there any realm better able to be defended than the City of Knowledge?

And with that understanding, the Gryphon made his decision.

The next day, the remaining drakes, including the females, were given passage from Penacles to the Dagora Forest. From there, the Green Dragon promised to send them north, to Kivan Grath and refuge under the wing of the Dragon Emperor.

The transfer went peacefully. Some among the spellcasters, including Solomon Rhine and Basil, lodged their protests, but all abided by the Gryphon's decision, especially once it was explained why this would benefit the rebellion.

The new master of the libraries revealed to the senior drakes among the refugees what he had to Lord Brown. Each of them saw what not only the one book contained, but rather *all* four did. Even the most stubborn drakes could not deny what they saw.

The message was clear. The Gryphon knew that it would also inevitably spread among all the drakes in all the lands no matter how hard the Dragon Kings might try to keep it from doing so. The Gryphon not only wielded the secrets of the libraries, but had used them to vanquish its former master in a most dramatic fashion.

Both the new monarch of Penacles and Nathan Bedlam hoped that spreading such fear would be enough to gain the rebels peace… and yet both knew that, in the end, it would only buy them time.

Four others of the calling had perished that final day. They were placed with Wade Arkonsson on a pyre in the city center and given the first of the funeral. Despite going first, though, they were not honored above the rest of the dead. Nathan felt that all lives lost were of equal value, a sentiment with which the Gryphon agreed.

The Gryphon also insisted that the dead defenders be honored as well, especially since most of the human ones still had family in the city.

Nathan watched as Basil, Tyr, Yalak, and Adam Gudwead dealt with the initial pyre. The Gryphon and Gwendolyn stood with him as for the last time they honored their comrades. Guided by magic, the flames burned fast and high but did not endanger the many mourners.

"Your treatment of the city's dead is to be admired," the enchantress commented quietly. "Many would not be so kind to the enemy."

"It will take a long time to heal the wounds here. This may help," the Gryphon replied. "Although a good number are happy to be free of the Dragon King's rule, there remain a large contingent who are not."

Nathan shook his head. "The advantage is yours, though. Once they knew the Purple Dragon was no more, his human soldiers surrendered in droves."

"Slaves come in many forms. Their support will be critical... once we ensure that there are no spies among them."

"We'll help you with that," the wizard promised.

Samir suddenly stood next to them. The dark-skinned mage looked as exhausted as any of them, but there was also a hint of eagerness behind the exhaustion.

"Lord Brown's forces have returned to the Adajian Fields, but not by his choice. It is confirmed by Tragaro that the Dragon Emperor has personally ordered him there."

The Gryphon clacked his beak. "They're trying to decide just how much access we have to the libraries' secrets."

"And with that in mind," Samir interjected, "shall I return to the libraries?"

He asked with such earnestness that none of the three could hide their amusement. At Nathan's behest, the Gryphon had granted Samir and two other Dragon Masters entrance into the libraries so that they could begin trying to decipher some of its elusive storehouse of arcane knowledge.

Nathan still had some questions in regard to the librarians and could not help thinking that the Gryphon knew more than he did on the subject. The wizard had noticed that his memories of certain incidents in the libraries had already grown oddly hazy, but had chosen not to confront the rebel leader with his suspicions just yet.

"You have my permission," the Gryphon said to Samir.

Eyes bright, Samir vanished.

"I hope he and the others are successful in their task...and quickly," the lionbird went on. "There's no telling how long before the Dragon Kings regain their nerve."

"In that case, let us savor this respite as much as we can." As the flames started to die away, Nathan's thoughts turned to another subject constantly nagging him. "Gryphon, if things continue to move smoothly with the funerals, I—"

"You want to find out where Dayn went...and where Azran is, too. I understand. I think we can hold Penacles long enough for you to do that."

"I thank you. It's not just—"

The Gryphon raised a hand to silence him. "They're your sons. No explanation needed. You can go now, even. Everything's calm enough."

Nathan exhaled. "Thank you."

Gwendolyn took his arm. "Let me help. I know Dayn well."

"I'd appreciate it. Gryphon, I just—"

The lionbird's eyes held amusement, although over what, Nathan could not fathom. "Enough. Go. Now. The Lady Gwendolyn will be the best aid you could *possibly* have."

Already distracted by the upcoming search, Nathan paid the Gryphon's exact words little mind. "Yes. Of course."

The wizard and the enchantress faded away.

THE GRYPHON EXHALED. A part of him wished that he could have gone with the pair, but that was not to be. With the rebellion such a daunting mission, he had never thought past the actual struggle. Now, he found himself leader of not merely an armed force, but an entire realm...and, worse, that with the war *still* on.

I'm no ruler, he insisted to himself not for the first time. *If this all ends well enough, Nathan can find someone better to oversee Penacles. This is just temporary, nothing more. I'm a soldier and always will be...*

A mournful horn announced the next funeral. The Gryphon straightened. This next pyre would include men and women who had fought for him. For their sacrifices, he had to see to doing what was best for the rest. That meant securing the City of Knowledge and giving his followers a place where they could recoup, at least temporarily.

It won't be forever. Just long enough. Then, if we manage to win this war, someone else can take on the headache of ruling...

"ALL RIGHT, I'VE brought them. Where are you?"

"Right beside you, Azran Bedlam."

Despite aware of just who he dealt with—and having killed him once already—Nathan's youngest gasped. Immediately after, anger over being treated like a child made him draw his sword.

Shade put up a gloved hand. "There's no need for that. Not this time."

"Don't play games with me!" Azran growled, brandishing the Horned Blade. "Just because we made an agreement—"

"Which I will live up to." The hooded warlock cocked his head. "Thank you for following my instructions to the letter. You had no trouble in the libraries?"

"None. I went in using your spellwork, took the books, and left right away, just as you recommended." Azran chuckled. "No trouble whatsoever, unlike you, from what I heard."

Shade said nothing, but Nathan's son thought the warlock might have frowned in momentary anger. It was impossible for the wizard to tell, of course, but he liked to think it the truth.

"I played a role for the Dragon King that offered rewards of its own if things went as planned," Shade at last grudgingly remarked. "They did not, and there was always the great possibility that they would not. That is why I moved ahead with our own agreement even in advance of the other situation."

Azran shrugged. He truthfully did not care about anything else that had happened in Penacles. "Well, the books are here. I don't know what good they'll do; the pages are all blank…"

The warlock extended his hand. The heavy tomes materialized above the hand. He gestured and the books flew behind him into the darkness.

It was not night here, but it might as well have been. The towering mountains kept much of the region in permanent shadow.

Azran did not miss the irony that he and Shade met in the Tyber Mountains in a location not all that far from Kivan Grath. The fact did not bother him anymore than it likely did the faceless warlock.

"The potential contents of the tomes are not as important as the tomes themselves. I will show the three of you in return for what you've promised me."

Nathan's son did not contradict Shade even though to all apparent appearances the two of them were alone. "How soon? How soon do you think?"

"It may take quite some time. If you have some other intentions, I suggest you move on them until I contact you again."

"Now that you mention it—"

Before Azran could say more, the sword abruptly swung to his right. Both the wizard and the warlock glanced that direction.

The wind howled through the mountains. A few rocks gradually loosened by the incessant winds of the north tumbled to the ground nearby where they stared.

"It's nothing," Azran finally whispered to the air. "Nothing." He turned his attention back to Shade—but the faceless warlock was nowhere to be found. Not at all to Azran's surprise, the books were gone as well.

"Play your games," Nathan's son muttered to the absent warlock. "Eventually, you'll play ours." He cocked his head to the side, then smiled. "Still, if I have to wait, there *is* something I'd like to pursue in the meantime...or rather, *someone*. I think she'll prove quite useful, don't you?"

There was no response from the air, but Azran nodded as if he heard something. Sheathing the Horned Blade, the wizard faded away.

"THERE WAS NO call for that!" Dayn reprimanded his companion. "I had everything under control, Darkhorse!"

"They sensed you!" bellowed the shadowy stallion despite being right in front of Nathan's eldest. "Or rather...that *thing* in his hand sensed you!"

"You're mistaken...." But the mage's voice trailed away as he thought again about the encounter he had witnessed. How could his brother not see that this was a darker incarnation of Shade and not the one that had been aiding the rebellion? Had the warlock mesmerized him?

"Hear me, young Bedlam! You need to tell your father what is happening—"

"No!" Dayn turned from the eternal. Darkhorse had come upon him without warning while the wizard had been observing his brother, then, just as suddenly, teleported both of them to the hills near Gordag-Ai. Their quiet surroundings did not assuage Dayn in any way, though. "We tell him nothing! I'll deal with Azran. I'll make this right. He's just gotten carried away. He was always wilder, but he still means well. I know that."

Darkhorse pawed the ground in frustration. "Very well. He is your brother, after all. You know him better than I...but you *must* be cautious and *must* tell your father if Azran goes any farther with this! I will insist!"

The wizard raised a placating hand. "Don't worry. I'm going to keep a very close eye on Azran. If he does anything I feel is too great a transgression, I'll let Father know immediately."

The ebony stallion snorted. "As you desire...but I urge you to be very careful, Dayn Bedlam. Very careful, indeed."

"Don't worry. I know all the stories about Shade."

"I was not referring to Shade...but Azran. Be wary of him."

Dayn glanced back at Darkhorse. "Be wary of *Azran?* We've often only had each other when Father was away on one quest after another. I'd give my life for Azran and I know he'd do the same for me!"

"I did not mean—"

"Thank you for helping me, Darkhorse, but I'm fine now. I don't need you anymore."

The shadow steed started to say more, than grudgingly nodded. Without a word, he raced away, leaving Dayn alone with his thoughts.

"I'll keep an eye on him, Father," the younger Bedlam finally murmured as he stared at the rolling hills. "He's just confused. I think it's that sword most of all. All I need do is somehow convince him to rid himself of it." He nodded confidently to himself. "He'll be fine then, Father; he will be. I just have to make him listen to reason...that's all. Just *listen...*"

-END-

ABOUT THE AUTHOR

Richard A. Knaak is the *New York Times* and *USA Today* best-selling author of *The Legend of Huma*, *WoW: Wolfheart*, and nearly fifty other novels and numerous short stories, including works in such series as Warcraft, Diablo, Dragonlance, Age of Conan, and his own Dragonrealm. He has scripted a number of Warcraft manga with Tokyopop, such as the top-selling Sunwell trilogy, and has also written background material for games. His works have been published worldwide in many languages.

Currently splitting his time between Chicago and Arkansas, he can be reached through his website richardallenknaak.com. While he is unable to respond to every e-mail, he does read them. Join his mailing list for e-announcements of upcoming releases and appearances. He is also on Facebook and Twitter.

BOOK

IS COMING

PERMUTED
PRESS

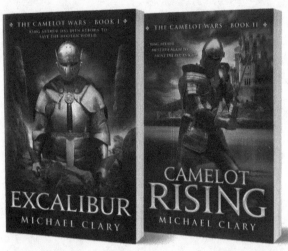

THE ULTIMATE PREPPER'S ADVENTURE.
THE JOURNEY BEGINS HERE!

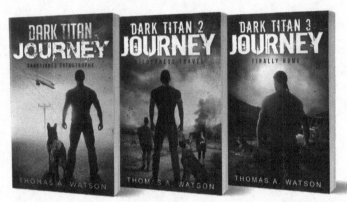

The long-predicted Coronal Mass Ejection has finally hit the Earth, virtually destroying civilization. Nathan Owens has been prepping for a disaster like this for years, but now he's a thousand miles away from his family and his refuge. He'll have to employ all his hard-won survivalist skills to save his current community, before he begins his long journey through doomsday to get back home.

PERMUTED
PRESS